Gaslighter

Gaslighter

The 11th Percent Book 5

T.H. Morris

Published 2018 by Creativia
Cover art by Cover Mint

This book is dedicated to Artenas, who always illustrated through his life that even in the midst of adversity, strife, and the trials of life, one still had a purpose. See you again one day, brother.

Also by T.H. Morris

The 11th Percent (The 11th Percent Series, Book 1)
Item and Time (The 11th Percent Series, Book 2)
Lifeblood (The 11th Percent Series, Book 3)
Inimicus (The 11th Percent Series, Book 4)
Grave Endowments (Chronicles from the Other Side, Book 1, with Cynthia D. Witherspoon)

Coming Soon
Six (The 11th Percent Series, Book 6)
Nemesis (Chronicles from the Other Side, Book 2 with Cynthia D. Witherspoon)
Black Roses (Chronicles from the Other Side, Book 3, with Cynthia D. Witherspoon

Acknowledgments

Five.

I am actually at the fifth book in The 11th Percent Series. To think that at one point, this entire thing was just an idea in my head, a random dream I had on a Thursday night in 2011. But I put pen to pad, and here were are! Since that time, some things have changed, from a personal standpoint, an emotional one... all ways. For one, this is the first book that I have published from my new home of Denver, Colorado! It is amazing just how fast this place became home. There was no awkwardness whatsoever! This is also the first book that is being released with my new publishing home of Creativia Publishing! Many thanks to Miika Hannila for giving me the opportunity to be a member of the family, and for extending the platform to showcase The 11th Percent Series in ways that I had not been able to previously. I am honored in ways that I cannot describe. Thank you, more than words can say. To my beautiful wife, best friend, and first fan, Candace, thank you continuing to push me, challenge me, inspires me, and motivate me to be better in all ways. Thank you for always reminding me that what was true yesterday, what was *comfortable* yesterday, may not be the case today. It always vitally important to evolve and grow; move past comfort zones, and get things done. Thank you for reminding me of that always, for continuing to be my first fan, and always letting me know what can be done to make a good scene, chapter, or book even better.

I love you more than life itself, and cannot thank you enough. Cynthia D. Witherspoon, my collaborator in the Chronicles of the Other Side series,thank you for always being a great friend, collaborator, supporter, and inspiration. I'm so glad to be an inspiration for your own works, and I look forward to seeing them reach even higher heights than they already have!! Lily Luchesi, I cannot thank you enough. Your help and insights were a badly needed shot in the arm for me at a time when I was in a creative quandary, and not really sure how to proceed. Sometimes, it takes a leftfield approach to bring about clarity and fresher perspective, and you provided that immensely. I appreciate that more than I can say. Thank you, and let's keep sharing our respective creative lights with the world!Tiffany Wyke, Melannie Johnson Savell, Ashley Uzzell, S.A. Gibson, Joseph "Jano" Mitchell, Christine "Chrissy" Carter, Ariel Mathis, Jessica Wren, Amanda Hoey, Craig Fields, Vernon Smith, Jillian Welsch, Margot Robinson…all of you are invaluable, and have had influence and input in my evolution. In some respects, all of you have provided inspiration and material! Paying homage to people in that regard…it gets no better than that. Thank you all.

Last but certainly not least, to Matthew William Harrill, my brother across the pond, workout buddy, and administer of The Acid Test. Man, I don't know what state my material would be in were it not for your watchful eye, sharp insights, and poignant suggestions. It is an honor and a pleasure to know you, and I am happy to now be privy to your own creative contributions! Like Lily Luchesi, your creative outlooks proved to be salient and game-changing. A thousand thanks to you.

Now, without further ado, I present to you the fifth stop on the wild journey of Jonah and the gang…Gaslighter!

Contents

1

The Negative Affirmation

Jonah lay face down, confused.

The thing that pulled his attention at the moment was the powerful scent of grass in his nose. But the grass wasn't the only scent. There was another one present. Jonah didn't know how he could smell it, but he did.

It was the smell of evil. In its purest form.

Jonah rose to find himself on the crest of an extremely elevated hill. Another thing that he knew, once again without knowing how he knew, was that the hill wasn't natural.

It had been constructed…just for him.

The hill overlooked a valley that was strangely barren; it was the complete opposite of his lush hilltop. It would have been entirely unremarkable except for some type of movement that Jonah could only make out in his peripheral vision. If he looked head on, he saw nothing. What was the source of that movement?

He tried to adjust his head so as to accommodate his peripheral vision a bit more when a bee stung him on the back of his arm. Immediately he reached there, but saw nothing. Then he felt a sting on his neck.

"Ah!" Jonah swatted at the area, but felt nothing there, either.

There was another sting on his back, and then front of his neck. Through his pain and anguish, Jonah realized something.

There were no bees.

He'd diligently hunted around, but there were no bees, or any other stinging insects for that matter, to see. Unless he was experiencing some type of physical hallucination, the source of the issue was something else.

It was when a sting caught the side of his head (which prompted him to jerk his head in discomfort) that he saw something.

There was another abstractly elevated hill miles away to the west. It mirrored the one that Jonah was on; it was even lush and green like his. But whereas his hill was only large enough to accommodate him, the other hill strained under the weight of dozens of people. Even though Jonah couldn't make out their faces, he knew that they were all focused on him, with their left hands raised like engaged students in a classroom. The strange thing was the fact that their hands all gleamed specific colors, with the exception of four or five, which had faded to black.

Wait.

Five hands were pitch-black dark. Jonah had experienced five stings. Were they the source of it, then?

He saw a hand go from green to black, and felt a sting on his left arm. Three more darkened. Three more stings.

Jonah felt like the stung portions of his body were on fire. He didn't know what to do about it. His mind went into panic mode, but he had no way to defend himself. What if all the hands went dark at the same time? Would the stings stop his heart, or something like that?

Jonah collapsed to his knees as three more hands went dark. The more this went on, the worse the stings felt. He didn't know how much more he could take.

Then, out of the corner of his eye, he saw a third hill elevate from nowhere. It, like his, only contained one person. Jonah couldn't make him out, but the man didn't waste any time with attempts to be seen or recognized. He yanked that largest bow that Jonah had ever seen from his back, notched an arrow that gleamed gold, and fired directly into the crowd atop the second hill.

Through the haze of pain, Jonah wondered if the man had enough arrows to make a difference on that hill, but he needn't have worried. The archer's first arrow downed almost a half-dozen targets, but the man hadn't shot at random. He'd aimed for the people whose hands had gone dark. When they were attacked, the colors returned to their hands, and Jonah's pain subsided.

The archer sent two more gold-gleaming arrows into a crowd, but with the disarray it caused, it may as well have been a volley. The crowd was in utter chaos; they trampled over each other, and fell to the ground. Some even threw projectile weapons at the third hill, but with an ease that was almost frightening, the archer shot arrows at each weapon and derailed each one. Once he'd destroyed the weapons, he resumed shooting arrows into the crowd. The mass of people there was in true panic now, like Jonah had been earlier. He watched as many of them collapsed to their knees, and many more fell flat on their backs.

And then a final arrow flew from the archer's bow, and the last enemy fell. Jonah tore his eyes from the second hill and looked over at his savior in awe.

"Who are you?" he called. "I mean, thanks and everything—I'm grateful and all that—but who are you?"

The archer looked in Jonah's direction, but he was still too far away for Jonah to see his face. "We've met before, you and I," he said.

Jonah frowned. The voice definitely triggered something in his memory, but he didn't remember much else.

"I can do this no longer," said the archer, but why did it seem like it was more to himself than Jonah? "Not this way. The lost spirits do all they can to survive."

It was in that moment that Jonah noticed it. It was as if his Spectral Sight decided to function on a delay. The movement on the barren land below the elevated hills were spirits. Hundreds of them. They looked to be the most defeated spectral beings that Jonah had ever seen. Under other circumstances, Jonah would have wondered why he'd had trouble seeing them at first, but that wasn't the most troubling thing.

It was how they looked that troubled him the most. The poorest, most malnourished alms beggar on the street would have looked healthier than these spirits and spiritesses. Their spectral skin hung from their bones. Lifeblood dripped from nicks, cuts, and bruises from all over their bodies. Most of them tried to pull themselves to standing, but simply couldn't make it.

"Why are they like this?" he shouted in the archer's direction. "What has happened to them?"

"Jonathan told you long ago that spirits and spiritesses could still be hurt, even in the next life, Rowe," the archer called back. "It's crystal clear—or should be, anyway—who would benefit from this."

The second Jonah thought about it, thought about him, a shadow darkened the hills and the valley. Both he and the archer threw their gazes skyward.

A huge crow flew over the landscape. Its eyes were full of hate and intelligence as it surveyed the scene. Jonah was horrified, not only because of the crow's presence, but because it wasn't new. There was no way he'd forget that overlarge monstrosity.

But if he was seeing this crow again, that meant…

At that moment, the crow realized that it was being watched. It ignored the archer completely, made a smooth turn, and flew straight for Jonah.

"Run, boy!" the archer snapped. "You must run!"

Jonah heard him, but it took a few minutes for his legs to cooperate with what his brain told him. He finally turned to flee, but then he felt claws at his shoulders, and hit the ground chest first. For some reason, he didn't hear the archer anymore, and everything had gone dark. That didn't matter. Those claws were still on his back, ready to tear at him like so much meat—he had to bat them away—

Then he stopped struggling, confused.

If there claws on his back, then they had to be by far the dullest ones he'd ever felt, not that he had any point of reference.

He reached behind his back, grabbed at what was there, and grimaced.

It was a wire hanger. No, two of them.

Then that meant—

Jonah looked to his left, and saw the empty bed. He shook his head.

He hadn't hit the ground chest-first, he'd hit the floor, when he'd rolled out of bed. The two wire hangers he'd left on the night stand must have fallen on his back when his ungraceful thud jostled the thing.

There was no crow. No hills, no lost spirits, and no archer. And everything had gone dark because he'd awakened in a dark room.

It had been a damn dream.

Now that he'd had that realization, his chest smarted with discomfort. He heaved himself off of the floor, and plopped down on the bunched mass of sheets and blankets on the bed.

It had just been a dream. He was glad that he was alone, and no one was around to see him make a fool of himself over a nightmare just now.

But there were some truly odd things that stuck out about that dream. Those people, the multi-colored hands that brought about stinging pain whenever the colors turned dark. It was no mystery who they were.

The Deadfallen disciples.

They'd been malicious as hell in that dream, the way they'd consolidated their endowments on him like that. But the Deadfallen disciples were all killers, so they wouldn't balk at causing agony.

Then there was the archer. Jonah was willing to swear that he'd seen him before. He'd definitely recognized the voice. Even though it had been a dream, it was nice to have had someone on his side in it. And those lost souls...Jonah didn't know what to make of them. He had seen shackled spirits before. They'd been emaciated and drained; looked as though they'd never known a moment's peace. But those spirits in that dream...

Life never ended. It merely changed form. But if that was what the spirits' lives had become, then he was just glad that it just had been a dream for their sakes.

And that crow—that had to have been Creyton. Or some representation of him, anyway. No wonder he ignored the archer.

Jonah closed his eyes. Creyton wasn't just a Spirit Reaper. He was *the* Spirit Reaper. He was looked upon as fearfully amongst Eleventh Percenters as the Tenth despots of old. But Creyton didn't call himself "Chancellor," or "Fuhrer" or the things that the dictators in the past called themselves. He called himself the Transcendent.

And the Transcendent was Jonah's mortal enemy.

They'd crossed paths before, and through luck, or testicular fortitude or whatever, Jonah managed to beat him and (or so he thought) force him to the Other Side. But the latter part hadn't happened. Through ethereal circumstances that Jonah still didn't understand, Creyton had been killed, but his spirit never went to the Other Side. He spent the equivalent of many years researching the means of a resurrection—a fact made possible by the lack of influence that time had on the Astral Plane—and had achieved Praeterletum, a literal return from the grave. He was the first Eleventh Percenter ever to manage it. His plan had come to fruition through the actions of his most loyal disciple, Inimicus, who was Jessica Hale. Jonah had very nearly lost his physical life—

Jonah swore loudly and smacked his own head with an open palm. He didn't hit his head too hard, though; he'd suffered a concussion that night Creyton achieved Praeterletum, which had only been rectified through ethereal healing. Still, he wouldn't help matters by scrambling his own brains.

He fought the thoughts each time his mind wandered to Creyton. He pushed them down as far as they would go whenever they reared themselves. Most of the time, his brain was pretty quiet, but then thoughts of that house, Jessica's betrayal, and that cold fire that burned Ant Noble to nothing but bones—

Jonah punched a nearby pillow. The thoughts had reared themselves again that quickly!

He abandoned his seated position. Sleep wasn't an option at the moment. He went to the bathroom, and silently surveyed himself in the mirror.

Jonah's profile had changed since he'd discovered that he was an Eleventh Percenter. His brown hair had elongated somewhat in the absence of barbers that he knew and trusted. His hazel eyes, upon inspecting them, very much resembled his mind at the moment; slightly haunted, confused, and full of memories that he didn't want. But there were two marked changes that had only occurred since he'd been road-tripping along the Outer Banks.

His waistline was trimmer now than it had ever been. He didn't smile at his reflection in the mirror, though, because he was of two minds about it.

Jonah was very pleased about it, no doubt about that. He'd always been between twenty and thirty pounds overweight throughout his life, so the fact that he was nearer to a flat stomach now than he'd ever been in his life was a great thing. The-not-so-pleasing part of the thing was the fact that, through his whole weight loss process, he'd discovered that it was simply wasn't in his genes to have a washboard stomach, or even visible abs. It wasn't a huge blow or anything such as that. It wasn't ever Jonah's life ambition to grace the cover of *Muscle and Fitness*, anyway. It was just that Reena had almost convinced him that through fitness gains, the sky was the limit. For his stomach, however, it seemed that the limit was the sky. Oh well.

Jonah's eyes rose back to his face, and he pondered the second change.

He'd grown a beard.

It wasn't even a deliberate thing. It was more attributed to laziness than anything else. But it was a new dynamic. The facial hair was nothing dramatic or overly dignified, but it did make him look older, more mature. It made it look as though life had shown him a thing or two. And that was a good thing, because that dream scared the hell out of him.

"Just great," he muttered to his reflection. "What is a summer without shit?"

Jonah managed to get back to sleep for several more hours before he officially began the day. He showered, dressed, straightened up the bed out of respect for the incoming maid, and checked out of the motel. It was the last day of the "vacation" that Jonathan mandated. He was cool with the fact that it was over, but he had to admit that he'd taken a great liking to this final stop.

The town, Coastal Shores, was mere miles from Manteo, and very quiet. Maybe twenty-eight hundred people resided there, which made it even smaller than Rome. But as Jonah took in the morning sun and the ocean, he couldn't make a single complaint about the place.

Despite his newfound affection for the place, Jonah still felt that it was time to return home. And it wasn't because of the dream.

Throughout his road-tripping, he'd stayed in contact with Terrence and Reena. Even though they'd always kept the conversation short out of respect for his being on "vacation," they'd kept him up on things around Rome. There had been nothing of note to report on their end, which relieved Jonah because his friends hadn't experienced any discord, but also unnerved him because it felt like Creyton wanted to lure them into a false sense of security while he and his disciples planned something even worse than what they had the last time. But Terrence and Reena hadn't spoken of anything sinister; Terrence spoke about helping the other janitors get the high school ready for the kids to come back at the end of summer break, while Reena spoke about assisting Kendall in self-defense now that she knew about the Eleventh Percent.

But something had changed in the past few weeks. Terrence and Reena were still upbeat and cheerful whenever Jonah spoke to them, but something in their voices was different. The positivity seemed a bit contrived at times. It was nothing obvious, but Jonah knew his brother and sister well. And he also knew a falsely cheerful voice when he heard it due to the fact that he had so much experience with using one himself.

Jonah wanted to know what was bothering them, but he also knew why they chose to hold back on him. Jonathan had probably told them that giving him negative information would be antithetical to his time away. But, oddly enough, Jonah didn't know how appreciative of that he was. He was beyond grateful for the time to collect his thoughts, but the estate was his home, too. He wanted to be in the know as much as everyone else. Especially if they really needed him. He still couldn't believe that Creyton had figured out that phobia.

Task at hand, Jonah, he reminded himself rather forcefully, but seconds later, he sighed.

The night he'd escaped Creyton and the Deadfallen disciples, he'd used anger to offset his fear and worry. It'd worked well enough, so he'd attempted the same approach whenever Creyton fell on his mind. But the tactic that saved his physical life that night just wasn't a healthy one to do in everyday life. He wasn't in threatening situations on the pier. Or at the beach. Or at the movies.

Or at breakfast in a diner, where a waiter had just seen his momentary scowl and began to back away in apprehension.

Smooth.

"I really wasn't trying to bother you, sir," said the waiter meekly. "I was just trying to make small talk, forgive my curiosity—"

"No, no," said Jonah hastily, "I wasn't even listening—"

The man deflated, and Jonah sucked his teeth. Not a great thing to say.

"You didn't hear anything I said?" said the waiter, who looked forlorn.

"I didn't mean it like that, sir." Jonah shook his head so as to play up the confusion of the situation. "I didn't mean that I was ignoring you, it was just—just a brief bout of reticence. I've got a lot on my mind."

Jonah waited, and breathed a sigh of relief when the man looked less depressed.

"Is that right, son?" he asked, sounding rather surprised. "You don't look like you're old enough to have a mind full of stress. Don't look like you've been in the world long enough to even have enough life to analyze."

Jonah gritted his teeth. It aggravated him something fierce when older people said things like that. He'd just turned twenty-six, and that was more than enough life to analyze. Hell, he had enough life to analyze with just the three years he'd known he was an Eleventh Percenter. "Right," he mumbled. "Now, what was it that you asked me?"

"I was asking you if you were thinking of putting down roots down in Coastal Shores, or were you just passing through?" said the waiter.

"Just passing through," replied Jonah. "Took the whole summer to myself to quiet my brain. De-stress and all that. Been throughout the Outer Banks, and Coastal Shores is my last stop before going back home."

The waiter nodded as he topped off Jonah's iced tea. "I've always said that young people move through life too fast," he remarked. "But I promise you that there isn't anything going on in your life that church can't fix."

Jonah swallowed. Not one of those types. "I suppose you're right."

The waiter regarded Jonah with narrow eyes. "You religious?"

"Not in any real sense," said Jonah, trying hard not to roll his eyes, "but I go to church."

"Really?" The waiter didn't even say it like a question. "What's the name?"

Jonah started to think that maybe he should have allowed the man to think that he was reticent a few minutes ago. "Serenity Road Faith Haven," he muttered. "Senior Pastor is Cassius Abbott."

Jonah waited with almost bated breath as the man regarded him further. But then he nodded, and he breathed a sigh of relief.

"You've got a good foundation, son," he said. "Get more involved, and you'll be fine."

"Right," said Jonah, mentally willing the man to leave.

Mercifully, the man remembered that he had a job, and left Jonah be. He glared after him for a moment. Some people in the world were just so damn nosy. And of course the nosiness had to be followed by free advice. If the man had known who Jonah truly was, then he would know it would take more than couple Sunday morning invocations to assuage his issues.

He was just about get up and pay his bill when a man lowered himself into the booth. He was lanky and thin, and stank of cigarettes and beer. The color of his stained teeth went along with that. His hair was a rat's nest, and his beard looked as though it could comfortably lodge a flock of birds. His presence annoyed Jonah even further.

Great. First, the religion-fixated waiter wanted to help me with salvation, and now the town drunk wanted a meal.

"Look, man—"

"Silence, Rowe," hissed the man as he bared those nicotine-stained teeth.

Jonah's eyes hardened for a half-second, but then he realized the guy referred to him by his last name. Now every sense was on alert. "How did you know my name?" he demanded. "What do you want?"

The man looked at Jonah with a kind of hungry delight. "Nothing in particular. Just having some fun by showing you how easy it is for you to be gotten to."

Instinctively, Jonah moved a hand to his pockets, where his batons lay, but the man shook his head warningly.

"I wouldn't do that if I were you," he said quietly. "One wrong move, and I'll kill everyone in this place. Surely you don't want another diner massacre, do you?"

Jonah's eyes widened. "Creyton—"

"The Transcendent," corrected the man.

"Yeah, him," snapped Jonah. "He wouldn't appreciate you drawing attention to yourself like this."

It was a gamble. Jonah hoped that it was true.

The man chuckled, and then a middle-aged woman sitting near the bar shook her head slightly and coughed. The man with her looked at her in concern.

"Honey? What's wrong?" he asked.

"I...I don't know," responded the woman. "I couldn't catch my breath for a moment. Think I might need my inhaler."

The woman's husband patted her back, still looking concerned. Jonah looked at the man in front of him utter horror. He was still chuckling.

"Who's drawing attention?" he asked politely. "As quietly as a rat, I could bring about a repeat of the Crystal Diner. And I know you don't want that, Rowe."

Jonah used every ounce of resolve he possessed as removed his hand from his pocket. The man smiled evilly, like he was in total control.

"Backup is an option for me as well, just so you know." He pointed to bruising at his throat. "You're outnumbered, unendowed, and stuck in the middle of all these precious, delicate Ungifteds. So if you want them to be safe, you will sit there like a good little boy."

Jonah's fingers gripped the table. If everything this Deadfallen disciple said was true, then there was nothing he could do without endangering the Tenths around him. Why did he stop here for food? Why didn't he just roll on back to Rome? These two dozen people in this diner would be safe right now if he'd done just that.

No. This stupid disciple of Creyton was the one endangering people. He had his finger on the proverbial trigger, not Jonah.

"This isn't about any of them." Jonah kept his voice very quiet, so as to not bring attention to the two of them. "Let's step outside, and handle this there."

The man flashed those badly stained teeth again. "No thank you," he said gleefully. "Now answer this question: Did you have the dream?"

Jonah's eyes widened. There was no way he could know about that.

The man smiled. "I can see by your expression that you did have it," he said. "That's all I wanted to know."

And the bastard actually rose to leave. Jonah looked at him, shocked. Was he serious?

"Oh, hell no," he snapped. "What was that dream supposed to mean?"

The man ignored him and headed for the exit. Jonah, temper and alarm rising with each passing second, followed him.

"What does it mean?" he demanded. "Answer me!"

The man said nothing, but Jonah distinctly heard another chuckle. That pissed him off even more.

"You hear me talking to you?" snarled Jonah, who didn't really notice that his words were now attracting stares. "You will not leave here without answering me!"

He reached for the guy's shoulder, but then the woman at the bar started having breathing issues once more. Jonah looked at her, concerned, but then his expression returned to anger once he looked at the man again.

"Stop that!"

The man's chuckle became a full on laugh.

"Leave her alone! If you want a victim, take me!"

More laughter.

And that was when Jonah lost it.

He threw a wild haymaker. The man slammed against the wall before he slid down to the floor. There were exclamations of shock and horror, but Jonah turned his attention to the woman who'd had her breathing obstructed.

"Ma'am! Are you okay—?"

But strangely, the woman's husband shielded his wife from Jonah, looking ready to throw a punch of his own. "Don't you come near her!" he yelled.

Jonah looked at him in confusion. "What? I meant no harm, sir!"

"No harm?" repeated the pious waiter in disbelief. "Are you joking?"

Jonah frowned, but then realized the situation. "You don't understand!" he tried to shout over the angered and panicked people. "That man over there was—"

He paused. What could he tell them? They wouldn't believe a word of it. Plus it seemed like they'd formed their own opinions of Jonah anyway.

He looked at the man on the floor, whom (conveniently) no one paid any attention to. But Jonah wasn't thinking about them at the moment.

The man rubbed his throat roughly…and wiped away the bruise. It had been makeup.

Makeup?

The guy's bloodied visage showed nothing but joy as he glanced outside. Jonah did the same.

A woman stood outside, calmly resting her weight against a trucker's rig. She ignored the commotion completely and looked straight at Jonah.

It was a white-haired woman. India Drew, one of Creyton's Deadfallen disciples.

She smiled widely as she gave Jonah a mock salute, and then—nothing could have prepared Jonah for what she did next—shape-shifted into a crow. She literally shrank into that accursed avian shape in the span of three seconds, cawed once, and took flight. Her bloody-nosed accomplice slunk out of the diner's entrance, but no one was the wiser.

And Jonah was in the middle of the diner, having just assaulted someone in front of multiple witnesses and having no explanation to give.

The fresh hell had descended. On the very last day of his vacation, his negative affirmation had come true.

2

Patience, Not a Virtue

"I won't ask again."

"You said that five minutes ago."

"Do you not understand this situation, boy?"

"My situation is that I'm entitled to a phone call, but instead I'm in here talking to you."

This had been going on for the past twenty minutes. The religious waiter at the diner had called 911, and Jonah had gotten carted away to the sorriest, most disorganized sheriff's department in America. He wasn't expecting due process. He wasn't sure that anybody in the station could even spell it.

The deputy sheriff, a man who would probably be less than insignificant had it not been for the gun and badge, had been, at least in his own eyes, bullying Jonah for information, but Jonah hadn't budged. Partly because he didn't appreciate the whole farce, and partly because if he told them what had actually happened, his next stop might be a padded cell.

The deputy ran impatient fingers across a weather-beaten brow. "You got a name, boy?"

"Wow." Jonah didn't even try to hide his frustration. "This whole time you've been badgering me, and you never even bothered to get my name, Deputy—?"

Jonah looked at the idiot's badge, and then raised his eyes to his face in disbelief. "Your name is Deputy Dumbass?"

The deputy sneered. "It's *Dümhass*."

"Well, it looks like—" began Jonah, but the man spoke over him.

"It's a misprint!" he snarled. "The engraver had bad vision!"

"Whatever, Deputy Dumbass," muttered Jonah under his breath.

Deputy Dümhass took a leveling breath, and tried to control his temper. "In all my years of being a citizen of Coastal Shores, boy, and I've been here all my life—"

"Explains a lot," murmured Jonah.

"—I have never seen such calamity," finished Dümhass in a louder voice than Jonah's. "This here's a quiet, sweet-natured, God-fearing town, boy. I wouldn't expect a drifter like you—"

"I'm not a damn drifter!" snarled Jonah. "I'm a tourist!"

"You watch your mouth, boy!" snapped Dümhass. "I've put away tougher men than your disrespectful—"

"First of all, you don't know anything about me," interrupted Jonah, whose opinion of the town went from the sky to the cellar in the past half hour, "and second of all, I've always been taught that in regards to respect, you have to give to get. You haven't given me any respect at all; you took the diner situation at face value. All this time that you've been flapping your gums about the sanctity of this town, you could have been asking for my version of what happened in the diner. You put the handcuffs on so tightly that I couldn't even feel my fuckin' fingers, and for almost half an hour, you've been trying—and failing, I might add—to frighten me. And, once again, you have not once asked me for my side of the story! So forgive me if I haven't shown you any respect. I'm only reciprocating what I've been getting from you."

It wasn't in Jonah's nature to be this disrespectful; his grandmother had drilled good manners into him. But this pack of imbecilic townies had pissed him off. He'd been trying to help that woman and the other Tenths, and he got lured into a trap by India Drew.

But why the hell had that Tenth man pretended to be an Eleventh Percenter? Even stranger, why had he pretended to be a Deadfallen disciple?

But Jonah didn't need to expend too much energy on confusion at the moment. He was in this station being questioned (by the loosest definition, anyway) for a panic that he did not personally incite. And if there was something that was guaranteed to piss Jonah off, it was being accused of things he knew he hadn't done.

Dümhass sat in silence for several minutes. It was clear to Jonah that his words had the deputy seething. But he couldn't care less.

"You really enjoying sassing people, don't you?" he said in a voice barely above a whisper. "Well, I know just what to do with you. Let's see if an overnight stay, compliments of the beautiful state of North Carolina, will make you cooperate."

At that very moment, there was a knock at the door. Dümhass' head snapped to it.

"What?" he snapped.

The man who'd been at the front desk opened the door rather timidly. Dümhass' angry face loosened somewhat at the sight of the other deputy's face.

"What is it, Hawkins?" he asked in a much more level tone.

"Sir," said the younger deputy sheepishly, "we have a visitor. For him."

He jerked his head at Jonah. Dümhass scoffed.

"This is not the Marriott, Hawkins," he said in an aggravated tone. "Tell them to get out of here."

"Um, I don't think that's gonna work, sir," said Hawkins. "See—"

Someone else pushed themselves past Hawkins into the room, and both Jonah and Dümhass flinched.

It was a black man with wire-rimmed glasses, very focused eyes, and posture so erect that Jonah wondered whether or not he'd ever curved his spine in his life. He wasn't necessarily imposing, but there was still something about the man that made Jonah feel the need to be wary or something. It kind of felt like the feeling that people got when they got around a tax auditor, or a health inspector.

The meek little deputy had said that this guy was a visitor for Jonah. But Jonah hadn't ever laid eyes on the man in his life. Was this some new crap? Some new danger?

The movies were right. The strangest things did happen in the tiniest towns.

"Deputy—" the man looked at Dümhass' nameplate, slightly raised his eyebrows, but maintained his composure, "—I'm just going to call you Deputy. I hope that that's okay."

"Who—?"

"My name is Toland Mathers," said the man, who fluidly flashed a badge and pocketed it before anyone actually noticed it. "I am here to take this man, Jonah Rowe, into my custody."

Dümhass' eyes shot up, and he rose from the seat. "Like heck you do!" he spat. "This—this Rowe man here was disturbing the peace at of this town's oldest establishments! And don't come in here with that above my pay grade horse pucky. I didn't even really see that badge; it wouldn't happen to be fake now, would it? Who are you even with, anyway?"

Mathers was neither impressed nor unnerved by Dümhass' tirade. "I'm part a department that doesn't take too kindly to gun-toting ma-and-pa law enforcement establishments who apprehend law-abiding citizens and deny them due process and access to legal counsel. And according to my information, you didn't even read Mr. Rowe his Miranda Rights."

Dümhass looked dumbfounded. Mathers turned to Jonah.

"Did any of these things happen, Mr. Rowe?" he asked.

Jonah didn't know this man from Adam, but he liked him. Dümhass caught his eye, with a pleading look in his own. Jonah smiled at him assuredly, but then muttered, "Nope."

Dümhass whimpered. Hawkins gawked at Mathers in disbelief.

"You didn't read him his rights, sir?" he asked.

"Shut up, Hawkins," said Dümhass, who now looked as fearful as the younger deputy did earlier.

Mathers nodded in satisfaction. Both deputies stared at him in silent terror.

"This is the part where you leave me to question Rowe, and no longer hinder me from now until the time we leave," he said to them.

Dümhass, though still rattled, looked as if he'd been force-fed something bitter. "Move along, Hawkins," he grumbled, and the two of them left.

Mathers stared at the door for several seconds. Jonah stared at Mathers.

"What—?" he began, but Mathers waved a hand at him for silence. He shut his mouth, more confused than ever.

Several more seconds passed, and then a pleased look crossed Mather's face. He sat in the chair that Dümhass had just vacated, and stared at his watch.

"That took longer than it should have," he muttered. "Nine whole minutes. I'm getting slow."

Jonah frowned. "Um, what are you talking about?" he asked. "Why were you staring at the door? While we're at it, who are you? How do I know you?"

"You don't know me, Jonah," said the man. "You just know of me."

"Begging your pardon, sir," said Jonah, "but I can't say that I do. I'm grateful that you got Deputy Dumbass off my back, but I've never heard of a Toland Mathers."

He snorted. "Toland Mathers isn't my name," he told Jonah. "That was merely a pseudonym. My real name is Ovid Patience."

Jonah's eyes widened. "Patience?" he repeated. "As in Mr. Decessio's friend? Networker?"

"The very same," nodded Patience, who extended his hand. "Nice to officially meet you, Rowe."

Jonah shook the extended hand, still rather dumbfounded. "Pleasure is mutual, but—why are you here? How did you know I needed help?"

"I'm a Networker, Jonah," said Patience. "We've been heavily trained to detect the involvement of ethereal humans in Tenth Percent crimes."

The earlier irritation rippled across Jonah's shock. "I didn't do anything."

"Of course you didn't." Patience didn't sound doubtful or disbelieving. "People see only what they want to see, and Tenths, bless them, do that more than anyone. Now before we proceed, please tell me what did happen in that diner."

Full of gratitude that someone believed him, Jonah told Patience about the Tenth impostor with the makeup on his throat who played a part while India Drew perpetrated the whole thing from the parking lot. His frustration, which had been dulled momentarily after Patience's arrival, reared itself once more during the recounting of the story.

"And once they'd made up in their minds that I was the one in the wrong, they didn't pay any attention to anything else," he concluded. "They didn't even notice it when the guy snuck out of the place, or the fact that a fully grown woman outside turned into a damned bird and flew off."

Patience took a deep breath. "A Tenth Percenter was doing the bidding of a Deadfallen?"

Jonah noticed that it sounded more rhetorical than anything else. "Um...does that mean something that I don't know?"

"I fear that it does." Patience rose, and invited Jonah to do the same. "But it's time to leave here."

Jonah glanced at the door of the interrogation, puzzled. "Are you going to show that Networker badge again? Because I think Deputy Dumbass will pay more attention to it this time."

"Networkers do not carry badges." Patience's voice was full of distaste. "One shouldn't need to carry such a gimmicky device so as to denote their affiliation. This thing in my pocket was merely a prop to throw off this sheriff's department. But they will not be a bother to us."

"How can you be so sure?"

"Jonah, I am involved in Spectral Law," Patience told him. "Taking the reins of an ethereal matter from Tenth authorities is my job. Besides that, these people have screwed up twice. First, they denied you your rights. Second, they tried to eavesdrop at the door."

"Seriously?"

"Yep," said Patience. "Why do you think that I stared at the door for a little while? But I'm not supposed to know what they were doing, of course."

"I'm just saying," said Jonah, who felt the need to be devil's advocate, "this is a police station—"

"Son, this is a joke." Patience didn't laugh, but his eyes were full of mirth. "*Mayberry, R.F.D.* was more organized than this, and that was a T.V. show. Trust me, I've got this."

Finally, Jonah believed him. If he'd been doing this for years and was that confident in his abilities, why should he worry? "Alright, sir. I'm ready to get back to Rome, anyway."

"Ah." Patience looked at Jonah, and some of the mirth left his eyes. "We're not going to the estate. I can't take you straight home just yet. We're going to the Decessio's house first."

"Huh?" said Jonah, taken aback. "Why?"

"There are…things you need to know first," said Patience evasively.

"What things?" Jonah's frustration was back. Surely, Terrence and Reena would have let him know if something was wrong, vacation or no. Was the reason that he couldn't go straight home the same reason that he'd detected something different in their voices when he'd spoken to them in recent weeks?

Patience scratched his brow. "We won't talk about it here," he said finally, "not in this place. But the thing that you need to know is that while you've been on your Jonathan-ordered sabbatical, the—world changed. Our world changed. Creyton returning from the grave screwed up a lot of things, for a lot of people."

3

Cult Status

Patience hadn't lied. He and Jonah walked out of the sheriff's department with nary a peep from anyone. Deputy Dümhass glared, but he knew he had no legs to stand on. Jonah wondered whether or not the deputy's blunder would cost him his job. Dumbass.

Jonah was just about to mention that he needed to get back to his car and pick up his stuff, but Patience beat him to it.

"It would not be in your best interest to be seen around that diner again," he said, "so we took care of your car. It's been towed."

"What?!"

"Pipe down, boy," said Patience shortly. "It was in appearance only. I had it taken to the Decessio home. Arn and Connie had no issue with that. It will probably be there before we get there ourselves. But I wanted to make it look like it had been towed, so as to please the patrons once they got so bloodthirsty."

Jonah looked away, feeling foolish. "Thanks. But hang on a second. You said that my car will be there before we get there? How can that be? Aren't we using the *Astralimes*?"

"No." Patience pointed to a black Trans Am. "It will behoove us to travel sans ethereal means as much as humanly possible. Trust me on that."

Jonah frowned. Did that have to do with these oh-so-major world changes as well? What had Creyton done that was so bad that it subjected Jonah to a ride in a Trans Am older than he was?

Patience raised an eyebrow at his expression. "Do you have a problem with my car?" he asked quietly.

"No," lied Jonah. "It's just that—"

"It's been fully restored," interrupted Patience, with just the faintest trace of annoyance in his voice. "I've been restoring it for the past several years, and I change the oil every month. Like Arn Decessio, cars are my hobby as well. My engine is probably more solvent than your own."

"I'm sure it is," said Jonah sycophantically. "Let's just please get out of this town."

Patience lowered himself into the car, and Jonah followed suit. Upon entering, he was never more thankful to have lost weight over the summer than he was now. If he'd been heavier, this tight ride would have been even more unpleasant.

Jonah was happy to see the *You Are Now Leaving Coastal Shores* sign. It was just so odd, because just that morning, he'd viewed the town as one of the nicest places he'd ever visited. Now he couldn't get out of the place fast enough. He wondered if he should blame India Drew or the townies for that.

Patience made very little small talk for a long while, and did much of the driving in silence. When they were within fifty or sixty miles of the Decessio house, however, he broke the quiet. "How many places had you gone?" he asked Jonah.

"Mainly places up the coast," responded Jonah. "Not the tourist traps or anything, but just the quiet places where I could relax."

"Did you grow up in the Outer Banks?" asked Patience.

"No, the Inner Banks," answered Jonah. "Nana didn't really care for beaches because she didn't really like leaving her garden. So when I got my driver's license, I started frequenting the places myself."

Patience nodded. "And had no incidences with dark ethereality?"

"Not until today," sighed Jonah.

For some reason, Patience looked guilty for a moment. "I'm sorry, son," he said.

"For what?" asked Jonah.

Patience sort of shrugged. "You were, at least until today, having a good time of things," he said. "Now, I'm pulling you back into the thick of things, and I just felt the need to apologize. Especially after that less than delightful dream—"

He froze. Jonah, who'd been paying attention to Patience's words the whole time, widened his eyes at that.

"How did you know I'd had a bad dream?"

"I didn't," said Patience.

"Don't lie to me, sir," said Jonah. "I never mentioned having a dream, not even when I told you what happened at the diner."

Patience said nothing. Jonah's eyes narrowed.

"Are you an informant?" he questioned.

"No, boy!" Patience's eyes widened. "If I were in league with Creyton, would I have saved you from the Yokel Patrol back there?"

Jonah deflated, realizing just how idiotic his accusation was. "My mistake. It's just that in the past several months, I've put trust in a lot of wrong people—"

"I know what you've been through, Jonah," said Patience. "Jonathan has kept us up to speed. But I am not on the side of the Deadfallen disciples. Just the mere thought of being on the dark side makes my stomach turn."

"Apologies," muttered Jonah. "But I want to know how you knew about the dream."

Patience switched lanes so as to get close to the highway exit. "Because I had the dream, too."

"That so?"

"Everyone had it, Jonah," said Patience. "Every Eleventh Percenter we're aware of had that dream. Even the sazers had it. Felix and Prodigal told us."

Jonah turned his attention back to the highway and let that sink in. He thought that knowing that he hadn't been alone would bring him some relief, but he felt just the opposite. It felt like isolation. Like the entire ethereal world was in danger together and sequestered from the rest of the population, who would never understand what they, the Eleventh Percenters, dealt with.

So that was why Terrence and Reena sounded so strange—

No. That odd thing had been in Terrence's and Reena's voices before that dream; the dream had only occurred the previous night.

So what else was going on?

"Patience," Jonah said it slowly and clearly, "what else has been happening? Why can't we just go to the estate? Going to the Decessio house feels like a—a pit stop. It's like I need to be mentally fortified for something."

Patience took Exit 81. "Let's just get to the house, son," he said quietly. "Your morning was crazy enough."

Jonah hadn't been to the Decessio house since the opening game of Bobby's last football season. He also remembered that at that time, they'd received information about a resurgence of Eighth Chapter crimes, which denoted crimes perpetrated by Creyton's followers. That had been bad enough. But he couldn't shake the feeling that whatever he was about to learn would make last year's revelations downright tame.

He exited the car, hurried to the door, and knocked. He was so eager for information that he didn't even check to see if his car had sustained any damages during the towing. The door swung open, and Mrs. Decessio wrapped her arms around Jonah seconds later.

"Jonah!" There was relief in her voice. "It's so great to see you! Everybody is waiting, so come on in. And Patience! How are you?"

She greeted Patience with kiss on his cheek, and he got a hug of his own. Jonah made it three feet before Terrence and Reena were there with him.

Terrence gave him a half-smile and a mock salute. Reena wrapped him in a one-armed hug, and then stepped back to take him in.

"Look at you," she said approvingly, taking in his frame.

"Love the beard!" laughed Terrence. "Keeping it?"

"Yeah, I think so." Jonah ran a finger over his facial hair. "I've already gotten past the barbs-on-my-face phase. Wouldn't make much sense to shear it off now."

Reena didn't say anything, which led Jonah to believe that she had mixed emotions about his new feature. Whatever.

"Vera might like it," added Terrence. "Makes you look more dangerous."

Jonah rolled his eyes. "Yeah, and out-of-work accountant with writing aspirations," he said. "I'm quite a bad boy."

"You're more bad to the bone than you think, man!" said Terrence.

"Uh-huh." Jonah turned serious. "Now are you going to tell me why you guys sounded so funny on the phone these past few weeks?"

Terrence and Reena looked at each other. Jonah impatiently tapped his fingers on his pants pocket. But Jonah's informal siblings were spared by Mr. Decessio, who came into the hall and greeted Jonah.

"Glad to see you safe and sound, son." He shook Jonah's hand with both of his own. "I've been ordered to collect the three of you. Connie's got food ready."

"Score!" Terrence clapped his hands together and headed that way. Reena gave Jonah another look of apprehension, and followed Terrence. Jonah frowned behind them.

All of that was a clear red flag to him. Since when had Terrence allowed his mom to cook on her own? Whenever she was in the kitchen, Terrence was on her like a shadow. Mrs. Decessio couldn't even make yeast rolls without Terrence checking and re-checking whether they rose properly, or were sufficiently buttered. She never made complaints about it, because Terrence was almost a better cook than she was. So why had she cooked alone?

What was going on here?

He reached the dining room, and was caught by surprise once again. He expected the only occupants to Mr. and Mrs. Decessio, Terrence, Reena, Alvin, Bobby, and Patience. Liz was also a possibility. While those people were all present, there were other people he hadn't expected to see there: Raymond, the oldest Decessio child, and June Mylteer. Ray wasn't a huge surprise, because he could have easily dropped in on his parents just to say hi, or something. But this was Friday afternoon. Shouldn't he have been at work?

But June Mylteer, on the other hand, had no reason to be in the Decessio household that Jonah could think of.

He'd only met the man once, and that was a few months ago, when Mylteer functioned as a consigliere for Sanctum Arcist once they'd gotten it into their minds that they were going to besiege the estate. He'd acquitted himself as a halfway decent guy, however, and Jonathan had even said later on that he was on board with them against Creyton. That was all well and good. But his presence amongst people that he'd recently been strategizing against in a near-war?

Red flag number two.

"Hey man!" crooned Bobby, who high-fived Jonah. Liz, ever his de facto baby sister, gave him her trademark beam and embrace. Ray acknowledged Jonah's presence with a nod, but he couldn't do further than that because he wielded two pitchers of water and lemonade. June approached him slowly, extending his hand as he did so. Jonah took it, but eyed him warily. Mylteer snickered.

"Surprised to see me, eh?"

"Very," admitted Jonah. "What are you doing here? Shouldn't you be in Florida? At Sanctum?"

"I haven't resided at Sanctum for over eight years," said June. "And besides, I'm keeping a cordial distance from them, especially right now."

"Huh?" said Jonah. "Why is th—?"

"Please, boys." Mrs. Decessio's voice was stern. "No shop talk until after the meal. Now sit and eat."

As everyone complied with Mrs. Decessio's wishes, Jonah realized that the spread was majestic: Oven-fried chicken (Reena would love that), rolls, vegetables, mashed potatoes, salad, cheese slices, rice bread, and Mrs. Decessio's world-famous bacon macaroni and cheese. It all looked flawless. Wonderful.

And it made Jonah more suspicious than ever.

The fact that Mrs. Decessio made such a hearty meal wasn't shocking. She was entertaining guests, and always went above and beyond. But these dishes contained the holiday fanfare. It also seemed the glorious cuisine had a "last supper" vibe to it.

Red flag number three.

But Jonah's suspicions weren't enough to prevent him from piling his plate high, though. Everyone else did the same, except for Reena. And if he thought that June Mylteer would be discreet, he was very wrong.

"This is amazing, Mrs. D!" He dropped two rolls on his plate despite the fact that he didn't really have the room for them. "I hope that you weren't expecting me to eat like a canary."

Mrs. Decessio raised her eyebrows. "Doesn't Emily feed you, June? Ever?"

"My mother hasn't cooked like this since she found out about her hypertension and cholesterol issues," said June. "Dad and I have been in a dietary abyss ever since."

"Surely, you aren't complaining about that, June?" said Reena in a voice that was a step above chiding. "One would think that you and your father would be supportive of your mother's valuing her physical life, and amassing healthful gains."

"Oh, we're proud of her, Reena," said June through a mouthful of mac and cheese. "Very much so. It's just that... well, we aren't the ones with hypertension."

"You know," said Liz delicately, "Mrs. Mylteer can get that righted with a properly proportioned tonic. I could whip her up one, no problem."

June shook his head. "Mom is aware of that, but she refused," he told her. "She said that if she got a Green Aura's cure, it would be no better than getting a free pass to screw herself up all over again. So she's managing it Tenth style."

"Admirable," murmured Terrence under his breath, "but I'd take the tonic and let that crap go."

From there, people broke off into tangential conversations, which Jonah listened to with a mixture of amusement and impatience: Liz spoke about how she needed to "buckle down" this year, which Jonah couldn't understand, because she'd always been a brilliant student. Bobby was telling a very disapproving Mrs. Decessio that he planned to double his intakes of eggs, chicken, and tuna so as to pack on more muscle.

"Say you got hurt and were forced to take time off of weight training, Bobby," said his mother. "If that happened, most of your musculature and tone would fade. And you're talking about putting on more?"

"Mama, you worry too much," said Bobby, unabashed. "I'm durable. Always have been. And you forget that my girlfriend is a Green Aura?"

Liz, still conversing with Reena, blushed when she heard that, but Mrs. Decessio looked even sterner.

"That's your grand plan, Bobby?" She narrowed her eyes. "To run yourself full throttle every time you play football, and then use Elizabeth's talents as your crutch? That makes no sense—"

"Oh, Mama," said Alvin suddenly, "let Bobby have Liz's help. If he gets injured, who do you think will have to rehab the injury with him?"

That actually elicited some laughs, even from Mrs. Decessio. Jonah couldn't help but notice that Mr. Decessio, Raymond, and Patience spoke amongst themselves a great deal. He didn't know what they were talking about exactly, but was certain that they weren't observing Mrs. Decessio's shop talk rule.

Jonah spent the whole meal using his ethereality to balance his impatience, and it worked somewhat. But now, the meal was winding down, and the time had come. He pushed his plate away and took a deep breath.

"Alright, everybody." His voice was level, but from the way everyone eyed him, he may as well have shouted. "Mrs. Decessio, this was a wonderful meal. Best in the world. And for that, I thank you. But it's very obvious that all of you wanted me sated and satisfied for a reason. Well, mission accomplished. Now I would greatly appreciate it if you all would tell me what is going on. What is it that everyone knows that I don't?"

Mr. Decessio sighed. "Jonah, I'm sure Patience has told you that things have changed," he said.

"He did, sir," said Jonah. "Has Creyton done something?"

"Yeah, he's done something," said June. "He returned from beyond the grave."

Jonah rolled his eyes. "I know that," he said rather tersely. "I was there. I mean has anything happened since then."

Mr. Decessio cast an annoyed glance at June, and then looked back at Jonah. "Son, none of us know what Creyton is up to," he said. "His planned magnum opus of making us obliterate ourselves came to naught, thanks to you, so he was forced back to the drawing board. Creyton has done what he's always done, which is screw things up. But that is on a much deeper level now."

"How do you mean?" asked Jonah.

"Jonah, life is all about balance," said Patience. "There is a time, period, and position for everything. And then, it is time to move on, continue the spiritual journey, whether that's staying on Earthplane, becoming a Guide of some kind, or completely passing on to the Other Side. But Creyton's Praeterletum has...made things foul."

"Huh?"

"Know anything about history?" Raymond chimed in. "Know the story of the early settlers into the New World? How they brought diseases that the indigenous people had never experienced, and things were disastrous because of it? It's kind of like that."

Jonah straightened in his seat. "So—Creyton's return is making people sick?"

"From an ethereal standpoint, yes," said Mrs. Decessio resignedly.

Jonah looked at the woman. It was clear that she didn't want to be having this conversation, but felt that Jonah had the right to know.

"Creyton's return has made some people act negatively again," she continued. "Make them more prone to volatility."

Anger flashed across Jonah's consciousness. "He's blocked the paths to the Other Side again?"

"That's the weird part, Jonah," said Reena. "He hasn't."

"He hasn't blocked the paths?" said Jonah, confused. "Then why are people acting volatile again?"

"It's a confusing thing, Jonah," said Mr. Decessio. "Creyton and his disciples have resumed their Spirit Reaping ways once again, but the path to the Other Side remains clear. It's like Creyton isn't bothering to block them, because he isn't allowing any spirits to reach that far, anyway. But Creyton's return has changed nature. No ethereal human has ever backpedaled from spirit back into physical life. Life functions like a machine. If one cog is disrupted, the whole machine malfunctions. That's what Creyton's resurrection has done to Earthplane and the Astral Plane. He's caused them to malfunction."

Jonah took several breaths. "So there are people who are acting out of their minds and behaving out of character because Creyton's return to physical life has thrown a monkey wrench into life itself?"

"Something like that," said June. "So now you can see that when I said Creyton had 'done something' by re-emerging into physical life, it wasn't sarcasm."

Jonah stared around the table. "Then why aren't we doing something?" he demanded. "Isn't this an all hands on deck situation? Felix, the rest of the S.P.G.—better yet, drag Sanctum Arcist along, those fools adore fighting—"

"Never gonna happen."

June was the one who said it. His voice was so matter-of-fact on the subject that it wasn't even funny.

Jonah raised his eyebrows. "Um...what's going on with them?"

"Jonah, Sanctum Arcist has become synonymous with bull—" June paused, and glanced at Mrs. Decessio, "—uh, bovine fecal matter. It's like the family issue that everyone in the house is aware of, but nobody talks about. I truly hate to say it, but Mr. Kaine and G.J. got off easy compared to the cesspit that Gabriel and the rest of them had been left in. And the remaining members of The Network? They should have been fed to sazers; The Plane with No Name is a kindness."

"I'm stopping you right there," said Patience firmly. He even raised a hand so as to accentuate the point. "First of all, June, to imply that all sazers are wild cannibals is about as bad as the vampire's hemocentrism. Seeing as how your father is a sazer, I'd like to think that you understand that. And speaking as a Networker with three campaigns on his resume, I've been to The Plane with No Name countless times. It is not a kindness."

June rolled his eyes. "Dial it back, man," he murmured. "I'm simply saying that Sanctum isn't a good place to be at the moment."

Patience ignored June, and turned to Jonah. "Jonah, what June should have said is that it's not that simple a matter," he said. "There are other things that you haven't been told yet."

Jonah braced himself for the next wave of bombshells. Patience plodded on.

"The Phasmastis Curaie has been cracking down on those of us who know the truth," he said.

Jonah felt another prickle of anger. "What, they don't believe what I said about Creyton being back?"

"Oh, they believe you." Mrs. Decessio actually laughed, though it void of mirth. "No one ever doubted what you experienced, Jonah. There can be no question that Creyton is physically alive once again. The problem is where they decided to place the blame."

Jonah's brow contracted. "They blame all of Sanctum Arcist?"

"You wish," said Terrence. "They blame us all."

Jonah gaped. "Excuse me?"

"The Curaie hold us all responsible." Alvin entered the conversation for the first time. "According to Patience here, they've said that the plots, bloodlust, and treachery led to—uh, what was it, Patience?"

" '*An environment susceptible to this ongoing unprecedented phenomenon,*' " recited Patience in a hollow voice. "That was their very statement."

Jonah's mouth dropped.

"Uh-huh," said Bobby, clutching Liz's hand. "That's exactly what I said."

"But how—how can that be?" cried Jonah. "That's not fair at all! That's like the last person at the crime scene gets slapped with the charge! Did anyone mention that Creyton used his disciples to plant those seeds of bloodlust and treachery in the first place?"

"It fell on deaf ears, Jonah," said Reena. "They're convinced that we all had a hand in creating this mess. They believe that we've had too much free rein to experiment with the Eleventh Percent."

"You've got to be kidding," said Jonah. "I thought that the Spirit Guides were intelligent!"

"Jonah, it's not a question of intelligence," said Patience defensively, like he felt compelled to go to bat for them, "it's a lack of reference. This has never happened before. They are afraid. We all are. And they're Spirit Guides, so their perspective is very different from our own."

"That may very well be," argued Jonah, "but blaming us for Creyton's achieving Praeterletum is full-blown stupid. We need to be fighting him and his Deadfallen disciples. We're no match for anyone if we squabble amongst ourselves."

"It all comes back to fear, Jonah," said June. "And that is a fear that was exacerbated last night, when every known Eleventh, sazer, and herald had that freakin' dream."

Jonah gave an involuntary twitch. "Patience told me that in the car. That many had that dream?"

"Yes," said Mr. Decessio. "The lush peaks, the barren valley full of lost spirits and spiritesses, the Deadfallen disciples' aura colors going dark, the archer and the crow. We all dreamed it."

Jonah didn't know what to think. Didn't know what to feel. "And I take it that that's never happened before, either?"

No one answered.

"Great," muttered Jonah. "Did the archer tell all of you to run, too?"

Reena looked confused. "No. Were you told to run?"

Now it was Jonah that didn't answer. So a legion of ethereal humans had the same dream, but only he was told to run? Why did that seem like it had something to do with his being the Blue Aura? After all, he *really* needed to stick out from everyone else even more than he already did.

"For what it's worth, Jonathan's not pleased in the least by the Curaie's stance, either," said Raymond.

"It's nice to have some support from the Spiritual side of things," Jonah ground out. "I'll probably be in need his counsel a great deal, and for an indefinite amount of time."

Liz swallowed. "Indefinite is a really long time, Jonah," she said delicately. "You might need to lean to your own understanding."

"And what in the world does that mean?" Jonah turned his eyes to Liz.

She didn't respond. Everyone at the table exchanged glances. Jonah almost said something bad, but caught himself at the very last second.

"I would be quite grateful if you guys would stop doing that," he said with measured calm. "Just spill it!"

Reena licked her lips. "Jonah, we might not be seeing too much of Jonathan for the foreseeable future," she told him. "His presence, especially for extended periods of time, might make things worse."

"Make things—?"

"We're being investigated as a cult, Jonah," Terrence blurted out.

Jonah stared at him. "I'm sorry, but for a moment I thought you said we were being investigated as a cult."

"Yep," said Terrence, surprisingly serious.

Jonah couldn't believe it. He refused to believe it.

"Started about three or four weeks ago," said June. "You've been watching the news, haven't you?"

"Not if I can help it," admitted Jonah. "Far too depressing."

"Eh, that's fine." June got out his phone, pulled up a YouTube video, and showed it to Jonah. "That guy. He's the investigator."

Jonah looked at the man in the video. He looked to be in his early fifties, and his face seemed ready-made for glares and sneers. His eyes, gray like Jonathan's, shone with a cold brilliance. He was yelling passionately about something, but as June's phone was silent, Jonah heard nothing. But it seemed that he was angry about something in the video as well.

"His name is Balthazar Lockman," revealed June. "Former right-wing congressman-turned cult buster after his daughter was murdered by what he thinks was a cultist nine years ago."

"What do you mean, 'what he thinks was a cultist?' " asked Jonah.

"The man his daughter was involved with was named Davis Powell," said Patience.

Jonah stiffened. "Wait. I swear I've heard that name before."

"You have, Jonah," said Reena. "It was one of those Deadfallen disciples that Felix told us about last fall."

"Back up," said Terrence, looking at Patience, "you said he *was* named Davis Powell. He isn't on The Plane with No Name? Did he escape?"

"No one has escaped The Plane with No Name," said Patience with pride in his voice. "Powell was placed there, yes, but he passed into Spirit under very mysterious circumstances once Lockman began investigating."

"Would it have mattered what Lockman found?" asked Jonah.

"Yes, it very well would have," said Raymond. "The Deadfallen disciples are integrated into Tenth society, remember? Exposing our world like that would have been bad for all Elevenths, and of course, bad for Creyton."

"Creyton had one of his own disciples killed?"

"Jonah, he has done it at least once before in the past," Reena reminded him.

Jonah looked away. "Oh yeah. I forgot."

"But at the time, Lockman went nuclear when he found some information Powell had written in a journal about the Transcendent, spiritual endowments, and being ethereal," said Patience. "The man obviously doesn't know about the Eleventh Percent, or where we put our prisoners, but he did get a hold of that journal. Before we could tie Powell to his crimes in a way that would appease the Tenth side of things, Creyton had him killed, and then had Wyndam O'Shea burn down his home."

Jonah frowned. "That was awfully sloppy for Creyton," he remarked.

"Made to look sloppy," corrected Patience. "By making it look like a bumbling cover-up, Creyton provided misdirection from his and his disciples' actions. Then he punished Powell by having him killed; I have no doubts that he got a message to one of his disciples on the Plane to do Powell in. Anyway, when all was said and done, Balthazar Lockman was an angry, hurt father with no answers."

"And the anti-cult crusader was born," supplied Bobby. "He is after us now."

"He doesn't even know—" Jonah shook his head. "How did we even get on the man's radar?"

"Specifics are unknown," said June, "but Creyton and his usual schemes are in there somewhere. That's why I'm here. Jonathan and I have our differences, but I'll be damned if all the good he's done at your estate and in the ethereal world go up in smoke because this guy never got vengeance for his daughter's murder."

Jonah nodded. His blood simmered, but he figured that June's aid was better than nothing at all. "So Creyton's resurrection has made people crazy, again, the Curaie hopes that all the problems will go away if they ignore it, and are mad at us for supposedly causing, it, and then there is this nut job cult hunter, whose presence is making Jonathan go semi-incommunicado. Does that about cover it?"

"Yeah," murmured several people around the table.

Jonah narrowed his eyes. "And why did no one see fit to tell me?"

Reena looked at him with caution. Terrence meant to say some bracing remark, but Jonah shook his head.

"Don't say because you wanted to respect my vacation," he said. "Don't say that you thought that you were doing me a favor, either. It was not a favor for me to be tucked away in the Outer Banks while you guys slogged through hell. Wanted to protect me, did you all?

I'm a member of this team, and of this huge family. When something happens that concerns the estate, it affects me just as much as it affects all of you."

"Jonah, you're mad at the wrong people," said Reena steadily. "After all that you witnessed, everyone just thought—"

"Who says I'm mad?" said Jonah quietly, disregarding everything else that Reena said. "I ain't mad at all."

Reena sighed. "Yeah, you are," she said. "Your essence is—"

"Don't do that, Reena." Jonah felt his nostrils flare. "Don't presume to think that you know everything about me, because you sure as hell don't. You were wrong to keep me out of the loop on this for so long, and that's all there is to it."

Reena looked angry herself now, but she said nothing. No one else did, either, and Jonah was glad for that. If anyone said anything about wanting him to be safe, there just might be an outburst.

"I'm going home," he muttered. "See you when you all get there. Mrs. Decessio, thanks again for the meal."

He turned his back on them all without another word, got into his car, and sped off.

4

Homecoming

By the time Jonah neared the estate, most of his frustration had given way to regret. And maybe even shame.

No, he didn't appreciate being kept out of the loop. That part hadn't changed. But maybe Reena had been right.

Oh, damn it all, she had definitely been right. Jonah's anger was misplaced.

Terrence, Reena, and the rest of them weren't the ones bringing this hellacious crap onto the Earth and Astral Planes. They weren't the ones who put the estate at the mercy of a right-wing, vengeful cult investigator. It was Creyton doing those things. Who had he used this time? Wyndam O'Shea? Charlotte Daynard? A nameless disciple Jonah didn't yet know? Or his beloved Inimicus, Jessica Hale?

And because of the fires that they created, Jonah had just snapped at, and very likely pissed off, the people that were on his side. And that was after getting arrested in Coastal Shores.

He was batting zero for life right now.

Swearing to himself, he pulled into the gate and soon saw his home beyond the trees. It stood as resolutely and majestically as it always had, but something was different.

Very different.

There were many more dark windows than there were lit ones.

When Jonah left for the Outer Banks, it seemed like every room had been occupied. The estate had been bursting with life. But now it was emptier. Quieter. Even a little forlorn.

As Jonah surveyed the setting in confusion, he felt eyes on him, and turned. It was Bast.

"Hey Bast." Jonah knelt to scratch her ears.

"*Greetings, Jonah,*" she intimated to him. "*How are you doing? Was your time away all that you hoped it would be?*"

Jonah's mouth twisted. "For the most part," he grumbled. "But never mind that. Where is everybody, Bast?"

The herald looked a bit crestfallen. The emotion on her small face was entirely new. "*Too much for me to intimate,*" was what flashed across Jonah's mind. "*Creyton's return—and subsequent actions—have created ripples that are most far-reaching. Are you aware of the current investigations of our home?*"

Jonah looked at the grounds, which were much less visible now that the late afternoon had turned to evening. "Yeah, I am. Can you tell me exactly—?"

Bast began to shrink away. Jonah frowned at her. She didn't intimate anything else into his mind. But then he tensed. Someone was directly behind him.

"Stand," commanded a vaguely familiar voice. "Now."

Very slowly, Jonah complied.

"Who are you, and what are you doing here?" said the person behind Jonah. "And don't even think of running. That'd be a very stupid thing to do right now."

The word *running* made it click. But wait…how could that be? Jonah hadn't actually heard that voice in his real, physical life. It had just been dream, and that Spectral Event…

Very cautiously, Jonah turned around to an arrow notched about two feet away from his face. When the archer saw his face, which was illuminated by the arrow, which gleamed gold, he exhaled in relief and lowered his weapon.

"Jonah Rowe." His voice sounded much more pleasant now that it was free of suspicion. "It's you. Even if I'd seen you from afar, I wouldn't have recognized you with that beard. My awareness is not what it once was."

Jonah took in some of those words, but he was more focused on the figure who'd voiced them. "How are you here?" he asked. "I remember you from the Spectral Event, but you said that I wouldn't remember your name."

"Indeed I did," said the archer. "And my name is Daniel."

"Daniel." Jonah memory flooded back the second he'd heard the name. "I remember now. The Spectral Event wasn't the most recent time I saw you. You were the one—"

"—from the dream that all of the Eleventh Percenters had," finished Daniel. "I'm sure that you've already heard many things at the Decessio residence. Why don't you and your friends come on in and we can speak more?"

"My friends?"

Daniel pointed, and Jonah turned. Bobby, Alvin, Liz, Terrence, and Reena were there. Jonah hadn't even felt the breeze when they came through the *Astralimes*. Bobby had a rather awkward look on his face, as did Terrence. Liz regarded him with caution. But Reena got right up in his face.

"Are you in there, Jonah?" she demanded. "Or is the asshole still out of the box?"

Jonah ran his tongue across his teeth. "It's back in the box," he muttered. "I apologize."

Reena's face cleared somewhat. "Accepted. Now that you've met Daniel, let's head on inside."

* * *

Jonah's outward assessment of the estate had been an accurate one. Many of his friends weren't there. He did see Magdalena, Malcolm, Spader, Akshara, and Maxine, but several others, like Ben-Israel, Noah,

Barry, and Sherman were nowhere in sight. Jonah didn't even see Nella, Liz's youngest sister. Liz waved away his concern.

"She might be around later this week," she told him, "but right now, she's visiting my Aunt Clara with Mom and Sandrine."

"Really?" asked Jonah, curious. "How did you get out of it?"

Liz snorted. "Green Aura reasons," she murmured.

Jonah shook his head at the lame excuse, but filed it away. "Where is everybody?"

"I'll tell you everything that you need to know, with Jonathan's help," said Daniel, who removed his bow from his back and placed it within reaching distance. "It's about twenty-six people here, give or take. Probably the ones who flat-out refused to leave, or the ones that Jonathan simply couldn't place anywhere."

That sounded very odd. What did it mean?

"But I thought you said Jonathan wouldn't be around," Jonah said to Daniel, but at that very moment, the Protector Guide appeared, a small smile on his face as he surveyed the family room's occupants.

"I won't be as visible as in the past, Jonah, it's true," he said. "But that applies to the grounds. The interior of our home is fair game. At least sometimes, anyway."

Although Jonathan had a smile on his face, Jonah noticed that it didn't reach his eyes, which were focused, determined, and a little hard. He wondered if Jonathan was hiding something again, or if he simply had one too many thoughts in his head.

Jonathan looked at Daniel with a slight frown. "Daniel, is it true what Bast intimated to me? Did you point an arrow at Jonah?"

"It was an honest mistake, sir," said Daniel. "In the present climate, one can never be too careful. My cognizance has greatly diminished since...you know."

"Nonsense," dismissed Jonathan. "You are as sharp now as you ever were. Even so, Jonah offers no threat to our home. Do not do that again."

"Yes, sir," said Daniel.

Jonah was a bit mystified by Daniel referring to Jonathan as "sir." With his charcoal-grey hair, he looked to be Jonathan's elder. But he knew that chronologically, Jonathan outstripped the archer by several decades.

Or did he?

"Hold on," said Jonah. "Daniel, you're a Protector Guide, too, aren't you?"

Daniel had his eyes focused on an arrow, which gleamed gold in his grasp once more. "No," he replied. "No longer."

Jonathan looked at Daniel with respect. Jonah looked at Terrence and Reena. Terrence widened his eyes and shook his head, and Reena pointed a finger at Daniel and mouthed, "*Pay attention!*"

"Daniel is the one that stopped the Deadfallen disciples in that dream you all had, Jonah," said Jonathan.

Jonah's mind went back to the dream. The numerous Deadfallen disciples, the myriad of aura colors which turned dark and caused the stinging pains, and the archer—Daniel—who laid them all out. And of course, his warning to Jonah to run, which no one else was told. Now was as good a time as any.

"You told me to run in that dream, Daniel," he said to the man. "But no one else was told that. Why was it just me?"

"You're the Blue Aura, Jonah," said Daniel. "The hatred that they have for you is more concentrated than anyone else."

Jonah took a very slow breath. So he was right. It happened with only him because he was in more danger than anyone else. Because, of course.

"When Creyton achieved Praeterletum, the Curaie quickly realized the natural abhorrence that he had caused," Daniel went on. "They tasked us all with damage control. That included the Protector Guides, the guardians, the Elect and Very Elect spirits and spiritesses—all of us."

"Who are the guardians?" asked Jonah quickly. "And the—did you say Elect and Very Elect spirits and spiritesses?"

"Yes, I did," said Daniel. "The Very Elect ones are just a couple rungs beneath the guardians. The ones directly beneath them are simply called the Elect ones."

"I know the terms from Dad," said Terrence, "but who are they all? What do they do?"

"Daniel," said Jonathan warningly.

"Worry not, Jonathan," said Daniel, who then looked at Terrence. "I'm not at liberty to say, son. You are still a physically living being; there are some things about Spirit that you are better off not knowing. You wouldn't comprehend most of them, and I don't mean that as an insult. It is simple fact."

Terrence made a face, but didn't say anything else. Jonathan nodded at Daniel, who continued.

"My brother, Broreamir, and I were assigned with preventing any more spirits and spiritesses falling victim to being usurped if we could," he continued. "But we discovered that Creyton hadn't re-blocked the paths. He was actually voiding spirits and spiritesses of the personalities and essences, making them something like barely functioning shells."

Jonah's fists tightened. "Were they the lost spirits and spiritesses in the dream?"

"Yes," said Jonathan.

"Broreamir was so fascinated by Creyton's new range of power after his resurrection that he betrayed us," said Daniel, who stared into the empty fireplace. "He chose to renounce his Guidanceship, embraced life as an ethereal human, and joined the ranks of the Deadfallen disciples."

"What!" demanded Jonah, but the word was echoed all around the room. So he wasn't behind in everything, it seemed.

"Yes," said Daniel. "He defected around the time Balthazar Lockman made it his goal to investigate you all. Then that dream happened, and I could stand by no longer. I invaded Creyton's little ethereal excursion into all of your minds, trying to figure out what was going on, and what he was doing."

"Did you?" asked Reena.

"No," said Daniel in a cooler tone than he'd had previously. "And I don't even know what they were trying to achieve with those stings. So I just fought them. Hard."

"You did that to save us?" said Jonah, awestruck.

"Yes," said Daniel, "and I also wanted to muddy the waters from Creyton if I could. But I put my neck on the line with my actions."

"How so?" asked Liz.

"The Phasmastis Curaie is trying to handle the situation as best they can," said Daniel. "As I am sure all of you are tired of hearing by now, no other Eleventh Percenter has ever done what Creyton has. He's changed the status quo. Between Broreamir dispensing his Guidanceship to become a Deadfallen disciple and Balthazar Lockman bringing in his Tenth skeptic brigade, not to mention the unconscionable actions of Gamaliel Kaine and his little Network, we were all ordered not to interfere. We were told to follow orders and do nothing else."

Jonah's eyes narrowed. "And, even though you saved us, invading our dreams was looked upon as defiance."

Daniel smiled humorlessly. "I didn't even let them judge me," he said. "I took the same path Broreamir took, and renounced my own Guidanceship and became an ethereal human. I'd do anything for Jonathan, anyway, so here I am."

"But we only met you today," breathed Reena.

"Yes," said Daniel, who didn't get her point.

"You renounced your Guidanceship and flouted the Curaie since that dream occurred?" Reena looked thunderstruck. "But that only happened last night!"

Daniel looked Reena in the eye. "How many times must you young ones hear that time means little to nothing on the Astral Plane?" he asked.

"Wow," said Liz, "and all day long, I just assumed you were here to help out Jonathan."

"Never mind that," said Terrence. "Like Reena said, Daniel, we just met you this morning, and Jonathan kept things pretty quiet until we could all get together. But I got to ask you something: You felt the need to become an ethereal human? This situation is that bad?"

"Yes," nodded Daniel. "It's that bad."

Jonah shook his head. He had no idea what the day would bring when he woke up that morning. Then again, the morning itself had brought about that damn dream.

"Who is Broreamir again?" he asked.

Daniel looked at Jonathan, who nodded. Then he sighed. "You've encountered him before, Jonah," he said. "He was the pale, dreadlocked behemoth you saw in that bookstore vision you had back when your essence was still raw."

Jonah shot up from his seat, horrified. "*That* guy?"

Daniel nodded.

"But then...the crows in the dream..." Jonah thought that that dream had lost its meaning when he'd gotten past Creyton back then. But now...it couldn't be coincidence that it was revisited right now.

"Jonah," said Reena suddenly, "you said that the largest crow never landed in that bookstore vision. Was it similar in size to the crow in the dream we all had?"

"No," muttered Jonah, "the one last night was even larger."

Terrence made a derisive noise. "And it had to coincide with this cult garbage," he grunted.

Jonathan closed his eyes. "Jonah, this is why I wanted us all to speak inside here," he said. "Being that I can't be seen outside at the moment due to Lockman's spies, Daniel will function as the estate's physical bodied representative. If Lockman comes knocking, Daniel will be the one he sees. It is also the reason why so many of our friends aren't here. The ones that remain here, like Daniel said, are either here of their own volition—"

"—or they are too old for their parents to tell them what to do anymore," added Bobby. We're here for you, Jonathan. We're loyal. That's not to say that our friends who are at their homes are disloyal, just saying we want to be here to help you out against Lockman. And, of course, Creyton."

Jonathan grinned at Bobby rather shrewdly. "I appreciate that greatly, Bobby," he said, "but are you absolutely certain that you can do that?"

Bobby snorted. "Of course."

Jonathan continued to smile. "And Constance acquiesced to your plan when, exactly?"

"Come again?" asked Bobby, while Alvin laughed.

"Right before we left the house today, sir," said Terrence.

This got a quick laugh out of everyone. Bobby muttered, "Snitch" at Terrence, but he was laughing, too. Jonah was glad to laugh; the levity siphoned off some of the crap out of his consciousness. But his laughter abruptly stopped when he had a stab of memory from the morning.

"Jonathan," he asked, "why would a Tenth follow the orders of a Deadfallen disciple?"

Jonathan and Daniel looked at each other. "Jonah, Tenth Percenters who do the bidding of Deadfallen disciples are referred to as suuvi," said Jonathan. "Suuvus is the singular term."

"Suuvus?" said Malcolm. "But Jonathan, that means slave! Creyton and his disciples have Tenth slaves?"

"It's more akin to indentured servitude that pure slavery," clarified Jonathan. "Although it is equally as atrocious. The suuvi do things for Creyton, and in return, they lay down their physical lives one day for him to make them minions."

"But Creyton has no further interest in making minions," said Jonah. "He's reactivated his disciples!"

"We know that," muttered Daniel, "but the suuvi don't."

Reena sat back on the sofa, fingers at her temples. "So India Drew got a suuvus to rile Jonah, and then she left when the fire was lit."

"Not only that," said Daniel. "She murdered the man about an hour later."

Jonah flinched. "What? Why?"

"Loose end, Jonah," said Jonathan. "What if the Networkers got a hold of him? He'd have caved in an instant."

"Damn," said Jonah. "I almost feel sorry for that bum. But that's aplenty for this evening. I'm calling it a night."

"One more thing, Jonah." Jonathan had a rather inscrutable look in his eyes. "In three days' time, I must escort you to an audience with the Phasmastis Curaie."

Terence and Reena looked at Jonathan, just as confused as Jonah was. He looked at his mentor like he'd sprouted gills.

"Why do I have to see the Spectral High Court?" he wanted to know. "I haven't done anything!"

"Of course you haven't," said Jonathan rather impatiently. "It's not a trial; you'll only be meeting the Five."

Jonah blinked, clueless.

"Oh, my apologies," said Jonathan. "The Five Spirit Guides who created the Phasmastis Curaie. There are thirteen, of course, but you will meet with the original Five."

"Oh, okay." Jonah tried very hard to fight the sarcasm and impatience in his voice. "Once again, may I ask why?"

"They've tired of the second and third party information they've been receiving about the occurrences on the night of Thaine's return, I'd wager," said Jonathan. "They desire to hear things from you directly."

Jonah had the distinct feeling that Jonathan was holding something back. But he decided not to pry at the moment. "Why now?" he asked instead.

"You've recently turned twenty-six," began Jonathan. "You've only been that age for about a month and a couple weeks. One's spiritual and ethereal composition is always at its sharpest near the time of their spirit's sojourn into physical life. They chose this time period by design, as you will remember more details. I don't think that they would have had a problem though. You're the Blue Aura, after all. Your retention can be very profound."

Jonah didn't feel pride from that praise. If anything, he felt more isolation. He had to meet with the Curaie. It felt like...he couldn't say. When Terrence had explained to him who they were a few years ago,

Jonah had simply viewed them the way an average citizen viewed a celebrity; he knew they were in the world somewhere, but he probably wouldn't ever lay eyes on them. Now he had to see them, recount a tale that he didn't want to revisit, and deal with whatever thing that Jonathan wasn't telling him.

He hoped that he wasn't supposed to be thrilled.

"Look at the time," said Jonathan. "Get you rest, everyone. Peace and blessings."

He vanished, and Daniel returned his focus to whetting the ethereal steel tips of his arrows. People dispersed in a very drowsy fashion, and Jonah, Terrence, and Reena ascended the steps together.

"That Daniel guy makes me nervous," said Terrence once they were out of earshot. "He just sat so still. He was so quiet most of the time. Like a crazy beast that'd been medicated or something."

Reena sighed. "Terrence, the man has been human for literally a day," she said. "Cut him some slack. Besides, what he's done—what he's sacrificed—noble is an understatement. It takes more guts than I have."

"Me, too," said Jonah. "I can't believe that that dreadlocked freak from my dream is his brother."

"I can't believe he embraced humanity to join Creyton," said Terrence. "But it messes with your head; if he's willing to give up a Guidanceship to be a Deadfallen disciple—Creyton's new plans must be sick."

"Time for a subject change." Jonah had had enough dark ethereality talk for a day. "I want to ask after some people. Doug?"

Terrence snorted. "Doug had to go to Asheville with his grandmother. They're visiting Silas, her youngest son. The one that's only like ten minutes older than Doug, remember?"

"The one with the little brat that Doug's grandmother favors over him and all her other grandkids?" asked Jonah.

"Yep," said Terrence. "I told him to take a lot of pictures."

"Trip?"

"Gig with his band in Charlotte," said Reena.

"And Vera?" asked Jonah.

Something flashed across Reena's face. "In her room," she said. "But she's probably really tired. She had a long day."

"Did she road-trip for a play, or something?" asked Jonah.

"Nah, man," said Terrence cautiously. "She's been—cleaning."

"What is up with all the esoteric around here?" Jonah felt that impatience stir in him once more. "She was cleaning what?"

"Cleaning up 810 Colerain Place," answered Reena.

Jonah looked at them, stunned. "Why?"

"I guess—in the event that things got too hot here at the estate," said Reena. "But Jonah, let her rest. Don't bombard her with questions tonight."

"'Specially after the day you've had yourself," added Terrence.

"Of course not," said Jonah blankly. "I'm just going to bed. See you in the morning."

Terrence nodded, and walked away. Reena shot Jonah a doubtful look, and then left as well. When they were gone, Jonah headed straight for Vera's room.

Cleaning in the event things got too hot here at the estate…Jonah didn't buy that dreck for a second. Vera inherited that house and hated everything about it. It had been the site of a horrible fight with her crazy older sister that had left her with scars, physical and otherwise. Creyton, in disguise, had even tried to kidnap her there. And even before she'd discovered that she was an Eleventh Percenter, she'd only stayed there out of convenience, because she was a waitress and struggling stage actress.

And he was supposed to believe that she would voluntarily go back?

He reached her door, which was ajar. And her light was on. Good.

He knocked? "Vera?"

No answer.

"I swear," murmured Jonah to himself, "if she's got that damn yoga CD on again—"

He pushed the door open. Vera had fallen asleep in a position that showed that she had been reading beforehand. Jonah moved forward, smiling when he saw the book. It was an encyclopedia of female playwrights, his present to her the previous Christmas.

He shook his head at her awkward angle, and wondered how comfortable she was in her tank top and yoga pants. Her right arm hung limply off the bed. That was going to ache her something fierce when she woke.

Jonah took the book out of her hands and placed it on the nightstand. Then he gingerly lifted her hanging arm to her chest and covered her with her blanket.

"On second thought," he murmured to her slumbering form, "we'll talk tomorrow."

5

Katarina Ocean

Jonah awoke very early the next morning, which was a surprise. But it was also a blessing that he didn't remember any of his dreams. If they'd been noteworthy, he would have had some idea of what had run through his mind. He didn't.

This day was off to a great start based on that fact alone.

He pulled on a T-shirt and headed downstairs for some cereal. As there were only twenty-something residents at the entire estate, he didn't have to worry about waking the world.

Jonah was still having issues with that. Yeah, there had only been a handful of people when he'd arrived here a few years ago, but there had been a reason for that. The estate had been bustling the next time he'd come, and had been that way ever since.

Well, until now.

Before Jonah knew the truth about what he was, he'd been a bit of a loner. But, if he were honest with himself, he'd gotten accustomed to being around the like-minded individuals. He liked the packed trainings. He like all the creative, artistic people (except for Trip, anyway). He'd gotten used to it all. It was a shame that he didn't find that kind of camaraderie until he was well into his twenties, but it was what it was.

And now, a two-pronged attack was throwing off the routine that had become his life. Creyton was one prong. His second existence was enough of a scare by itself. But of course, it couldn't stop there. Creyton had to go and psych out dozens and dozens of Eleventh Percenters with that infernal dream. What did it mean?

And that stupid Tenth. Balthazar Lockman. He was investigating them as a cult? Seriously? Jonah couldn't help but wonder exactly what it was that got Lockman on their case. June Mylteer had said Creyton's scheming. But that could mean a great deal of things. To call Creyton an evil genius was akin to calling the Atlantic Ocean a "place with some water."

All these things had prompted Jonathan to send many of the residents home. Jonah was sure that Creyton was a higher concern than Lockman, though. Jonathan wanted to know what Creyton was up to; Lockman simply happened to be the shit they'd stepped in on the side of the road.

Jonah hoped that was the case, anyway.

These things were in his mind when he reached the kitchen, which was already occupied.

It was Vera.

Jonah laughed quietly when he figured out that it was her, because his mind went to the previous night. The sound caught her attention.

"Morning, Jonah." She smiled when she saw him. "So you are part of the skeleton crew still here."

"Indeed I am," said Jonah, who joined her at the table. "And a good morning to you too."

Vera's expression turned curious. "When I woke up, I was wrapped up, stretched out, and my light was off," she said. "Did you do that for me?"

Jonah laughed. "Guilty. Didn't want you to wake up with your limbs hanging off the bed, stiff and aching."

"You have my thanks," said Vera.

"No problem," said Jonah. "Summer go well for you?"

"You first," said Vera.

Jonah was about to state what he thought was obvious, but then he remembered that Vera had been in the city all day yesterday. She hadn't heard anything. With a sigh, he told her about how his summer had been a piece of cake until the previous day in Coastal Shores. She listened to him intently, and her eyes widened with each new detail.

"Shit," she murmured. "I was freaked out by that dream, too, but it seemed like your day went downhill from that. Good thing Daniel was there to protect us."

"So you met Daniel before you crashed for the night?"

"Yeah," nodded Vera. "He was traipsing the grounds when I returned from Colerain Place. Things must be dicey if he willingly gave up being a spectral being. But he's doing a solid for Jonathan concerning this Lockman idiot, right?"

Jonah barely registered many of Vera's words pastthe mention of Colerain Place. He sat forward so as to be nearer to her. "Colerain Place. Why the sudden interest in your old house, Vera? What's the deal?"

Vera looked away. For some reason, a fraction of the gleam faded from her eye, and it was like her mind was elsewhere, just like that. Jonah frowned. Should he be concerned?

Then she abruptly rose from the chair.

"Let me show you something, Jonah." She took his hand. "Before I answer that question, let me show you something."

They were back upstairs almost as quickly as Jonah had come down. It was so early in the morning that it was still dark, so they didn't hear stirrings from anyone else.

"Vera, why are you up so early?" he asked her.

Vera pulled him into her room and shut the door, with the moonlight from outside as the only source of illumination. "I had probably been asleep for three hours before you came and wrapped me up, Jonah," she replied. "So after a couple more hours, I actually had a full night's sleep. I'm not awake at this time for my health. I had just gotten an early start on my rest."

"Huh." That actually made sense to Jonah. "Gotcha. Now what did you want to show me?"

Vera had moved from the moonlight, but he heard her tinkering with something. It didn't sound too heavy. He heard Vera flick a switch, and then there was a whirring, rhythmic sound.

"Close your eyes, Jonah," she warned.

"Huh—?"

Suddenly, Jonah's eyes were bombarded by a luminous onslaught that seemed to shoot from all angles. With an exclamation, he shut his eyes tightly, but could still see a blinding white light through his eyelids. He heard Vera openly laughing at him, and then felt her hand on his shoulder.

"I did tell you to cover your eyes," she chided, but Jonah could hear the humor in her voice. "Try looking at the walls, not directly at the box."

Jonah did as he was told, and found himself dazzled by what looked like white flames dancing harmlessly across the walls of Vera's room.

"Isn't it the most beautiful thing you've ever seen?" asked Vera.

"Um, what exactly is it?" asked Jonah, squinting.

"Snow and Fire," breathed Vera. "It's a visual inspiration of a dream."

With some effort, Jonah brought his eyes to the source of the debilitating light. It was some sort of wooden contraption, like a free moving puzzle box. Different components changed their stance across a bright white light fixture, which provided the illusion of white flames across the walls.

"Did—did Malcolm make this?" he asked Vera.

"Yes!" said Vera jubilantly. "He did me the favor after I told him about an idea I had! So whenever I have too many thoughts in my head, I get a spiritual endowment, come in here, and fire it up."

Jonah moved closer to the box, marveling at Malcolm's mastery of woodwork. "So the white light is from your aura?" he asked. "That's ethereal steel in there?"

"Yes," grinned Vera. "It's one of the nicest things I've ever had."

Vera left Jonah's side and sat near the box. Jonah sat next to her.

"What is the significance of Snow and Fire?" he asked.

"Vera smiled. "It's the name of my play."

"Your play?" repeated Jonah. "The one you were telling me about when–" Jonah froze. The last time Vera spoke about her play, the moment had been ruined when she discovered a gift that Jonah had gotten Rheadne. She hadn't it taken it well. "Um…the play you never finished telling me about?" he finished.

Vera ran her tongue across her lips. She knew good and well what Jonah had been about to say, but seemed to keep her mind focused on the here and now. Her smile returned, and Jonah breathed a sigh of relief. Dodged that bullet.

"It is," she said. "It's not my play exclusively; Eden Bristow, one of my actress friends, wrote it with me."

"You actually wrote a full play, Vera." As a writer who couldn't yet complete a book, Jonah gave her his full admiration. "Tell me about it now."

"It's about a woman named in the early eighties named Juliette Nightingale," began Vera. "She spent several years as an assassin. That's how she got the alias of Snow and Fire. When she did her deeds, she did them quickly, effortlessly, and accurately…a shooting star across a black night, Snow and Fire through the heavens."

Jonah raised an eyebrow. "You guys put some thought into that, didn't you?"

"You couldn't possibly imagine," said Vera. "Anyway, she got out of all that after having a crisis of conscience. She found love, and moved to a farm with a widowed father of two. They begin to build a life together when loose ends from her old life begin to threaten her new one. She has to tie off those ends by any means necessary. Even if those means include the usage of the prowess from the former life that she tried so desperately to escape."

Jonah looked at Vera in amazement. "That's epic," he remarked. "that'd make an awesome movie."

Vera shook her head. "Much more freedom as a play," she told him. "You can tinker, experiment, and tweak. Eden and I had pretty much hashed out all the details before…before the Time Item business forced me here."

There was prominent duality in Vera's facial features as the while light illuminated them. It was like a cross between longing and slight bitterness. Jonah had to fight the urge to take her into his arms and say…anything that'd comfort her.

"You miss it, don't you?" he asked.

"I do, Jonah," she said quietly. "Jesus Christ, I do. I'm not myself on the stage. Or maybe I am. When I'm bringing characters to life up there, creating those emotions—it's like the creativity is my reality, and the stressors, the drama, and all the garbage that I went through is the fiction. Don't get me wrong; I'm grateful that you saved my physical life, Jonah. I'm grateful to know that there is a reason that I'm the way I am, and I'm not just some odd woman with a shitty past. But—I miss it. Very much."

Vera's words made a realization fall into Jonah's head. It buzzed on the outer fringes of his mind during this little interaction, but her impassioned words made things really clear.

And made him really uneasy.

"Right before last Christmas," he said cautiously, "you told me that you'd re-established connections with Eden and your old actor friends. They—Eden—have been persistent, trying to get that play up and running, right?"

"Indeed they have," confirmed Vera. "That's why they were looking for me so hard."

"So you and Eden can get it running?"

"They tried themselves," said Vera, "and it fell flat. Even with retooling, it still didn't click. They all came to the conclusion that they need to go back to the original vision…with me as the lead. That had been the original plan anyway, but then I got threatened."

Jonah stared at her. "That's why you wanted to show me the box. That's the sudden interest in Colerain Place. You want to sell it, and move back to Seattle."

Vera, who'd been looking away, turned suspicious eyes to Jonah. "I never told you about my time in Seattle. How did you know that?"

Jonah sighed. Way to go, Mouth Almighty. "Back when we first met you, Reena wanted to make sure that you were on the level. She looked you up."

Vera's expression cleared somewhat. "Wait…Something Liz told me…before you met me, you'd dealt with that minion. Marla, or something?"

Jonah nodded.

"So there was that," murmured Vera, nodding herself. "You were probably looking over any new people with a fine-toothed comb. I can let that go."

Jonah could have smiled. Whew. "Why did you come back from Seattle at all, Vera?"

"To do what I could to make my mother's final physical days her happiest before she passed into Spirit," answered Vera. "Heaven knows—" Vera shook her head, "—Heaven knows her other daughter wouldn't have done it."

Jonah looked at her steadily. "What's your sister's name, Vera?" he queried.

"Maddie," mumbled Vera.

"What does she look like?"

"Like our dad."

"And you have no idea where she is?"

"I don't want to know where the bitch is, Jonah," said Vera. "We're not family anymore, so the hell with her."

The finality in her voice was striking. The matter was even further closed by Vera's seemingly unconscious stroking of the scar at the base of her jaw. Jonah decided to respect her. After all, it didn't matter if she was willing to share information about Maddie or not. It was clear to him which one was the better woman, and that was without ever having met Maddie. Jonah couldn't help but wonder if Vera's sibling, wherever she may be, was an Eleventh Percenter too.

"I moved back from Seattle prepared to be a caregiver for as long as it took," said Vera, who clearly wanted to move on from her sister. "But my mother passed into Spirit after only four months. I'd dropped everything to come back, and when the inevitable happened, I just wasn't able to return to Washington. Eden stayed, and found another roommate. We kept in touch, ironing out Snow and Fire and whatnot. But now, she and all of our friends want me to go back up there."

Jonah dared asked the question, though he wasn't sure he wanted to know the answer. "Do you do it?"

Vera clicked off the box. Although the morning sky had finally given way to the early light, the rough treatment they'd just done to their eyes still made it seem dark. "Depends on what happens with Colerain Place, Jonah," was her almost silent reply.

* * *

"Reena, you knew, didn't you?"

That was the first thing Jonah asked her when he found her later that morning, working on a new painting for Kendall. Terrence sat nearby, eating a large breakfast sandwich and trying hard not to laugh.

"Of course I knew, Jonah," said Reena. "Terrence, did, too."

Jonah rounded on Terrence, but Terrence shook his head, pointing to his full mouth. He seemed to have purposefully stuffed so he wouldn't have to speak. Shaking his own head, Jonah turned his attention back to Reena.

"It wasn't ours to tell," said Reena before Jonah could say anything else. "You heard the information from the very person that you needed to. And besides, what was more important for you to know when you returned from the coast? The current status quo, or Vera thinking about moving away? It isn't like your relationship with her has clear definition or anything."

Jonah really hated it when Reena a point. Come to think of it, he hated that more often than not. "You win," he grumbled.

Reena rolled her eyes. "Quit trying to placate me," she grumbled back.

"Anybody still hungry?" said Terrence.

It was such a random question that Jonah and Reena were shocked into laughing. It lightened things hugely.

"What are you painting for Kendall?" he asked.

"I call it *True Me*," said Reena with a rare note of pride in her voice. "It's all of the things that I couldn't tell her when I first fell in love with her, in the form of paint and canvas. Now that she knows that I'm an Eleventh Percenter, she sees me completely for who I am. And this will be a reminder of that when we are away from each other."

"You must really love this woman, Reena," said Jonah, shaking his head. "I can remember a time when no amount of convincing would get you to remove any of your paintings from here."

Reena looked defiant as she moved black and scarlet strands from her face. "I'm a woman," she said. "I reserve the right to be complicated."

Jonah looked at Terrence, who'd swallowed his food and mouthed, "Or whipped."

"And you would do well to get someone of your own before labeling me whipped, Terrence," said Reena calmly.

Jonah snorted. Terrence looked at her incredulously.

"There is no way that you picked that up out of my essence!" he exclaimed.

"How right you, are," said Reena calmly. "One needs not be an essence reader when they can see their friend's snide comments from the corner of their eye."

It was in that moment that Terrence realized that Reena had removed her hair from her face. His eyes narrowed.

"You win," he grumbled.

Jonah spent the rest of the day answering questions about his summer travels, which was a great way to pass the time. Magdalena revealed that when she'd had the dream, her father attempted to forbid her from coming back to the estate, but she'd changed his mind almost instantly.

"What did you do?" asked Terrence. "The age-old case of Daddy not being able to refuse his little girl?"

"Hardly," said Magdalena. "I simply told him that I was here at the estate, there was a much higher likelihood that Mama wouldn't learn that I bought her birthday present for him, because he'd forgotten the day."

Maxine stared. "That was low, Magdalena."

"Nope," replied Magdalena, "it was fun. Why? Because I'll never have to tell. Mama already knows. She's even thanked me."

They all shared a big laugh over that.

Spader mostly kept to himself, and spoke when he was spoken to, but spent most of the silent assembling and disassembling his locks. Bobby had entertained several card games with him, but then pulled Jonah to the side later on.

"He's faking indifference," he revealed. "But it bothers him that no one trusts him anymore."

Jonah wasn't surprised, nor did he have much pity. Spader had made a disastrous judgment call earlier in the year that made the estate extremely vulnerable. Had it not been for Jonathan and, of all people, Trip, there was no telling what would have happened. Some of the residents had suggested grievous punishments for him when they held something called Family Court at the estate, but Reverend Abbot had approved Jonah's suggestion that Spader abdicate all of his illicitly obtained funds to charitable causes, which he did. Despite those actions, he had not regained the negligible amount of trust that he'd had.

"I told him that it would be uphill, and he was gonna have to give it some time," Bobby went on. "But it's been rough."

"I'd imagine," said Jonah. "Spader really messed up. It'll take a miracle."

Bobby didn't reply, but his expression let Jonah know that he agreed wholeheartedly.

Liz was still making bearded necklaces with Maxine, but to Jonah's surprise, she had improved since he'd been gone. She happily displayed the jewelry they'd fashioned together, and they were some nice pieces, but Jonah judged Liz's improvement by Maxine's behavior. She now had contacts in, rather than shield her eyes with her usual thick glasses. That, above all else, let him know that Liz had gotten better at it.

Douglas returned the next afternoon completely up in arms about the dream, but by that time, everyone had gotten tired of talking about it that Alvin told him to drop it before he went into more detail. Douglas was shocked that everyone had had the dream, but was even more shocked to see his savior in person.

It happened right after Alvin curtailed Douglas' plan to rehash the dream. Daniel walked out of the kitchen with a cool drink in his hand. Douglas mumbled a nonchalant "Hello," but then did a double take and nearly jumped out of his skin.

"You!" he exclaimed, pointing a trembling finger at Daniel. "You...you...you..."

"Yes, boy," said Daniel calmly. "I was in your dream. I was in all of them. I am Daniel, formerly a Protector Guide, but have since become a mortal Eleventh Percenter because I could no longer sit idly by. My brother Broreamir has become a mortal Eleventh as well, but he chose to join Creyton's Deadfallen disciples."

"You—" Doug's voice sounded blank, "you were a Protector Guide? Like Jonathan?"

"Was," said Alvin wearily, "but he isn't now, Douglas. "We've heard it already. Please, be content that he is on our side and leave it alone."

"Right," said Douglas absently. He hadn't taken his eyes off of Daniel. "Who is Bror—Bohr—your brother?"

"The guy from my dream with the crows," said Jonah. The dreadlocked guy. Jonathan told you about that one, right?"

"Yeah..." Douglas frowned slightly. "B—but that can't be. That can't be your brother."

Daniel paused, and moved nearer to Douglas. He even lowered his bow across the table. "Why not, son?" he queried.

Douglas looked around at other people like he couldn't believe that the question was even raised. Jonah had to admit that he was bit intrigued himself, because he wanted to know what Douglas meant.

"Jonathan told me about that dream, sir," said Douglas slowly. "I recall the description. That guy in Jonah's dream, Brore—him, had grey dreadlocks, and was Caucasian. You, sir, are black. You can't be brothers."

Jonah frowned. He'd put so much effort in forgetting the dreadlocked guy that he'd forgotten than fact. But Douglas was telling: Broreamir had been white, and Daniel was black. And they were brothers?

Daniel looked like he already knew the question Douglas would pose. "The race question," he murmured. "Let me let you in on a little secret, Douglas, is it? All the individuals in this room, at this estate, the town, the whole world? You're all one race—human. A focus on color and ethnicity is a purely mortal thing; it's not a concept anyone bothers with in the spirit world. A person's skin color is immaterial. So Broreamir chooses a skin color that differs from the one I have, and that means that we can't be family?"

Now Douglas looked awkward. His face was almost as burgundy as his travel bag. "I...I..."

"Do you not refer to yourselves as a family here?" asked Daniel.

"Yes, of course—"

"And did you waste time bothering to make note of the shades of skin of these young men and women at this estate before you labeled them family?"

"Well, no—"

"There you go, then." Daniel lowered the glass of water and retrieved his bow. "No matter one's color, people can still be family. This conversation is done."

He headed for the kitchen. Douglas plopped down next to Terrence, skin rather blotchy due to the blushing.

"Well, that was...strange," he mumbled.

"No, son." Daniel wasn't quite out of earshot. "The fact that skin color is such a big deal to certain people on Earthplane is what is strange."

Finally, he went into the kitchen. Terrence stared after him.

"Dear Lord," he said. "As if Jonathan wasn't philosophical enough, now we've got him, too?"

"You've got to admit that the viewpoint is rather refreshing," said Reena. "Ethnicity is immaterial."

"It's not his viewpoint," snapped Terrence, "I was talking about his need to give a mile when he was asked for an inch. I don't need to hear the racial lecture, Reena—I'm biracial, remember?"

"And I'm not?" demanded Reena.

Terrence paused. "Point," he muttered.

Jonah couldn't help it. He laughed. Douglas turned to him, confused.

"What's funny?" he wanted to know.

Jonah relaxed his head against the back of the sofa. "It's just good to be home," he said. "No matter what goes on inside here, no matter what goes on outside here. It's just good to be home."

Jonah shook himself awake early on that Friday.

The day that Jonathan would take him to converse with the Curaie.

He remembered that thing about the meeting having to be in close proximity to his birthday, which made him think of that day. He'd been in Rhodanthe at the time, had a steak dinner, and allowed himself a rare glass of wine. Nothing too fancy or special. The funny thing had been the fact that Jonah didn't feel any different on his birthday. The fact that he was healthier now than when he was younger was something, but he felt that with the things he'd been through, twenty-six summers didn't feel like enough. He'd felt much older than that at time.

Jonah pulled his mind back into the present. This was the day that he had to meet with five members of the Phasmastis Curaie. He hoped that the meeting would be quick. He wanted to spend this day at the estate doing a whole lot of nothing.

But that glorious reality had to wait until after the meeting.

He sighed. He was sure that he had to make a good impression. He looked into his closet, and a navy blue polo caught his eye. He grabbed it and hung it on his door. He then grabbed some tan khakis. That outfit ought to get him there and back.

He showered, put on a tank top and loose-fitting boxers, and made sure that his beard was neatly trimmed. Then he headed back to his room, where he found Reena holding his chosen clothes in her hands, surveying them with distaste.

"No," she said simply. "Sorry, but no."

"Reena?!" Jonah taken completely by surprise, and none too pleased. "What are you doing here?"

"Because you need my help," said Reena, who tossed his outfit on his bed. "That won't cut it."

"What is wrong with my clothes?" he demanded.

"Watch your tone," snapped Reena, "I'm on your side. But seriously; khakis? A polo? This is the Phasmastis Curaie, Jonah. If you go in there looking like some reject cabana boy, and they'll never take you seriously."

Jonah narrowed his eyes. "And you know all of this how? Have you ever met them yourself?"

"No." Reena began to riffle through Jonah's closet. "I've been here since I was fourteen, Jonah, and I've had many conversations about those Spirit Guides with Jonathan. They have been around a long time, and if there is one thing that they haven't quite mastered, it's progression.

Jonah frowned. "Reena, I wasn't going in there looking like a damn vagabond—"

"Of course you weren't," said Reena impatiently, "but the clothes you were going to wear would not be endured. These guides have been around for a couple centuries. Ralph Lauren chaps and an Old Navy polo would be—what's the term older folks use—newfangled."

Jonah blinked. Reena took no notice.

"You have to be impeccable, Jonah," she said. "With all you've been through, the last thing you want is for the five most prominent Spirit Guides to think of you as a hothead slouch who thinks of the meeting as a joke. Please let me help you."

Reena actually wanted to assist him. She didn't want to dress him up like a damned Ken doll or something. It was something, if nothing else.

"Fine, Reena," he sighed. "What do you have for me?"

Jonah descended the stairs in a black button down and olive dress slacks. The get up was finished by a pair of loafers that he hadn't worn since his days at Essa, Langton, and Bane. By the time Reena declared herself satisfied, he felt utterly ridiculous.

The whole process with Reena had taken most of the morning, so when they went downstairs, several people were in the kitchen eating breakfast (Jonah looked enviously at their pajamas and robes). Vera, who was eating a muffin next to Liz, caught sight of him and her eyes widened for a moment. It wasn't unnoticed by Jonah.

"What?" he asked, instantly on alert for some imperfection with his clothes.

"N—Nothing." Vera lowered her head. "Nothing."

He looked at her in confusion, but then saw a devilish grin on Reena's face. The nothing made sense after that. Huh. Maybe this outfit wasn't so tacky after all.

"You are superbly attired, Jonah," said Jonathan, who was near the back door. "It's a great thing that you had the wherewithal to dress so sharply. One would have thought you'd throw caution to the wind and chanced one of your favored polo shirt and a pair of khakis."

"No, sir," said Jonah, glancing at Reena. "I had this hiding in my closet, and decided to give it a spin today. Have to be impeccable, right?"

Jonathan smiled. "You're a great young man, Jonah," he said, "but an abysmal liar. Thank you so much for assisting him, Reena."

"Yes, sir," said Reena, eyes on her feet. A couple of people laughed.

"Come into the backyard, Jonah." All mirth was gone from Jonathan, and he was all business. "Getting to where we're going can be a bit tricky, but you needn't worry whilst you're with me."

They went into the backyard, near the path that led to the Glade. It was there that Jonah gave Jonathan a curious look.

"Where are we going?" he asked. "I assumed that since these are Spirit Guides, they wouldn't have an office or anything, right?"

"Not exactly, no," said Jonathan. "Spirit Guides are not like us Protector Guides or the other spirits in the employ of the Curaie. They only have form when they desire to. So the way that you will see them today, is how they look in corporeal form. But I'm getting ahead of myself. We both are, actually."

"Huh?"

"Grab my arm, Jonah," said Jonathan. "*Astralimes*."

Jonah complied, took the two steps, and looked around in wonder.

He and Jonathan stood in a very cozy lobby area that resembled the hub of a business complex. Jonah didn't see a single window, but the place didn't seem claustrophobic. Every surface seemed to be made of highly polished cherry wood, and the air had that new car scent, which was beyond odd. Jonah saw dozens of doors along both all four sides of the walls. They were cherry wood as well. Strangely, though, there were no identifying markers of any kind on any of them. How did people know whose office was whose?

"Where are we, Jonathan?"

"This is called the Median," answered Jonathan. "It is a place where the Earthplane and the Astral Plane have been made to overlap, which makes it an ideal place to occupy before anyone goes to where their goal is."

"Goal?"

"Yes, Jonah, goal," said Jonathan. "Not everyone goes to the same destination. Take those Networkers, for example."

With a jolt, Jonah realized that he and Jonathan weren't alone. Several men and women stood here and there, or were seated on simple sofas and sectionals. All of them were engaged in conversation, but a few looked at Jonathan and nodded respectfully. How had Jonathan not noticed them before? He really needed to pay more attention to things in this strange place.

"They aren't meeting with Curaie." Jonathan hadn't even noticed Jonah's realization. "They're meeting with Elect Spirits to triangulate locations of ethereal crimes, namely Eighth Chapter ones. They make the request, and Katarina links them."

"Katarina?" said Jonah curiously.

"Jonathan, sir?" said a sweet, businesslike voice. "I'm ready for the two of you now."

Jonah turned his eyes away from the group of Networkers and saw a woman seated at a desk. Jonathan nodded in her direction, beckoned Jonah forward, and they walked to her desk. When she rose to greet them, Jonah regarded her.

She couldn't have been older than late twenties, but there was something timeless and classic about her look, like Hedy Lamarr or Audrey Hepburn. She had milky white skin, but didn't look unhealthy or malnourished. Her black hair was in a very tight bun, and she had eyes so blue that they actually appeared violet. Jonah found himself wondering when this woman had passed into Spirit, but Jonathan, who caught his expression and chuckled.

"She isn't a spiritess, Jonah," he said. "Katarina is very much physically alive, just like yourself."

The lady turned those violet-looking eyes on Jonah and frowned. "You thought I was in Spirit?" She sounded like a Southern Belle from a long-forgotten era. "No. Not at all. My name is Katarina Ocean."

She extended her hand, and Jonah took it. She allowed him a very brief shake, and took back her hand. She then picked up a pen, which gleamed purple, and handed it to Jonah.

"Please sign the Ledger."

Jonah looked at the ledger, which was about the size of Jonathan's Masonic bible. He signed the thing and handed the pen back to her, intrigued. "You're a Gate Breacher?"

"I am a Gate *Linker*," corrected Katarina, slightly annoyed. "Breacher is looked upon as a pejorative term in most circles. I do not perform selfish actions with my ethereality. It is sacrosanct, and should never be violated."

Jonah half-smiled. He wondered if Turk Landry was aware of that train of thought.

"Katarina, we are meeting the Founding Five, as you know," said Jonathan. "Please Link that for us."

"Certainly, Jonathan, sir," said Katarina, while she extending what looked like a silk pouch to Jonah. He looked at it, frowning.

"It's for any ethereal steel you may have on your person," she explained.

"Oh." Jonah removed his batons in dormant form and reached for the pouch, but Katarina pulled it back. Her eyes widened, while Jonathan's narrowed.

"Elongate them!" she cried. "Full size!"

Puzzled, Jonah did so. Katarina took them with a look of awe on her face.

"The batons," she whispered, handling them as though they were fragile jewels. "Older than any of us here, and the previous owner—"

"Katarina," said Jonathan firmly, "the Linking of the gate?"

"Oh, yes." Katarina came back to her senses. "Right, sir."

She reverently slipped Jonah's batons into the pouch, and then walked to one of the unremarkable doors. Jonah raised an eyebrow at Jonathan.

"What was that about?" he asked. "Is she a weapons fanatic or something?"

"Not at all," said Jonathan, staring after Katarina. "She is just a young woman who has a knack for history."

"What was she talking about just now?" asked Jonah. "The previous owner of my batons?"

"She was mistaken," said Jonathan. "Her young mind is blending stories."

Jonah didn't buy that, but he knew that Jonathan wasn't going to be cooperative at the moment, so he reluctantly let it drop. "Okay, yeah. So what is Katarina doing?"

"Linking," said Jonathan. "See, this is the Median, but Astral Places cannot be contained. There aren't actually offices behind those doors. Nothing is behind them until Katarina links them to a destination."

Jonah's brow furrowed, and he looked at Katarina. She had her hand on the third door on the wall to his left, which was purple in her grasp. She also had a strong look of concentration and focus on her face.

"There is nothing behind those doors?" Jonah looked at his mentor once more. "Jonathan, exactly what kind of place is this—?"

"Link has been made," announced Katarina, who wiped a faint trace of sweat from her brow. "Sorry, but the Link to the Curaie is always more challenging than the others. But that's neither here nor there. The Founding Five will see you now."

6

Five across the Face

Jonathan nodded in Katarina's direction and gave her thanks. Then he beckoned Jonah forward. Right before they entered the door, Jonathan paused again and looked him square in the eye.

"Forgive this, Jonah," he said. "But I implore you to remain respectful, tactful, and maintain a level voice. At all times."

Jonah frowned. "Are you telling me to mind my manners, Jonathan?" he asked disbelievingly. "I always do that, particularly with new people. Why would you need to tell me that?"

"It's the most commonplace things that are the easiest to forget," he said.

Jonah wondered, but nodded. "Right," he muttered. "Let's just get this over with."

"Indeed." Jonathan opened the door.

The place resembled a cordoned off room that was set up for a panel discussion or the like. There weren't any windows here, either, but the place was well-lit. Jonah felt some of his unease fade. He'd imagined one of those spots straight out of the movies with some clandestine group issuing him cryptic threats while shrouded in shadows. But this place was just as cozy as the Median had been. And the occupants weren't shrouded in shadow at all, which was a huge plus. None of the five Spirit Guides looked like he expected. When he thought of Guides higher than Jonathan, he'd pictured extremely ancient individuals in corny thrones and probably in white robes or something. But he was zero for three.

Jonathan left Jonah to engage the spirits in conversation, so Jonah continued to take them in. The Founding Five Spirit Guides were three women and two men. They represented several ethnicities, and were all dressed like Jonah was. He was never going to tell Reena that she was right about fixing him up to the nines. And the thing about thrones? Nah. They were seated in high-backed, comfortable-looking chairs.

At that moment, Katarina entered the room, and seated herself in front a prehistoric manual typewriter. Jonah glanced at Jonathan to make sure that he was still in conversation with the Founding Five (which he was), and walked to her.

"Hello again," said Katarina without looking at him.

"Hi," murmured Jonah. "But... a typewriter? How old are you, Katarina?"

Katarina raised her eyes at him, looking surprised. "I'm twenty-six, same as you."

Jonah blinked. "How do you—?"

"Blue Aura, please seat yourself."

Jonah turned to see who'd spoken to him. It was the Spirit Guide standing at the center of the Founding Five. She was taller than all of them, even taller than Jonathan. Her hair was light brown with streaks of gray here and there, and her brown eyes looked intense and focused, as though there weren't too many things that escaped her watch. He remembered that Jonathan said only had corporeal form at certain times, but this lady's chosen form made him think of another statuesque woman he remembered seeing on television when he was a kid. Iman, he thought her name was? Yeah, that sounded right.

They seated themselves, and he followed suit.

"It is a pleasure to make your acquaintance, Blue Aura." The woman's diction sounded as out-of-time as Jonathan's. "I am Engagah, Overmistress of the Phasmastis Curaie and Spirit Guide One."

Quite a title, thought Jonah. More than I'd ever bother to memorize. "Pleasure is mutual, ma'am."

"These are my fellow Spirit Guides Silver and Lorelei," said Engagah, indicating the other women, "as well as Hilliard and Ephraim," she indicated the men. "Even though there are thirteen of us, you are only meeting the five of us."

That piqued Jonah's curiosity yet again. "Is there any particular reason for that, ma'am?" he asked.

"Certainly, there is, Blue Aura," said Engagah. "We only appear as the full collective when an ethereal individual is on trial. You are not on trial; this is merely a private conversation."

Although Jonah felt some ease at those words, he also felt low-level impatience. It didn't sit very well with him that they were so bent on referring to him as "Blue Aura." He did have a name, after all. This little thing hadn't even begun yet, and he already wanted it done. Jonathan, who stood at the side, maintained an impassive face.

"Glad to hear that, ma'am," said Jonah. "Is there anything else you need to know about who I am?"

"We know exactly who you are, Blue Aura," replied Engagah.

"Wh—?" Jonah caught himself. "I mean, ma'am?"

Engagah looked at Katarina, who'd been typing everything. Jonah even saw that the typewriter's keys each gleamed purple when her spiritually endowed fingers touched them. "Katarina?" she said.

"Certainly, ma'am." Katarina pulled a slip of paper from another silk pouch that was full of them, and then took a small breath. "Jonah James Anderson Rowe," she recited. "Born June 28th, 1987, in Radner, North Carolina. Son of Luther Coy and Sylvia Rowe, illegitimate conception. Raised by maternal grandmother, Doreen Rowe, now in Spirit. Briefly majored in Social Work, but switched to Accounting, where Bachelor's and Master's degrees were earned. Has recently completed courses in Creative Writing and Narrative Foundations—"

"That is quite enough, Katarina," said Engagah, who'd never taken her eyes off of Jonah. "I assure, Blue Aura—in regards to who you are, we are quite knowledgeable."

Jonah narrowed his eyes. That had been a strong arm. A power play. And he didn't appreciate it at all. They would never get a true viewpoint of who he was simply from reading that neatly summarized snapshot on that piece of paper. Son of Luther Coy and Sylvia Rowe? Those people weren't his parents. They were two irresponsible fools who happened to have a kid. His connection with them ended there. And what the hell had been the point of highlighting the fact that he'd been illegitimately conceived? What bearing did that have on this private conversation?

He looked at Jonathan, whose face remained impassive. Very painstakingly, Jonah emptied his own face of emotion. The act didn't go unnoticed by Engagah, whose eyes flashed in a mysterious sort of way.

"Now, Blue Aura," she said quietly, "we asked you to these chambers to obtain a firsthand account of the events that led to Creyton achieving Praeterletum."

The urge to get up and leave this place grew within Jonah with each passing word, but with a tight swallow, he told them everything from G.J.'s murder to Creyton's resurrection. Katarina typed the entire thing, and Jonah saw her eyes widen at points during his story. As aggravated as he was, he felt the minutest trace of pity. She was a Gate Linking secretary. Her life must not have all that much excitement.

When he finished, Engagah looked around at her counterparts, and then returned her eyes to Jonah. "That is a very interesting story," she commented.

Jonah bit his tongue rather painfully to avoid responding to that with, "You think?" The resulting clamp on his tongue caused his face to twitch involuntarily, which Jonathan noticed. He widened his eyes at Jonah, who sighed and gave him a subtle nod.

"The fact that you preserved your physical life in such spectacular fashion was most admirable," said Engagah. "But it is also continues to send a dangerous message to the ethereal world."

Jonah sat back. "I don't understand what that means."

"Well, Blue Aura, we had received information that there was a secret outfit with Sanctum Arcist, which Gamaliel Kaine had the audacity to designate as The Network," said Engagah. "So that part of your story was out-of-date to us. The fact that Gamaliel not only conceived a plan to usurp Jonathan's spirit, but convinced others to follow in said plan, lets us know that you all have had too much free rein."

Jonah almost loosed an exclamation, but Jonathan was at his side faster than thought. Jonah hadn't even seen him move.

"Engagah," he said steadily, "I have stressed to you, time and again, that while Gamaliel's plans were unconscionable and he did not have my best interests at heart, he was being psychologically manipulated by a Deadfallen disciple in Creyton's inner circle by the name of Charlotte Daynard. The entirety of the blame falls on Creyton personally. He was the spider at the center of the web—"

"But Gamaliel Kaine feared you ever since he discovered that you didn't cross to the Other Side, Jonathan," interrupted Engagah. "He had planned to betray you anyway. We know this. And since you brought up the fact that Gamaliel was being influenced by one of Creyton's disciples, we'd be remiss if we didn't remind you that the Blue Aura here allowed himself to be influenced by one of Creyton's disciples as well, despite a vitriolic hatred he had for her."

"You mean Jessica?" blurted out Jonah. "Yeah, I hated her with a passion, but I thought that Wyndam O'Shea was stalking her! She played a part! They both played their parts well—"

"These are the things that let us know that you are ill-equipped and dangerously impressionable, Blue Aura," said Engagah softly. "A trained representative of Spectral Law would have instantly seen the signs of Eighth Chapter influence—"

"The hell they would've!" said Jonah with heat. "Jessica Hale was Inimicus. The embedded enemy; the one you didn't know you didn't know. If she'd been working for Creyton all of that time, why hadn't she been discovered before his plan for Praeterletum could move forward?"

The Spirit Guide named Hilliard sat forward. "That is a wonderful question, Blue Aura," he said. "And the answer is a simple one: Vigilantism."

Jonah felt Jonathan's hand tighten on his shoulder. "I'm afraid that I don't see what you mean, Hilliard," said the Protector Guide. "Vigilantism?"

"You do not see it, Jonathan?" asked Hilliard. "Why, the events of the past year alone are enough to make Katarina's typewriter burst into flames! You went along with the antics of Sanctum Arcist. You even went as far as granting haven to a man you didn't trust."

"Hilliard, to blame all of Sanctum Arcist for the actions of The Network is closed-minded," said Jonathan. "They were duped just as much as we were. And I granted haven to keep an eye on Kaine and his students. I also meant to prevent harm from befalling them—"

"And that was unsuccessful, Jonathan," said Engagah. "Despite their duplicity, the murders of Gamaliel Kaine and his eldest son happened despite your haven. And a young man was nearly burned alive on your very grounds."

"That had nothing to do with Jonathan!" said Jonah. "That was because of Trip's chain-smoking! And Kaine and G.J.'s murders were the work of Jessica Hale, who did it for Creyton!"

"Creyton again." It was Lorelei who spoke this time. "His return has become your crutch, no?"

Jonah felt his eye began to twitch. Never a good sign. Jonathan moved forward.

"We can have these circular conversations until the end of time," he said. "But they surely cannot be the reason of this conversation. Can we get to that, please?"

"Certainly." Engagah crossed her hands in front of her and returned her focus to Jonah. "After due consideration, Blue Aura, we've decided that the best course of action is for you to return home."

"Amen to that," said Jonah, who rose and headed for the door. "It has been interesting."

He grabbed the door. It didn't budge.

"What the—?"

He grabbed at it again. No change.

"There is nothing out there, Blue Aura," said Katarina fearfully. "No Gates are currently in play."

"And why not?" demanded Jonah.

Katarina looked ready to shrink away from him. "Because this isn't yet over."

"What?"

"Katarina is right, Blue Aura," said Engagah. "This isn't over."

Jonah turned to see that every eye was still on him. The Founding Five looked at him with something like triumph, while Jonathan looked at him with something like disappointment.

"What is it now?" he asked. "You told me to go home. I'm just complying with your wishes."

"We did not mean the estate, boy," said Engagah. "We meant your former home, where Jonathan discovered you."

Jonathan closed his eyes, clearly trying to corral anger. But Jonah ignored it.

"What?" he whispered. "Are you serious right now?"

"Yes," said Engagah.

"What for?"

"Because it will be safer for everyone involved," said the Overmistress. "You get to have peace, and get to be away from the daily reminders of ethereality. The vigilantism can now quiet down."

"I'm not a vigilante!" snapped Jonah. "I get why you guys have cracked down on Sanctum, but why in the world am I taking blame?"

"You were in the midst of it all, Blue Aura," said Engagah. "No one forced you to pursue Charlotte Daynard that night. No one asked you to go to the home of Jessica Hale—Inimicus. Your curiosity is just as much to blame for Creyton's resurrection as Creyton is himself."

Jonah stared. Once again in his life, he'd heard something so absurd, so asinine, that he wanted impatiently to hear a laugh track somewhere. "You're blaming me for Creyton's Praeterletum?! You're sending me away from my friends? Who is going to stop Creyton? Who is going to stop the Deadfallen?"

"My my my," said Engagah, surveying Jonah with those eyes of hers. "The fact that you thought the task was your own shows that you have an issue with ego as well as impertinence. The job of stopping Creyton and his disciples is ours. And of course, the men and women who have been trained to neutralize Eighth Chapter crimes."

"I'm not abandoning my friends!" snapped Jonah. "You can't move me around like that! I'm not a damn ottoman!"

"You aren't a docile individual either, Blue Aura," said Engagah almost lazily. "Katarina stopped at your collegiate achievements. If we'd allowed her to continue, we would have heard all about how you once obtained aid from spectral forces so volatile that they actually fatally endowed an Eleventh Percenter once—"

"I was fighting Creyton and his minions!" snapped Jonah. "What were you expecting me to do? Go and ask to make sweaters in exchange for my friends?"

"You conducted unsupervised time experiments despite the fact that they were outlawed—"

"That was a mistake!"

"You've also performed countless Mentis Caveas and unauthorized *Astralimes* traveling at your merest whim—"

"Okay, you spouting all these half-way stories is really starting to piss me off—"

"And most recently," Engagah's voice didn't elevate a single decibel, "your arrest in Coastal Shores for assaulting a Tenth Percenter. It took a Networker's intervention to prevent your shenanigans from becoming public record in Tenth circles."

"THAT WAS—!"

"Jonah," said Jonathan in a calm voice, "the stance of the Curaie will not change. The decision is made. We are done here."

Jonah was livid, but he heard an undercurrent of anger in the calm of his mentor's voice as well. It was that—the simple fact that not everyone in this room was a damn automaton—that calmed him.

Somewhat.

"I have one question, though." Jonah had managed a voice so calm that he shocked even himself. "You want to move back to the city. Am I supposed to sleep in my car?"

Engagah rose. "Arrangements have already been made, Blue Aura," she told Jonah. "Whatever you may think of us, we are not evil."

"Mmm hmm," mumbled Jonah, "yeah."

"And you need not worry of Creyton," said Lorelei. "If all he had done is caused seventy percent of the ethereal world to have one dream, he is bound to fail. We will stop him."

Jonah didn't even dignify that last part with a response as he headed over to Katarina. "Can we leave now?" he asked.

Looking apprehensive, Katarina looked past Jonah to the Founding Five. They must have O.K.'d it, because she rose, touched the door for several seconds, and then opened it.

"Median," she announced unnecessarily.

Jonah overtook her on the way to her desk. "Give me my damn batons."

"Pardon me?" said Katarina.

"Give-me-my-batons," repeated Jonah, his voice slow and cold. "Do I have to spell it for you?"

Katarina removed them from the pouch and extended them. Jonah snatched them and stalked off maybe ten steps when a hand grabbed his shoulder.

"Jonah," Jonathan's voice was equally as cold, "look at me."

With a deep breath, Jonah turned. "What?"

Jonathan glared at him, and Jonah sighed.

"Sir?" he mumbled.

"You will apologize to Katarina."

"Say what?" asked Jonah.

"You heard me, boy," said Jonathan. "Now go."

"For the love of–Jonathan, we are all adults here!" Jonah exclaimed.

"Are we, Jonah?" asked Jonathan.

Jonah opened his mouth to respond, but then sensed eyes on him. Looking around, he saw that every eye was on him. The clique of Networkers, other Elevenths, several heralds, a group of spirits and spiritesses—they all had their eyes on him.

He'd made a scene. No one knew or cared that he was the one that had been wronged, because all they'd seen was his outburst. The injustice of it made him even angrier, but there was shame mixed in. The feeling of shame was exacerbated when he saw Katarina staring down at her desk, tears dripping down her face.

Aw, hell.

Feeling like a bully (which sickened him), he returned to Katarina's desk.

"Katarina, I'm sorry," he murmured. "You're not why I'm angry, and I shouldn't have taken my anger out on you. I have no excuses."

Katarina wiped her eyes and stared up at him. "Apology accepted."

Jonah nodded once, and returned to Jonathan, whose anger with him seemed to have dulled. Mostly.

"Are we using the *Astralimes* now?" asked Jonah.

"No, sit down," said Jonathan.

Jonah's eyes widened, but Jonathan shook his head.

"You're not about to hear a lecture," he said, "not just yet, anyway. I asked you to sit down because I estimate that the arrangements that Curaie have made for you are near fruition."

Not even five seconds after Jonathan said that, Jonah's phone rang. He answered it with a frown. "Hello?"

"Jonah!" Jonah recognized the voice instantly. "It was P.J. Bell, the landlord at his old apartment complex. "This was quick! Unexpected, and quick!"

"I'm sorry?"

"I got your request to reinstate your old lease agreement," said P.J. "Accepted! And the security deposit and two month's rent was a nice touch, son! Have you published one of those books of yours?"

Jonah heard, but it may as well have been a foreign language. Security deposit? Two month's rent? "Um, not yet, sir," he answered. "I'm...just really frugal."

P.J. laughed on the other end. "Whatever you say, son," he said. "You're a paying customer, and that's all I care about!"

Obviously, thought Jonah.

"But your apartment will be 7A now," P.J. went on. "That fine with you?"

"Yes, sir," said Jonah. "Thank you so much."

He ended the call, and looked up at Jonathan, but he quickly raised a finger to silence him.

"Hang on," he said, and Jonah's phone rang once more.

"Hello?"

"Jonah! Glad I got you!"

Jonah's eyes widened. "Mr. Steverson?"

"Right!" said the old man.

The voice was so welcome that Jonah actually smiled. Bernard Steverson was a jovial Vietnam veteran who'd given Jonah a job at his bookstore, S.T.R. It had been a fun experience working there, until Jonah damn near destroyed it when he stopped a disguised Creyton from killing Vera. He'd never felt the need to enlighten Mr. Steverson with that information. To this day, he believed a shelf collapsed and made a mess of things. He'd never felt the need to enlighten Mr. Steverson with that information. To this day, he believed a shelf collapsed and made a mess of things.

"Listen, son," Mr. Steverson went on, "I've re-opened S.T.R."

"You have?"

"Yep!" said Mr. Steverson. "Two months ago! I brought back Harland, and what's-her-name—you know, the one who watches the accounts—"

"Amanda?" asked Jonah, almost laughing.

"Yeah, her! I didn't call you because I imagined that you'd moved on; found something else somewhere far from here. But not even ten minutes ago, my mind fell on you. Like you needed help or something."

Jonah's eyes widened. There was no possible way the Curaie could do that, could they?

"What do you have going on professionally?" asked Mr. Steverson. "Would you like to have your old job back?"

Jonah looked up at Jonathan, his silent question obvious.

"Time doesn't have much merit with ethereal beings, Jonah," he mouthed.

Jonah lowered his eyes. What could he think? He was being forced away from the estate, back to the city he'd left nearly two years before. They always said that you could never pick up where you left off, because the world kept spinning. But now, because of the Curaie, Jonah had to do just that.

But it meant being away from his family.

Away from Vera.

Jonah had some seriously mixed emotions about the events of this day.

But none of that was Mr. Steverson's fault.

"I'd be honored, sir," said Jonah. "I'd love to have my old job back."

7

"Homecoming"

Jonah and Jonathan employed the *Astralimes* to return to the estate, and wound up at the same point in the backyard that they'd left earlier. Jonah looked at his watch and shook his head.

"You mean to tell me that my life was turned upside down in just two hours, Earthplane time?" he muttered. "Well, ain't that a—"

"Over here, Jonah." Jonathan was in the shadow of several trees.

Jonah walked over to him, puzzled. "What now?"

"What did I tell you?" Jonathan demanded, his grey eyes blazing.

Jonah, not expecting the temper, was taken aback. "What rattled your cage?"

"Don't be cute with me, boy," said Jonathan tersely. "I warned you to stay level, and remain respectful. I told you to maintain tact. But you threw that out of the window the minute you heard an opinion contrary to your own! It was immature, Jonah. More immature than you realize."

Now Jonah was furious again. "How the hell do you get off calling me immature?" he snapped. "I will not tolerate that bullshit, Jonathan, no matter who it is! They took things grossly out of context, and used achievements against me! They'd made up in their minds what they were going to do long before they even saw me, and that was even in this corporate jackass outfit! I should've worn whatever, given what happened—"

"See that right there?" Jonathan actually pointed a finger at Jonah. "That is the very type of attitude that retards progress, Jonah!"

"Jonathan, I'm getting a little sick of everybody's selective blindness!" Jonah matched Jonathan in voice tone. "It seems like nobody sees anyone's actions but my own! You were right there in that windowless room with me! You heard how everything was perverted, changed around, and made to point me in a bad light, not to mention everyone else—"

"And your goal to make it right was to react like a moody, temperamental loose cannon?" asked Jonathan, completely unabashed. "Jonah, I am well aware of the unfairness of this situation; I am infuriated by it as well. But they ignited that need in you, Jonah. That intense need of yours to defend your every action as righteous. You flew off the handle, and never looked back. You have to be smarter than that, Jonah, and no, I am not implying that you aren't smart, so do not bother twisting my words."

Jonah regarded the Protector Guide, breathing deeply. "So I was supposed to sit there and smile and nod while they tore me apart?"

"Of course not, Jonah," said Jonathan. "But you could have exercised more diplomacy. Objectivity is not the enemy of passion. It was not necessary to immediately jump to defensive mode when they riled you. They're spirits; they aren't like you and me."

Jonah contemplated Jonathan. "And what are you, Jonathan?"

"I am well aware of my status as a spirit, Jonah," said Jonathan impatiently. "What I mean to say is that while I am a spirit now, I was a physical being once. I have experienced the complexities that go along with a human existence, and not only that, but an ethereal human existence. The Spirit Guides never did that. They have always been spectral. They do not have the point of reference that you have. That I have. All of us have."

Jonah frowned. "They don't even know what it's like to be human?" he said blankly.

"No, Jonah, they do not," said Jonathan. "That is why I said to be respectful and respectful. You learn understanding through respect, see? And only with understanding can there be growth."

Now Jonah felt a bit bad. Yeah, he'd gotten angry, and that hadn't changed. But maybe he could have gone about it differently. At the same time, though, the notion grinning and bearing it in the name of understanding was full of holes. "I don't entirely follow that, Jonathan." he admitted.

"Three dimensional mind, son," said Jonathan, but Jonah knew that it wasn't meant to condescend. "That's been the tradition for them for many, many years."

"Yeah," said Jonah. "But Creyton didn't bother taking tradition into account when he returned from the grave. So how can they handle him traditionally?"

Jonathan paused, and gave the question some thought. "I don't agree with every decision they make, Jonah," he said at last. "Not by a long shot. But I do maintain that there are better ways to convey your position. Learning to exert control over your emotions will better shape your destiny, whatever that is. It is imperative that you learn that, Jonah. Train, practice, hone, perfect. Not just for yourself, but for all of us."

Jonah sighed. "I got you, Jonathan."

Jonathan didn't look fully convinced, but he still nodded. "Will you need support?" he asked.

Jonah looked at the estate, truly unaware of what to feel. What he knew for sure was that he was not looking forward to going inside. He thought that this must be what it felt like to be a parent looking at their home before they walked in and broke the news of a layoff.

"Nah," he murmured. "I got it."

Unfortunately, entering through the kitchen put Jonah in close proximity to the absolute last person he wanted to see: Trip.

He was polishing his saxophone when Jonah entered, and gave Jonah the usual glare that changed to curiosity when he saw Jonah's outfit.

"Funeral or job interview, Rowe?" he muttered. "Although I'm sure the two of them would be interchangeable when they involve you."

Jonah felt his face twitch again, but he shook his head. "Not doing this with you right now," he said, heading for the door.

"Oh wait," said Trip slowly. "You had the meet with the Curaie this morning. That's the reason for the getup. I take it that it didn't go well?"

Jonah froze. "What do you know about it?"

Trip didn't answer. "Sucked that bad, eh?"

Jonah turned around for the door once more. "Mind your damn business," he snapped.

"Did they kick you out of here?" asked Trip.

Jonah pushed the door open. To hell with Trip. But unfortunately, the closed door did nothing to drown out Trip's gleeful voice.

"They did, didn't they? My God! It's like my birthday! Pity you can't channel your stresses with your groupie anymore!"

That brought Jonah right back into the kitchen, and into Trip's face. "What did you just say to me?"

"Eh, you know," Trip lowered his eyes to the saxophone, "once upon a time, when you had a bad day, you'd spend the night with your little groupie from Sanctum. But alas, she's gone, buried under problems like the rest of those dumb fucks. So with no ass to enjoy, what will you do now?"

Jonah threw a punch at Trip, but Trip, without even looking up from the saxophone, raised a hand and caught his fist. Trip lowered the instrument with his other hand, and then slowly rose cold, menacing eyes at Jonah.

"You'd better check that shit," he warned. "You might have gotten lucky in days past, but you've never been in a one-on-one fight. I can embarrass you—or maim you. Got no issue with either one."

Just then, Bast wandered through the cat flap in the back door. She froze when she saw Jonah and Trip, but then her amber eyes seemed to flash. She was one of the direct sources of information to Jonathan, and everyone knew his stance on fights in his home. With everything going on, internal spats would probably lead to more bullshit.

"Get off me." Jonah wrenched his fist from Trip. "And go hang yourself."

"You first, asswipe," retorted Trip.

Jonah put as much space between the kitchen and himself as he could. He knew Trip was an efficient Eleventh, but he had been ready to throw caution to the wind.

He was heading for Reena's art studio, and he knew that Terrence wouldn't be too far away—

Wait.

Reena was at work by now. Terrence was, too; the custodians at the high schools were hard at work getting them ready for the new semester.

Great.

Bobby was probably out killing himself with weights, and there was no doubt in Jonah's mind that Alvin was with him. Malcolm was at work. And since he didn't see Liz, that meant that her mother, Nella, and Sandrine were back in town.

So who was left?

Then someone fell on his mind.

He went up the stairs, headed for Vera's room, and rapped on her door once he'd reached it.

"Vera? Are you in there?"

"Yeah!" she called. "It's open!"

Jonah entered. Vera was pulling an oversized T-shirt over her sports bra, so she must have doing yoga, or something. Jonah caught the briefest glimpse of the scar on her torso before the shirt was completely down, but decided not to mention it.

"Okay, Jonah," said Vera, "now how did—?"

She saw the look on her face, and her own face fell.

"Yeah," muttered Jonah. "It's like that."

"What happened?"

Jonah told her. Vera stared.

"Are you serious?" she demanded. "They did that because you lost your cool?"

"Nope," said Jonah in a dry voice, "they'd already made up their minds what they were gonna do. Me losing my temper was just an added bonus. Then I had to go and make the secretary cry, for which Jonathan made me apologize."

Vera shook her head. "Jonah, what are you going to do? You have no job, no place to live in the city—"

"Oh, don't worry; the Curaie took care of that, too," muttered Jonah ungratefully, and he filled Vera in on the Spirit Guides' "special arrangements" concerning his old apartment complex and his old job.

"That old bookstore," said Vera in a pensive voice. "Which was next to that sad excuse of a coffee shop."

Yep," said Jonah, with the merest trace of a smile. "The Southern Bean."

Jonah and Vera hadn't known each other then, and Jonah had actually frightened her when he'd tried to offer his assistance at first. Eventually, she realized that his intentions were good, and came looking for him. She'd checked The Southern Bean because Mr. Steverson had some leeriness about her when she'd tried the bookstore. The whole thing had been rife with tension at the time, but it was rather amusing now.

Then Jonah remembered what had happened earlier, and the mirth fell away.

"What do you think about it all?" asked Vera.

"What do I think?" cried Jonah. "I think it's—wait."

Vera tried hard to look innocent, but she failed miserably. Unless Jonah was mistaken, there was something in her voice and expression that sounded like…relief?

"What's the deal, Vera?" he asked her, point blank.

Vera hesitated, then sighed. "Okay, fine. I—I know you're not pleased about all the displacement, but I'm—I'm not sorry that you have to move back to the city."

Jonah, who had been hunched over, straightened. "And why is that?"

"Because I'll be going back to Colerain Place," said Vera.

"What?" Jonah blinked. "Why? Is something wrong? Please don't tell me that they kicked you out, too—"

"No no," said Vera hastily, placing a hand on his shoulder to calm him. "Nothing like that. I'm trying to sell it, remember? I couldn't very well be here, trying to spruce something up there. It was going to be hard enough leaving Liz and everyone, and the estate—I love this place. I have to focus on priorities, though. But then you said that you have to go back to the city as well, so I figured…this situation wouldn't suck so bad if you had a friend close by."

Vera's voice trailed off. Jonah raised an eyebrow. There was no denying that this entire situation was messed up. He'd been forced out of his home, where he needed to be so that he could help his friends figure out Creyton's new plan, even if that goal would be ten times more challenging due to the cult hunter Balthazar Lockman. But he was stuck with this situation, and he'd have to make it work one way or the other. Being around Mr. Steverson would help for sure. There was always Nelson and Tamara. And to have Vera back at Colerain Place around as well…

Something caught Jonah's and Vera's attention. Once again, the two of them had been close enough to lock fingers. With a snort, he let her fingers free.

"It's a great boon, Vera," he said. It'll help. I'm glad that this wasn't bad news for you. Because the worst is yet to come."

Reena had her thumb and forefinger at her brow. Terrence looked ready to break something.

"How in the hell is this fair?" he kept saying. "If it weren't for you, no one would have ever known Creyton had come back from the grave!

Both the estate and Sanctum would have been crippled! And this is your reward? Our reward? Being shunted sideways, or should I say, backward—"

"Terrence," Reena didn't even raise her head, "stop talking. I'm certain that Jonah has already gone through this a million times in his head already."

Jonah was thankful that Reena said that, but strangely, he was also thankful for Terrence's ranting instead of him. By the time the evening came, he had no more emotions to spare. He was just exhausted.

"It'll be like it was in the beginning." Jonah still wanted to rationalize it in his mind. "When I came when I could, and stayed for as long as I could before I had to get back."

"But Jonah, that's just bullshit!" said Terrence. "We're only gonna survive together! What'll we do without you?

Jonah's head shot up. "Terrence, stop right there. You talk like I'm some savior, and we all know that I'm not. I'm just another guy—"

"That's a lie and you know it, Jonah." Reena's tone was sharp. "You are the most powerful ethereal human. You're the Blue Aura. Terrence is right. This is bullshit."

Jonah rolled his eyes. The one time that Terrence and Reena agree, and it's on this? "Reena, I thought you were all for respecting them," he said. "I thought I needed to be impeccable and compliant, and the like. Now you're flip-flopping on that?"

"Maybe my opinion has changed now that they've punted one of my brothers away from our home," said Reena, looking Jonah in the eye.

"But you know what, though?" Jonah frowned slightly. "Something struck me as odd. I've had hours to think about it, and the more I do, the stranger it gets."

"What are you talking about?" asked Terrence.

"The way that the Five already had everything arranged," answered Jonah. "I mean, talk about speedy. They saw to it that I had a security deposit, plus two months' rent at my old apartment complex. Then they put some random thought in Mr. Steverson's mind that I needed assistance."

"Wasn't it always Mr. Steverson's plan to hire you back, Jonah?" asked Reena.

"The door was always open," said Jonah, "but he hadn't called me when he re-opened S.T.R. because he thought I'd moved on to bigger and better things."

"Hell," said Terrence, "in a bunch of ways, you did."

"That's beside the point," said Reena. "What is it that you find strange, Jonah?"

"Something was up with the Curaie," said Jonah outright.

"What?" said Terrence, incredulity in his face. "You think that the Phasmastis Curaie is working for Creyton?"

"Hell no," said Jonah. "Antiquated, out of touch, and rigid, but not evil. I think that they wanted to tuck me away for other reasons that just my supposed impulsivity."

"What, they're afraid that you might do their job?" snorted Terrence.

Reena looked pensive. "Now that you mention it, that's a good point, Jonah," she said. "Jonathan always said that the Curaie were dispassionate, and coolly logical. But what they did for you was extremely generous."

"Huh." Jonah looked at his best friends. "I don't think they are as dispassionate and logical as they have been in the past."

When Jonah broke the news to the others, he was annoyed and grateful. Grateful at all the fervent protests, and annoyed that no one seemed to realize that said fervent protests only made things more difficult.

Liz and Magdalena were both in tears, but for different reasons: Liz was worried that Jonah wouldn't fare well alone, and Magdalena cried when she got really angry.

"You guys make it seem like you'll never see me again," Jonah told them, though their tears made him angry with the Curaie all over again. "It will just be like it was before, when I was new here."

Magdalena nodded, but Liz wasn't appeased at all.

"What if you sustain an injury, Jonah?" she asked. "What if there are too many Deadfallen disciples to handle? What if—?"

"Liz, calm down," said Jonah seriously. "Since when were you the one who thought up all worst-case scenarios? Be happy that I have a home and a place to work!"

He still had mixed emotions about that. He noticed that Terrence sneered faintly, and cynicism was all over Reena's features.

"Why don't you make a big dinner, Terrence?" suggested Alvin.

"I will not," said Terrence flatly. "It's not like Jonah is going away forever. Spaghetti, garlic toast for you guys, and French bread for me. Take it or leave it."

To the surprise of no one, Trip loved every second of it. Jonah had never seen him, Karin, or any his buddies in such sunny moods. It was rather off-putting, and definitely infuriating. But what did surprise Jonah was that one of Trip's cronies, Grayson, told him in a quick undertone, "Take care of yourself, Rowe. I mean that."

Jonah looked at the guy, wondering when he'd stop being Trip's bit player.

"You want to ride together?" Jonah asked Vera the next morning at breakfast.

Vera looked apologetic. "I would, Jonah, but I promised Nella and Sandrine that I'd check in on the progress of their new gardens before I left. I got Jonathan's permission to use the *Astralimes* later on."

Jonah nodded. "I also meant to ask you whether or not you have a job lined up, too."

"My old waitressing one." Vera tried not to sound bitter. "It's a means to an end until I get this house gone."

Jonah was no stranger to crappy jobs, so he knew that no bracing statements would make her feel better. He hoped that she could go ahead and get that house off of her back so that she could go chase her dreams.

Well, it sounded right enough when he told himself that that was what he ought to be thinking, anyway.

"Terrence and Reena are at work, right?" asked Vera.

"Yeah," said Jonah. "You should have heard Terrence swearing about not being able to help. I told him that it wasn't the energy, because it's not like I hauled everything I owned here when I moved. Most of it's in storage, so it's still close to the old apartment complex."

Vera looked at her breakfast, seemingly lost in thought about something. Jonah could have remained seated and spoken to her all morning, but putting off the inevitable wouldn't help anything. So he took a deep breath and rose.

"I'll see you soon, Vera," he said.

She nodded, still lost in thought. He wondered what was bothering her, but didn't think that this was the time to ask. So, reluctantly, he left her there.

He was so preoccupied with thoughts that he didn't realize someone standing against his car. It was Daniel.

"Daniel?" Jonah frowned. "Why aren't you asleep?"

Daniel pulled a wry face. "I'm new to this life, Jonah," he said. "I have never had to do such a thing as sleep, and even now I can't grasp why anyone would want to waste eight hours of your physical life a night. That lost time accumulates, you know?"

Jonah blinked. "Right. Later."

Daniel pulled an arrow from his quiver and blocked Jonah's path with it. "One moment," he said. "I know that you're angry with the Curaie. They did what they thought was best."

Jonah sniffed. "I've already heard this—"

"However," Daniel continued as though there had been no interruption, "what they think is best is not always sensible. I'm glad that you spoke your mind to them."

Jonah hadn't expected to hear that. At all. "You're going against Jonathan?" he asked suspiciously. "He was going on and on about how diplomacy is the best way."

"I'm not going against Jonathan," said Daniel, lowering the arrow. "Jonathan is a much more serene being than I. The Curaie's stance concerning handling Creyton was the final straw for me, so I became mortal. Jonathan is still of two worlds, and two minds."

That wasn't the first time that Jonah had heard that about Jonathan, but now it seemed to take on a new meaning. "You think Jonathan needs to take a harder line?"

"I do," confirmed Daniel. "Jonathan needs to learn how to get nasty. The qualities that he exhibited during Sanctum's time here, like when he scared the piss out of the Kaines and broke that bastard's jaw? That's the Jonathan that he needs to be now. Words will not be enough to end this problem. Which is why I want you to have this."

He unclasped his fingers from around the arrow, so Jonah could take it. Jonah did so, surprised.

"What about my batons?" he asked.

"They have their purpose," replied Daniel, "but sometimes blunt force isn't enough. Sometimes, it takes something sharper. Safe travels."

Jonah lowered himself into his car, having no intention to ever use the arrow.

* * *

Jonah stepped out of his car and surveyed Cremo Ridge Apartments. He couldn't help but think about what an amusing thing perspective could be.

There had been a time when this place had been his haven. His refuge from Essa, Langton, and Bane. Many a night had passed when he'd driven into the parking lot in the late afternoon or early evening, cursing Langton and Tony Noble while mentally thinking of ways to cause Jessica Hale bodily harm and make it seem accidental (while he'd come to regret the former practice, the latter one had picked up a brand new intensity in the past few months, with the only change being that he no longer cared about whether or not it was an accident). How many nights had he looked forward to returning to this place just to take yet another stab at writing, eat greasy pizza, and catch a glimpse of Leta, the woman who'd lived in 7C?

But so much had changed since that time. He had changed so much since that time. And in those days, he'd been a voluntary tenant. Now he'd been forced here, away from where he belonged, away from where he was the most useful.

His mind went to his old job. He knew that Jessica was still employed at the accounting firm (the Curaie, so Jonathan told him, lacked anything concrete to tie her to her ethereal crimes, plus they'd have to deal with the whole Tenth side of the law as well. Typical.), but, thankfully, he didn't have to worry about his two closest friends colleagues. The receptionist, Mrs. Souther, was now happily retired and living in Sarasota. His pal, Nelson Black, had taken his wife Tamara's advice and started his own accounting firm, so he was no longer under Jessica's eye. That was awesome, but the bitch was still around. And he had no idea what she and her "Transcendent" were cooking up now. Life had been a huge mystery since that damn dream.

Jonah closed his eyes. And the Curaie said that sending him back here would prevent him from having to think about stressors of the ethereal world. Those spirits had no idea.

With a sigh, he slung his bag over his shoulder, went inside, grabbed his new key, and hopped into the elevator. When Jonah stepped out on the seventh floor, he burst out laughing. In all the time he'd been gone, P.J. still hadn't fixed that crack in the wall that been there since before Jonah lived here the first time. At least he'd been consistent.

He unlocked his apartment and entered. The place was empty of course, but a trip to the storage facility would remedy that. No big deal.

There was just one last thing to do before he found the new location of S.T.R.

He closed his eyes tightly, and willed the curtain to open and the actors to perform. When he opened his eyes, he saw that there was a paleness over everything. It was like a thin layer or coating had been used to modify his vision. But if this misty film was present, then that meant there were too many spirits to see. That was great. A high spirit count in any given place meant that there was no dark ethereality present. Still, Jonah could never be too careful. He would go into Spectral Sight in every single room. He'd be damned if he got blindsided ever again.

He was about to go check out the bathroom when a voice said, "One moment, Eleventh Percenter."

A spirit took form in front of him. It was a young man who could have been Jonah's age, with shoulder-length brown hair and rather shabby clothes. But Jonah imagined that clothing types didn't matter much in the spirit world.

Why did he see fit to present himself from the misty mass?

"Um, hello spirit," said Jonah. "Is there something I can help with?"

"There is something I can help you with," said the spirit. "I have a message for you, and a package from the Networker named Ovid Patience."

He reached into his pocket and then handed a pocketknife to Jonah. The thing was in good condition, but Jonah looked at it with curiosity.

"Patience sent you here to give me a pocketknife?" Jonah hoped that the sense of anticlimax he felt couldn't be heard in his voice.

"An ethereal steel-bladed, pocketknife," corrected the spirit. "He wants you to carry it with you everywhere you go, and make imperfections on the thresholds that you don't trust. He said you'd understand the significance."

Jonah did. He'd been tricked into crossing a Threshold of Death, which took him to the location of the site where Creyton achieved Praeterletum. He'd been leery of crossing an unfamiliar threshold ever since, but usually convinced himself to get over it. Now he had the means to prevent falling victim to a Threshold of Death ever again.

Suddenly, Patience's gift wasn't so anticlimactic after all.

"He also wanted me to tell you that he didn't think your batons would be very subtle if you tried to use them to do it," joked the spirit.

Jonah grinned. "When you see him again, tell him many thanks," he told the spirit. "I'll get to work as A.S.A.P."

The new location of S.T.R. was a bit of a surprise. By no means had Mr. Steverson relocated to some swanky part of town, but the last location had been surrounded by establishments equally as antiquated, maybe even more so. That wasn't the case in this new area.

There wasn't actually any rhyme or reason to the collection of businesses here. It was like whoever had handled the zoning here had simply phoned it in. There was a quaint Italian restaurant, an auto repair shop, a yoga studio, a Baskin Robbins, and, perhaps the most interesting thing of, a tattoo parlor situated two doors down from S.T.R. Blood Oaths Tattoos by Bryce Tysinger sat atop the place in scarlet, cursive letters.

The sight of the place sparked a long ago memory in Jonah's mind. He'd once asked his grandmother what she thought about tattoos because he'd had a vague idea about getting a skull on his arm.

It had been no go.

"*If we were meant to write on ourselves,*" she'd scoffed, "*they'd have never invented paper.*"

He smiled at the thought, and then filed it away as he entered S.T.R.

The interior of the new site was very nice. It was larger than the previous S.T.R. had been, but not so large that the personal touch had been lost. The rows were lined with books of all ages and titles, and Jonah also saw that that all the shelf foundations were strong.

"Can I help you, s—?"

Jonah's attention shifted to the man who stopped speaking so abruptly. It was Harland.

"What?" he said excitedly. "Jonah?"

In spite of everything, Jonah grinned and shook his hand. It was such a surprise that Harland showed such enthusiasm. He was a taciturn man by nature, but it wasn't the case at this particular point in time.

Harland hadn't changed much. His hair was bit longer than before, and he had some stubble under his chin. Other than that, same guy.

"Guess I can't call you 'kid' anymore," joked Harland. "Beard and everything! How has life been treating you?"

An interesting question. "Kept living, kept learning," said Jonah easily, and then his eyes lowered to Harland's knee. "How did that heal?"

Harland had an old football injury that Creyton had caused to re-aggravate him, which resulted in a car accident. But Harland's road to recovery got expedited when Liz and Reena performed some surreptitious ethereal healing.

"Healed just fine," said Harland, shaking his leg somewhat to demonstrate the absence of ill effects. I was even able to start running again last summer."

Jonah nodded. Great things, great things.

"Amanda is going to be mad that she missed you," said Harland. "But she'll be back tomorrow. Wait till Mr. Steverson sees you."

He beckoned Jonah forward, and they moved through the shelves to the register, where Mr. Steverson was on the phone. Harland pushed Jonah to a position where he'd be in Mr. Steverson's direct line of sight when he turned around. Jonah decided to humor him.

Mr. Steverson chatted away, but something that the person on the other line said must have given him pause, because he sighed, turned to lower the phone, and saw Jonah. He looked stunned for the briefest of moments, then broke into the widest smile.

"Hey there, son!" Mr. Steverson completely abandoned his phone call and came around the table. Jonah extended his hand, but Mr. Steverson ignored it and wrapped him in a huge hug. Jonah grunted in surprise. For a disabled veteran, Mr. Steverson was still pretty strong. There was more gray in his hair since Jonah had seen him last, and he'd probably gained a few pounds, but none of that mattered. He was still the same jovial, pleasant-tempered, and wizened bookworm that he'd always been.

He stepped away from Jonah and looked him over. "You look so different, son!"

"The same can be said about you, sir!" said Jonah, knowing Mr. Steverson would see it for the silly banter that it was. He was not disappointed; Mr. Steverson punched him in the shoulder, laughing as he did so.

"I want to show you something." Mr. Steverson pointed to a row near the wall. "Harland, please finish that call. It's Amanda. The girl just left, and she has already called with new advice to eliminate 'excess expenditures,' or whatever she said."

Harland snorted at that, nodded, and went to the phone. Jonah and Mr. Steverson headed down Mr. Steverson's desired row, and Jonah had an inkling of what the man wanted.

"Did you bring me here to show me the new shelf reinforcements, sir?" he asked.

"No, I didn't," said Mr. Steverson, and Jonah was surprised to see that all the laughter had left his face. "I wanted to ask you how things are going."

Puzzled, Jonah shrugged. "It's—I mean, y'know—"

"Quit rambling, son," said Mr. Steverson quietly. "You look different."

"How do you mean?" asked Jonah. "The beard? The face that I'm slimmer?"

"No, son." Mr. Steverson waved an impatient hand. "I mean you look different. You have the exact same look in your eyes that I had when I got back from Vietnam: haunted, seen too damn much, and don't know what to expect next."

Jonah stared. How had Mr. Steverson pegged it like that? He'd been pleasant and friendly, smiled all around, and it was still obvious that he'd been through things?

"Thought so." There was triumph in Mr. Steverson's eyes. "Now talk to me, son. What's up?"

Jonah swallowed. "It would take way too long, Mr. Steverson—"

Mr. Steverson interrupted him with a sly smile. "We can finish *Hamlet* in the time Harland gets rid of Amanda," he said. "We've got time."

8

The Reminder

The situation was garbage. That's all there was to it.

But wallowing in self-pity wasn't going to help Jonah at all. So he forced himself to roll with it.

Mr. Steverson had been no problem at all, which was a bright side. The man was observant and receptive, but also very thoughtful and respectful of people's experiences, and how they chose to deal with them. Maybe that stemmed from the fact that he still dealt with survivor's guilt that he'd had since Vietnam. When Jonah worked at S.T.R. before, he'd done Spectral Sight one day and discovered that there were two soldiers that Mr. Steverson hadn't completely forgiven himself for not rescuing in Saigon. Their spirits were still around him, no doubt assisting him in getting past it. Nearly forty years after Vietnam, it still hadn't happened.

Jonah bore that in mind when he carefully told Mr. Steverson that he'd been betrayed by someone he thought he knew, and had experienced the loss of two individuals that he felt it should have been in his power to save. Mr. Steverson immediately looked understanding, and Jonah knew what he said had done the trick. Jonah knew that Mr. Steverson would pry no further on the matter, nor would he hit him over the head with pity.

"I won't be as bold as to say I completely understand, son," Mr. Steverson had said, "but one bit of advice I will give you is that it won't do you any favors to handcuff yourself to past regrets. The handcuffs can evolve into a prison. It's like liquor, son. It'll creep up on you, and then the next thing you know, you're a different person. You've got so much life ahead of you, Jonah. I don't want to see you change for the worse."

Jonah wished that he could tell Mr. Steverson the whole story, but since he was free of the man's suspicion, he knew to leave well enough alone. He also wished that he could tell Mr. Steverson that a change within him was already well underway.

He found himself slipping into a routine. The business was steady, which was a good thing, because busyness was a distraction from Creyton, that dream, and his quasi-exile.

He'd only been back to the estate three times in the four weeks since the Curaie put their shit decision in motion, but he stayed in contact with Terrence and Reena. They kept him updated on the goings-on at the estate. Terrence told him that Trip had been nothing short of ecstatic concerning Jonah's situation; he'd nearly come to blows with Bobby over it. He also labeled Daniel as an "alright guy."

"He's like—I don't know—Spock, without all the logic, and just a *bit* more display of emotion," described Terrence. "He'll be cool, and really still, with patience that you or I could never achieve. Sociable enough, but spends more time observing. But if you get him on a subject that he's passionate about...well. That's where the emotion comes in."

Jonah was reminded of the ill effects of Creyton's resurrection when he'd spoken to Reena, who'd revealed an experience at her job. Jonah knew that it had to be bad; Reena never spoke about her job if she could help it.

"Brent Shane, the guy from HR, robbed the custodian's truck. When the guy confronted him, Brent punched him so hard he ruptured his eardrum. In front of us, Jonah! I didn't know that he was capable of such a thing. The man only weighs about a hundred pounds! We had to restrain him long enough for a couple deputies to show up."

Jonah frowned, pushing the phone nearer to his face. "And this guy has never acted that way before?"

"Never," said Reena. "He's a wimp. I've had to stop people from bullying him in the past."

Jonah sighed. "If he got walked on all the time, then that's not suspicious activity, Reena," he told her. "That just means that the doormat finally had enough, and fought back."

"I thought that, too," said Reena quietly, "until Brent got arrested and said that he never wanted to hit the custodian, he just 'felt like he had to.' And remember, Jonah, he was the one in the wrong. He robbed the custodian. So why would the guilty one rob someone, and then lash out when confronted?"

Jonah shook his head. Leave it to Reena to see every perspective. "Well, it's a good thing that he didn't attack you, Reena," he said, for humor. "You'd have probably killed the man and provided more fuel for the Curaie that we're all crazy."

Jonah decided to visit Vera's place of work, an eatery simply The Stop. The place was too small to be all that remarkable, but also too large to have "hole in the wall" status. He hoped that Vera was making the most of her situation as well.

He couldn't have chosen a busier time; 12:15. Everywhere was full, and The Stop was no different. There were men complaining about fries not being hot enough. A middle-aged woman whined about not being able to smoke near the door. There were two children who had the most useless parents Jonah had ever seen. They did absolutely nothing about the fact that there was more of their children's food on the floor than on their plates. Jonah wasn't about to activate Spectral Sight in here. The sights of spirits and spiritesses would only serve to make the place appear even more erratic.

Then he spotted Vera. She was near a particularly portly man who griped on and on about something, and she was attempting to handle it maturely. She looked comfortable enough in the quaint uniform of a hunter green T-Shirt and black pants, with her brownish-blonde pulled back into a ponytail. Jonah wondered how she felt about that, because needing the ponytail put the scar on her jaw in full view of everyone. She had grown comfortable around the estate residents, but these weren't residents. He hoped that she wasn't getting flack or heckling.

She must have felt eyes on her, because she turned and spotted him. The relief that came over her face was almost laughable, and she headed straight for him, face flushed, and a light sweat across her forehead.

"Jonah," she said breathlessly. "Finally, somebody rational! Go out and stand by my car. I'll meet you there in five minutes."

Jonah did as he was told, and, true to her word, Vera was beside him, but it was only four minutes later. Jonah glanced at his watch and snickered.

"Does it ever get annoying being a minute early for everything?" he asked.

"Used to it now," said Vera, who unclasped her hair so that it hung like usual. "It makes getting to work easy most of the time, and I can take as long as I want on breaks."

"We didn't have to talk out here if you didn't want, Vera," said Jonah. "I would have gladly ordered—"

"No," said Vera flatly. "I bless the moments that I'm not in that madhouse."

Jonah snorted. "Fair enough. So how have you been?"

Vera ran a finger along her facial scar. "Well, the house is completely clean. Patience—who is the coolest guy—placed many protections around my place, and put slash marks across all of my thresholds."

"He did that for you?" said Jonah with mock envy. "He sent a spirit to give me an ethereal steel pocketknife to make the slashes myself."

Vera looked at Jonah, in all seriousness. "You're not as cute as I am."

"Got me there," grumbled Jonah, but his frustration was all for show. They were laughing about it seconds later.

"I think that Patience has done that for many folks," said Jonah. "He is one of the few Networkers who has loyalty to Jonathan and isn't really following the Curaie's hard line. He did it for the Decessio house, and Kendall's place, too."

Vera nodded. "Good stuff," she said, and then resumed silence that Jonah was pretty sure he'd correctly interpreted.

"I don't want to be here either, Vera," he said quietly. "I miss them all. I've only managed to go back three times in the past month. I'll be there tomorrow, staying till Monday. But this back-and-forth thing takes a toll."

Vera nodded. "I was on Skype with Liz last night, once I was done Skyping with Eden. The girl actually cried a bit, Jonah, because she missed us so much. One would think we've been gone for years. I told her that it wasn't a big deal, and we could be there at any time."

"But she got you misty-eyed as well, didn't she?" said Jonah shrewdly.

"Yeah," conceded Vera. "I admit it. So what are you doing here, Jonah? Not that I didn't want to see you, but you could have easily asked me how I was doing over the phone."

Jonah blinked slowly. He really needed to work on being so obvious. "Okay, Vera," he began. "There is a reason I came here, beyond seeing how you were doing. I figured—since you were here, and I was here—there was no point in us hiding in our homes and going out of our minds trying to figure out what was going on in the ethereal world. I wanted to know if you'd be amenable to…to making up for that night."

Vera looked puzzled for a few moments, but then her face cleared. "Oh," she said. "*That* night."

Jonah knew that he'd taken a gamble. Last summer, he and Vera had had a date. He'd gone above and beyond for it, too; a blank check from a rich idiot and some imagination would prompt that. They'd had a nice dinner at an upscale restaurant named The Maiden of the Rose, and then watched a play. It had gone so well, even with Jonah's arm in a sling. But then they'd experienced a tire blowout, which was remedied by a Good Samaritan…who happened to be a gorgeous woman later revealed to be an Eleventh Percenter. That hadn't sat well with Vera.

So, once again, Jonah knew that this was a gamble.

"No," said Vera.

Jonah's guts twisted. No? Had she actually said no? Had Rheadne altered their lives that much?

"No?" he repeated somewhat stupidly.

"No," said Vera once more. "I am not amenable to making up for that night. I am, however, amenable to creating a new one."

Jonah's insides ceased their erratic activities at once. So she didn't want to have a night based on the previous one. She wanted a brand new experience. She had him going there for a minute. Man, she shouldn't have done that!

"Of course," he said smoothly, leveling his voice so as to not sound like a relieved child. "When's the end of your shift?"

Vera had had her eyes on Jonah the entire time, and she didn't look fooled in the slightest. "A quarter to six."

"Pick you up from your house an hour after that?"

"I'm game," said Vera.

"Good deal," said Jonah. "See you then."

Vera smiled, and went back into The Stop. Jonah made sure that he was safely in his car before he heaved the hugest sigh in the history of the world.

Jonah played it cool for the most part. He didn't go all out like last time. There was no point. But he did eschew any weight training, and triple, quadruple, and quintuple-checked his tires.

His mood hadn't escaped Mr. Steverson's notice, who smiled when he saw Jonah check his tires for the fifth time.

"Don't know what you're up to," he said, "but you certainly look happy about it!"

Jonah ran into Amanda, who was very pregnant. It was a good thing, because it had been Amanda's life ambition to have a baby the last time he'd seen her. Now, she was expecting. He hoped that when the kid came along, the experience was everything she dreamed it would be.

"They told us that we were having a girl," she told Jonah, "but then Mr. Steverson touched my stomach and said that they were wrong; I'm having a boy. Not even an hour later, they called and told me they'd made a mistake, and we're having a boy!"

Jonah frowned and looked over at Mr. Steverson, who was helping a patron. "When did he become the Baby Whisperer?" he asked.

"No idea," said Amanda, but I'm glad he filled me in before Danny and I turned the nursery into a pink nightmare."

Jonah was still laughing about that when he pulled in front of Vera's house on Colerain Place, but he wasted no time in sobering and going into Spectral Sight. But he was pleasantly surprised, not to mention thankful, to see that the neighborhood was a far different place than it had been the last time he'd been here. The spectral activity was much more prevalent; Jonah even noticed when a young spiritess grinned at him and waved. He smiled and waved back. Vera met him outside before he'd deactivated the Sight.

"So you just met Wilhelmina," she said as she lowered herself into his car.

"That's the spiritess' name?" asked Jonah.

"Yeah," said Vera. "She's been a here a long time. I used to catch glimpses of her before I knew I was an Eleventh Percenter, and just thought I was crazy. Apparently, she helps families with small children. Helps them adjust to their new surroundings."

Jonah raised his eyebrows, interested. "Sounds like you've made friends with her," he commented.

Vera nodded. "She's a very sweet spiritess. She told me that working with children from a spectral standpoint is cake. Even Tenth children are receptive to spiritual activity at that age."

Jonah shook his head as he pulled off from the space. "Imagine if the whole world knew the truth about spirits and spiritesses."

Vera cracked her knuckles. No doubt her fingers had been overworked many times over that day. "I wouldn't get my hopes up," she muttered. "The information would likely be suppressed or regulated, just like everything else."

Their conversation smoothly carried over to their destination, which was dinner at a neat little Italian restaurant. Jonah didn't put much thought into it. He was simply struck with inspiration after having a taste for lasagna. It wasn't anything ostentatious, but in Jonah's mind, that was fine. No grand plan, and no forced intelligent design filled with numerous variables. And it worked out very well.

When Jonah held the door open for Vera when it was time to leave, many patrons were still inside, but the parking lot was sparsely populated with people who'd yet to have entered their vehicles: there was a man busily shuffling papers in his backseat, a couple who were trying and failing to coax their overly energetic children into car seats, a guy—Jonah felt for him—who was battling a car that wouldn't start, and a dark-haired woman some distance away, savoring a cigarette. Vera shook her head.

"I have always hated cigarettes," she said in an undertone as they neared the smoker, who they had to pass to get to Jonah's car. "Such a revolting habit."

"And Trip makes it seem like mother's milk," murmured Jonah. "He once told me that he wasn't worried about cigarettes screwing with his music career—"

Jonah froze. Vera looked at him, puzzled.

"What's wrong?" she asked him.

"Vera." Jonah spoke as clearly as he could, because he didn't want to repeat himself. "Let's go back in the restaurant. Now."

"What?" frowned Vera. "Why?"

"Vera, please," urgency was in Jonah's voice now, or maybe it was panic, "just listen to me—"

The smoker flicked the cigarette away and smoothed out her shirt. Jonah recognized that profile. He would have recognized it even if he'd seen it from another state.

"Vera, just listen to me, we need to go back in—"

Jonah had taken too long. The woman turned to go into the restaurant and saw him and Vera. She surveyed them with as much shock as Jonah had, but she was quicker to recover, and smiled maliciously.

Jessica.

"Well, well, well!" Jessica blocked their path with an athlete's grace. "Jonah! Who'da thunk!"

Vera looked at Jessica, wide-eyed. Jonah knew how she felt; Jonathan had had Jonah describe every Deadfallen disciple he could recall seeing that night of Creyton's Praeterletum, and Reena had sketched them. The images were now burned into everyone's memories. And now, Vera had the unfortunate experience of seeing one of those images, live and in color.

But with one stark change. Jessica saw that Jonah's eyes were on said change, and she grinned.

"I know, I know," she said, swinging her hair a bit. "You barely recognized me. It's the hair, I get it. The strawberry blonde was great for a time, but I figured that I'd dispense with it once I was free to stop playing characters. Brunette is more of my speed nowadays. But look at you! Trying to butch up with a beard! Was that supposed make you look more dashing?"

Before Jonah could respond, Jessica looked Vera over, then back at him, and then down at their clasped hands. It was at that moment that she smiled. It was a sweet, pleasant smile, but when Jonah saw it, it was one of the most terrifying things he'd ever seen.

"And you've got company," she said hungrily. "What is this? A causal benefits arrangement?"

Vera's hand tightened in Jonah's. To hear Jessica describe Vera like she were a plaything to be violated made him angry. The fear hadn't left by any means, but that emotion now had a friend.

"Let's leave your practices out of this, Jessica," he grumbled. "How's the arm, by the way?"

Jessica's smile faltered for just a second. Much to his displeasure, Jonah saw that her arm, which had been badly broken the night of Creyton's resurrection, showed no ill effects at all now. Creyton had fixed her up perfectly.

"My arm is doing as well as your jaw," said Jessica smoothly. "My Transcendent is good to me. I'm forever faithful."

"What do you want?" demanded Jonah.

Jessica widened her eyes in an obvious sort of way. "Italian restaurant...food...eating." She said it slowly and clearly, like Jonah wouldn't make the connection. "I'm taking a meal amongst the Ungifteds this evening!"

"Cute touch," said Jonah, whose nostrils flared. "Who are you waiting for? Are you planning to kill him after he buys you dinner? Or her, since I recall that that doesn't really matter to you?"

Jessica's eyes narrowed. "Don't condescend, Jonah," she said softly. "It's unbecoming."

"If you don't get away from here, I'll do more than that," promised Jonah.

Jessica laughed. Jonah hated it now as much as he ever did.

"You realize that I could make your little friend here traipse in traffic, don't you?"

"I'd love to see you try, bitch—" Vera had found her voice, but Jonah didn't let her finish.

He let go of her hand and stood in front of her. He knew that Vera was a strong-willed woman and probably wouldn't appreciate the gallantry much, but he didn't care. She had no idea what Jessica was capable of doing.

"One step closer, Jessica," he warned, "and you will have the fight of your life."

Jessica licked her lips, but she backed away and raised her hands in an innocent fashion. "Don't worry, Jonah," she said sweetly. "I'll not mess with your Alpha male moment. I didn't even expect to run into you tonight. But since you're here, I may as well give you a reminder, from my Transcendent: You are on borrowed time."

"What's he planning, Jessica?" Jonah wanted to throttle her, but that would mean putting space between him and Vera.

"Like I'd tell you," scoffed Jessica. "Patience is a virtue, Rowe."

"So is chastity, but you dropped the ball on that one long ago," countered Jonah.

Jessica's eyes flashed. "Just don't shit yourself when the hammer drops, Jonah."

"They'll find you, Jessica," said Jonah viciously. "And I pray that they torture the truth out of you."

Jessica flashed that maddening smile again. "They'll never catch me. Want to see why?"

Before Jonah could blink, Jessica's form compacted, and a crow stood before him and Vera.

"Son of a bitch," hissed Vera, who clutched Jonah's arms from behind him.

Jonah just stared, stupefied. When India Drew had done it back in Coastal Shores, it had been so slow. So deliberate and methodical. But Jessica had done the shape shift in the blink of an eye, like a damn magic trick, or something. None of the Tenths noticed, because of course.

The crow looked them over with spiteful, intelligent eyes, and then gave a sharp *CAW,* and took flight. Jonah's eyes followed its progress, and he knew Vera's had done the same. It was late, so soon there was nothing to see, but neither Jonah's nor Vera's eyes lowered from the sky.

"What the—?" One of the patrons noticed the crow when it cawed and flew off. "You ever seen one of those in the evening?"

"They always said that those birds represented death," said the man with car trouble. "It's fitting that I'd see a damn crow, given my poor engine."

Those words were mere background noise to Jonah. He couldn't care less about cars or superstition at the moment. Vera grasped his hand and broke the silence.

"That...was...scary," she managed.

"Understatement," said Jonah. "India Drew did it too, back at the beach. That's why they didn't find her, either."

"Right." Vera's response almost sounded like autopilot. "I'm ready to go home now."

"Of—of course," said Jonah. "I'll take you; I'll even walk you in—"

"That's the thing, Jonah," said Vera. "I don't want you to leave me."

Those words actually pulled Jonah's eyes from the sky, and he looked at Vera. "Seriously, Vera? You're not uncomfortable with me spending the night in your house?"

"Yeah, Jonah." Sarcasm actually crept into Vera's alarmed voice. "I'm about as uncomfortable with it as I am with seeing a woman shape shift into a crow and flying into the night sky."

A great deal of Jonah's awkwardness faded at once. "Point. Want me on the couch or the floor?"

9

The Popular Ones

Jonah and Vera didn't speak on the drive back. It made Jonah think about the last time that had happened, but he reminded himself that that situation had been worlds different. Vera wasn't ignoring him this time; she was just freaked out and preoccupied with her own thoughts. On top of that, she actually wanted his company this time around.

When they arrive back at Colerain Place, Jonah turned off the engine and removed his seatbelt. "Wait for me here," he said.

"Hell no," said Vera immediately. "We're together on this."

Sighing, Jonah didn't say anything when Vera followed him to his destination, which was her young spiritess friend Wilhemina. They found her easily, and she greeted them with a bright smile that faltered when she saw the looks on their faces.

"Trouble, Eleventh Percenter?" she asked Jonah warily.

"Not here," answer Jonah. "Elsewhere. We just want to be prepared."

Willow's eyebrows rose. "Is it Creyton?"

"One of his disciples," said Jonah, who felt that she didn't need any more than that.

Willow nodded vigorously. "You have been endowed," she said, even endowing Vera for good measure.

With the endowment coursing through him, Jonah thanked the spiritess, grabbed Vera's keys, and unlocked her front door. With one foot across the threshold, he paused.

"Jonah, it's alright," said Vera. "Patience slashed all my thresholds and put up protections—"

"No," said Jonah, "it isn't that. Did you re-rig that little security system of yours?"

"Oh." In spite of everything, Vera actually laughed. "I did, actually. Hang on."

Jonah breathed a sigh of relief. When he'd first met Vera, he'd discovered that she employed a clever-but-crude security system which involved looping spools of yarn through holes in tin cans, which were full to the brim with spare change. It was laughably low-budget, but Jonah knew that the ensuing commotion, and potential injury, simply wasn't worth it.

"Safe," announced Vera in a quiet voice. The momentary glibness was gone.

Jonah walked in, and looked over Vera's living room. She hadn't been lying; she had been busy. The areas looked so naked of belongings that if Jonah hadn't known any better, he'd have thought someone had just moved in. Which, technically, Vera had.

"It's just bare essentials." Vera noticed Jonah's inspection. "I don't want a whole lot of work to do if and when I sell this place."

Jonah closed his eyes. Just that quickly, he'd forgotten about that. "Right. I'll...I'll just park it here on your couch."

Nodding slowly, Vera retreated to her bedroom, where Jonah heard water running a few minutes later. Figuring that her nighttime ablutions would take a bit, he tried to distract himself with television. Didn't work. Nothing could pull his attention. Jonah couldn't even distract himself by watching Maggie Q kick ass on reruns of *Nikita*. Jessica's appearance had rattled him that much.

With a sigh, he gave up, and sat back on Vera's couch. He had no doubts that it was only a coincidence that they'd seen Jessica that night, because she had been just as shocked to see him as he'd been to see her. But the way she carried herself, with that smug and self-righteous demeanor, was unnerving.

And then, there was her little reminder about him being on borrowed time.

He had escaped Creyton that night by pure luck and good timing. There was no denying that. But the fact that he had actually gotten away, luck or not, had gotten him thinking about his chances. He didn't know how much of a threat he was to Creyton. He thought that the more he got lucky, the more Creyton would come. And he'd be more and more sadistic with it each time.

Creyton had returned to physical life. All Jonah had returned to was his old apartment building, and that hadn't even been his choice.

Those feelings of isolation began to seep into his mind once more. They were quickly followed by frustration. How was he supposed to look after his well-being even a tiny bit when he was away from the estate? Away from his friends, and the ability to train? Creyton was out there, doing God-knew-what (not to mention the activities of his disciples), and Jonah and his friends were practically on ice, with him stashed all the way up here, rehabbing books and ducking tenant's meetings. He couldn't see the justice in that.

He thought of the Phasmastis Curaie, and his blood began to boil all over again.

"Jonah?" said Vera, who'd returned from her bedroom in a snug tank top and pajama shorts.

Jonah, mind lost in anguished thoughts, responded, "What?" rather sharply.

Vera blinked, and Jonah cursed himself.

"I'm so sorry," he said hastily, shooting up from the sofa. "No malice intended. Jessica just got me on edge, and I was just—I was just wrapped tightly. I'm sorry."

It was the truth, and Vera bought it.

"I know what you mean," she said. "The sooner this night is behind us, the better."

"Couldn't have said it better myself," muttered Jonah.

He meant to lower himself back to the sofa, but Vera grabbed his hand.

"Please," she said. "Come into my bedroom. At least until I'm asleep."

Jonah couldn't help it, but some of the awkwardness rose in him once more. It was all he could do to ignore how it felt to be hand in hand with Vera, headed to her bedroom. It was also hard to ignore how cute she looked in her overlong shirt and pajama shorts, which were shorter than he remembered. She had always been a fuller-figured woman, which Jonah loved about her, and her bedtime wardrobe worked perfectly. Did she always look this attractive when she headed to bed?

Wrong thoughts, J, he scolded himself. *Ain't the time, or the situation. Shut it down.*

He used his ethereality to balance himself out, and it worked. Kind of.

Once they were in her bedroom, Vera lay in her bed, and brought the blankets to her waist. Jonah compromised by seating himself in the wicker chair next to her bed. He winced as he felt the criss-cross design dig into his back when he sat down. His back would probably resemble a country ham when he rose. Whatever.

Vera watched him with a small smile. "Comfy?" she asked.

"I'm adaptable," murmured Jonah evasively.

Vera propped herself up on pillows, and began to idly pick at a small hole in her tank top. "So that woman we saw tonight," she ventured, "Jessica. You knew her beforehand?"

That would definitely kill discomfort and awkwardness. But it was at the expense of talking about Jessica. Relief and irritation at the same time. Oh well. "I did," Jonah went with it. "She was working at my first job out of grad school when I got there."

"What was she like then?"

Jonah had no trouble with that question. "I could call her a bitch, but that would be an insult to bitches. Being around Jessica Hale was like—like witnessing a master class in solipsism, pontification, manipulation, and whore-mongering. And she happens to be a Deadfallen disciple. You know the funny thing, though?" Jonah had a sudden realization. "I hated her from the second I saw her. It seemed to go almost beyond the fact that she was a skank bitch. It always had this—this different level to it. I could always see through her, even when other people couldn't. It was almost like a part of me could sense that there was more to her. I should have trusted my instinct. I probably wouldn't have fallen into her trap. Creyton's trap. Damn Inimicus."

"Creyton's most loyal," murmured Vera. "What do you think the nature of their relationship—?"

Jonah made a noise to cut Vera off. "Not touching that," he said flatly. "It's bad enough thinking about the people and spirits that they hurt. But—but I'm not touching that one."

Vera seemed to think it over, and then nodded. "On second thought, you're right," she decided.

"I know that there are a bunch of Deadfallen," said Jonah, "but Jessica…that one's personal. Forget Charlotte, forget O'Shea—Jessica still cuts me. She is just an evil, murderous bitch. Plain and simple. She and everything associated with her is just backwards, evil, and wrong. I find it very ironic that there was a faction like Creyton's Deadfallen for her to be involved in. She was ready-made for a life like that."

Vera nodded and looked away. Jonah could tell that she was more than a little disturbed by his words. He didn't want to scare her or anything, but she could never understand the depth of his hatred for that woman. He may very well hate her more than he hated Trip.

"What's on your mind?" he felt the need to ask.

"It's strange," said Vera instantly. "It's just…strange that there are people in this world who are so twisted. Makes you wonder about who to trust, you know?"

Jonah nodded. "I know what you mean, Vera. You're thinking about your situation, being up here alone and all that. But you needn't worry. You're with friends. You probably have the nicest, sweetest best friend in the world. Patience put up all these protections for people, yourself included. You have Jonathan looking out for you, and now Daniel—you aren't alone. We will get through all this shit. But you've got support."

It seemed like Jonah was telling Vera things that he needed to hear himself. But it was about Vera right now, not him. And it did the trick.

Vera half-smiled and lowered herself to a more comfortable position on her pillows.

"You forgot you," she said quietly, with her eyes closed.

Jonah looked at her near-slumbering form absently. "Sorry?"

"I have you, Jonah," whispered Vera. "I have you."

Jonah stared at her. But there was no point in making further inquiries. Vera was asleep now.

He had no idea what he meant, but chose not to worry about it. At least for the moment. He pulled out his batons and brought them to full size, making sure to gather his hands in his sleeves so that his endowment's illumination wouldn't frighten Vera awake. Placing them in an X across his lap, he sat there as his mind swirled with a mixed bag of thoughts.

"Jonah."

It felt as if someone was trying to pull him into a brighter place, but he was reluctant to comply. This darker place was more comfortable.

Actually, it wasn't. He felt a strange resistance at his back, and his neck was killing him. When had his futon become so uncomfortable?

"Jonah."

Wait. He recognized that woman's voice, and she had no business in his bedroom—

"Jonah!"

Finally, he was awake. He frowned at Vera for a moment, and then everything fell into place. Vera was not in his bedroom, he was in hers. He'd slept in that wicker chair the entire night.

And damn if he wasn't paying for it now.

His neck was sore as hell, his shoulders experienced a dull, smoldering burn, and his right arm was still asleep. When Jonah moved forward, he sucked his teeth. That infernal wicker chair had left indentations all down his back, which all smarted at the same time when he parted from the source. Vera watched all of this with concern and pity on her face.

"Oh, Jonah," she muttered, "you're a damn mess. I never meant for you to sleep in that chair. You said you'd crash on the couch—"

"I did say that, didn't I?" said Jonah grumpily, but he was more annoyed with himself than anything else. "I got to get to work. I'll just soldier through this—"

"Jonah, shut up," said Vera. "That bookstore doesn't open till nine. I remember that much. It's too early for your job, the sun just came up. I woke you up because I knew what it would feel like in that chair. Come here."

Painstakingly, she guided him to the floor, which was welcoming because it was soothing to his soreness. Vera then began to massage his back and shoulders.

"What were you thinking, sleeping in that chair?" she demanded. "I hadn't even put the padding back on it yet!"

"I wanted to be closer to you than the couch," mumbled Jonah. "It seemed too far, especially given how these people work."

Vera was silent for a moment. "I wasn't worried, not after the protections that Patience placed up," she said. "But thank you so much for that."

Jonah nodded, and then wished he hadn't. One just never knew how interconnected things were in the human body until something was hurting. But a memory flickered in his mind that allowed him to ignore the pain somewhat.

"What did you mean last night?" he asked. "About having me?"

Vera's fingers slowed on Jonah's shoulders. "What?"

"Last night, before you went to sleep," said Jonah. "You said that you had me."

Now Vera removed her fingers entirely, and Jonah looked at her in confusion.

"I'm sure I don't know what you're talking about," she said. "What did I say, now?"

Now Jonah felt idiotic. Had Vera just been night rambling, or something? It was possible, but she'd sounded lucid enough. Maybe he'd lost her at the tail end of it. "Never mind," he said. "Must have been a dream. Dealing with this Deadfallen shit just has me wondering who has whose back."

"Oh." Vera nodded. "That I can see."

Jonah returned to his position, and Vera resumed massaging his shoulders. So she didn't recall saying that. It had been nighttime rambling. Jonah supposed it was just as well, but he couldn't help wonder what she'd meant, even if it had just been sleep mutterings.

"You don't have to worry about who has whose back, Jonah," said Vera. "You've got support, just like you told me last night."

Jonah nearly rolled his eyes. *That,* she remembered. "Right you are, Vera," he said. "Speaking of people at your back, did you want to call out of work? Did you want to come with me to the estate later?"

"Can't, Jonah," said Vera apologetically. "I'm working a double shift today and tomorrow. Liz will be sad, but I got stuck."

Jonah's eyebrows rose somewhat. "You're staying here this weekend?" he asked. "After last night?"

"Jonah, I was frightened out of my mind," admitted Vera. "But something that Jessica said last night got me thinking. I don't think she'll be messing with me at the moment."

Jonah rose from his position. His affected areas were much more cooperative after Vera's massage. "May I ask why you think that?"

"That thing she said about patience being a virtue," answered Vera. "Now, I'm not an expert on deduction like Reena, but I think that if Creyton is planning something, he doesn't want extra attention on his activities. That said, I think Bird Girl bothering me, a known mentee of Jonathan's, would qualify as unwanted attention."

Jonah looked at her. Try as he might to poke holes in that, it made sense. Still. "Vera, you weren't thinking along those lines last night."

"I told you, Jonah, I've had time to think about it," said Vera. "We had a spiritually endowed sleep, remember? Clearer head, clearer thoughts."

"Oh yeah..." Jonah was disarmed again. "Speaking of that, where are my batons?"

"Here you go." Vera retrieved them from her nightstand and gave them to him.

"Huh." Jonah noticed that the ethereal steel remained grey when he touched them. "When did Wilhelmina remove her spiritual endowment?"

"Not sure," replied Vera. "Right before we woke up, maybe?"

Jonah nodded, and shoved them into his pocket. Then he regarded Vera once more. "Are you sure about being here alone, Vera?"

Vera actually smiled. "I'm not a damsel, Jonah," she said. "It's not like I prowl the streets looking for trouble. I can freeze people in time if I need to, remember? Shit, I won't even have time to get into trouble tomorrow. I'll be fine."

Jonah didn't like it. In the slightest. But at the same time, he knew he couldn't make her do anything, or boss her around. That wouldn't have been the right thing to do, anyway, and in any case, he wasn't in any position to play that role, anyway. He took a deep breath. He just had to be a gentleman. "Okay, Vera," he said reluctantly. "I'll...I'll be respectful of you."

Vera placed a bracing hand on Jonah's arm, as if she knew of the mental battle he'd just had. "Thank you, Jonah. And thank you for staying with me. I appreciate you more than you know."

Jonah nodded. "I could see myself out, if you want. You know, just in case of nosy neighbors."

Vera rolled her eyes. "To hell with them, Jonah," she said. "And their opinions. They don't know me."

Jonah snorted. Sometimes he forgot how Vera could be concerning people's approval.

He followed her through the living room, around her crude trap, and finally, to the front door.

"Have a great day and weekend, Jonah," Vera told him.

"To you, the same," responded Jonah.

He walked to his car, but turned to give Vera a two-fingered, informal salute. She waved back, and Jonah frowned slightly.

Were there tears in Vera's eyes? Or was it the fact that the sun, recently freed from cloud cover, had blasted her unprepared vision?

Jonah couldn't tell for sure. And he wasn't about to find out at that particular moment, either, as Vera turned her back on him and shut her front door, presumably to continue her morning routine.

After a day at S.T.R. that Jonah enjoyed, he hit the highway without even returning to his apartment. It had been a good day, but there had been two things that had stuck out. There was that moment where he though Vera had had tears in his eyes, and the moment when Bryce Tysinger, the owner Blood Oath's Tattoos, gave him a very strange look. Jonah knew that it was idiotic to think that the man's particular look was any different from any other random look that he might get a million times a day, but there was something about Bryce's look that simply didn't seem random. It seemed…Jonah didn't know.

But as he reached Exit 81, he'd pushed it to the back of his mind.

Jonah knew that Daniel would be making his circuits around the estate when he got there, so it was no surprise to see him outside, sharply scanning everything his eyes could see. Jonah turned off his car, and quietly walked to the estate's front door.

"I'm approaching the front porch," he announced once he was in earshot of Daniel. "I'm so close to it…getting closer now…and what do you know? I'm on the front porch."

Daniel turned his full attention to Jonah. "Tell me, Jonah," he said coolly, "was that supposed to be droll?"

Jonah's grin faded slightly. "Yeah. Wasn't it obvious?"

Daniel almost smiled. "Keep trying," he advised, and then turned away to continue his circuit.

Jonah shook his head. All he'd managed was an almost-smile. It made him wonder whether or not Daniel even had a sense of humor.

Jonah knew that it was practically a skeleton screw at the estate, so he wasn't expecting any bustle.

And he certainly didn't expect someone to pounce from the shadows and wrap him in an oxygen-depriving embrace. But he smiled nonetheless. There was only one person who was full of that much energy.

"What's up, Liz?" he laughed.

"Nope!" said another voice happily. "She's out with Bobby!"

The young woman flicked on the light, which illuminated her form. Jonah's mouth dropped.

"Nella?" he breathed.

"Yep!" she said.

Jonah couldn't believe it. Nella's sixteenth birthday had just been back the past May, but in the short time since he'd last seen her, she'd changed. Her hair was longer, she'd grown at least four more inches (which would actually make her taller than Liz), and her voice sounded less high-pitched. A great deal of her precious pudginess had faded.

Nella noticed Jonah's expression and smiled. "Not a little girl anymore, huh?" she asked, spreading her hands.

"You've grown so much!" exclaimed Jonah. "It's like I was gone longer than just the summer!"

"And that's not all!" said Nella. "Look!"

She pointed to her mouth, and widened her grin. The braces were gone.

"Nice, Nella," smiled Jonah. "Think you're a little woman nowadays, huh? But why were you in the dark just now?"

"Oh, I was just hanging up my coat," said Nella. "I just got here, too!"

"Did you use the *Astralimes*?" asked Jonah.

"Nope!" squealed Nella.

Jonah frowned, but then noticed the extra thrill in her voice. It made things crystal clear. "When did you get your driver's license?"

"Tuesday!" gushed Nella. "It was almost too easy! Sandrine let me have her old car! But I wasn't driving it tonight, though; Dylan let me drive his vintage GTO—"

Jonah felt his smile fade. "Dylan?"

Nella rolled her eyes. "Yes, Jonah, Dylan."

Jonah's mouth twisted. "How old is this boy?"

"Sixteen, just like me!"

"Nuh-uh," said Jonah. "Is he sixteen as in recent birthday, or sixteen as in kicking seventeen's door down?"

Nella shook her head. "Jonah, don't worry," she insisted. "You know that I'm a good judge of character. Dylan's harmless."

Jonah said nothing at first. No, he didn't know this boy, but, having been sixteen himself once, he knew that harmless might be a stretch. Eventually, he manufactured a smile. "If you say so, Nella," he responded. "Congrats on your driver's license!"

He hung up his keys, and took maybe ten paces when he saw Kendall and Reena kissing. He cleared his throat loudly, and they parted and looked at him.

"You probably should take that upstairs," he advised. "There aren't that many people here, sure, but still—nosiness is nosiness."

Both Kendall and Reena laughed. They knew that Jonah's taunts were in jest and meant nothing.

"Nice to see you again, Jonah," said Kendall, who hugged him. "When I have more time, you can tell me all about your summer. Excluding the shitty part at the end, of course."

Jonah frowned. "When you have more time?" he asked. "You're leaving?"

"Yeah," said Kendall. "Training just got done, and I was down there going over things with Reena. Akshara and Bobby helped out, too. But I've got to get rest now."

"Yeah, baby, you better," said Reena. "I'll see you out. Be back in a second, Jonah."

The two of them went outside, and Jonah waited patiently for several minutes before Reena returned. He regarded her with curiosity.

"You have Kendall out there training in the Glade, with everyone else?" he asked.

"Oh yeah," said Reena. "Not about to treat her like a waif."

"But it gets pretty hardcore," said Jonah. "Particularly when we're endowed!"

"True," said Reena. "But I don't want Kendall to be caught unawares by anything. Now that she knows about us all, I can give her self-defense pointers and all that."

"Yeah, Reena, I get that," said Jonah. "But I assumed that you'd give her private lessons, or something."

Reena looked away. "I tried, but that didn't work. Private lessons proved counterproductive."

"Why? Because you couldn't use your cold spot trick?" snorted Jonah.

"It wasn't that," said Reena. "It was the fact that after exchanging a few holds, the workouts always transformed into sex."

Jonah snorted again. "Got it. Well, I'm glad that you found a solution to the, um, issue."

They shared a laugh over that, and then found Terrence in the living room, surrounded by Little Debbie snacks and watching the WWE Network.

"Hey, y'all!" he said. "Zebra Cake?"

"Don't mind if I do," said Jonah.

"Pass," said Reena.

They joined Terrence on the sofa, where Jonah looked the particular pay-per-view Terrence was watching.

"You do this every Friday night?" he asked.

"Nowadays," said Terrence. "I've always loved wrestling, as you know, but it's an even better stress reliever, given everything that's going on."

"Speaking of Friday night activities," said Jonah, suddenly serious, "who is this Dylan boy that Nella was telling me about?"

Terrence laughed at Jonah's consternation. "Don't worry," he said. "He is about as dangerous as a box full of newborn heralds."

Jonah immediately focused on Reena, who shrugged.

"Seemed clean when I met him," she said.

He turned shrewd eyes on Terrence. "So what, did Bobby tell him that he'd hunt him to the ends of the earth if he ever did anything to hurt Nella?" he asked.

"Nope," said Terrence, who bit into a frosted cake with great relish. "Liz did that."

Jonah tore open the Zebra Cake and smiled. "Love that woman," he said.

"Where's Vera, by the way?" asked Reena. "Why didn't she come with you for the weekend?"

"She's pulling two doubles this weekend at that food hole where she works," said Jonah. "But wait until you hear this..."

He filled the two of them in on seeing Jessica after he and Vera had had dinner. When he was done, they looked at him in silence.

"I know," he said in response to their expressions. "I know."

Terrence abandoned the Donut Stick he'd just unwrapped. "But that...that..."

"I know," said Jonah once again, "but I'm certain that seeing Jessica was just a coincidence. It didn't stop her from taking advantage of the situation, though."

"And she said that you're on borrowed time?" asked Reena.

"Yep," said Jonah. "And then she turned into a crow, and jetted like a bat out of hell. She makes the second Deadfallen disciple I've seen do that, and I still don't think I'll ever get used to it."

"I bet," said Terrence. "How did Vera take it?"

"Rattled her something fierce," answered Jonah. "But she calmed down after I spent the night with her."

Both Terrence and Reena looked at Jonah in pure shock, and Jonah sighed.

"Not remotely what I meant," he muttered. "I slept next to her bed in a damn wickerwork chair."

"Ohhh..." Terrence nodded, but then frowned. "Wait. She was rattled, but was calm enough for you to leave her?"

Jonah sighed again. "We were spiritually endowed when we fell asleep," he told them. "She claimed that she had some clarity in her dreams, and then came to the realization that Jessica wouldn't bother her at the moment. Something about Creyton having no desire for unwanted attention."

"Wise words," said Reena.

"Eh, Vera will be fine, now that I think of it," said Terrence. "Remember, if she needs to, she can stop someone in time. Maybe if Jessica comes for her, she can just pause her in time, bend her forward, and then let her face plant on concrete, or something. The bitch deserves worse, but it'd be a start."

Not that Jonah hated the futon in his apartment, but the bed in his room at the estate was almost euphoric. He was surprised that it was so easy to relax, especially after conversation with Terrence and Reena.

Particularly Reena.

They'd left Terrence to the Network—insightful conversation was impossible with Terrence whooping after every high-risk move he saw in a match— and spoke further in private. As usual, Reena provided insights on everything that Jonah and Terrence never would have achieved. But it was when the conversation moved to Vera, Reena's viewpoint was very interesting.

So much so that Jonah's head was still full of the things she said now that he neared sleep.

* * *

"Of course Vera wanted to be alone, Jonah," Reena told him in her trademark obvious tone. "She'd been frightened, and then rationalized it in her own mind. She rationalized it quite well, it sounds like. It had nothing to do with you; remember that Vera has had her own share of trials and tribulations, and deals with them as she sees fit. It was awesome that you were there for her. But you were also right to respect her wishes to be left alone."

Jonah took in Reena's words, but had to ask her something else before she went to bed. "Reena, there was something else I want to ask you. Something that might need the…gleanings of a woman."

Reena gave him that pensive look of hers. "Okay," she said with some uncertainty. "Go ahead."

Jonah told Reena about his conversation with Vera concerning *Snow and Fire,* and then he told her about Vera's muttering in her sleep, and her complete ignorance of it in the morning. He even mentioned the moment when he thought he saw tears in her eyes when he left. It felt good to get it out, but he didn't know what else to do past that. Hopefully, that was where Reena could assist him.

"I mean, should I just let her have her moments?" he asked. "I know that she misses acting, and I know that she probably has to relive shit being back in that damn house on Colerain Place. And she's at The Stop again, working herself crazy. She's got stress, which I get. But...could it be something more? Something that I might need to confront her about?"

Reena didn't give Jonah a quick answer, for which he was very grateful. When she did speak, it was measured and deliberate. "Jonah, we women are complicated creatures," she said. "We keep a great many things about ourselves jealously to our chests. Sometimes for preservation, and other times out of fear. When people try to prise those things from us, particularly men, they can be met by an almost unfathomable resistance. Oftentimes, unsolicited assistance and free advice do more harm than good. For that reason, I'll tell you this: If there are things that Vera hasn't shared with you, then allow her to do so at a later time. Give her that; she will appreciate it more than you can ever imagine. Don't prompt, and don't pry. Just support."

* * *

Those words were still in Jonah's mind when he fell asleep, and also when he woke up.

Don't prompt, and don't pry. Just support.

Okay, fine. That was what he'd do. For now.

He rose for a quick treadmill walk because he wasn't in the mood for weights, and then went to the kitchen, where Terrence had his usual morning spread. Daniel, who was new to human sustenance, seemed to have taken a great liking to toast. Jonah watched him eat a slice, wrap a stack in a napkin, and head outside.

"It's a damn shame that he grew an affinity for wheat," remarked Reena.

Magdalena, Malcolm, and Maxine greeted Jonah warmly, and Liz bowled him over with glee. Bobby grinned in his direction, and Alvin, whose arm was heavily wrapped, simply nodded his way. When Jonah inquired about the wrap, Terrence laughed.

"Bobby goaded him into doing supersets," he explained. "He suffered a triceps tear, kind of like you did way back when. Liz put a healing salve on it, and he'll be good as new in two days."

Jonah sighed. "Bobby is going to kill us all in that weight room," he murmured.

"Yep," said Terrence, "I think that's his personal goal."

Spader greeted Jonah with a nod similar to Alvin's, and Douglas still had indignation about the decision the Curaie made, despite it being old news. Luckily, he had the wherewithal to keep it to himself. Everyone had tired of it long ago. Terrence got Jonah's attention and motioned to Douglas.

"He and Ray would get along so well," he said. "Raymond was pissed about you being run back to the city, too."

Jonah looked at Terrence, Alvin, and Bobby pensively. "I meant to ask you earlier, but I hadn't gotten around to it. I see that Ray is helping us out. What about Sterling?"

The brothers all looked down. Jonah raised an eyebrow.

"Sterling won't be helping us out with this one," said Terrence. "He can't."

"Can't?" repeated Jonah. "What does that mean?"

Alvin looked annoyed. "It's because of that Lockman bastard," he grumbled. "Sterling works with children, see, and if he got implicated in a situation where it even looked as if he might be affiliated with a cult, it would damage his livelihood."

Jonah stared, and then banged his fist on the table, which made everyone jump and look at him in alarm. He couldn't have cared less. "We're not a damn cult!" he said heatedly.

"Bring it down a thousand, Jonah," said Bobby. "Sterling said the same thing. He didn't back out quietly. He said he would stand with us no matter what, because we had right on our side. But Dad told him that although were not involved in the occult, his mentoring program would be irrevocably damaged if he tried to assist."

Before Jonah could make an angry retort, a familiar voice spoke directly behind him, which turned everyone in their seats.

"You do realize that the word occult actually means *secret*, Bobby? It's yet another word that was bastardized by history."

"Felix!" Jonah rose from his seat and extended a hand, which Felix took, but released very quickly. He was obviously wound very tightly. Reena looked at him warily.

"Felix, your presence is a gamble," she warned, "Trip is upstairs—"

"Fuck that fool," said Felix instantly. "I need to see Jonathan."

Daniel, who had reappeared as soon as there was a new presence in the estate, shook his head. "For obvious reasons, Jonathan's appearances are kept to a minimum—"

"I don't give a—" began Felix with heat, but then everyone tensed. Felix realized their unease, and slowly employed some diaphragmatic breaths. When he spoke again, his voice was level. "I need for Jonathan to make an exception. I've got bad news."

The skeleton crew all gathered in the family room. As usual, no one was cramped or uncomfortable. Liz sent the herald Laura to summon Jonathan, and while they waited, Trip, Karin, and Markus showed up, though they stayed near the door. Jonah also noticed that, for some strange reason, Maxine had removed her glasses when Felix turned up. That made no sense, because Max couldn't see two feet in front of her face without those damn goggles. Jonah hoped that she would have remembered that when she nearly flipped over the couch, to no avail.

Felix sat near the empty fireplace, with the bottle of 'Vintage in its usual spot near his person. Spader regarded it, puzzled.

"Aren't you a recovering alcoholic?" he asked Felix.

"Yes," said Felix without looking at him. "Nine years."

"Then why the hell do you keep liquor on you?" Spader questioned.

Jonah sucked his teeth. He already knew the story, and also knew that it was a personal thing for Felix, and he didn't appreciate prying. Indeed, Felix looked as though he was about to respond sharply, but ultimately, he just sighed.

"It's a reminder that I'm powerless," he obliged. "A reminder that if I slip, I could be right back at square one. My abilities and my strength could make me very cocky and arrogant if allowed them to. But at the same time, I cannot safely take another drink again. So this bottle keeps me grounded. Lets me know that there are things more powerful than I am."

"You don't need the liquor bottle for that, Felix," grunted Trip. "Go into a vampire nest, and you'll have about fifty things more powerful than you right then and there."

Felix rose, but reconsidered, and sat back down. "Not the time or the place to deal with your horseshit, Trip," he murmured. "But yeah, Spader. That's why I have the bottle."

"It takes balls to have something you're afraid of so close to you," commented Spader.

"I don't fear alcohol, boy," said Felix. "I respect it. Like one would respect a poison. You don't have to fear poison, but you can respect its abilities enough to not put in your body."

"All the more reason for that bottle to remain sealed, son," said Jonathan, who appeared near Trip and Karin. "What is the trouble?"

Felix scrambled to his feet, looking anxious as hell. "Bad news, sir," he said. "It's Creyton. He's sending Deadfallen disciples into the sazer underground."

Jonathan stiffened. "He is wiping out sazers?" he asked.

"Worse," said Felix. "He is showering them with gifts."

Jonah felt his eyebrows contract. Douglas frowned at Felix.

"Why would a murderer be charitable?" he asked.

"Seriously, Chandler?" snapped Trip. "You have to ask that question? Creyton is putting out feelers to re-amass the power base that unraveled in his absence."

"For probably last time in physical life, I agree with Trip," murmured Felix. "That's exactly what Creyton's doing. If he augments his movement with sazers—"

"But what about the vampires?" interrupted Jonah. "Wasn't he working with them?"

"Creyton works both sides of the street when he needs to," said Felix. "But he isn't keen on working too closely with lifeblood looters nowadays, because of what the 49er did. Vampires would only care for the lifeblood. But sazers…sazers care for many things."

"Like what?" asked Reena. "What kind of the gifts are the Deadfallen disciples giving them?"

Felix seated himself again before answering Reena's question. "Food. Toiletries. Clothing. The kind of stuff that will spoil a deprived mind and body. If he gives the sazers just enough to need him, then the Curaie will have a hell a lot more to worry about than they did before."

"But—but surely they can listen to reason," said Liz, desperation in her voice. "Look at sazers like you, Prodigal, and June Mylteer's dad."

Felix shook his head. "You can't understand, Elizabeth, because you're not an addict. I am. Sazers will do anything for resources. And the Curaie treats sazers as expendable, like objects to be disregarded once their purpose is done. But Creyton is treating them a completely different way. Some sazers won't even care if he's using them. If he continues to provide that fix, be it with food, clothing, and clean items, who do you think will look better in the sazer's eyes? Who do you think will be the popular ones?"

Liz had no answers. Jonathan focused on Felix with laser precision.

"I surmise that this information came from Prodigal," he said. "First and foremost, is he safe?"

Felix nodded rigorously. "Prodigal knows how to fly under the radar," he said. "He did it for years. Of course, ducking social services and ducking Creyton are two very different things. But the boy has my respect. He manages."

Jonah was relieved to hear that his friend was safe. That same relief was on Terrence's and Reena's faces as well.

"Did he describe the Deadfallen disciples that he saw?" asked Jonathan.

"He did," said Felix. "From his descriptions, I recognized Kenneth Hardy, Donovan Fleming, Janet Dane, but he said that there was someone else. He said that he was a scary guy…scarier than the rest of them, I mean. Well over six feet, bearded, dreadlocks—"

A sharp snap made everyone jump. Daniel had broken an arrow in half.

"Broreamir," he said in a voice slightly above a whisper.

"Bro-what?" said Felix.

"My brother," said Daniel.

"Your brother?" demanded Felix. "Wait, who are you? You—" Felix was back on his feet, eyes wide. "You're the man from that dream."

"Indeed he is," answered Jonathan for Daniel. "This is Daniel. Formerly a Protector Guide, now a resident of the Grannison-Morris estate."

Felix looked at Daniel with raised eyebrows. "You're a Guide no longer? You're an ethereal human? And the dreadlocked dude is your brother?"

"Yes," said Daniel simply.

Felix still looked curious, but shrugged. "Hey, I'm adaptable," he said. "Glad one of you is on our side."

Jonathan nodded at Felix. "I'll consult the Curaie on your behalf, Felix," he said. "You came to me to act as a liaison, which is understandable."

Jonah remembered Felix's words from the previous Thanksgiving: "*That's what the Curaie think of sazers. We're good enough to clean the kingdom, but not good enough to live in the kingdom once it's clean.*"

It made him think of what the Curaie had just done to him. Those Spirit Guides may not be evil, but they weren't endearing themselves to anyone by sweeping folks under the rug. Felix was lucky, because his parents had left him a sizeable nest egg. Other sazers didn't have that. They were desperate, prone to violence, and some were even cannibals. But Felix and Prodigal were living proof that if sazers just had support and access to resources, they could function well in society, ethereal or otherwise. At the same time, Jonah realized that he wasn't quite over his aggravation with Jonathan, either. The way he'd just gone along with the Curaie's decision, despite the fact that he said that he disagreed, was almost like a punk teacher who went along with the principal's decision just to keep the peace.

Where was the sense in that?

"Jonah," whispered Reena, knocking him out of his thoughts, "tell Jonathan about Jessica."

"Oh yeah," said Jonah. "Jonathan, sir, there's something you need to know—"

Jonathan raised a hand, cutting Jonah off. Jonah narrowed his eyes, irritated. Jonathan looked in the direction of the front door, looking rather irritated himself. "A Gate Breacher just entered the grounds," he announced.

Terrence rose, fire in his eyes. "Gate Breacher?" he demanded. "Is it who I think it is?"

"No," said Jonah, "but unwelcome nonetheless."

Douglas reached the door a second before Jonah did, and froze when Katarina smiled sweetly at him.

"Um—um," he stammered, "who—who are you, exactly?"

Jonah pushed Douglas aside. "Hello, Katarina," he said in a dull voice.

Katarina's smile faded somewhat when she saw Jonah. "Blue Aura," she said with manufactured brightness. "Wonderful morning to you!"

Jonah wasn't so sure of that. Especially now. "Everyone, this is Katarina Ocean," he announced with no excitement. "She works for the Curaie. Now what do you want, Katarina?"

Katarina looked even more unnerved. "I—I just wanted to see how you'd been doing—"

"Bullshit," said Jonah lazily. "Your masters sent you here to make sure I was being a good little boy while I was at the estate, didn't they?"

Katarina winced as pinkness rose in her pale face. "I do what I'm told, Blue Aura," she said softly. "Is that so wrong?"

"Oftentimes, yes," said Jonah. "Now—"

He was interrupted by shrill meows. They all looked in that direction.

"What the—?"

There was another shrill meow, this time accompanied by a howl of pain.

"I think a herald's got somebody!" shrieked Spader, and before anyone could react, he jumped off the porch and tore off for a couple of trees. Jonah didn't know what to expect. Maybe a Deadfallen disciple, or a hungry sazer.

So when Spader yanked a thin man with plentiful scratches on his face, and a ruined camera around his neck from behind the tree, Jonah was just a bit taken aback.

"Let me go!" shouted the man. "You don't know who you're dealing with!"

"Shut up!" said Spader. "Or the next thing I'll let Anakaris scratch up is your balls!"

He shoved the man down in front of everyone. Katarina flinched, appalled.

"Such barbarism," she whispered.

"You think that's barbaric?" said Terrence. "You should see us train—"

Reena viciously stamped on Terrence's foot, and he yelped. Daniel moved forward, followed closely by Felix.

"What is this?" Daniel asked.

"This guy was taking pictures behind that tree," said Spader coldly. "Anakaris found him, scratched him up, and he fell on the camera when he tried to run."

Jonah surveyed the man. He was definitely a Tenth. But what was he doing taking pictures?

"Explain yourself, man," commanded Daniel.

"You don't know what you're doing!" snapped the man. "This is making your situation even graver than it already is!"

"I know you." Felix's tone suddenly went arctic. "You're Wyatt Faulk. You work for the Lockman Association. But why are you here? You people only rear your ugly heads when you think you've found cults."

"Two points for Felix," grunted Trip.

Felix clearly hadn't been aware of the Tenth problem that the estate had. Now that he knew, he looked ready to snap the man's neck. Jonah looked at the man with a newfound dislike. So this was one of Lockman's goons, huh?

"How right you are," said Faulk sharply. "And I remember you too, Felix Duscere! Last I saw you, you were attempting to stir up vagrants in New Orleans. What did they call themselves? Sazies, or something?"

Felix growled in his throat. Jonah did not want to see him Red Rage on a Tenth. Even if that Tenth happened to be a part of a cult hunter's association. But before Felix could say anything else, Faulk continued on.

"And what was that that I just heard? Blue Auras?"

"You've never heard of auras?" asked Daniel calmly.

"Of course I have!" replied Faulk. "But so-called auras are supposed to change with each passing whim, so what makes blue so special?"

No one said anything, and the silence spiraled terribly. Jonah could have sworn aloud.

Faulk turned to Katarina. "Ocean?" he said. "Is that what that boy called you? Tell me, how are you doing?"

"Blissful," said Katarina steadily. "Life is utterly blissful."

Jonah could have sworn again. He heard Reena groan, which meant that she was on the same wavelength. Katarina may have actually believed that life was blissful, but to a cult investigator, a response like that served as fuel for the fire.

Faulk looked at Katarina with such triumph that Jonah wished Anakaris would scratch him some more. But it was of no consequence at that point. Damage done.

"You have compromised every courteous approach in existence," said Daniel in a dangerously calm voice. "You have violated the sanctity of these grounds, and worst of all, you have no respect. I have no respect for those who have no respect for others. Retrieve whatever is left of your infernal contraption and depart, or else."

Spader released Faulk's shirt, but there was a look on the man's face that Jonah didn't like. He picked up the remains of his camera, murmuring something about how Lockman would love all this. Jonah just watched the guy stump off in silence. Between the abusive herald, Felix's anger, Daniel's cool threat, and Katarina's pure vapidity, he smelled a recipe for disaster.

10

No Introduction Necessary

Everyone returned to the family room, irritated and unnerved by this new development. Douglas invited Katarina in, and she immediately began to scope the place out, like it was a museum of some kind. Terrence looked at her in wonder.

"Who is this Ocean woman?" he whispered to Jonah.

"I just told you, Terrence," said Jonah, "she works for the Curaie."

"Is she—" Terrence scrabbled for words, "is she—playing with a full deck?"

"Damned if I know," muttered Jonah, flinging himself on the sofa. "All I know is that she is my age, a Purple Aura who prefers to be called a Gate Linker, and, evidently, quite blissful."

Daniel alternated between tightly and loosely clutching an arrow. It was clear that Wyatt Faulk's—and by extension, Balthazar Lockman's—audacity really irked him. Jonah felt for him. He may have knowledge of humans as a Protector Guide, but to experience them as an actual human himself, along with the emotions that accompanied said experience, was probably jarring.

"You've got to get Jonathan back here, Daniel," said Douglas, who paced back and forth. "I understand why he had to vanish and all that, but get one of the heralds to call him back—"

"Not an option, Douglas," said Daniel, who tossed his arrow back into his quiver. "You know that Jonathan can't do multiple appearances in the daytime. It's draining. If he hadn't vanished at all, that would have been one thing, but to risk coming back so early—"

Jonah was already aware of this information, but a part of him still couldn't resist the urge to think, *Convenient.*

"That dude had some balls!" snapped Bobby. "It's bad enough that Lockman's begun his investigation on us from afar, but to send spies—"

"Faulk wasn't the first," muttered Reena. "He can't have been. No first time visitor to the grounds would have been that close, let alone have video and audio equipment. You didn't pick up on that, Trip?"

Trip's eyes narrowed. "Electrical sound and ethereal sound exist on two frequencies, Reena," he said. "I have only been focused on the latter, so the device Faulk was using slipped through the cracks."

Liz took a sharp intake of breath. "Who knows what he's been hearing," she whispered.

"Or seeing," said Jonah slowly. "Nobody's been training or taking endowments outside, have they?"

"All residents present have been prohibited from any ethereal activities in the open," said Daniel.

Jonah stared. "So how are people honing skills?" he asked. "Jonathan would never—"

"It didn't come from Jonathan," said Malcolm in an uncharacteristically cold voice, "it came from the Curaie."

"What!"

"They are aware of the Lockman situation," Malcolm went on, "and want us to keep our training slim to none."

"Um…what about the other situation?" demanded Jonah. "The Creyton situation?"

"They said they'd take care of it," muttered Bobby. "At least, that's what Jonathan said."

"I know, I was there," fumed Jonah. "Their idiocy is going to get us all killed—"

Reena coughed loudly, but the cough sounded very much like, "*Jonah!*"

Jonah glanced at her in alarm, but then understood. He was bad-mouthing the Curaie, in front of one of their representatives. He'd almost forgotten Katarina's presence. But when he looked at her, it wasn't with apprehension. It was with pause.

"Katarina," he said steadily, "did you drive here?"

Katarina turned the shockingly blue eyes on him with surprise. "I can't drive," she said. "I never learned. I opened a Gate—"

Jonah flung his hands into the air. "Fuck! You opened up a Gate out there while Faulk was watching!"

Several people grimaced. Katarina's mouth dropped.

"I—I didn't know," she said. "I didn't know. I'm sorry."

Once again, her eyes were bright with tears.

"Oh no," he murmured, "for the love of Christ, don't cry—"

Liz and Nella sat down on either side of her, and tried to comfort her. Even Reena frowned at Jonah. Now he felt awkward again. He decided to turn to Felix.

"How do you know Faulk?" he asked in hopes of misdirection. "What was that stuff about New Orleans?"

Felix had brought out the lighter with the *fleur-di-lis* design on it that had once belonged to his father, and lit it intermittently. "I saved a group of sazers from a nest of vampires in the French Quarter," he said. "Lockman was also in New Orleans at the time, outing what he said was a supposed necromancer cult. His boy Faulk was mugged by one of the sazers when I was trying to get them to safety. He said something along the lines of, 'We sazers deserve whatever we get.' Yeah, that was what he said. Faulk knew of me because my dad was rich and all that. Since the sazers were hiding amongst the Cities of the Dead, Faulk tried to tie them—and me—to the necromancer cult thing. He failed."

"You know better than to say dead, Felix," said Jonah.

"Read a book, man," said Felix. "They refer to the above-ground tombs in New Orleans as Cities of the Dead."

"So what you're saying is that he knew the name Duscere," said Trip with a cold smile, "and you were still dumb enough to engage in a sazer rescue?"

Felix stood up again, but Daniel put a hand on his arm.

"No infighting on my watch," he grumbled. "Now shut up, Titus. And Felix—sit down. I think we need to allow emotions to lower before we continue any further discussions."

With that, several people took the opportunity to leave. Bobby went to the weights, while Alvin, still recovering from the last workout his brother put him through, went upstairs to ice. Malcolm went for the woodshed. Maxine attempted small talk with Felix, while Nella went off to the side and began to text her little boyfriend, Dylan. Jonah didn't even bother to wonder where Trip and his crew went, and he passed Liz and Katarina on the couch while idly noticing that Douglas had taken Nella's abandoned spot at the woman's side. Spader returned to his lock disassembly, and gave Jonah a strange look of gratitude. Jonah had been on his way outside, but that look stopped him in his tracks.

"What's the deal with that look?" he questioned.

"People 'round here hate me, remember?" said Spader cheerily. "I can't win from losing nowadays. But if you keep losing your shit like that and making people uncomfortable, you will take the focus off of me for a change!"

Jonah scowled, and went to the gazebo. If his temper received an endorsement from Spader, he knew he had to do better, and quick.

Jonah closed his eyes when he heard footsteps coming his way. He already knew who it was, so he kept his eyes shut.

"You really need to check that, Jonah," said Reena.

That popped Jonah's eyes open. "Reena, you know that flare up had nothing to do with Katarina."

"Of course," said Reena, "but she doesn't. I don't want you to jump down the wrong people's throats."

"I'd have been pissed, too," muttered Terrence. "Katarina can open a Gate and *poof*, she's nowhere in sight. But her little screw up was here, meaning Faulk can lump us all into one category and tell Lockman."

"I know, Terrence," said Reena coldly. "And are you aware of what that means? That we can't further complicate matters by tearing down an employee of the Curaie, who will undoubtedly repeat every word she heard!"

Jonah fastened on to Reena's words. "So she's definitely here to snitch and spy?" I could have told you that from minute one—"

Reena shook her head. "I don't think that she came here with ill intent, Jonah," she said. "I read her essence."

"And what did you pick up?" asked Terrence in a sarcastic voice. "The fact that she's an air-headed ass kisser who's probably fascinated by shiny things?"

Very slowly, Reena turned her eyes to Terrence. "No, actually. She's a very serene and gentle Eleventh Percenter, who is even more sensitive than Liz."

Jonah hung his head. What were the odds of that?

"She believes wholeheartedly in the Curaie's methods, and dislikes confrontation," Reena went on. "And unfortunately, Jonah, she's a little afraid of you."

"Great," grumbled Jonah. "Just great."

"She is afraid of you after meeting you one time?" asked Terrence.

"Second time," corrected Jonah. "I met her when I had the private conversation with the Curaie. I made her cry then, too."

"Oh yeah," said Terrence, looking away. After struggling with himself for a second, he muttered, "Maybe you do need to keep your frustration in check."

Jonah rolled his eyes, and pulled himself up from his seat. How was it possible to feel irritated and ashamed at the same time? "I'll go apologize to her," he told them. "Again."

"Please do," said Reena. "Then she can leave."

Jonah looked at her, surprised at the terseness. "Come again?"

"You heard me," said Reena.

"But what about my outburst?" asked Jonah. "Hurting her feelings and all—?"

"I stand by all that," said Reena, "but she is so goddamned sensitive. It's disgraceful. I cannot stand overly sensitive women; they hold us all back almost as much as sluts. Now go apologize to her, Jonah. Make it right, so that her delicate ass can leave."

The rest of the day was quite enjoyable. Jonah discovered that the fitness room now doubled as a training area, though they still had to remain unendowed. Apparently, this was working out quite well. No one was ever cramped or uncomfortable at the estate, and the fitness room was no different. Jonah was pleased to see that the skills he'd sharpened as an Eleventh Percenter hadn't escaped him. Moreover, he seemed to move much more smoothly. Maybe that was due to the weight loss, or the simple fact that he had been at this for a good little bit now.

"I don't get why it's such a significant change," he said to Reena when they ended about two hours later. "I've only lost about eleven pounds. It's not like I'm going to grace any magazine covers."

"Doesn't matter how much weight you've lost," said Reena, who looked very approving of Jonah's physique. "You reap benefits on the journey, not the destination."

"You just wait," said Terrence. "You'll be giving me a run for my money soon!"

"So sayeth the guy lucky enough to be mesomorphic," said Jonah.

Terrence laughed, and went to get some water. Reena poked Jonah's shoulder.

"You just might wind up in better shape that Terrence," she said, her tone serious. "His mesomorphic body type is a crutch, but you've been steadily working. Maybe you will give him a run eventually."

"Thanks for that, Reena," said Terrence, who'd overheard, but was grinning. Jonah smiled, too, but there was just a bit of bitterness.

"I just wish we could be in the Glade," he said. "I wish the Lockman crap will pass soon, if for no other reason than that. Why do you think that he's been so subtle? The estate hasn't been on the news or anything. What's his holdup?"

"He probably wants to devastate us," hypothesized Reena. "I started thinking that after seeing that Faulk weasel this morning. I bet Lockman has done his crap from afar because he wants to build as much firepower as humanly possible, and then strike."

Jonah looked at Douglas, who was being walked through a counter maneuver by Bobby. "I wonder what Creyton did to get Lockman on our case," he said.

"Nobody knows," said Terrence. "Not even Jonathan."

Jonah took a leveling breath as frustration reared itself again. Reena caught the mild change in his mood, and slightly widened her eyes in warning.

"Jonah, we've told you before—" she began, but Jonah cut across her.

"Save it," he said. "Jonathan doesn't know everything. I've heard it a gazillion times. I swear to God, if you say a mesomorphic body type is Terrence's crutch, then selective ignorance is Jonathan's."

Now Reena's eyes narrowed. "Back in the box, Jonah," she said, her voice slightly heated.

"Yeah, okay," said Jonah. "It just seems like the lapses in memory and lack of information are getting tiresome, especially with the people who are supposed to know stuff."

"We're all in the same boat with this, Jonah," Terrence reminded him.

"Yeah." Jonah pocketed his baton. "Same boat. Let me educate you, Terrence. That is *not* the case. Have you forgotten that nowadays, my boat is three hours west of here?"

He chucked his water cup into the trash, and left the fitness room without another word.

He was within ten paces of his room when he realized he'd screwed up. Again.

Shit.

Terrence and Reena were on his side. Why did he let frustration get the best of him again?

Terrence simply said they were all in the same boat. Jonah could have easily said words of appreciation, even if he was irritable about the whole thing. But no—he dropped the ball, and opted to be a moody prick. Once again.

He was a better man than this. Nana had taught him better than this. He had always been a bit of a straight shooter, but he had never been the one that was the asshole. That had always been someone else.

Now he was pissed at himself. He hadn't had close friends as a kid, and would have given anything for that to have been different. Now, as an adult, he had friends like that, and he was pushing them away because of anger and frustration.

He'd already been on Terrence's bad side once, and it had taken a grievous cut, a broken foot, and cannibal sazers for them to bury the hatchet. And he didn't want to be on Reena's bad side. She wouldn't cry like Katarina; it would be everyone else who'd be in tears if Reena got in a fit of anger.

Felix hadn't been lying. Unresolved anger could really come back and bite you if you allowed it to.

He had to go back and apologize. He regretted throwing away the water cup now. It would have helped tremendously with washing down his foot.

Five feet away from the door to the fitness room, Jonah felt a painful buzz at the back of his skull. He grabbed his head by reflex, and grimaced. Had he gotten dinged by someone during training?

But then he realized that that wasn't what this was. He knew this feeling, although he'd only experienced it back when he'd first discovered he was an Eleventh Percenter.

It was a Mindscope.

But it hadn't ever been this powerful. Never been this all-consuming.

Never been strong enough to make him black out…Jonah barely felt the floor when his body slammed against it…

He was standing in that weird dream place again, but this time, there was no grass, or greenery of any kind. The area was completely barren. The sky vacillated between grey and black, as if a severe rainstorm would strike at any minute. But if storms were possible, why was the place barren like this?

The emaciated, voided spirits and spiritesses were there as well, but they appeared to be trying to crawl away from a figure that was above them. The figure had his back turned to Jonah, and didn't even seem to register his presence.

"Daniel?" said Jonah uncertainly. "That you?"

The man turned around. Jonah's blood froze in his veins. There was no way. No possible way.

But the truth stared him right in the face, with dark grey eyes that didn't have the merest trace of humanity in them.

"No introduction necessary, Jonah," said Creyton quietly. "You know my name."

11

The Desert of the Ethereal

Jonah looked at Creyton in stunned silence. He hadn't seen him since the night he achieved Praeterletum, and his appearance was a bit different now. His hair had lengthened somewhat, and it was nearer to his shoulders than it had been before. His face also bore a rather pronounced five o'clock shadow, which hadn't been present that night. But those aesthetic differences meant nothing to Jonah. It was still the same savage, ambitious Eleventh Percenter who'd violated everything involved with physical life.

"Looking over my appearance?" Creyton noticed Jonah's expression. "I'm not surprised. Preoccupation with image is at an all-time high these days. Although, I must admit, your own attempts to butch up with beard are amusing."

Jonah ignored that completely. "Is this a dream?"

Creyton snorted. "How long have you been doing this, boy? And yet, you still ask infantile questions?"

Jonah didn't know what to make of that. Creyton's words illuminated nothing. "Are you here to kill me?"

"As much as the desire to do so consumes my very being, no," answered Creyton. His already hard eyes hardened further. "As I had my darling Inimicus tell you, you are on borrowed time. The time for that will come, but alas, it is not right now. I can't even touch you here.

The Desert of the Ethereal is merely an ideal place to have dialogue. The Mindscope you experienced was a type of summons."

"The Desert of the Ethereal?" said Jonah. "This is not a dream place? This is a real location?"

"Real enough," replied Creyton. "And no, you can do nothing for these filthy spirits."

Jonah looked at the agonized spirits and spiritesses. He'd thought this place was a figment of his imagination. Or everybody's imagination, since so many Eleventh Percenters had had that dream. Now Creyton said that it was real. Jonah remembered the sight of it in the previous experience. The hills had been lush, but they had included Creyton's Deadfallen disciples. Now it was barren, and contained Creyton himself. And there was no question which scenario was worse. "I—I don't recall the Mindscopes being so powerful," was all he could manage.

"Well, if it hadn't been for your lucky break nearly three years ago, they wouldn't be," said Creyton. "But I'm enjoying many new levels of ethereality since having transcended death through Praeterletum."

Jonah glared at Creyton. "What are you doing to these spirits and spiritesses?" he demanded.

"Don't bother yourself with matters that don't concern you, boy," snapped Creyton. "Or better yet, matters that don't yet concern you, I should say. As I said, I wanted to have dialogue. There is another reason you're here, but we will get to that later."

"Quit the riddles, man." Jonah's frustration and impatience boiled over. It assisted with the fear and alarm. "You're frickin' worse than Jonathan."

Creyton took a deep breath. It looked as though he had just curbed a sudden spike of rage. "Don't compare me to that disgraceful echo," he growled.

"You don't want comparisons?" Jonah poured as much irritation into his voice as he could muster. He would not let Creyton know that he was afraid. "Get to the damned point!"

Creyton smiled at Jonah, as though he wasn't the least bit fooled. "Very well. How are you?"

Jonah blinked. "What?"

"How. Are. You?" repeated Creyton.

"What kind of question is that?" demanded Jonah.

Creyton shrugged, and once again surveyed the landscape that Jonah was trying hard to avoid. "With the horrible scene you caused in Southern Shores, not to mention the disastrous conference you had with the Founding Five of the Curaie, I was curious about your emotional state."

Jonah regarded Creyton with disgust. "What is this, therapy time? You and your little slave bitch, India, caused that scene in Southern Shores! And how do you know about the thing with the Curaie? That was a—"

"—private session?" finished Creyton for him. "Is that what you were going to say?"

That threw Jonah for a loop, because he had no idea how Creyton could know. But he didn't show it. "I find it funny that you are interested in my mental state," he deflected, "seeing as how you're the one that's the heartless murderer."

Creyton shook his head. "You're a barely evolved imbecile, Rowe. Let me explain it, so that even you will understand. You are a writer, yes? So you know that many things go into a great book. The kind of book that will greatly excite and ensnare the interest the masses. If one placed a raw manuscript into the world, it would be butchered, maligned, and lambasted. The book needs to be revised. Edited. Excess words need to be pruned. Some scenes may even need to be overhauled completely. It's a grueling process, and not everyone agrees with it. But at the end of the process, the product is crisp, sharp, and top quality. I am an author as well. But I do not scribe my words on paper. I scribe them in the world. And for the ethereal world to be perfect, some mentalities must be edited. Some practices need to be revised. Some ideals and perspectives need to be overhauled completely. And yes, some people need to be pruned. But in the end, the work is quality. I'm not heartless; no. I'm simply unafraid to do what's necessary to make quality work."

Jonah stared at him. Did Creyton really believe that? "Are… are you crazy?"

Creyton's eyes flashed, but then he just sighed. "It's the mark of a primitive mind to call progression crazy," he said in a cold voice.

"And it's the mark of a psychopath to refer to wiping out innocent people as quality work," countered Jonah.

Creyton smiled that hated smile again. "I suppose it was too much to expect you to understand," he said. "How can you comprehend what life should be, when you were never supposed to be alive at all?"

"What the hell is that supposed to mean?"

"Think, Jonah." Creyton's voice was sharp and terse. "Think. You're a bastard. If your father had been an honorable man, you wouldn't have even been born. I, on the other hand, am on my second life. Of the two of us, who do you believe has fate on their side in this scenario?"

Jonah closed his eyes. That was the second time someone mentioned the circumstances of his birth. First, the damned Curaie accentuated the fact that he was illegitimately conceived, and now this. When would these assholes get it through their heads that those things had nothing to do with who he was?

"I believe my inquiry has been answered," said Creyton suddenly.

"What?" said Jonah. "But I never even told you 'how I was!' "

"Yes, Rowe, you did," said Creyton. "And I must say, you're coming along nicely. But in case you've forgotten, that was only the first thing. I did tell you that there was another reason why you were here. I want to see just how far you're willing to go."

"Regarding what?" snapped Jonah.

Creyton looked Jonah in the eye, almost pinning him down just with his gaze. "Someone dear to you is going to die, Rowe," he said.

A chill ran down Jonah's spine. "Life never ends, Creyton," he said in a voice that he hoped was level.

Creyton laughed. *Laughed.* "Keep reassuring yourself of that. But it will happen, tonight. Unless you are willing to defy the Curaie."

"By doing what?" snarled Jonah.

"By finding and saving him," Creyton snarled back. "But here is the challenging part. It will require you actually thinking for yourself. It will require unfettering yourself from the leash of your Guide masters. And you had best make haste. People can be so transient."

Jonah's eyes widened. Did Creyton mean who he thought he meant?

"Not convinced of my sincerity?" asked Creyton shrewdly. "Go to Jonathan's study, and inspect the Vitasphera. You are aware that it darkens in times of crisis, are you not?"

Jonah didn't answer. Creyton smirked.

"When a loved one, a blind one, is marked for death, the gathering darkness in the Vitasphera is rimmed with red," he informed Jonah. "Go check it."

"Why are you doing this?" spat Jonah. "What is the point?"

Without warning, Creyton grabbed Jonah's throat and lifted him off of his feet. "You'd best get going," he said coldly. "Be quick. You don't have your pretty little Time Item friend to assist you with punctuality, do you?"

Jonah grabbed at Creyton's wrist. His grip was like iron. "I-I-I th-thought you c-couldn't touch me here," he gasped.

Creyton regarded Jonah with hate. "I did say that, didn't I?"

He threw Jonah from his grasp—

—and Jonah shot up from the floor.

It was like his consciousness had practically slammed back into his body. He looked around, momentarily wondering why his side ached. Then he remembered that he'd collapsed when he'd experienced the Mindscope. Had that been a dream? A vision? But it seemed so real. Creyton's vice grip on his neck had felt real. Jonah was surprised that he didn't have trouble breathing at the moment. It took a few moments for all the cogs to fall back in place, but as suddenly as they did, he remembered Creyton's words.

"*Someone dear to you will die. You must make haste; people can be so transient.*"

No.

He heard weird sounds from the fitness room. What was wrong now?

He pulled himself from the floor—a feat made painstaking by the soreness in his side— and hurried inside. His friends were all getting up from the floor. They appeared to have collapsed just like he did.

What the hell? Had they all experienced the Mindscope, too?

Bobby still lay on the weight bench. Thank God he'd racked up the weight before he'd collapsed. Some people sported minor injuries; Alvin flexed his already damaged arm, Spader had a busted lip, and Douglas had a knot already forming on his head, and Nella had a shiner. Jonah approached her, and helped her to her feet.

"Are you alright, Nella?" he asked.

Nella looked in the mirror on the wall. "It's nothing that a little foundation and concealer won't fix," she muttered.

"Huh?" said Jonah. "Why do you need to hide it? Liz can put a salve on it—"

"No time," said Nella. "Dylan's coming to pick me soon."

"Are you serious?" Jonah frowned at her. "Are you seriously thinking about a date right now—?"

"Yes I am, Jonah," spat Nella. "Need to relieve stress. Especially after what I just saw in my mind. Later."

She left before he said another word. He almost went after her, but then remembered the task at hand. There were bigger things going on than Nella's ill-timed date.

He located Terrence and Reena, who were lifting themselves from the ground, shaking off disorienting effects. He helped the both of them up, and then looked over at Liz. She'd had the fortunate experience of falling into a nestled position among the exercise balls.

"Call Vera, Liz!" he said in an elevated voice.

"W-what?" said Liz, trying to focus.

"The Mindscope!" said Jonah. "Everybody had it! Vera's working a double at the diner! Make sure she didn't pass out near the stove, or on anybody's kids, or something!" He then looked at Terrence and Reena. "I'm sorry for earlier," he told them. It was hasty, but sincere. "You can give me scathing rebukes later. I won't even protest. But I need the two of you to come with me now!"

He left before they could question him, and he was grateful to hear them behind him as he headed to the third story of the estate.

"Did you see all that?" asked Terrence. "That bone-dry place? The black skies? The spirits and spiritesses?"

"Every bit of it," said Reena, who looked angry. "It pisses me off seeing those spirits and spiritesses being ruined like that. It's a pity Daniel can't do anything for them anymore."

Jonah frowned. When were they going to mention the most important piece? "What about Creyton?" he asked of them. "Did he say something different to you than what he said to me?"

"What are you talking about, Jonah?" asked Reena. "Creyton wasn't even there."

Jonah paused at the top of the stairs, which nearly caused all of them to fall. He turned around and faced them. "You didn't see Creyton?"

"No, Jonah," said Terrence. "Creyton wasn't there. It was just that barren valley, full of voided spirits and spiritesses. It sounds like you had a nightmare on top of that crazy Mindscope."

Jonah just looked at them. So they hadn't seen Creyton. He was the only one to see the bastard? This wasn't the first time that something like that had happened, but he couldn't think about that now.

"Are you alright, Jonah?" asked Reena.

"Hell no," said Jonah. "Creyton was in my Mindscope vision—thing, whatever it was. He said someone was getting killed."

"What!" cried Terrence. "Who?"

"Hang on." They'd reached the door to Jonathan's study. It wasn't locked.

"Um, Jonah?" said Terrence. "This is Jonathan's—"

"I hadn't forgotten, man," interrupted Jonah, who flicked the light switch on but took in no part of the room except for the Vitasphera. He grabbed it and began to inspect with every bit of his attention.

"Jonah, what are you doing?" asked Reena. "We shouldn't be in here!"

"Creyton said that if someone we care about has been marked to lose their physical life, there is a red streak in the Vitasphera," muttered Jonah as he continued to inspect the sphere.

"Jonah," said Reena after a second of silence, "you are going on Creyton's information. He could have very well been lying."

"That's what I'm hoping," said Jonah. "Because if a red streak's in here, then—"

Jonah froze. It was there. Plain as day.

The darkness in the Vitasphera had a thin red lining. He dropped it, not even bothering to register the fact that it fell right back to its original state on Jonathan's desk.

"No," he whispered. "No."

"Jonah, you're scaring me," said Reena, who grabbed the Vitasphera and eyed the red lining herself. "What does this mean?"

Jonah felt the blood leave the tips of his fingers. He felt the aching cold there.

And it didn't even matter.

"It means that if we don't do something," he told them in a hollow voice, "then Creyton is going to kill Prodigal."

12

Slippery Slope

Jonah's words were met with blaring silence. Reena even let the Vitasphera fall from her hands, where it once again landed neatly on Jonathan's desk, completely unscathed.

"Jonah, are you serious?" she whispered.

"Quite," said Jonah.

"How do you know that he wasn't lying, though?" asked Terrence.

"Because Creyton revels in killing, we know that," said Jonah. "He'd watch us all fall one by one, and simply laugh. He just referred to murder as artistic editing in the Mindscope vision we just had."

Jonah half-desired to break something, but decided against it. As if he hadn't made a fool of himself enough today. He looked at Reena, seized by inspiration. "Reena, do you consider Prodigal close?" he asked.

Reena wasn't fooled, and ripped off her dampener. "Give me a second. Or a minute, since I'm not spiritually endowed."

She closed her eyes and clasped her fingers. Jonah glanced at Terrence, who still seemed to be holding on to some hope that Creyton was lying.

Reena's brow furrowed slightly. Jonah snapped his attention back to her.

"What's wrong?" he asked instantly.

"Prodigal is in Dexter City," said Reena as she opened her eyes.

"Dexter City?" said Terrence, who frowned himself. "Seriously?"

"Um, pardon me," said Jonah, "but where is Dexter City?"

"It's a township right over the state line in Maryland," answered Reena. "Prodigal is there right now."

"Is there something wrong with the place?" asked Jonah, recalling their expressions. "A bad spot or something?"

"It's ain't that, Jonah," said Terrence. "It's larger than Rome, but never mind that. Dexter City is like—like one of those Slice-of-Americana-type places. Old-school thinking, antiquated ideas about life...the kind of place where everybody goes to the same churches and are members of the same activities and all that."

Jonah understood. "Not the type of place that a sazer would want to attract attention," he offered.

Reena nodded. Jonah's eyes lowered.

"So Prodigal is up to something," he murmured. "Is that why you were looking so confused, Reena? You sensed that something was up?"

"It's weird," said Reena. "Prodigal doesn't have an evil bone in his body, so I don't feel malice or anything. But...something isn't right."

"He could already be in danger, then," Jonah told his friends. "And because of that, residents in this Dexter City place may be in danger, too. Creyton doesn't care who he cuts down in his path. We need to do something."

"We're being sanctioned and scrutinized, Jonah," Reena reminded him. "Faulk has already seen that Ocean waif use ethereality; what if—?"

"Prodigal is our friend, Reena," interrupted Jonah. "He might be responsible beyond his years, but he is still a kid and prone to stupid mistakes. Prone to being in grave danger."

"Not if he goes into Red Rage," said Terrence.

Jonah ignored that. "Creyton's all but guaranteed that Prodigal's physical life will end tonight. I don't give a damn about sanctions and scrutiny right now. We need to get to him and make sure that he is safe."

Reena looked away for a second. "I don't want our livelihoods, threatened any further," she said, "but I also can't stand idly by while a friend is in danger. I'm in."

Jonah nodded, and looked at Terrence, who didn't even waste time deliberating.

"Of course I'm in," he said.

Jonah nodded. He loved these guys.

"Let's summon spirits for endowments right here," said Reena. If we go back downstairs and do it, there will be questions asked."

After doing what Reena suggested, they were ready to go. Jonah already had his batons in his pockets, because he never kept them too far away. Terrence had his steel knuckles from training in the fitness room. But Reena, who was obviously nowhere near her javelin, reluctantly took a hunting knife off of Jonathan's shelf.

"I'll bring it back," she muttered aloud, as if Jonathan could hear her or something. "Maybe I won't even have to use it."

Jonah grimaced at her words. For a fleeting moment, he wished that they had been trained at Sanctum Arcist, where Eleventh Percenters were trained to use ethereality for combat from a very early age and actually used it to police certain areas from dark ethereality. But he pushed that thought aside. After all their training and skill-sharpening, Sanctum was in an even worse situation that the estate right now.

They employed the Astralimes, and then stepped out into the night in Dexter City. Jonah gaped.

When Creyton had given him that cryptic warning, his mind had gone to all sorts of dark places. He'd imagined Prodigal hanging from a ledge. Or being bludgeoned in a dark alley by a group of Deadfallen disciples, or even Creyton himself. Hell, he even imagined Jessica used that damned CPV power on him, and then forcing him to do unspeakable things…

But none of those thoughts included an impeccable two-story brick house with a two car garage, cobblestone path, and two bird baths, all in the shadow of a tall, majestic cedar.

"Um…" Terrence looked dumbfounded. "When you said that Prodigal's physical life was on the line, I wasn't expecting the TV sitcom house."

Jonah agreed. He had no idea what to make of this beautiful home, and no sign of Prodigal. What the hell was this all about? "Reena, are you sure that this is the right place?"

Reena, who'd been staring at the dwelling place just as dumbfounded as Jonah and Terrence, looked at Jonah with impatience. "Of course," she hissed. "There is definitely essence of an ethereal nature here. The place is saturated with it. But something…something just feels wrong."

"Hey look," whispered Terrence suddenly.

He pointed at one of the higher windows. Jonah looked up, and saw someone moving around by candlelight.

"Candles?" Jonah was puzzled as hell. "What the—? You know what, Reena? Hairpin, please."

He reached for it, and she obliged, but did so with a frown.

"You do realize that breaking and entering is a Tenth crime, Jonah?" she said quietly.

"Duh," said Jonah, unabashed, "I also realize that there is a possibility that a little B&E will be the least of our problems if we don't find out what the hell is up with Prodigal."

The door opened without a single creak, and a figure just out of sight nearly jumped out of their skin. When Jonah straightened, the figure gasped in recognition.

"Jonah!" said Prodigal in a stage whisper. "Hey friend! And you've got Terrence and Reena with you, too! This—this is a surprise!"

Jonah's eyes narrowed. He glanced at Terrence and Reena, the latter of whom was re-pinning her hair and regarding the sazer kid shrewdly. Jonah almost smirked; if Reena wasn't going to use her essence reading, then she was about to give Prodigal the third degree. Depending on what Prodigal was doing, that just might be fun.

"Prodigal," said Jonah quietly, "what are you doing?"

"N-nothing!" said Prodigal in a voice that fooled no one. "I'm not doing nothing at all! Why would you think I'm doing something?"

Now that Jonah's eyes had adjusted to the dim candlelight, he could see that Prodigal looked frazzled. His shoulder-length hair was a bona-fide rat's nest, and his clothes were wrinkled and grungy. He even wore mismatched shoes. Granted, he wasn't disgusting like he'd been when Jonah first met him, but he still appeared to have been roughing it for a while.

"Have you pissed away all of the money that Felix gave you, boy?" asked Terrence point-blank.

"No!" Prodigal actually abandoned his stage whisper. "Not even! I'm still good! Great, actually!"

"Then why do you look like life ain't treating you well?" quizzed Terrence. "You were a top-of-the-line apparel, Bluetooth-wearing bandit the last time we saw you. Now you look like you fell off the progress tree, and hit every branch on the way down. So what's the deal, kid?"

Prodigal looked to be on the verge of a panic attack, and Jonah contemplated using his balancing ethereality, but just then, the kitchen door swung open, which caught all their attention. Someone was walking through, lighting their way with a kerosene lamp. The sight of visitors at the front door was a fright to the person, and they dropped the lamp.

Terrence loosed an exclamation, and Jonah knew that he was too far away to make any difference, but Reena kept her head, and used her ethereal speed to catch the lamp inches from the floor. Meanwhile, Prodigal hurried to the other person before they bolted. He grabbed the boy's shoulder before he disappeared back through the door.

"It's alright, Constantine," he said hastily. "It's cool."

He looked back over at Jonah and sighed. "Alright, fine. Come…come down to the basement."

More confused than ever, Jonah, Terrence, and Reena followed Prodigal to the basement, having pulled out their weapons to contribute to the illumination (the kerosene lamp simply wasn't enough). When they reached the destination, Jonah heard hasty movements, but Prodigal said, "It's me and Constantine. And these are my friends. All Elevenths."

The basement was far brighter than the above rooms due to the collective candles and lanterns, and was populated by at least half a dozen other people. They all looked around Prodigal's age, and all looked rough and ragged. And despite Prodigal's reassurance, none of them had dropped their weapons, which consisted of old night sticks, ball bats, and box cutters.

A guy with uneven facial hair came forward, wielding a battered night stick with a sharpened edge. "Full-blooded Elevenths, Little Man?" he demanded.

Prodigal nodded. "They live a couple states away, with the Protector Guide Jonathan. Even though they're Elevenths, they're on our side, Nicodemus. You have my word."

The kid's face sort of softened when he heard Jonathan's name, and he lowered the stick. Jonah frowned. Constantine? Nicodemus?

Prodigal turned his back on his buddies once they'd lowered their weapons, and looked at Jonah, Terrence, and Reena once more. "These are friends of mine that I've made over the years," he explained. "Don't be confused if they call me 'Little Man,' because that's what everyone I knew called me before I started calling myself Prodigal. This is my best friend Nicodemus," the boy with the sharpened night stick made a less than enthusiastic gesture, "Stella Marie," a teenage girl with bushy hair gave a two-fingered wave, "Autumn Rose," the girl next to Stella Marie half-shrugged, "Alecksander, and no, it doesn't have an 'X' in it," a bald black young man grinned, "Obadiah," a teenager of Asian descent inclined his head, "and Gideon."

The last boy, whose hair rivaled Prodigal's in length, poked a thumb at his chest.

"I hope you don't mind my saying," said Terrence, "but you guys have some awesome names."

Prodigal snorted. "It's a sazer thing," he explained. "Almost none of us ever have anything of value. Ever. Most sazer parents feel that since they can't give their kids great lives, then they can at least give them great, upstanding names."

Jonah winced. That was just sad. All these kids had were nice names?

"We can't all be trust fund babies like Duscere," grunted Nicodemus, who saw Jonah's expression. "Lucky bastard."

"You got to let that go, man," snapped Prodigal. "He's helped us—"

"He helped *you*," corrected Nicodemus. "Yet another somebody who figured he could throw dollars at a problem, and magically make it fixed."

"It wasn't like that and you know it," Prodigal shot back. "Because of him, we don't have to rob people to eat. And that's real important right now."

Nicodemus shook his head, but remained silent. The girl named Autumn Rose removed brunette strands from her indelicate face and regarded Jonah, Terrence, and Reena.

"And how do you feel about sazers?" she asked with sharpness.

"Why should our opinions matter to you?" asked Reena quietly. "If we were to say we accepted you, or understood you, how stupid and hollow would it sound? Simple words can't convey how we feel about you, because we've only known you a matter of minutes."

Autumn Rose looked caught off-guard. "First impression is the lasting one," she muttered feebly. "That's what they say."

"I hope that won't be the case in this situation," Reena replied, "seeing as my first impression of you was the sight of you with a box cutter trained on my friends and me."

Prodigal shook his head. Jonah couldn't help but smirk at Terrence, who smirked back. It was always so fun to watch Reena shut people down.

The boy named Edwardious snorted. "Hot Eleventh lady, one, Autumn Rose, nothing."

Jonah sucked his teeth on that one. If that boy referred to Reena as hot again, he might be the one who got shut down next.

Prodigal grabbed a burger from a makeshift dinner table that consisted of cardboard boxes, and took a couple bites off of it. It was at that moment that Jonah noticed that the others had been eating combo meals as well.

"Why are you guys chowing down in the basement?" asked Terrence. "There is a kitchen upstairs, with saucers and a table. You guys could be up there taking advantage."

All the teenagers looked up at Terrence, with expressions bordering between coldness and shame.

"Never had saucers to put on the table," muttered Stella Marie.

"Never had a table," said Obadiah.

"Never had a *kitchen*," said Nicodemus.

Terrence looked downright foolish. Reena gave him an angry look, while Jonah shook his head.

"Dude, really?" he asked.

"My fault." Terrence's voice was sheepish. "I'm sorry. And I know better. I was homeless myself at one time."

Constantine piped up. "You were? Spoiled Eleventh like you?"

The awkwardness faded from Terrence's face, and his eyes narrowed. "You'd be surprised, boy," he muttered.

Nicodemus, who looked at Terrence in a new light, beckoned him over to the section of the basement floor where he and Constantine were seated. "Let's talk," was all he said.

With a shrug, Terrence joined the two teenagers. He'd gotten Stella Marie's, Obadiah's, and Edwardious' attention as well. Autumn Rose said she needed to walk around so as to rectify leg stiffness, grabbed a lantern, and left the basement. Prodigal looked after her suspiciously.

"She's going to check on Jael," he murmured.

"Who's Jael?" said Jonah quickly.

Prodigal's face twitched. "She's upstairs. You haven't met her."

Jonah remembered the candlelight he saw upstairs. This whole situation didn't add up. He decided that now was as good a time as any to get information, while Terrence had the other sazers distracted. "What are you doing here, Prodigal?" he asked again. "I've been told that this isn't the type of town one would want to lay low in."

Prodigal sighed. "Did Felix give you the information I got for him?" he asked. "About Creyton—?"

"—sending Deadfallen disciples into the sazer underground with blankets, food, and toiletries?" interrupted Jonah. "Yeah, he did."

Prodigal took a deep breath, but Jonah assumed that that had more to do with maintaining his temper. Sazers were prone to Red Rage if their tempers went unchecked. "He's been channeling his inner Santa Claus, and many sazers have been eating it up," he grumbled. "But some of them want nothing to do with Creyton and his disciples. They think that getting in bed with those assholes will make all of us sazers look even worse in the eyes of the Curaie and the ethereal world. They already view us as dangerous bums who are only good for fighting vampires and nothin' else. What would they think if we linked up with Creyton?"

Jonah looked at Reena, who seemed to be putting something together that she wasn't ready to share just yet. He looked over at Terrence, but he was still playing the role of keynote speaker with Prodigal's buddies. "Sazers get a raw deal, there is no disputing that," he said, "but what does that have to do with you and your posse squatting in this house?"

"Because the sazer underground isn't safe anymore, thanks to Creyton," said Prodigal heatedly. "The sazers that aren't cool with Creyton's showers of blessings are being ousted, for fear that we'll mess it up for the ones who want all the charity. Some have even gotten killed, or even eaten by cannibal sazers. We had to move, and out in the open, we are more vulnerable to vampire attacks, so we have to take shelter where we can."

Jonah shook his head. Leave it to Creyton to stir things up from the top to the bottom of everything in the ethereal world. But there was still something about this situation that didn't smell right. "I get your plight, Prodigal, and I do," he said stubbornly, "but you've been in trouble before. I didn't see you breaking into houses then."

"It's not like that!" said Prodigal hastily. "It's a new foreclosure. They don't expect anyone to look into this place for three months at least. We only need it three or four weeks, hopefully—"

"Ding!" Reena finally broke her silence. "Now we've gotten somewhere. Three or four weeks, Prodigal?"

Jonah didn't know what was going on, but Prodigal looked at Reena, his eyes wide with fear. "I—I mean—I didn't want to be specific with time, Reena. I meant to say—"

"Stop talking, Prodigal," said Reena. "Like most men, you are an abominable liar. Why is Jael not down here?"

Prodigal licked his lips. Jonah wondered just where the hell Reena was going with this.

"You don't have to tell me," she went on. "It's because she can barely move. She's practically on bed rest, isn't she?"

Jonah's eyes widened, but Terrence was the one who ruined it all.

"Bed rest?" He completely abandoned his conversation with the other sazers. "Who is pregnant in here?"

Every sazer in the basement tensed, and looked at their guests. But Reena only had eyes for the teenage sazer quailing under her gaze.

"Jael is expecting a baby," said Reena flat-out. "That baby is coming soon, and you didn't want her on the run from vampires and recently spoiled sazers." She looked at Jonah. "That's why things felt off. One of the essences I read was undeveloped. Prodigal's girlfriend is having their baby soon."

"I—wait, how did you know I had a girlfriend" asked Prodigal.

"Because Felix said that one of the reasons you spent so much time in the sazer underground was because you were sweet on someone there," said Terrence, who rose from the floor. "And now you're about to be someone's daddy."

Prodigal shook his head. "You're right about everything 'cept that last part," he said. "That kid ain't mine, and Jael's not my girlfriend."

Reena's stern look morphed to confusion. Jonah wasn't doing much better. Terrence was completely lost, but that might have been because he'd been in another conversation the whole time. The other sazers actually snickered.

"What do you mean?"

"Jael's not my girlfriend," repeated Prodigal. "Her sister is."

"Her sister?" said Jonah.

"Yep." Prodigal said it like it should have been obvious.

Jonah looked over at Stella Marie, who shook her head.

"Not me," she said as she pointed up to the ceiling. "It's the one your friend there just owned, Autumn Rose."

Within moments, everyone was in the master bedroom, with the exception of Edwardious, who remained downstairs.

"He doesn't get to eat very much," explained Stella Marie, "so he'll finish that food and then join us."

Reena seated herself next to Jael, while Autumn Rose, who'd grudgingly given Reena her respect after being verbally put in her place, sat on the opposite side. Jonah looked at Jael's young, freckled face, and shook his head. She reminded him of Nella. He promised himself that he would have a talk with her about that Dylan boy. That thing about her keeping her date with him after the Mindscope event sent up a bit of red flag in his mind. He hoped that that boy's influence wasn't changing her.

"She's an Eleventh," Reena told Jonah and Terrence. "And she's your sister, Autumn Rose?"

"Yeah," said Autumn Rose, whose eyes remained on her younger sister. "Our dad was an Eleventh, and mama was a sazer. Jael had daddy's gift. I wasn't so lucky."

"Don't put yourself down—" began Terrence, but Autumn Rose waved an impatient hand at him.

"Fuck the pep talk," she muttered. "I'm focused on my sister."

Reena inspected Jael further, and half-smiled. "She's having a boy," she said.

Jael turned her gaze to Reena, as did Autumn Rose. "S-Son?" she whispered. "How do you know? Can you read his essence?"

Reena smiled down at the young girl. "His essence is a little fuzzy because he is still unborn," she explained. "I'm wearing my dampener now, anyway. I figured it out when I felt your stomach."

Jonah frowned, distracted. "You know, Mr. Steverson did that same stomach-feeling thing with Amanda at work. How—?"

"Don't even worry about it, Jonah," said Terrence. "Speaking for myself, I'm completely fine with not knowing."

Reena eyed Nicodemus, Constantine, Alecksander, and Obadiah. "Are any of you the father?"

"No," answered Jael, bitterness in her soft tone. "It was an Eleventh that I met last year. He was the sweetest guy at first—"

"Of course he was," snapped Autumn Rose. "They're all sweet at first, then they get what they want, and reveal who they really are—no offense to you, baby," she threw a look at Prodigal.

"I'm sorry that I chastised you, Prodigal," said Reena. "Assumptions got the best of me."

Prodigal waved it off. "These are my friends. Very, very dear to me. I didn't want to break into this house, but it was too many of us for a motel room, and I wasn't gonna have Jael out there trying to survive with us in the elements. Way too much danger nowadays."

Jonah was about to praise Prodigal's actions, but then he remembered the whole point of this visit. The boy's devious behavior, the other sazers, and the revelation that one of their number was with child greatly distracted him. Prodigal brought it back to Jonah's mind when he mentioned not wanting his dear friends in danger. "Prodigal," he said slowly, "have you encountered any dangers since you all left the underground?"

Prodigal looked at Jonah. "Vanquished a lifeblood looter or two, but that's nothing for us sazers," he said. "So I guess I can say no."

Jonah frowned. That response was weird. "So you're not hiding from anyone?"

"Nope," answered Prodigal. "We know how to hunker down for vampires, and keep out of sight. We made sure no one saw us traveling."

Jonah's eyes narrowed in puzzlement. "So you're saying that the only reason that you guys are squatting in here is because of Jael's limitations?"

"Of course, Jonah," said Prodigal, who looked at him like it should have been obvious. "I didn't even break into people's houses *before* Felix gave me money! Like I said, I wanted my friends out of the underground, and there was no way I was gonna have my girlfriend's pregnant, barely mobile sister out on the ground somewhere. Why? What's up?"

Jonah was confused as hell. Creyton specifically stated that Prodigal would be killed tonight. There was the scarlet trace in the Vitasphera that someone had been marked for murder. But here was Prodigal, safe and sound, looking out for his friends. Jonah couldn't have been played. Creyton enjoyed killing too much for that—

Then a horrible thought occurred to him.

"What's wrong, Jonah?" repeated Prodigal, who now looked concerned.

"Prodigal," said Jonah with a low-lying level of desperation, "is there any reason at all for you to think that your physical life is in danger?"

Prodigal looked at Jonah like he'd grown an extra eye or something. "Nah. I mean, the lifeblood looters want to kill us all, but that's old news. No one knows we're here, 'cept you guys."

Jonah felt like the ground beneath his feet had shifted, just like someone had activated a Threshold of Death. Creyton had done that damned Mindscope, yet only conversed with Jonah. He all but promised him that Prodigal would be killed. He'd said that he wanted to see how far Jonah was willing to go. But it was a trick.

Jonah had screwed up. Big time.

He scrambled to his feet, which made everyone start.

"Jonah, what is it?" demanded Terrence.

"That lying bastard," snarled Jonah. He knew that his tone alarmed everyone, but didn't care. "Reena, get Jael out of this house. Use the Astralimes to get her to Liz—"

"What?" snapped Autumn Rose. "You won't move my sister! She can barely walk!"

"Shut up, Autumn Rose," Jonah fired back, anger and fear engulfing him again. "We don't have time for your personal shit—"

"Hey dude!" Prodigal got in Jonah's face. "Don't tell her to shut up! What's wrong with you, Jonah?!"

"What *is* wrong with you, Jonah?" asked Reena, who looked at him with alarm.

"Please get Jael out of here," said Jonah again. "I messed up. I messed up bad—"

Just then, Edwardious burst into the room. Crumbs from the burger bun were in his stubble, but he either didn't care or was too frightened to notice. "Kill the candles! Now!"

"What?" cried Prodigal. "What the hell—?"

"It's a trap!" cried Jonah. "They weren't looking for Prodigal, they were following me!"

"WHAT!" Nicodemus had his sharpened night stick out as he neared Jonah . "This damn Eleventh done brought some hell down on us?"

"You need to get back boy, I'm trying to help—"

"WILL YOU ALL SHUT THE FUCK UP!" shouted Reena, which instantly silenced the entire room. Jonah and Terrence looked at her, stupefied. Reena never used that word. "The essence of the house has changed! Blow out the candles!"

The edge in Reena's voice was such that no one questioned her, not even the defiant sazers. Jonah intensified the air flow, and the bedroom was pitch-black dark like the rest of the house. He listened with everyone else while impatiently waiting for his eyes to adjust to the dark.

Then the silence was broken by the unmistakable signs of twigs snapping. It was so striking that it carried up the stairs. Jael gasped, which prompted Autumn Rose to whisper, "Quiet, sis!"

Jonah tried hard to regulate his breathing. He'd been baited into looking after Prodigal's welfare, and because of that, a bunch of people were now at risk, and one of them was pregnant. This was all on him.

Again.

"Alright, here's the situation," rasped a voice from downstairs. "Blue Boy took the bait, and led us to this nest of ungrateful sazers. One of them is Duscere's little roadie. If you vampires wanna get back into the Transcendent's good graces, you will kill everything in this house. And be quick about it. Sunrise isn't too long off."

Jonah immediately heard hushed obscenities, Jael's petrified whimper, and a hiss from Nicodemus.

"Nice friends you got there, Little Man," he said in a nasty whisper. "Led lifeblood looters straight to us, corralled by a Deadfallen disciple!"

"Quiet, Nicodemus!" said Prodigal. "We need to improvise! The stakes are all in the basement with our food!"

"And you Elevenths may as well keep your flashy ethereal steel in your pockets," said Stella Marie's voice in the dark. "Wood or silver is the only way to go."

"We've fought vampires before," snapped Reena. "Now, Terrence, Jonah, we need to be intelligent about this—"

"To hell with intelligence." Jonah had bumped into a chair when the candles got blown out, so he didn't need to see it to grab it. "If these bastards want to play, then I say game on."

He bashed the chair against the floor, which resulted in gasps from his counterparts in the room and sounds of surprise from downstairs. He ignored them both as he picked around in the dark for broken pieces of wood.

"What in hell's name are you doing, Jonah?" demanded Reena.

Jonah barely registered the words as he tore still-attached wooden chair pieces apart. "Use me as bait, will you?" he muttered to himself. "I'm nobody's bait…I will end you all, I swear to fuckin' God…"

"Um, Prodigal?" said Autumn Rose. "Your pal here's scaring me."

Jonah couldn't have cared less about the girl's fear. He was so sick of being toyed with, all that mattered was vanquishing the vampires, then getting hold of that Deadfallen disciple. "Reena, get Jael out of here," he repeated in a voice most unlike his own. "Take her sister with you. The rest of you can sit here for all I give a damn, but I'm going out there."

"What?" Terrence sounded as though he were afraid of Jonah, as well. "Jonah, don't be a fool, man!"

Jonah walked out of the room, hoping that he could rely on his senses, since it was too dark for his eyes to be helpful—

Wait.

What was he thinking? He was the Blue Aura. He could alleviate darkness even if the power company had disconnected the service.

He closed his eyes and concentrated—

Every light in the house popped on, lack of electrical service be damned. He couldn't have timed his decision more impeccably, either. A vampire was on the stairs, inching toward him. The lifeblood looter could see in the dark, but he hadn't expected his night-trained eyes to be blasted by the lights of the house. He yelped and shielded his eyes like the bulbs were the sun itself, and Jonah seized his chance and staked the disoriented fiend on the stairs. When he heard the howl of agony, he kicked the bastard off of the stake and watched him fall down the stairs. The thing rolled down the stairs in a most grotesque fashion before slamming to the floor, a hollowed out husk of its former self. One down.

Jonah continued down the stairs, where the living room was empty. There was no furniture in the family room due to the house's status as a foreclosure. Why then was everything still set up in the kitchen?

Jonah's musings cost him. Another vampire emerged from a room while Jonah's focus was elsewhere, and before he knew it, he was on his back, doing his damndest to avoid the fangs nearing his throat.

Jonah made his fingers sting with current, and tapped the vampire's forehead with two fingers. The resulting spark literally knocked the vampire completely off of Jonah. The thing tried to break his fall with his arm, but it made a sickening crunch when his full weight landed on it. Jonah hopped back to his feet, unmoved by the streak of luck. He was well aware that the vampire's break would heal soon, and the electric shock did nothing more than just piss him off. He staked him while he was still off-balance, barely even breaking stride as he headed for the den.

Where he got tripped up.

There was no longer a rug there, but some sort of fabric had been expertly pitched at his feet. Jonah tried to control the fall, but had too much momentum. He completely wiped out, and got all the breath knocked out of him in the process. And the stake flew away from his grasp, because of course it did.

"I'm glad that worked," rasped a female voice, "because I wasn't gonna chase you."

Dazed, Jonah turned to see an emaciated, ruddy-complexioned vampire mere feet away. Despite her sickly, slight frame, he was smart enough to know that she was anything but weak.

"That's two of my friends you vanquished, right?" she went on as she strolled toward him leisurely. "Then it's only fair that I break some of your own bones before I take your lifeblood."

She knelt down next to Jonah's disoriented form, but then froze, eyes wide. Both she and Jonah looked at her upper body, where scarlet bloomed at her chest and made a hasty descent. She fell on her face, and Jonah saw a sharpened night stick lodged in her back. Nicodemus had thrown it at her from the stairs. It had been a remarkable toss, but the sight of him annoyed Jonah something fierce.

"Come to help at last?" he grumbled.

With a sneer, Nicodemus came forward and wrenched his night stick out of the vampire's back. "I'm not down here to help your dumb, reckless ass," he spat. "I came down here to distract any vampires from going upstairs while your friend got Jael and Autumn Rose out of here."

Jonah forced himself to let the jab pass. "So they got them out?"

"That's what I said, isn't it?" said Nicodemus.

"So where is everyone else?" asked Jonah.

"Looking for other vampires, duh," said Nicodemus. "Your guy Terrence vanquished one in that upstairs bathroom. He was trying to stop you from coming down here and making an ass of yourself, but got distracted by the vampire. I told him that I'd find you. It wasn't hard; all I had to do was follow the noise."

"You know, you're a snarky little shit—"

Jonah stopped. He heard something outside. From his expression, it looked like Nicodemus had heard it, too.

Twigs snapped somewhere out there. But that didn't make any sense. Surely the vampires wouldn't be dumb enough to bring backup this close to sunrise.

"Go make sure everyone's okay," he threw at Nicodemus. "I hope that's not too much trouble, seeing as how it requires you to work something other than your mouth."

"What'd you say to me?" demanded Nicodemus, but Jonah flicked him off, and headed outside.

What first struck him was the quiet. He'd heard twigs snapping, which meant usage of portals. But now it was simply quiet.

That was odd, now that Jonah thought about it. Vampires could move silently, without footfall. It was one of the many reasons why Elevenths feared them and sazers hated them. One could be coming up behind him now—

Out of pure instinct, he jabbed his stake behind him, but there was nothing there. Open space. Paranoia was a bitch.

"Stupid move, Jonah," he mumbled. "Rank amateur."

Another twig snapped, and Jonah wheeled around to see a figure hurrying from the house. With a jolt, he realized that the twig-snapping he'd heard wasn't the arrival of vampire reinforcements, it was the sound of the Deadfallen disciple who'd brought them in the first place. He must have decided to flee once he realized the vampire siege was a fail.

But why would he flee? Couldn't he have used a twig portal? Or shape shift into a crow and just fly away, like India and Jessica had?

Maybe it was better if Jonah asked the guy himself.

He tore off after him, and to his surprise, caught him much faster than expected. The man attempted to fight back, but Jonah overpowered him with no effort at all, frowning as he did so.

This was an embarrassing performance; Liz could have fought better than this guy. Hell, Jonah imagined that Katarina Ocean could do better than this guy. What was the deal? Creyton hadn't taught this man well at all. Did he doze off while the other Deadfallen disciples were in dark ethereality class with their boss?

The man flailed his arms like a baby, and Jonah rapped him hard near his temple. The man howled and brought his hands to his head. This fight was over. It was a joke. For some reason, that made Jonah angrier.

"I hate to break it you," he growled, "but you suck. I can't believe Creyton let you out of the gate! You should have turned into a crow before I reached you!"

The man looked up at Jonah through one eye, as the other was swollen. "The Transcendent will deliver me from you!" he said with confidence.

"Uh-huh," said Jonah. "Well, your vamp buddies in there failed, and Creyton didn't come to deliver any of them. So where are your buddies?"

"What buddies?"

Jonah couldn't resist the urge. He impatiently slapped the guy across the face. "The other Deadfallen disciples, genius! Where's O'Shea? Charlotte? Jessica?"

"You speak of the chosen," said the guy in a weak tone. "We stand apart—"

Jonah grabbed the man by the collar, and grabbed the stake with his other hand. "I'm sick of this shit circular talk!" he shouted. "Creyton sent the Mindscope, warned me that Prodigal would be killed, and your little lifeblood looting team failed. I have half a mind to let you go, just so you can tell your lord and master that his little plan failed."

The man gave Jonah a bloody smile. "The Transcendent was right," he said. "You are just a gullible country boy."

Jonah's eyes widened in anger. Those were bold words from a guy that was such a bloody mess...who didn't have a scar on his throat...

Jonah's eyes remained wide, but the anger diminished to make way for confusion, then realization...

"Help!" cried the man. Suddenly, his voice was strangled, terrified, higher than before. "Help me, please!"

"Who the hell are you talking—?"

"Get off of that man and raise your hands," said an angry voice.

Jonah looked around. A police officer stood several feet away, his sidearm trained on him.

"Get off of him before you make things worse for yourself, boy" growled the officer.

"Officer, you don't understand—"

But then Jonah remembered what was in his hand. He'd foolishly picked up the stake, for no other purpose than to threaten. There was even blood on the tip of it. And he held it near the bleeding head of another suuvus.

A suuvus who, from the officer's standpoint, resembled a victim of a brutal assault.

"Aw, shit," he mumbled.

13

Gamed

"That man is in danger! You need to send some police up to the hospital to watch him!"

Jonah started his intonation from the minute they sent the suuvus to the local hospital, and repeated it the whole trip to the police station, up the steps, and into the holding cell. His arresting officer practically ignored him during all this, but once Jonah was locked in the cell, his entire demeanor changed.

"I was waiting for you to stop on your own," he snapped, "but you just wouldn't shut up! So tell me, why the hell do you keep saying that?"

"Because they're going to kill him!" Jonah fired at him. "He doesn't understand!"

The officer's eyes widened maliciously. "So you have accomplices, boy? Are they going to go up to the hospital and finish the job you started?"

"If I had accomplices headed for the hospital, would I have told you to send police?" demanded Jonah. "The people threatening that man are not affiliated with me! He doesn't realize what's going to happen! They've got him so turned 'round that he doesn't get it!"

The officer gave Jonah a scathing look. Jonah almost felt guilty. But his anger outweighed it. He was not the criminal here. He was the one that had been wronged. He tried to preserve physical life, yet here he was, the only one behind Tenth bars. He had half a mind to kill all of the electricity in the police station, just to be as big an asshole to the officer as the officer had been to him. But he knew that would probably make his situation worse. The staff would have no way of knowing that Jonah had done it, but Jonah also had no doubts that they'd take it out on him regardless.

"Right now, boy," said the officer, who surveyed Jonah through narrow eyes, "the only one 'turned 'round' is you. Now sit down and shut your mouth. I have a feeling we will be here for a little bit. Thanks to you, I'm probably gonna miss my daughter's solo in church this morning."

"Like I give a damn about your crotch spawn," mumbled Jonah.

The officer wheeled around, eyes smoldering. "What was that?"

Jonah glared at the guy. "Nothing."

Giving him another scowl, the officer turned and walked over to the receptionist. Jonah's didn't bother to eavesdrop. His focus went internal.

The way that Creyton gamed him was crystal clear now. Jonah thought that the setup at the foreclosed house with the vampires was the big play, but that was just violent misdirection. Creyton was well aware that a combination of sazers and Eleventh Percenters would stamp out the vampires, and he was also aware that Jonah would do his damnedest to take down the Deadfallen disciple that brought about the chaos. And it turned out to be a suuvus. Then there was the convenient incident of the cop showing up to "save the day."

Creyton had played a long game. But why?

And Prodigal. He was perfectly fine. It was Jonah who screwed things up for the young sazer. And he screwed things up for all of the boy's friends. Their only goal was securing the well-being of Jael and her unborn son.

God, Jonah hoped that Jael hadn't gotten hurt. He hoped the events of the night hadn't sent her into false labor or anything…

Jonah gave himself a mental shake. Reena would have been superbly efficient, as she always was. He wasn't even mad that she didn't use the Astralimes back to check on him. At least as far as he knew, anyway. And Terrence–Terrence had likely seen the police officer from the one of the upstairs windows, and realized that he couldn't do anything personally for Jonah. He probably used the Astralimes to alert Jonathan or Daniel. With a sneer, Jonah hoped that it was Daniel. It wasn't like Jonathan could appear in the police department in spirit form, anyway.

To make matters worse, the officer that had arrested Jonah wasn't anything like Deputy Dumbass back in Southern Shores. He read Jonah his rights. His only blunders were the fact that he accepted the suuvus' word as gospel , and not investigating the foreclosed house. Accepting the suuvus at his word was certain to result in that idiot's passing at the hospital, since Jonah knew that Creyton wasn't interested in making new minions. The strange thing was the fact that not checking the house turned out to be a blessing, because it allowed the sazers to escape.

The sazers…

What would they think of him now? Autumn Rose was sure to be pissed, and Nicodemus probably wanted to kill him by this point. But Stella Marie, Edwardious, Alecksander, and Obadiah…Jonah hadn't actually gotten a full read off of them. Not that it mattered. He just hoped that Jael was okay, along with her unborn son.

Most of all, he wanted to speak to Prodigal. The sazer kid who befriended Jonah in LTSU's parking lot because Jonah had showed him kindness. What was Prodigal thinking about his "kind friend" at this point?

Jonah had no way to find out, because he was stuck in this stupid holding cell in Dexter City, Maryland.

If only Nana could see him now—

Jonah rapped his knuckles hard against the side of his skull. He was almost thankful for the resulting pain and the distraction that it caused. That thought had to go, plain and simple.

The click of high heels pulled his attention out of his own mind, but once he saw the person in the heels, his attention was pulled out of the cell.

It was Reena.

But not like he'd ever seen her.

She was clad in a sharp outfit, and the glasses she wore even had frames that matched the suit. Her black and scarlet hair was pulled back into an unyielding bun, which was a look that Jonah had to admit worked very well for her. But there were two things that really stuck out. Apart from the heels, of course.

The first was that Reena had painted her fingernails. Jonah had seen paint on her clothes, hands, hair, and even her face. Not once had he ever seen her with painted fingernails.

But the second thing made even the painted nails a throwaway: The outfit ended with a skirt.

Reena had on a skirt.

Jonah's mouth dropped. Reena abhorred dresses and skirts. To Jonah's knowledge, she didn't even own one. She once joked to him and Terrence that when she and Kendall got married, she was going to Men's Wearhouse to get a tailored tux. But she was far from a tux right now. Granted, the skirt was quite conservative and went past her knees, but still. Reena was wearing a skirt.

"Who are you, ma'am?" Jonah's arresting officer asked Reena.

Jonah's eyes narrowed. The guy used a lower voice register than he'd used with him, and even the receptionist mere minutes ago. The guy had a wedding band on his finger, so he shouldn't have been gawking at Reena like that. Jonah saw that the receptionist had narrowed her eyes at him as well.

Reena remained stone-faced. "A more important question is who are you, officer."

"Ralph Feldman." His answer was instant. The man even righted his posture; he'd been slouching earlier.

"Well, Officer Feldman," said Reena, coolness in her tone, "I would like to speak to my client in private, and also inform you that anything he has said up to this point is inadmissible."

"Wait, what? But—"

"His legal counsel wasn't present, seeing as I'm his legal counsel," interrupted Reena. "Unless of course you are attempting to deny him due process."

Feldman paled. "No, of course not," he murmured. "How did you know he was here so fast? We haven't allowed him any phone calls."

Reena rolled her eyes and didn't answer. "What has he done? Why are you holding him?"

It's just that...he beat a man to a bloody pulp on foreclosed property, and he has been spouting something about the man would surely die if we didn't send police to protect him in the hospital—"

"Really," said Reena, whose eyebrows inclined only by a couple of inches. "Well, God only knows what he's said, since he's been neglecting his meds."

"What!" said Jonah aloud, which made several heads snap his way. With everyone's attention off of her, Reena took the opportunity to widen her eyes at Jonah. He'd just have to roll with it.

"Um, what—what day is it?" he said with much less certainty and coherence this time. "What day is it? Funday?"

The receptionist regarded Jonah with alarm. He felt a bitter taste creep into his mouth. Now he had to be a crazy convict. Swell.

"He sustained a traumatic brain injury late in his adolescence, and now there are intermittent violent episodes and speech," invented Reena. "So there are times when he speaks that it is truly prattle."

"Is that right?" asked Feldman.

"Indeed," said Reena in a rather deliberate tone. "You never know what he will say."

"Did I ever mention that I talk to spirits?" said Jonah loudly. He didn't have to be a brain surgeon to figure that one out. "I talk to them, deal with them, and they speak back to me! And when I touch certain metals, they turn blue!"

"I know the *spirits* you've been messing with," said the receptionist with disgust. "You godless loon."

Feldman, on the other hand, narrowed his eyes. "He wasn't doing that before," he said slowly. "Nor did he sound so foolish. He was adamant when he was talking earlier, and then he just went into dead silence."

Jonah felt his face twitch. Uh-oh. A smart, observant one. Now he really missed Deputy Dumbass back in Coastal Shores.

"I did just state that the outbursts were intermittent, Officer Feldman," said Reena, undeterred. She even allowed some impatience to seep into her tone. Assuming it was fake. "And of course he would sound certain, seeing as he's not well."

Jonah almost glanced at Reena in admiration. For an artistic person, she had this shtick down to a science.

Feldman looked disarmed. "I'm seeing what you mean, ma'am," he said in a voice that still carried a trace of displeasure, "but surely you must understand that someone with potential homicidal ideation cannot be taken lightly."

"Very true," nodded Reena. "I never sought to impede your job responsibilities. Now," Reena made her voice provocative, "please be a gentleman and refrain from impeding my own."

Jonah saw Feldman's half-smirk. It was all he could do not to roll his eyes. Within seconds, he'd walked to the cell, unlocked the door, and beckoned to Jonah with his eyes still on Reena.

"You can take him to interrogation room two," he said. "You can't miss it; we only have four of them back there. But I'll take you back there. It's no problem."

Jonah walked out of the cell and smirked at Reena, but she didn't return it, which he regarded with puzzlement. Feldman led them into the place interrogation room two, and shut the door behind them. Jonah opened his mouth to speak, but Reena silenced him by widening her eyes.

"Use your endowment to kill that camera in the corner over there," she commanded. "Don't look up there. Keep your eyes on me."

With a trace of a shrug, Jonah concentrated on the camera he'd seen when they first entered the room. He heard a spark or two, and knew that it was no longer active. Reena motioned for him to sit down.

"Where did you get that skirt suit?" asked Jonah.

"Magdalena," answered Reena quietly. "We're near enough the same size."

"I appreciate what you're doing for me," said Jonah, "but the mental health illness thing might've been a bit much—"

"The hell it was," snapped Reena, who still hadn't raised her voice. She didn't need to; the venom in her tone made it unnecessary. "Mental illness is about the only thing I can think of that would explain your behavior back at that house!"

"What?"

"What the hell were you thinking, Jonah?" demanded Reena.

"What the hell are you talking about?" Jonah demanded back.

"You endangered the lives of almost a dozen people!" hissed Reena.

Jonah's mood instantly acidified once more. "I was gamed, Reena," he responded. "Creyton played me, made me think—"

"I don't mean that!" said Reena in a brusque tone. "I mean your blatant disregard for any kind of planning to deal with the vampires! Did you forget that one of the innocent people in there was pregnant?"

"Wow, how did I miss that?" Jonah's voice stank of sarcasm, and he didn't care. "Oh wait, I didn't! I was trying to salvage the situation, and preserve physical lives. I had it under control."

"Did you, now?" said Reena, wrenching the glasses from her face. "Did you secure Jael? Did you make sure we could defend ourselves before you ran out of the bedroom, balls to the wall, channeling your inner Van Helsing? And while we're on the subject, did you go into Spectral Sight in order to ascertain the possible presence or spirits and spiritesses? Since they would have been just as vulnerable to the fangs of the vampires as you, me, Terrence, and everyone else!"

Jonah paused. He'd done none of those things. His only thought was that he'd been made a fool of, and making the vampires hurt as much as he could. Leave it to Reena, for the zillionth time. "How is Jael?" he muttered.

"We got her to Liz," answered Reena. "She's fine."

"Good," said Jonah. "And Autumn Rose—?"

"They're all fine, but Autumn Rose hates you now," said Reena in a voice that made it sound like she was in full agreement. "Nicodemus, too."

"Lovely," muttered Jonah. "Just lovely! Put it all on Jonah, since that's the 'in' thing to do nowadays! Ignore that I tried to help. Ignore that I vanquished two lifeblood looters. Ignore that Creyton's plan stretched to me getting tricked by that bastard suuvus outside—"

Now it was Reena who paused. "Suuvus?"

"Yes, suuvus." Jonah could almost taste the belligerence in his voice. "The guy who told them that they had to kill us before sunrise to 'get back in Creyton's good graces?' Him."

Reena looked confused, which was such a rarity that Jonah would have savored it had he not been pissed. "That voice we heard was from a Tenth?"

"Yes," responded Jonah. "I caught him before he ran away, and roughed him up. I thought he just sucked at ethereality, or something, because he couldn't fight worth a damn. But he was so cocky and collected, talking about how Creyton would deliver him. Then that Feldman guy showed up and he did a complete flip-flop and acted like I'd battered him just because I felt like it. Creyton had something to do with that tip. I'm sure of it."

Reena raised an eyebrow. "What do you mean?"

"What I mean," said Jonah, "is that he didn't trick me in to leading those bastards to the sazers. He wanted us to get the upper hand. He wanted me to take down that suuvus, and he must have influenced the cop in some strange way. Or hell, maybe just spun it dramatically enough...I don't know. But Creyton is playing a long game here, Reena. I know it."

Reena looked away. "Sothat stuff Feldman said about you saying that they guy would be killed if they didn't put police around his hospital room—"

Jonah nodded. "He wants to lay down his physical life and become a minion. He has no idea that Creyton will simply have him killed, and then usurp his spirit. I told that cop out there to send someone to watch the guy—"

"And he assumed that you had accomplices to assault him further, or worse," finished Reena with a grimace.

"Uh-huh," responded Jonah.

Reena sighed. "I'm sorry, Jonah," she told him. "I still disagree with the way you handled the trap, and you did put us all in danger, but it's messed up that Creyton's games landed you in here."

Jonah felt his irritation toward Reena ebb away. It was what it was. He didn't know how to respond, so he gave her a slow nod.

"And Jonah, I meant what I told you a couple weeks ago." The edge in Reena's voice had dulled, but it was still present. "You really need to do something about your temper. It's a very telling thing when an Eleventh Percenter's temper scares a sazer, and they have the vulnerability to Red Rage. Do you see what raw emotion does?"

Jonah drummed his fingers on the table. Yeah, Reena was right. And no, he didn't have to like it. "What happened to Terrence afterward?" he asked instead. He remembered what Nicodemus had told him, but hearing it from another perspective would do him well.

"He and Nicodemus checked for stragglers," said Reena. "Being that Jael was pregnant, her essence was just as volatile as her hormones. The scent of her lifeblood...the vampires may as well have been sharks. But it so happened that the number of them was small. They knew sazers would be there, but they didn't count on how vicious they were, or how far they would go to protect Jael. Anyway, Terrence vanquished a vampire in the upstairs bathroom, and then saw that cop arrest you. He used the Astralimes to his dad's house. But he left without waking anyone when he saw Sterling's car."

"Why'd he leave because of that?" asked Jonah.

"Because Sterling would have wanted to help," answered Reena. "And he just can't. Precious time would have been wasted arguing over it. So he went to the estate, grabbed me from Jael's bedside, and told me what happened. He's waiting around the corner."

Jonah whistled. "That's a great deal of unauthorized Astralimes travel," he commented.

"Oh, we're going to pay the price," said Reena, sounding resigned. "But we couldn't leave you in here."

Jonah nodded. He loved Terrence and Reena. "Did you guys inform Daniel?" he asked.

"No," said Reena, "it would've taken too much time. But I'm hoping this ruse will work. It's a good thing that Terrence didn't have to wake up Mr. Decessio. If he had, then the Networkers would have been alerted, and the Curaie would have their latest excuse to make our lives miserable, and that would be double for you. They can't know—"

"They already do," said an unfamiliar voice that turned Jonah's and Reena's heads in surprise.

There was a woman in the corner, who hadn't been there before. She was about Reena's height, looked to be in her late thirties, and surveyed them with stern eyes behind square-fashioned glasses. Her coat looked windswept, which signified the Astralimes. The new appearance was shocking, but Reena recovered first.

"Hello," she said uncertainly. "Who are you?"

"Name's Dace Cross," said the woman. "I'm not surprised to see you again, Blue Aura."

Jonah frowned, but then his face relaxed somewhat. "I do know you," he said slowly. "You were in the Median that day that I had to meet with the Curaie."

Dace nodded. "Yes. And you flew off the handle at Katarina."

Jonah blew off that last part. "Are you a Networker?"

"No," said Dace.

Jonah snorted. This lady looked like a retired librarian; she didn't look the least bit hardcore.

"I was discharged at the beginning of my third campaign because I enjoyed violence too much."

Oh.

"So what do you do, ma'am?" asked Reena. "You may not be a Networker, but you definitely work for the Curaie in some significant capacity."

"Oh, I do Ethereamency," mumbled Dace.

"Huh?" said Jonah.

"I am one of the ones who scrub Eleventh infractions from Tenth public records," clarified Dace.

"They've got people for that?" said Jonah, puzzled, "then why did—?"

Reena kicked him, hard, underneath the table. Jonah swallowed his exclamation.

Dace raised her eyebrows. "Why did what?"

"Why did—it take so long for you to get here?" finished Jonah rather lamely. He had been about to say that if the Curaie had a branch of Spectral Law that handled those matters, then why did Patience bail him out back in Southern Shores? But after Reena's kick, he wondered whether or not Patience's favor was widely known. If Dace learned that, it just might send the wrong message.

The woman didn't look convinced in the slightest, but she didn't speak on it. "Because you have a problem," she responded. "Normally, a fancy-looking badge and bogus credentials are enough, but you didn't know when to quit."

"What are you talking about?" said Jonah.

"You played an insane man, didn't you?" asked Dace.

"Huh?" Jonah blurted out, and Reena grimaced.

"Figured," said Dace. "You did too good of a job, Blue Aura. And using your endowment to kill the camera? Overkill."

"Wait, that wasn't Jonah's idea," said Reena loyally. "That one was my suggestion. It's on me."

"A suggestion you wouldn't have had to make if he hadn't gotten you all into that situation at that house," countered Dace. "So actually, it's all on him."

Jonah's blood warmed. And he'd just calmed down. "Is there a point to this?" he grunted.

"Your nut job act was a very convincing performance," said Dace in a cold tone. "You really rattled that Feldman guy out there. But when the camera went out, he began to fear for her," she threw a finger Reena's way, "and he called a criminal psychologist."

"He did what?" exclaimed Reena.

"I'm not crazy!" spat Jonah.

"No," said Dace in the wintry tone again, "you just have a gift for acting as though you are."

Jonah stood up, but Reena clamped onto his arm before he could jerk free.

"Who is it?" she asked Dace. "The criminal psychologist?"

"Oh, you'll find out soon enough," said Dace, her tone warmer for whatever reason. "Do yourself a favor, woman. Get your pal waiting down the corner, and get back to the estate. I'll even see to it that your numerous unauthorized Astralimes will be considered actions under duress. I no longer think that assisting the Blue Aura is a prudent action. He should be left to the ether."

Jonah's eyes widened in fury, and he tried to step forward, but he didn't have the positioning or the leverage to break Reena's grasp. She probably did that for a reason.

"The ether?" demanded Reena. "I'm not abandoning my friend!"

Dace shook her head sadly, and then regarded Jonah after stealing a glance at Reena's grip on his wrist. "Spirits among us," she murmured. "You need to find yourself some dignity, woman. Falling on swords for stupid men will get you nowhere."

Now it was Reena who moved forward, freeing Jonah in the process. He boxed his anger long enough to realize that what might happen next wouldn't bode well.

"Reena, no!" he cried while he restrained her.

Reena struggled herself, but Jonah had it under control. When they first met, such an exploit would have been laughable, but Jonah had gotten smaller in the gut and bigger in the arms since that time. Reluctantly, Reena was forced to yield.

Dace shook her head. "Pray to whoever you pray to," she said, a bizarre urgency in her voice, "because you're about fresh out of miracles, Blue Aura."

With a step back and a gust of wind, the woman was gone. Reena growled in frustration.

"That bitch had some nerve!" she snapped. "Why did you stop me?"

"Would have looked a tad bit messed for us both if my legal counsel got into a fight with a representative of the Curaie," said Jonah. "See what raw emotion does?"

Reena stepped back from Jonah and straightened her blazer. "Point," she grumbled. "Now I wonder who this—?"

The door opened, and it became a good thing that Jonah had parted from Reena. Had they still been entangled, there was no telling how Feldman would have reacted. As it was, he opened the door while looking in another direction.

"Right in here, sir," he was saying as he opened the door.

"Thank you," said a steady, firm voice.

Jonah didn't recognize the voice, but Reena's eyes widened. Her anger was replaced by what looked like terror.

"What, Reena?" whispered Jonah, but the new arrival entered the room, and eliminated all need to ask Reena why she looked so afraid.

Because now he was as well.

The new arrival was Balthazar Lockman.

"Lockman?" said Jonah loudly. "The cult dude?"

He probably should have remained silent. Maybe even feigned ignorance. He was supposed to be insane, after all. But once he looked into those gray eyes, his mouth moved fast than his brain could check it.

Lockman's eyes gleamed, but his expression didn't change. Feldman's eyes narrowed again.

"How would you know that?" he asked. "I'm starting to wonder if you're actually crazy."

"There, there, Ralph," said Lockman, which raised Jonah's eyebrows again. Lockman was on a first name basis with the police officer? "His lucidity may be present now, but it could very fade soon."He turned to Jonah. "I am indeed a cult buster," he said, "but I am a criminal psychologist as well. That was my profession before I went into Congress. And you," he narrowed his eyes at Reena, "you're his legal counsel, so you said? Leave your contact information with Irma at the desk, along with the name of your firm. Now go."

Reena had no choice, but Jonah saw muscles working in her face. Very slowly, she left the room. Feldman gave her another appraising look, which Jonah hoped that she caught on her way out.

"Get on to the church now, Ralph," said Lockman in an oddly paternal voice. "And tell Liv I wish I could have seen her solo."

"Absolutely, sir," said Feldman.

They shook hands, and Jonah saw it. It was smoother than silk, but he saw it.

Lockman gave Feldman money.

Jonah didn't know how much, and he didn't care. But that handshake play was the oldest trick in the book. Jonah knew that now; hanging around Spader always gleaned useful gems.

Lockman closed the door, and though his expression didn't change, his eyes hardened. "Now we can dispense with this coy shit," his voice remained calm, "Jonah."

Jonah felt dampness on his palms. At the moment, he was just glad that he hadn't uttered, "Huh?" "How are you here?" he asked. "Why are you here?"

"Dexter City, Maryland is my home," said Lockman, who lowered himself into the seat Reena had had earlier. "I was born here, and I still live here. When I'm not going across the country outing scum, of course."

Jonah gritted his teeth in disgust. Prodigal sure did know how to pick a town. But then again, Creyton probably knew that this was

Lockman's hometown. He started to wonder just how far Creyton's little scheme was supposed to reach.

"Before you say anything else," warned Lockman, "I know your supposed mental issues are bullshit, so we can dispense with that as well."

Jonah shrugged to show an indifference that he didn't feel. "I've got nothing to hide," he said in a terse tone.

"Oh, I know several people who would disagree with that," replied Lockman. "Namely, my dear friend Wyatt Faulk."

"You mean the Peeping Tom?" said Jonah.

"I mean the assault victim who happened upon some very questionable things," said Lockman. "For example, why is there such a focus on people's aura colors at that dwelling place?"

Jonah's stomach flipped, but he kept his face neutral. "We didn't invent that," he said carelessly. "That notion's been around a long time."

"True," conceded Lockman, "but how does it tie in with carrying weapons that supposedly gleam with these aura colors?"

Yow. Faulk had seen people training? How? Daniel and Jonathan had forbidden outside training for this very reason. "I have no idea what you're talking about," said Jonah.

Lockman's demeanor hadn't changed at all. It was almost like the possessed tendencies of a cyborg; cool, in control, unflappable. For that reason, Jonah paid attention to his eyes. There was plenty of emotion there, and no warmth whatsoever. Finally, he nodded. "Okay," was all he said. "Who is Daniel?"

Jonah had clamped his tongue between his teeth because he didn't want to betray anything. At this question, he released it slowly so as to not reveal any tells or twitches. "The Overseer of the estate," he answered.

"Is that a fact?" Lockman's voice rose slowly to convey curiosity. "Daniel is the overseer, you say?"

"Uh-huh."

"Then who is Jonathan?"

"Huh?"

Jonah could have sworn. Lockman did it so expertly. He lured Jonah in with that false notion of leisurely inquiry, and then dealt a hammer blow to his already shaky shell of security. Jonah had to remember that the guy had a background in this type of thing. He wasn't going after information for his health. He'd attempted to keep his answers short and sweet just like in the movies, and Lockman adapted, and switched tacks. So Jonah tried something else.

"You've confused me," he experimented. "Daniel… Jonathan… forgive me, but you're dropping names in freefall here. Who is Jonathan supposed to be?"

Lockman stared at Jonah a full six seconds, and then laughed. It was his first full show of emotion. It was neither boisterous nor jovial. It was full of certainty, with just a faint trace of coolness. It was a laugh that Jonah knew very well. It was reminiscent of a teacher who just knew that they'd caught a student in a lie. They had right on their side for no other reason than the fact that they were the one in authority. And because of that, they were content with being entertained by watching the student attempt to wriggle themselves out of said lie. It was juvenile. It was manipulative.

And it was sufficient enough fuel to stoke the kindling already smoking in Jonah's consciousness. Didn't Felix always say use anger as a tool?

"What are you trying to pull, Lockman?" he demanded. "You came in here on a bright Sunday morning, missing some little girl's church solo in the process. You threw around credentials that you probably haven't traded on in years, which didn't look necessary, because these people defer to your every whim. You did all that just to see little ol' me? Why is that? Are you trying to trap me? Are you trying to get me to drop some incriminating gems? Have a slip of the tongue? I hate to say it, but you're going to be disappointed. I'm not guilty of anything, and the other residents at the estate aren't, either. I'll tell you who is guilty of something, though. You are. And your little bit player, Faulk. And whoever else you've had spying on us. So you can kill this therapeutic invasion of privacy right now."

Lockman still hadn't flinched. Jonah had been defiant, insubordinate, and Lockman hadn't even shown aggravation. What was this man's angle?

Very calmly, Lockman picked up an ink pen that he'd lowered next to the pad where he'd been jotting down notes. He slowly ran his left forefinger over an imperfection in the plastic near its tip. "Tell me, Jonah," he said softly, "what is the Eleventh Percent?"

Jonah felt his face go cold; he hoped that he hadn't paled. That was leftfield. Unexpected. A very unpleasant shock. "What is—?"

"—the Eleventh Percent, yes," finished Lockman.

Jonah stared. It was either that or dart his eyes here and there like the cornered person that he was. "Sounds like—some kind of progressive rock band to me," he said, instantly wincing. That was the best he had?

Now Lockman's face changed, if only slightly. The impassive expression morphed into incredulous one. "A progressive rock band," he said in a voice that clearly translated to, 'Is this idiot serious right now?'

"Hey," said Jonah with a shrug, "they've got some funky names nowadays. I've even heard of one that call themselves The Incline Down—"

"Enough." It was quick and sharp, and it stamped out Jonah's rambling. "I have heard enough. All I need to hear for the moment, actually."

"What are you talking about?" asked Jonah hastily. "I've barely told you anything!"

"Quite the contrary, Jonah," said Lockman, and just like that, the impassive expression was back. "You see, what we hear is invaluable, but combined with what we see? That's a mighty force. I haven't just been listening to the things you've said, I have also been observing. Your callous exterior, terse responses, selective deafness, and instant proclivity to be apoplectic when cornered? All followed by the jocular assumption that you made just now? That all told me a great deal. It's something we, to use your phrasing—therapeutic invaders refer to as the truth behind the words."

Jonah frowned.

"I wouldn't expect you to understand," said Lockman matter-of-factly. "It's clear that you lack complexity and restraint. All you need to understand is that the time of sending representatives to that estate of yours has now ended. The matter now gets my personal attention."

Before Jonah could respond, and undoubtedly dig himself deeper, the door opened once more, and Jonah was relieved to see someone he trusted.

"Pardon me, sir," said Patience respectfully while showing a badge to Lockman, "I'm Officer Corbett. This man is a North Carolina resident, and will be extradited back there post-haste."

Lockman looked at Patience's badge, then at Jonah, and then back at Patience. He gave Patience a smile that missed his eyes by many miles. "How very convenient," he said quietly. "Carry on then, officer."

Patience beckoned to Jonah, and Jonah walked his way, thankful to get out of this godforsaken room. He was at the door when Lockman cleared his throat.

"I'll see you all very soon, Jonah," he said, even bothering to follow it with a little wave.

Jonah couldn't get out of this place fast enough.

"Thanks man—" he began, but Patience muttered, "Shut up. Not in the police station."

There wasn't anger in his voice. It was simply warning.

At a very expedited pace, they left the station and walked to an unmarked car that bore North Carolina tags.

"How did you find out about this?" asked Jonah.

Patience lowered himself into the car. "Jonathan," he said simply.

Jonah frowned. Huh. "How nice of him. Where are Terrence and Reena?"

"Around the corner," answered Patience. "It would have been really suspicious if we were all together."

Patience drove at a slow enough pace to avoid suspicion, but then picked up speed once they were clear of the place.

"Patience, there was another Curaie rep in there," Jonah informed him. "Woman named Dace Cross. She came to scrub me from the Tenth records or something, but decided that she didn't like me and left me to hang—"

"I'm aware of it all, Jonah," interrupted Patience, "I've handled it. You'll be losing your spiritual endowment in a few, so just relax."

Patience spoke in such a distracted manner that Jonah stared.

"What's wrong with you?" he asked.

"Whole new ballgame, Jonah," said Patience. "We are now on the other side."

"What?" said Jonah, eyes wide with concern for the Networker. "Like the Other Side of life?"

"No, boy," said Patience, rather impatiently. "The other side... of sanity."

14

When Worlds Collide

Patience reached Terrence and Reena, who seemed to have been waiting rather anxiously, and allowed them into the car. Terrence still looked slightly aggravated about Jonah's actions, but was relieved to see him safely out of the police station. Jonah glanced back at Reena and frowned.

"Lockman told you to leave your name and the name of your firm with the receptionist," he recalled. "How did you get out of that?"

"That flirtatious dumbass, Feldman," muttered Reena. "He said that he truly didn't want to see 'that loon's' crazy lies drag down anyone else. He told me to just walk away, head back to my firm, and he was certain that Lockman would deal with you."

Jonah turned and faced the road. Even though the insanity had been a ruse, it was annoying to hear himself described like that. And Lockman was supposed to "deal" with him, was he?

"Reena said something about an Ethereamency specialist showing, and then abandoning you," said Terrence coldly. "What the hell was the point of her even showing her face?"

Jonah felt his fingers dig into his knees. "She claimed to have been intending to help me, but then said her hands were tied when I played crazy and they called Lockman," he grumbled. "She had it in for me anyway; apparently making Katarina cry left a sour taste in her mouth concerning me—"

"You shouldn't judge her too harshly, Jonah," said Patience suddenly. "Dace has had her share of misfortune."

"Haven't we all?" said Jonah, unmoved.

Patience gave Jonah a stern look. "Dace began her first campaign when I did, and was discharged a third of the way through it."

"So she said," replied Jonah. "What for?"

"She killed a Spirit Reaper," said Patience.

"That can't possibly have been the first time that happened with Spectral Law," said Terrence.

"In front of the Spirit Reaper's ten year old son," added Patience quietly.

Jonah tensed. Terrence gave an awkward, "Oh."

"She is a rehabilitated Eleventh," said Patience. "Ethereal emotional management—that is a team of spirits who monitor our emotional states—saw to that. But she's come to despise reckless behavior."

"Wonderful," muttered Jonah. "So the impression is that I'm a reckless, bumbling fool. She paints me with that brush based on her past. Does everyone have some backstory in their history? Because this is getting tiresome—"

"Everyone does have a story in their history, Jonah," said Patience, "which is why it helps abundantly to understand people before you judge them."

"Yeah," Jonah shot back, "because everyone has been doing that for me."

"Jonah, perpetuating things only puts you even with people," said Patience. "I didn't help you just now only because you are an Eleventh, but because you're a great kid who's in a bad way. I could have judged you just based on the mistakes you made tonight and left you there to be fodder for Lockman, but I didn't. Think about it."

Jonah placed his left thumb and forefinger to each temple and gathered the flesh at the forehead. Were these lecture annoying because of their frequency, or because they were right? "What about the suuvus?" he asked.

Patience looked angry himself. "There was nothing that could be done," he said.

"You mean you were too late?" asked Terrence.

"Punctuality was immaterial," murmured Patience. "The suuvus was so eager to be a minion that he—nursed it along."

Jonah was confused. Reena spoke.

"Drugs?" she asked.

Patience made a wry face. "He would have passed away before the Deadfallen disciples had gotten to him. But when Charles and Marlowe had gotten there, his spirit had already been usurped."

Jonah shook his head. The poor, deluded fool. He had had no idea that Creyton wasn't ever going to hold his end of the bargain, and that there would be no more minions. He had even had a hand in ending his own physical life, only to be betrayed immediately after he started the next one. He almost pitied him, but then remembered that the guy had tried to get them all killed.

"Here is something I'm not understanding," Jonah said slowly, "Felix and Prodigal have both confirmed that Creyton is sending envoys to the sazer underground. And now he is granting vampires the opportunity to get off of his shit list? I'm not surprised that he would work both sides of the street—that's not it. But just say he brought both factions into his control. How would he control them? They're natural enemies."

"I was thinking about that myself," said Reena. "One would think that Creyton would have the good sense not to allow such dangerous and unstable elements into his regime."

"You kids are very intelligent," complimented Patience, "but still very young. Duplicity, like everything else, has its layers. Creyton could have disciples in both camps and neither camp would be the wiser. Remember, he has had decades of practice with playing people."

Jonah slammed his fist on his thigh. "If only that was all we had to worry about," he groused. "But Lockman has to be in the picture, too."

"I was waiting till we got to that scum," spat Terrence. "What all did he say to you?"

Jonah rearranged his weight in the passenger seat, scowling. "Well, I suppose that we have plenty of time, given that we have to trek from Maryland to Rome—"

"No, actually," said Patience. "Here is where we stop."

They had just passed a sign that said, *You Are Now Leaving Dexter City, We Pray For Your Hasty Return!*, and Patience immediately turned down a dirt road, pausing at an overgrown bend where the resolute clumps of grass and weeds actually shifted the car. The Networker put the car in park and exited without even turning the car off. Jonah, Terrence, and Reena followed him in confusion.

"Why exactly are we here?" asked Terrence.

"This is away from prying eyes," answered Patience, who looked around to double check this fact. "Plus, this is a good enough place to use the Astralimes, seeing as it's where I found this wreck in the first place."

Jonah looked at the immaculate white unmarked car, then back at Patience. "You found this car here?" he asked. "That's…odd."

"What? Oh." Patience smirked. "I almost forgot."

He placed his left hand, palm down, on the driver's door. When he removed it, there was an unmistakable portion of rust that hadn't been there. The rust began to spread in all directions, and in seconds, not only was the door rusted, it actually began to crunch in on itself somewhat, like it had been smashed in a wreck, and fell to the ground.

Jonah backed away, stunned. Reena suddenly grinned, as if she understood something. Jonah returned his gaze to the decaying car, not understand anything.

The rust traveled on, across the now-mangled hood, the bashed-in trunk, and the grille. The entire car was now affected, and the interior was not spared, either. The steering wheel came detached and fell into the seat, which was now aged, split, and missing great chunks of interior foam.

The pristine vehicle was now a hollowed-out wreck. The process hadn't even taken two minutes.

"What the hell just happened?" asked Jonah.

"It was a Spectral Manifestation," Patience explained. "It was a means to an end."

"But," Jonah circled the jalopy with wide eyes, "but we were just riding in this thing!"

"Yeah," said Patience, oblivious to Jonah's shock. "Again, it was a means to an end. Now let's proceed, so I can get you on back to the estate."

* * *

They were back at the estate within two steps, and there was already a reason to be tense.

Trip sat near a mimosa tree, a cigarette between his lips. Douglas and the sazer boy Nicodemus seemed to be arguing with them.

"But you could do something!" Douglas shouted at Trip. He was so passionate about whatever had angered him that sweat created a giant U-shape down the front of his gray button down. "You could tune a radio frequency to level things out, or something!"

Trip blew out the smoke carelessly. "I could, couldn't I?" he murmured.

Douglas roared in frustration. "Would it kill you to be show some humanity?" he demanded of Trip.

"In this case, yes it would," sneered Trip.

Nicodemus growled somewhere in his throat. "What is your problem, man?" he snarled. "Why can't you be cooperative?"

Trip flicked away the cigarette and made to light a new one. "I'll be cooperative," he said nastily/ "I'll be a paragon of cooperation, in fact—when you and the rest of the accidents are out of my home."

Nicodemus swatted the cigarette out of Trip's hand. "Call me and my friends accidents again, and I'll—"

Trip stood up, eyes on the reckless sazer. The boy slowly collapsed to his knees, like a heavy weight was on his shoulders. Seconds later, he was flat on the ground, writhing under some invisible weight. Trip just glared down at him.

"You'd better mind who you speak to like that, asswipe," he whispered. "Not everyone is intimidated by the fact that you're one of nature's mistakes."

"Trip, that's enough!" cried Douglas. "Come on, man!"

By that time, Jonah, Terrence, Reena, and Patience reached the fracas. Trip saw them first, and scowled.

"Oh Lord," he grumbled. "The fun continues."

"Let that boy free, Titus!" commanded Patience.

Trip regarded Patience. "I'm merely defending myself," he murmured. "Little bitch was going to attack me."

"Now." Patience was steadfast.

Trip rolled his eyes. "What the hell ever."

Nothing visible occurred, but suddenly Nicodemus was able to lift his weight. He came back to his feet, staring at Trip with the purest of loathing. Trip, on the other hand, looked bored.

"What is going on here?" asked Patience in a clear attempt to break the tension.

Douglas rounded on them. "That girl is having the baby!"

Reena swore silently. Terrence's eyes bulged.

"But she isn't due for weeks!"

"Well, the kid didn't get the memo!" exclaimed Douglas. "And Trip won't help!"

"Damn right I won't," agreed Trip. "They're made of tougher material anyway, right?"

"Jael is an Eleventh!" snapped Jonah.

"Oh." Trip looked just as indifferent as Nicodemus looked angry. "Want me to give her a cookie?"

"To hell with you," barked Nicodemus, who turned and ran into the estate, presumably to go back to Jael's bedside.

"Jonah," said Reena quickly, and she seemed to be holding on to her own anger by the merest of threads, "put your frustration into a more helpful outlet. We'll do what we can to help, Doug. Is Liz up there?"

"Yeah," nodded Douglas. "Nella, too."

"Great." Reena threw a final nasty look at Trip. "Let's get up there. You too, Terrence."

"I'm..." Terrence shook his head. "I—I'm good, actually—"

Reena grabbed his wrist.

"Aw, no!" he cried. "Come on, Reena! I ain't built for no babies!"

The tense group left the indifferent Trip and Patience at the tree and went up to the infirmary. When they got there, the hallway was full of people; estate residents and sazers alike.

"What are you all doing out here?" demanded Reena.

"We all tried to help," said Alvin, "but Liz ran us all out! She said something about too many cooks in the kitchen or whatever. I guess you had no luck with Trip, Dougie?"

Douglas' frosty silence answered the question for everyone. At that moment, Spader came up the stairs, towels in tow. Liz met them at the door, face flushed and hair a mess.

"Good, Spader!" she gasped. "I knew that you were good for something!"

"Hey!" snapped Spader, but she tugged the towels out of his hand and turned to Doug.

"I knew asking Trip for help was a long shot," she said resignedly, "but thank you anyway, Doug."

"I don't deserve your thanks." Douglas looked as though he'd let Liz down. "I didn't do anything. Imbecile didn't even put out his cigarette. But can I do anything?"

"Just get the heralds," said Liz, "they will see to it that the baby's spirit entity smoothly transitions into physical life."

Doug tore off downstairs, and Liz finally noticed the new arrivals. Her eyes filled with gratitude and hope.

"Thank God," she cried. "Come on in! The baby's coming any second—"

"Oh God Oh God Oh God," intoned Terrence, who sounded queasy. Jonah, not too certain himself, moved tentatively to the door, but got blocked.

"Oh hell no," said Nicodemus, who regarded Jonah with disdain. "She don't need your help."

That washed away some of Jonah's misgivings. He pushed the teenage sazer roughly to the side and stepped into the infirmary.

And the brief moment of resolution was gone just that quickly.

Prodigal was in the corner wringing his hands, while Stella Marie and Autumn Rose were at Jael's bedside. Jael, sweating buckets and clearly in unfathomable agony, kept uttering loud exclamations. Nella was the head of the bed, dabbing Jael's forehead with a cloth that had some sort of purple ointment on it. Jonah didn't know how she remained centered, but she did it pretty well.

"What are you doing?" he asked over Jael's screams.

"No idea!" said Nella. "Liz just told me to do it!"

"It's an herbal tonic," answered Liz for her sister. "It's being absorbed into Jael's pores. "I'm curing her."

"What?" Autumn Rose's head shot up. "What are you curing?"

Liz took a deep breath. "Jael has a condition called eclampsia," she answered. "I thought it was gestational diabetes, but I figured out my mistake."

"E-what?" said Jonah.

"Why the hell are we talking about an eclipse?" asked Terrence.

"Eclampsia?" cried Reena in horror. "Do you know how rare that is?"

"I'm a Green Aura, Reena," said Liz, aggravated.

"Oh, yeah." Reena looked foolish for a few seconds. "Right you are."

"What does that mean?" cried Stella Marie. "I've never even heard of that!"

"It's a pregnancy complication characterized by intense headaches and higher blood pressure, among other things," muttered Liz, who placed green-gleaming hands over Jael's belly. "It's why her mobility was so bad."

Now Prodigal moved to the group. "Jael's been complaining about migraines for days," he said. "That's why we broke into that house, because we didn't want her dealing with that outside on the dirt."

"Wh—wh—wh—" attempted Jael laboriously, "what about my baby?"

"Time will tell, Jael," said Liz, "but I want to take care of both of you."

"I don't care about me!" the girl gasped. "Just please take care of my baby!"

"I will take care of both of you," repeated Liz, her usually sunny voice firm. "And your eclampsia is healing. I just want it completely gone before the baby comes. Three minutes max, and we'll be good."

"Wait." Autumn Rose seemed to have come to a realization. "You mean if that crazy Eleventh there hadn't gotten in our business at the house, Jael might have—?"

"I won't be presumptuous enough to say that for certain," interrupted Liz, whose face looked more optimistic when she scanned around Jael's face. "But there was a possibility."

Autumn Rose looked at Jonah slowly, like she was stunned. But then, quick as a flash, it passed.

"Doesn't change anything," she told him. "You still pissed me off."

Jonah shrugged, and turned to Liz. "What's in the tonic on that rag?"

Liz placed her hands methodically, almost reverently, on Jael's belly, and then smiled. "It was magnesium sulfate," she said, "and it worked! The eclampsia is gone! Reena, help me!"

Jonah looked at Liz in confusion. "What do you want *me* to do?"

"Is this a question, Jonah?" cried Liz.

Jonah sighed. Of course it wasn't a question. He just wanted the privilege of having the last traces of his denial wrenched away. And Liz had done just that. Swell.

He went to the side of the bed near Nella and Stella Marie, because he had no desire to be near Autumn Rose. When Jael caught sight of him there, her agonized face hardened even further.

"I'm not talking to you," she spat. "You're a reckless nutjob."

Jonah grimaced. "Maybe I had that coming," he conceded, "but I was only trying to help you guys. Like I've been asked to do now."

"I need you to push, Jael!" cried Liz.

Jael's face scrunched up as more sweat poured from her brow.

"I'm going to try to balance out your pain while Liz and Reena deliver the baby," said Jonah loudly. "I'm the Blue Aura, so—"

"I know what the Blue Aura powers are," snarled Jael. "You're supposedly a big deal, right—?"

She cried out in pain.

"Keep it cruising, Jael!" encouraged Reena. "We're nearly in the home stretch!"

Breathing harsh and ragged, Jael turned her teary, scarlet eyes on Jonah. "You want to help me, Blue Aura? Hold my hand."

Like a fool, Jonah extended his hand. That was a simple enough task, right?

"Jonah, no!" shrieked Liz, but it was too late.

The second Jael wrapped her long fingers around Jonah's hand, she experienced another contraption. When she tensed, Jonah could have sworn that her hand transformed into a steel pincer, because that was what it felt like when she tightened her grasp.

Jonah was hurling just as many expletives as Jael during that period, while also trying to ignore the cracking that he swore he heard from his hand. He tried to wrench it free, but the more he yanked, the tighter Jael clamped. It actually reached the point where Jonah was pleading in a very graphic manner for Jael to let go of his hand—

Then, praise God, the air was pierced by the sound of a baby's crying. Autumn Rose gave a cry of pure delight, and then Jael freed Jonah.

"There," she exhaled. "That was for last night. Now we're even."

Jonah looked at his reddened, damaged hand, and then glanced back at the new mother in the room. "Now...we're even," he grumbled. He glanced at Reena, who looked like she was going to be sick.

"The smell," she murmured. "I need to sit down for a moment."

Now that she mentioned it, he could smell what she was talking about. However, he was too distracted by his hand to have cared about it.

"Wait, Reena." Liz grabbed at her shoulder. "You need to hold the baby so I can get Jael to push the afterbirth out, or else, if kept in, it will cause great damage."

Reena didn't look like she wanted to, on account of being sick and all. But she managed a smile and said, "Sure."

She held the baby in a small towel that didn't cover him much. She almost looked like a natural holding the baby.

Almost.

The sound of a trash bag being shook out caught Jonah's attention, and he had to face away for what came next.

"One last push, Jael," encouraged Liz, "then you're through."

As Reena was holding the baby, he was fussy. So she started walking around. She went to Terrence, as he was the closest, so she could show the baby off to him. When she did, they all burst out laughing, except for Terrence. He grumbled something incoherent as he ran a sleeve across his face.

"Sorry, about that, Terrence," Reena smirked.

She returned to Liz as she finished up her previous task. Liz took the boy, swaddled him into a cocoon of cloth, and handed him to his mother. Looking apprehensive, Jael cradled him. Jonah looked around, and saw Reena in a mental conference with the heralds, with Bast at the forefront. He hadn't even heard Douglas return with them. It must have happened when he experienced his hand getting crushed like a soda can. Her own work done, Nella handed Jonah an Ace bandage from a healing satchel. She did so almost on autopilot.

"You alright, Nella?" he asked, distracted.

Nella blinked rapidly, as though she couldn't quite recall how to articulate her thoughts and feelings through speech. She looked at Jonah, and for a moment, she resembled the girl he remembered before the summer growth spurt. "I—I'm fine," she finally whispered. "I'm... good."

Jonah got a savage pleasure out of Nella's shock. Maybe he wouldn't have to talk to her about Dylan after all.

But then she ruined the party when she said, "I need to call Dylan," and fled the room.

"May I ask what you're going to name him?" questioned Liz.

"Addington," said Jael without hesitation. "Addington Sebastian Vance."

Jonah raised an eyebrow. Terrence, still seething at the urine drying on his face and clothes, was taken aback as well.

"Nice," gushed Autumn Rose.

"Untouchable," smiled Stella Marie.

"Addington Sebastian?" said Douglas, his face caught somewhere between admiration and amusement. "That sounds almost dignified."

"That's the idea," murmured Prodigal.

Douglas made to ask another question, but Jonah shook his head. Mercifully, Douglas took the hint. Liz stood and smiled, but Jonah could tell that there was something forced about it.

"Jael, we're going to all step out and let all your friends here get acquainted with the new addition," she said, and with a pointed jerk of the head, Jonah, Reena, Doug, Spader, and Terrence followed her out. Surprisingly, Liz grabbed Prodigal by the wrist and pulled him out of the infirmary as well. Once they were in the hall, her contrived smile faded.

"Prodigal, did you know how sick Jael was?" she whispered.

Prodigal's eyes bulged. "No, I didn't. You said she was okay!"

"She is okay now," said Liz. "But when she first got here, I didn't know what to think. It took her having a mild seizure for me to realize what was going on! Had she had any of those before? In addition to the headaches?"

"A few," answered Prodigal. "But I thought that they were because of malnutrition or something—"

"No," said Liz. "Not even. I'm glad I thought of the Epsom salt, because it was the only source if magnesium sulfate I could find."

"Epsom salt?" said Jonah with a frown. "I know what that looks like, and it's not purple."

"Of course not, Jonah," said Liz. "I got Nella to mix some of it in. The purple stuff you saw was a stabilizing tonic to keep Jael from having a seizure during her delivery."

"Wait a second," said Douglas. "That's the reason why you sent me for the heralds. You wanted to keep Jael's spirit in place just as much as the baby's!"

Liz nodded. "I had to be sure."

"That's what I was communicating with the heralds about," said Reena. "Bast intimated to me that if Jael had remained in that house in Maryland, she may very well have passed into Spirit."

"Yeah," concurred Liz, who had settled against the wall now that her adrenaline had faded. "I'm just estimating here, so I'm giving or taking a digit. Without healing and proper ministrations, she'd have had a ten percent chance of surviving her childbirth."

Spader ran a finger across his forehead. "A tenth of a chance," he said.

"That's not what I said—" began Liz, but Spader waved her off.

"Close enough," he muttered.

With that revelation, Jonah looked Prodigal in the eye. "You still mad at me?" he asked point-blank.

"I had been," the sazer boy admitted. "You really did put us in danger, Jonah. But after what Liz just said, and after what Jael did to your hand, I'd say you've redeemed yourself."

Jonah nodded, relieved. The other sazers were strangers—he could live with their consternation. But Prodigal was his friend. "So what happens now?" he asked the young sazer. "She can't stay on the road with you guys. You know that, right?"

"Please tell me," said Terrence, "how did an Eleventh wind up on the road with sazers? No offense at all, I'm just curious."

"Jael has adoptive parents in Silver Springs," explained Prodigal. "That's why we were in Maryland in the first place."

"Did you know that the cult buster lived in the town where you guys were crashing?" asked Reena.

"Lockman lives in Dexter City?" asked Douglas, distracted.

"Later for that," said Jonah, putting the focus back on Prodigal, who continued.

"We thought they—they being Jael's parents—would be supportive now—"

"So they're like that, huh?" said Terrence viciously.

Jonah placed a calming hand on his best friend's shoulder. There was no point ruminating about the past.

"No no," said Prodigal. "They were great to Jael. It was Autumn Rose that they didn't care for. She doesn't even really mesh well with Elevenths, so Jael's Tenth adoptive parents? Forget it. Then Jael got pregnant, freaked out, and ran away. She made contact with Autumn Rose and the rest of us in the sazer underground."

"So I'm assuming that she ran right before she began to show," surmised Jonah. "But why did she run?"

"She was afraid of her parents' reaction," said Prodigal. "Jael was about to make them the youngest grandparents in their community, and she was afraid of shaming them. She didn't want to do that, because they've been so good to her."

"So what?" snapped Terrence. "Shaming them—they brought that girl into their family. They should support her! As for that shame notion, they're just going to have to drink some prune juice and let that shit go."

"Not every family is as wonderful as the Decessios, Terrence," Spader reminded him.

"Well, maybe they all ought to learn," Terrence grumbled.

Douglas snorted. "That's going to be a hell of a conversation when she sees her parents again," he said. "But her physical life is no longer in danger. Kudos, Liz."

Silence.

"Liz?" Douglas looked her way. "Wow."

That about it summed it up. Jonah had no idea how Liz had done it, but she'd fallen asleep while standing against the wall.

Everyone laughed, which jolted her awake. She looked around, wide-eyed and disoriented.

"What's up?" she said defensively. "I didn't fall asleep."

"Come on," chortled Douglas. "You may as well get some sleep, because that's exactly what Bobby will suggest if he sees you like this."

"I'm leaving, too," said Terrence. "I got to get this baby piss off of me."

With that, the tiny group dispersed, with Jonah and Reena in the direction of their rooms. Mere feet away, though, their path was blocked by Magdalena, who looked at Reena with an incredulous, hopeless look in her eyes.

"What's the matter with you?" asked Jonah.

Magdalena ignored him completely. She only had eyes for Reena. "Did you…just help to deliver a baby in my business suit?"

Jonah snorted. Reena's shoulders slumped.

"Right. I'm sorry, Magdalena. I'll put this into the cleaners. Hell, I'll buy you a new one!"

* * *

The members of the action-packed morning allowed themselves rest before they convened, once more, in the family room. Felix was present again, waiting to debrief with Prodigal as well as hear about Lockman. As usual, he and Trip were on opposite sides of the room. It was always best when volatile substances didn't mix, after all.

"Good afternoon, everyone," said Daniel, rolling an arrow in his finger as usual. "I believe that, before we discuss matters, there is good news to hear?"

"Yes!" said Liz, from her perch against Bobby's knees. "Jael has been completely cured of eclampsia, and successfully gave birth to a boy, and gave him the name Addington Sebastian. He is a red aura—"

"Do you have something to say, Trip?" said Felix coldly, making everyone start and stare at the pair of them. "Because all the teeth-grinding and sneering while Elizabeth is speaking is rather irritating."

"Oops," said Trip in a lazy voice. "It's just that I don't see how that's good news. What's that old saying? You should laugh at death and cry at birth?"

"Death isn't real," snapped Felix. "And that's a biblical quote, which is nothing but superstition and propaganda—"

"You don't believe, Felix?" asked Maxine.

"In God, yes, in religion, no," answered Felix. "End of story."

"And also the end of this bickering," said Daniel. "Felix and Titus, you will cease these tiresome displays. If you feel that strongly about things, you should go to the Glade and have it out, one on one. Jonathan taught both of you better than this."He turned back to Liz, ignoring Felix's look of discomfit and Trip's look of hate."Finish, Elizabeth," he practically commanded.

"What? Oh yeah." Liz had been taken slightly by surprise. "Addington is a red aura, and his spirit is a strong one. Jael has decided to return to her parents, and Patience agreed to assist with damage control."

"Wonderful," said Daniel, who gave that customary almost-smile. "Jonathan will be pleased to know that mother and son both came out unscathed."

"Speaking of Jonathan," said Jonah slowly, "where is he?"

"Right here," said the familiar voice.

Jonathan was near the fireplace, and many people smiled and greeted him. Jonah was not one of them. The Protector Guide gave him a meaningful look, like he might have sensed the coolness, but said nothing about it.

"I would like to hear your story firsthand, Jonah," he said. "I would like to know exactly what you know."

"Uh-huh," said Jonah, who felt a scowl pull at his face. Jonathan didn't ask about well-being. Didn't ask about the almost-assault charge, where he'd been abandoned by a member of the Curaie. He wanted to know what he knew. The odd thing was the fact that somewhere in Jonah's mind, he knew that he probably shouldn't interpret it that way, but he'd had a highly charged two days. Simple things like logic and reason didn't apply."Here it is, Jonathan."

He plunged into it all, from the Mindscope that affected everyone but how his own was the one that included a conversation with Creyton to the warning and the events that followed. He gave very little thought to the fact that some of this information was new to his friends, so he was surprised to hear gasps and sound of alarm when he spoke. Jonathan, by contrast, didn't move or speak. He didn't even blink. His very first movement at all was when Jonah reached Lockman.

"He gave that police officer money?" he asked quietly.

"Yep," said Jonah. "Apparently, they know each other well. Lockman asked about the man's kid."

Jonathan looked away. His grey eyes were blazing. "A bribery that you are in no position to prove," he muttered.

"Pretty much," said Jonah, who felt that a statement of the obvious helped nothing at all.

"And from the way that officer showed up when you attacked the suuvus, it seems like he had been tipped," said Daniel.

"Feldman seemed like his take on upholding the law was questionable," said Reena with disdain. "Not that I'm not glad to have had the way out, but he only did it because he thought I was beautiful."

"Please, Reena," said Terrence wearily. "This ain't the time to remind us of your hatred of men."

"I don't hate men," said Reena. "I just have no love for the stupid ones."

Jonathan tilted his head slightly, as if he paid little attention to the brief exchange that just occurred. He returned his eyes to Jonah. "And you say he knew about auras?"

"Jonathan," said Jonah, "he knew about Daniel."

"Means nothing," said Daniel, with true indifference. "He could have easily gotten my name from the cameraman. Besides, I am here to provide a physical presence in Jonathan's stead, anyway. If someone knows my name, whatever."

"Somehow, I knew you'd throw that at me, Daniel," said Jonah. "But here's the thing: Lockman knew about Jonathan, too."

Many heads turned Jonah's way. Even Trip's brow furrowed.

"He mentioned my name?" asked Jonathan quietly.

"Yeah, he did," said Jonah. "When I said Daniel was the overseer of the estate, he looked me straight in the eye and said, 'What happened to Jonathan?' "

"Jonah, why didn't you tell us that?" asked Patience.

"I was going to," said Jonah, "but then we got back here and got swept up in Jael's baby story."

He glanced at Jonathan, and noticed that his expression hadn't slipped. Either he was more concerned than he let on, or the information that Lockman knew about him already hadn't been a surprise. Jonah hoped that it was the former, because if Jonathan knew about Lockman and didn't warn them, that would be tantamount to betrayal.

"He also knew that ethereal steel reflects the colors of auras," he decided to reveal. "And he said that we now have his undivided attention."

"Just great," said Malcolm suddenly. "Jonathan, you decreased the population at the estate, have us training indoors, and have us modifying our conversations all in an effort to keep this man off our back, and now he's still going to drop the hammer on us?"

"Would have happened anyway," said Bobby. "I bet that it was always his plan. He was just looking for an excuse."

Jonah tightened his fists. "And he got it because of me."

"No, Jonah," said Jonathan firmly. "He got it because of Creyton."

When Jonathan said those words, Spader stood up.

"Hate to bring this up, and I mean that." The sincerity in his voice was genuine, for once. "But Jonah here said that Creyton told him someone dear to him was going to get wiped. He went to check on Prodigal after that warning, but we now know that was all one big trap. But Prodigal is still physically alive, as are the rest of the sazers. Hell, they even brought a baby into the world, so there is more life here than when we started."

Spader paused, like he truly didn't want to proceed. Liz scoffed.

"Spill it, Spader," she snapped.

Spader looked at her and sighed. "Fine. Since Prodigal is still alive, does that mean we're off the hook? Is the red streak gone from the Vitasphera?"

Liz's eyes widened, and Jonah's did the same. He hadn't thought of that.

Daniel looked at Jonathan, who said nothing for a few seconds. But when he finally spoke, it was with carefully measured precision.

"You pose a wonderful question, Royal," he said. "Let us find out."

Spader nodded, and headed for the stairs before he realized that Jonathan hadn't moved.

"Um, Jonathan?" he said uncertainly, but Jonathan concentrated on the coffee table...where the Vitasphera appeared.

Everyone crowded around it, looking hopeful—

But the hope faded.

The trace of scarlet remained.

"Damn," said Terrence.

"Jesus," said Reena.

"Yeah," said Bobby. "That's someone we all need right now."

Jonah said nothing. His mind was the most active thing at the moment. He thought of the miscommunication that Liz and Spader had after Jael had given birth, and wondered if Spader had been right.

Maybe someone around them only had a tenth of a chance.

15

The Power of Doubt

Jonah didn't think the summer would ever come to an end.

He actually didn't care that much for the summer months anyway, despite being a summer child. The hot months were for the teeny boppers, ne'er do wells, kids, and families on beach trips. He hadn't ever really gone through devil-may-care experiences, so he couldn't miss something he'd never had. But the thing he disliked the most about the summer was the thing that everybody else adored: the heat. He couldn't think clearly in thick, soupy warmth. His thoughts just didn't come together the way they needed to when it was hot. That had been a recurring theme throughout his life.

But this particular summer had just sucked. Between the Curaie, concerns over Creyton, and the added issue of Lockman, Jonah's thoughts were more convoluted than ever before. Plus, there was the unexpected issue of Nella. Her personality began to change the more she was with that boy Dylan. She quit HOSA, a clinical nursing program that had always been her pride and joy, because "it wasn't like it was going to lead to a job." She missed curfew a few times, but always explained them away as losing track of time. Jonah didn't know what to make of it, or what to say to her. Then again, he wasn't her father. Hopefully, Mr. Manville handled his business in that regard.

Jonah coasted through the remaining summer days, and spent as many weekends as he could at the estate, but, apart from seeing his friends, it wasn't enjoyable. Especially after Lockman made his next move.

"A realtor buddy of mine told me that the Lockman Association has rented out office space in Rome," June Mylteer told him one weekend that he visited the Decessios with Terrence. "God only knows what he plans to do from there."

Lockman's intentions became obvious very quickly. He and his goons began to make appearances all over town to ask the townsfolk questions about the "strange residents at the sprawling estate off of Highway 81." According to Terrence and Reena, a great deal of Rome's citizenry didn't know much about them, but the people that were known around town, like Liz the volunteer at the doctor's office, Bobby the football star, and Douglas (only because they knew his grandmother), all got glowing praise.

"That's good right?" asked Jonah during his next phone conversation with Reena. "He'll quickly discover that he won't have any legs to stand on, won't he?"

"If only it were that simple." Jonah had never heard Reena sound so pessimistic. "Balthazar Lockman is out for blood, Jonah. Especially after he discovered that you got out of the assault charge. He'll switch tactics soon, I'm sure of it."

Jonah didn't have to distract himself too much from the ongoing saga; he had more than enough to keep him busy in the city. S.T.R. always had steady business, which was something that kept a smile on Mr. Steverson's face. Jonah couldn't help but smile himself when he saw his boss interact with patrons, who always asked him about books that were popular in decades past. Some even didn't mind his occasional Vietnam stories. Mr. Steverson would cut the subject off rather quickly each time, but he always did so without a loss of composure.

"That man is on fire," said Harland one afternoon. "I don't know how he does it! He's knocking on sixty's door, and he gets around better than me!"

"That's an unfair comparison, Harland," Jonah reminded his colleague. "You've had two surgeries on your left knee."

"Mr. Steverson's had four," countered Harland. "Not to mention the back surgery. I can't blame my knee anymore."

Jonah snorted. "Maybe you ought to take up yoga."

Amanda had her baby, which, after the situation with Jael, Jonah was thankful to miss. Admittedly, the boy, Julian, was one of the most precious things he had ever seen. He also had quite a set of lungs on him.

"He does more crying than any child on earth!" Amanda told Jonah, Harland, and Mr. Steverson. "I consider arguing over the accounts a reprieve!"

Mr. Steverson calmly loped over to Julian, who was bawling and flailing his tiny fists, and gathered him expertly into his arms. The baby ceased crying at once. Amanda gaped at them.

"How did you do that?" she demanded.

Mr. Steverson smiled. "Just hold him up close," he told her. "Babies can always sense affection, and that's a soothing thing."

Amanda remained dumbfounded. "He did that so easily," she mumbled to Jonah and Harland. "I thought that this guy was a war veteran."

"I am, darling." Mr. Steverson had overheard every word. "I'm a war veteran who later became a husband and father of four daughters. There is no magic switch; you learn on the job. You'll do just fine, Amanda."

He made to return Julian to the stroller, but Amanda nearly hurt herself stopping him.

"No no," she pleaded. "Hold him for just a bit longer."

Harland laughed.

"What's so funny?" asked Jonah.

"Mr. Steverson has four daughters," he said. "No wonder he is so patient now."

Jonah enjoyed every day at S.T.R. His only problem was that when he left, he always saw the owner of Blood Oaths Tattoos, Bryce Tysinger, staring at him. The man always looked so fearful when he did so. Jonah simply didn't know what to make of it. Did his beard make him look like he was going to rob the place? Nah, that couldn't be it. The guy seemed timid and fidgety with most people—which was a personality that Jonah wouldn't expect from a tall, heavily inked guy—but it was only Jonah who got that particular look. Sometimes Jonah had half a mind to confront him, but he always decided against it. If he looked afraid, then trying to converse might just make him howl like Amanda's new son.

When Jonah focused on it, there were some things about the summer that were positive. But he still wasn't sad when the influence of autumn quietly bought up stock in summer's territory. It made the Curaie's forced arrangement more tolerable.

And Jonah enjoyed Vera's company.

She hadn't been wrong; the two of them being in the city together helped both of them a great deal. She went to the estate a couple of weekends without him, which was perfectly fine, but mostly she worked at The Stop. Jonah had even taken her some lunch a few times, since she didn't want to eat the greasy stuff that surrounded her every day, and she always paid him back, even when he insisted that it was on him. Given that disturbing night when they'd experienced Jessica's crow trick, they'd agreed that if one of them couldn't unwind alone, they were welcome to come to the other's place to hang out.

The funny thing was the fact that they wound up hanging out quite often.

It wasn't a big deal, though. It was just as comfortable conversing with Vera as it was Terrence and Reena, and sometimes more so. But there were times when Vera would look so concerned, so distant. And, if Jonah was honest about it, scared. During those times, though, he simply let her be. He didn't want to, but every time he felt the desire to pry, he stopped himself when he heard Reena's warning in his head.

Don't probe, don't pry, just support.

In Vera's presence, Jonah was even able to file away his recent aggravations.

But that got rattled one evening, near the tail end of summer.

It was September the sixteenth, and Jonah and Vera decided to spend the evening bingeing on *The Blacklist* over Chinese food. He knocked and she answered, concealing her scar with a few fingers, like she always did when her hair was pulled back.

"Oh, it's you." There was relief in her voice when she dropped her hand from her face.

"Of course it's me," laughed Jonah. "It wasn't like you didn't know I was coming!"

"What you got there?" Vera inspected the bag. "That's General Tso's, isn't it? You know I only eat—"

"Chicken and Broccoli?" Jonah pointed to the bottom container in his bag.

Vera eyed it and grinned. "Jonah, you are the best in the world."

Jonah mentally cheered. Vera was a woman of such simple tastes. It was quite refreshing.

"You can come on in and put that down." Vera backed away so as to let Jonah inside. "I'm wrapping up a Skype chat with Eden. Get comfortable, and I'll be right with you."

Jonah nodded once seated himself on Vera's couch which she went back into her bedroom. He began to spread their food out on her coffee table when a particularly loud commercial about some new smartphone came prompted him to mute the television. Unfortunately, that enabled him to overhear Vera's conversation. Not wanting to eavesdrop he raised the remote to un-mute the television, but he paused after he heard his own name.

"—Jonah guy you were telling me about?" The end of the sentence came from a woman whose voice Jonah hadn't ever heard. Eden, then.

"Yeah," said Vera in a nonchalant tone. "He stopped by to hang out."

There was a small bit of silence, then—

"So that's why you're on the fence about coming back to Seattle," said Eden slowly. "You've got a man."

"No, no." Vera's answer was hasty. "It's not like that, Eden...we're not like that. Jonah's my—my friend."

Jonah winced, suddenly overtaken by a feeling he couldn't quite place. He and Vera were indeed just friends. That was no secret. So why did it sound so off when Vera described him as such to Eden? He almost missed the next part.

"The two of you are just friends?" said Eden in a quiet voice. "The guy comes by your house regularly, and you talk about him a great deal, and he's just your friend?"

"People can do that, Eden," said Vera with a trace of impatience. "And why can't I watch TV and eat Chinese food with a pal of mine?"

"Is he aware of the pal designation?"asked Eden.

Damn, this woman's nosy, thought Jonah.

"Is he—Eden, why are you so concerned about it?" asked Vera.

There was silence again. When Eden spoke, it sounded genuine enough.

"Because I'm hoping that you aren't holding yourself back from the future that you deserve for a guy that's simply you're…pal," she told Vera. "If you guys aren't a couple, then there's no reason for you to still be in North Carolina."

Jonah felt a prickle of anger, but it was intermixed with confusion. Why did he feel this way? It didn't make sense. Vera describing him to her friend in such informal terms, and Eden making him sound like…like a hindrance, or a bane who'd gotten his hooks into Vera, just didn't feel right.

Was this how Vera felt after Jonah's encounters with Rheadne?

"I…I appreciate your concern, Eden." There was less certainty in Vera's voice than Jonah would have liked. "But this is truly none of your business. I have to go."

Jonah hurriedly un-muted the television and manufactured a neutral expression for when Vera walked into the living room. He looked over at her with a passable impression of polite curiosity.

"Everything cool?" he said with so much heartiness that he could have cursed.

Vera's eyes narrowed. "Did you hear all that?" she asked.

Jonah forced his face to morph into a frown. Man, this holding expressions was hard! "Hear all what? I've been out here, ready to see what Raymond Reddington is gonna do next!"

Vera gave him a questioning look, but then looked relieved and joined him on the couch. Shortly after that, she joined him in food and Netflix bingeing. Jonah was glad that she bought it, but was still confused by the way he felt.

But there was one thing he knew for sure.

He hated Eden Bristow.

* * *

Jonah pulled up at the estate very early on a Saturday morning about three weeks into fall. Autumn was taking hold nicely, and the cooler mornings were welcome.

A surprising sight, however, was Douglas Chandler. He was standing in the front yard, hitting golf balls into the trees. Jonah laughed. Douglas was a preppie to the core.

He stepped out of his car. Douglas hadn't even registered the presence of another person near him. Odd.

"Morning, Doug," said Jonah.

Douglas actually jumped a little, and looked around. Jonah's presence surprised him.

Once again, odd.

"Hey." Douglas' voice was so robotic that it wasn't even funny.

Jonah approached him, curious. "Something on your mind?"

"No."

"You don't want to talk about it?" pushed Jonah.

"No," said Douglas.

"You sure?"

"Yeah," muttered Doug, who hit another golf ball, which ricocheted off of a tree trunk. "I'm sure."

Jonah shrugged. "Suit yourself."

He headed for the door.

"Jonah?" called Douglas.

Jonah turned. "Yeah?"

"Do you consider me a man?"

Jonah blinked. "Um…I don't understand the question. Am I not supposed to?"

"I don't mean physically," said Douglas with impatience. "I mean…you know, through my actions."

"Actions?" Jonah repeated with a frown. "Doug, you've never done anything—"

Douglas' face fell. "There you go," he said as he returned to the golf balls. "The truth."

Jonah swore. He realized too late how his words would be interpreted. He returned to Douglas, but backed away just a bit, so as to avoid being struck with a golf ball by mistake. "I didn't mean it that way, man," he insisted. "I meant…I meant—"

"You meant that I am an unproven waste of skin," said Douglas. He looked angry, but it seemed to be more at himself than with Jonah. "They all agree with you."

"Who agrees?" queried Jonah.

"Everyone," answered Douglas.

Jonah cocked his head to the side. Suddenly, he realized what the problem just might be. "Everyone? Or just one?"

Douglas sighed, and placed his weight on the golf club. "Jonah, I love my grandmother," he said, "and I think that she just might be right about me."

"Concerning what?"

Douglas sighed again. "Jonah, the men in my family are all…I don't know, typical," he began. "Loggers, truck drivers, brick mason's laborers, that sort of thing. And they're also beer-swigging, manly men, if you catch my drift. And Grandma 'Dine adores them. Then there is me. I hate wearing jeans and flannel, and I like creases in my pants. I love graduate school. My favorite things are chess, golf, strategy, and re-watching *Downton Abbey* over and over again. Is any of that manly? What woman would want that? And on top of that, I'm a lousy Eleventh Percenter. God forbid I ever get into a real fight."

He made to swing at another ball, but Jonah snatched the club away.

"Doug, listen to me." His voice was stern. "Who you are is just fine. Can you imagine how sucky this world would be if we were all the same? You're as great an Eleventh as anyone in your family, as any one of us—"

"Now, Jonah, that one might be a stretch—"

"Shut up," said Jonah. "I ain't done yet. Your prowess on a chess board is second to none. You're getting your Master's Degree, man! In Urban Planning! And if you keep training, your ethereality will get better. The same is true for all of us. If you want to improve yourself, do it for you. Not some girl you might meet in the sweet by and by, not to match up with your brothers, uncles, and cousins, and certainly not for your grandma's approval."

Douglas still didn't look convinced. Jonah extended his golf club to him.

"Treat her opinion like one of those golf balls there," he suggested. "And smack it with this putter—"

"It's a nine-iron, actually," corrected Douglas.

"You see?" said Jonah with dramatics. "I didn't know that before! I just learned something because you were here to tell me!"

Jonah knew the "grasp at straws" technique was a long shot, but it was worth it. Douglas looked as though a little bit of the weight was off of his shoulders.

"I appreciate what you've said, Jonah." He sounded sincere. "Thank you. I still want the chance to prove my mettle, though."

"Be careful what you wish for, Doug." Now it was Jonah's turn to sound sincere. "Seriously."

Reena was feverishly sketching on a pad when Jonah found her. Conveniently enough, Terrence joined them soon after, with breakfast suitable to both of his best friends' tastes.

"Vittles!" he announced. "Jonah, there are some homemade bacon and sausage sandwiches with your name on them. That's your weekend treat, right?"

"You know me so well, brother!" Jonah unwrapped one of the greasy napkins and revealed the treasure within.

"And for you, Reena," chuckled Terrence, "I've got wheat-free, gluten free, and sugar free muffins. Eggs, butter—none of that's there, of course. You had better eat them up; I worked on them something fierce—"

"Muffins won't be enough," said Reena, who barely took her eyes off of her sketch. "Let me have one of those."

She pointed to something else on Terrence's platter that made both Jonah and Terrence look at her in alarm.

"Um, Reena?" said Terrence. "That's a bacon sandwich."

"I know."

"Pig bacon," said Terrence, "not turkey bacon."

"Duh," said Reena.

"On buttered bread!" said Terrence.

"I know, Terrence!" snapped Reena. "Now give me the damn thing!"

She grabbed for one, but Jonah jerked them out of reach, still alarmed.

"Reena, what the hell?" he demanded. "What is on your mind that is so heavy that you're willing to eat fried pork on buttered wheat?"

"I told you once that I'm a complicated woman," spat Vera. "Isn't that enough of an explanation?"

"No!" said Jonah and Terrence at the same time.

Reena looked at the both of them, exasperated. "Can't I enjoy an unorthodox food while I paint?"

"You ain't painting, Reena," observed Terrence. "You're sketching. And you only do that when you're stressed out."

Jonah looked at Terrence, intrigued, as did Reena.

"Wow," she murmured as she lowered her pad down to the table. "Kendall mentioned that, and I didn't think too much of it. But you of all people picked up on it, too. My girlfriend and my brother are on the same accord."

Jonah and Terrence waited. Reena sighed.

"There are two things." Reena reluctantly reached for the healthy muffin. "First, Kendall's been summoned by the Lockman Association for private conversation."

"Ahhh..." said Terrence.

"Shit," said Jonah, vacillating between annoyance and concern.

Throughout the end of the summer, Lockman had been sending out his lackeys to summon people all over town for his "private conversations." His official story was that he wanted to glean as much information as possible about Rome because of the temporary office space he'd gotten there. But Maxine and Magdalena quickly discovered from some of their Tenth friends that most of the questions posed there were about the residents of the Grannison-Morris estate, as well as their families. Now Jonah felt bad for labeling Reena a pessimist when Lockman hit those initial dead ends. He changed tactics, exactly like she said he would, when he started asking about the resident's personalities. Everyone at the estate knew that was a tactic that struck gold for Lockman. Eleventh Percenters were all unconventional people with habits viewed as weird by some Tenths. Their difficulties with jobs raised questions, and that got compounded by the fact that Lockman had wondered—via muses in the local paper—why so many adults would live at such a palatial estate and have no one question its funding or upkeep. For the crusading bastard, that question was what made everything click, and the doubts began shortly thereafter. Townspeople began to regard them with suspicion and distaste, among other things. Liz was told that her services as a volunteer at the doctor's office were no longer required, and Doug was told the same thing at the Brown Bag charity drive. And, because Reverend Abbott never denied his ties and friendships with estate residents, he saw a dip in the congregation at the Faith Haven.

So, bearing all of the recent events in mind, Jonah and Terrence could see why Reena was concerned about Kendall seeing Balthazar Lockman.

"Are you afraid she'll crack?" asked Jonah. "I mean, Kendall isn't easily broken. Look at the geezers she's had to deal with at LTSU."

"This isn't an old geezer, Jonah," said Reena. "This is a crusader who is vicious in his approach, and has a background as a criminal psychologist."

"Wow," said Terrence with heat. "Former congressman, former... what Reena just said, and now a cult buster. With all the jobs the guy's had, I'm surprised that he ain't an Eleventh Percenter himself."

"He also has experience with horticulture," murmured Reena. "He listed that on his website."

"So he knows plants as well," grunted Jonah. "Forgive me for not cheering. I left my pom poms back in the city."

"Hang on a minute," said Terrence suddenly. "You said two things were bothering you. What's the other one?"

Reena shook her head. "Ben-Israel called me about two days ago," she said. "He brought something to my attention."

"Really?" said Jonah. "What's Short Stuff been up to since he was sent home?"

"He's a volunteer at a free health clinic in Sharpsburg," said Reena. "He'd been afraid to contact us for obvious reasons, but he called me because he was stumped and a little worried."

"Something Green Aura-related?" asked Jonah. "How come he called you, and didn't call Liz?"

"He said he thought I had a 'stronger mind,'" said Reena. "He thought Liz would worry a little too much, I suppose. Plus he knew that I'm interested in healing myself."

Jonah raised an eyebrow. By-the-book, anal retentive Ben-Israel was concerned about something?

"Okay," said Terrence. "You got our curiosity. What did he find?"

"For the time that he'd been there, things had gone as smooth as one could expect from a health clinic," said Reena. "People came in, got treated and checked, and some got remarkable advice from Ben-Israel. Normal course of events in a medical practitioner's life, I suppose. But then, Ben-Israel said some people came in with odd chills, inexplicable fevers, and complaints that they, or so they said, 'couldn't get their bodies right.'"

Jonah frowned. "So, what did the Tenth doctors say?"

"They hadn't seen anything like it," said Reena. "Ben-Israel said it was crazy. People with temperatures of over a hundred, but their skin was ice cold. There was a presence of heart palpitations, and failure of equilibrium for absolutely no reason."

Now Jonah straightened. "That sounds like a Haunting."

"I thought that myself," said Reena, "but those effects are instantaneous. This thing was slow. Building over time."

"Wait," said Terrence. "Just wait. Building since when?"

"Since the Mindscope dream in the summer," said a voice not too far from them.

All of them wheeled around. Liz stood there, a solemn expression on her face.

"Liz!" Reena looked sheepish. "Um–"

"Not to sound egotistical, and I mean that," interrupted Liz, her green eyes blazing, "but if Ben-Israel figured out the anomalies, don't you think I would have, as well?"

Reena looked uncharacteristically ashamed. Terrence opted not to say anything at all. Jonah approached Liz, leery of her irritation.

"It's not that we didn't trust you, Liz," he placated. "We just didn't want you to worry."

"You didn't want me to worry?" demanded Liz. "Creyton. Deadfallen disciples. Lockman. My baby sister doing a one-eighty. I am already worried, Jonah."

Jonah sighed. "It was just to protect you, Liz."

"Yeah?" Liz looked Jonah in the eye. "Well, I'm a big girl, Jonah. Scratch that; I'm a woman. That means that you don't get to make that call. Not Ben-Israel, not Bobby, and not any of you."

"We're really sorry, Liz," said Terrence finally. "That not a façade; it's the truth. Here, want a bacon sandwich?"

Plainly, that was Terrence idea of a peace offering. A highly caloric and greasy peace offering, but a peace offering nonetheless. Liz glared at them some more, but that faltered quickly enough.

"I forgive you," she said in her usual sweet voice. "Of course I do."

Jonah sighed in relief. "So what do you know about this thing?"

Liz took her time chewing the bacon sandwich before she answered. Jonah couldn't blame her; the thing was delicious. "The anomalies, as I said, began to occur after that blanket Mindscope dream. It seems to begin as issues at the synaptic level, and spreads some sort of disturbance from there."

"So those people in that free health clinic that Ben-Israel saw were Elevenths?" asked Jonah.

"And there are some Elevenths who experienced that Mindscope dream and had these effects afterward?" asked Terrence.

"Looks that way, to both of your questions," said Liz. "But I have no idea what's causing it."

"I bet it has everything to do with Creyton," mused Reena. "His resurrection has changed things, after all. What if the ill effects he brought on by his leap-frog back to physical life left some type of harmful essence on some Elevenths that had that Mindscope dream?"

Liz's brow furrowed. "You know, that's an interesting theory, Reena."

"I know," said Reena. "That's why it worries me."

Terrence must have sensed the turn to the theoretical and the intellectual, because he whacked Jonah on the arm. "I don't think we're needed down here any longer, man."

"Wait," said Liz. "I did come down here for a reason; the eavesdropping was inadvertent. Someone is here to see you, Jonah."

Jonah tensed. "Who's that? One of Lockman's punks?"

"No." Liz's eyes almost had pity. "It's that Ocean woman."

Jonah took his ever-loving time on the stairs. That way he could get his frustration out before conversation with Katarina. He really wasn't fond of that woman. Every time he saw her, something unpleasant occurred. No, it wasn't her fault. No, she hadn't done anything to him personally.

But still, he didn't like her.

Terrence offered to join him, if only for damage control status, but Reena shot that down, reminding them that since Katarina was afraid of Jonah, the two of them might resemble a gang-up, and that would do more harm than good.

So Jonah walked up to the kitchen alone, where Spader and Douglas played a game of spiritually-endowed chess on Douglas' ethereal steel chessboard. It was a rather vibrant sight to behold, seeing the board flash red because of Spader and then silver because of Douglas. Spader shook his head when he saw Jonah.

"When you talk to that little waif out there," he didn't even bother to mask his disdain, "will you tell her that the fifties are over?"

"Why must she be a waif?" demanded Douglas. "What can't she just be a woman with classic tastes? What's wrong with a little class in the world? She does the look justice!"

Now Spader shook his head at Douglas. "That antiquated bull-shit—that right there—is why no woman but your grandma likes you."

Douglas struggled with himself, like he was on the edge of backing down, but then he squared his shoulders.

"And that mentality right there is why nobody but nobody likes you," he retorted.

Spader stood. "What did you just say?" he whispered. "What did you just say to me?"

As much as Jonah wanted to see whether or not Douglas had the nuts to match those words, he hurried to the family room, where Katarina looked over pictures on the wall.

Jonah had to admit that the Gate Linker looked as if she belonged in a few of the older ones. The timelessness of her look, the aged motif of her wardrobe…yeah. She belonged in some of the pictures.

Unfortunately, Jonah's positive comments about the woman ended there. He cleared his throat, and Katarina jumped, just like he thought she would.

"Blue Aura!" She said the words with the air of a child who got caught sneaking in past curfew. "I didn't see you!"

"Of course you didn't, seeing as how your back was turned to me," mumbled Jonah. "What do you want, Katarina?"

"Blue Aura, I'm just the messenger," she prefaced. "Any issue that you have can be taken up with the Curaie."

Jonah's eyes narrowed for two reasons. First, was she really that afraid of him, to preface it like that? And second, just what the hell had she been sent to say? "So...what is it? Spit it out."

Katarina seemed to take a steadying breath. "I was sent to take something from you."

"What's that?" snorted Jonah. "My self-respect?"

"No." Katarina's voice was impossibly soft. "Your batons."

"What?" demanded Jonah. "Why?"

Katarina closed her eyes. "I told you that I'm just the messenger, Blue Aura—"

"Well message on, then!" blazed Jonah. "Why do they want my batons?"

"To prevent any further incidents of vigilantism."

"Further—?" Jonah looked at her in disbelief. "Are you talking about what happened in Dexter City?"

"Yes."

"That was forever ago!"

"It was just a few months, actually—"

"Oh, be quiet," Jonah spat. "Are you aware that my vigilantism , which resulted in a troop of vampires being vanquished—"

"A plan that would never have come to fruition if you hadn't gone on a wild goose chase," said Katarina. "I know all about it, Blue Aura."

"Oh you do, do you?" Jonah didn't care how cold his voice was. "Are you aware that my 'rash' action resulted in the continued safety of several sazers?"

The look that Katarina gave Jonah was almost piteous. "You didn't do anyone any favors with that, Blue Aura. If vampires and sazers get into a fight and some get killed, it's not much of a crime."

Jonah's jaw dropped. No, Katarina did not just say that! "Was that you talking?" he asked. "Or did the Curaie just speak their opinions with your voice?"

"I believe in what the Curaie does for the ethereal world, not to mention the Astral Plane," said Katarina with conviction and passion. "Is that wrong?"

"No, it isn't wrong," responded Jonah. "I couldn't care less what you believe! But you just said that you don't care if sazers get killed! I count several sazers as friends!"

"They are dangerous, Blue Aura!" cried Katarina. "Did you know that Creyton has been sending envoys into both of the vampire and the sazer populations?"

"Katarina, almost all of Creyton's disciples are ethereal humans, just like you and me!" said Jonah with heat. "Would you want us rounded up and tagged? Or killed, just because a few of us are evil?"

Katarina actually paused. Clearly, she hadn't thought of that.

"Uh-huh," said Jonah. "Penny for your thoughts?"

"It doesn't take away from the fact both of those populations are frighteningly dangerous," said Katarina. "Where would you draw the line?"

"Where would you?" Jonah shot at her. "You and these Networkers are a piece of work, Ocean. Who threw me under the bus? Was it Dace Cross?"

"I wouldn't criticize Networkers were I you, Blue Aura," said Katarina. "A Networker went to bat for you. His name is Ovid Patience."

"Patience?"

"Yes," nodded Katarina. "Had it not been for him, and Jonathan as well, you would have spent a month on the Plane with No Name, followed by a year's prohibition from taking spiritual endowments."

Now Jonah was the pensive one. He really liked and respected Patience, but Jonathan? With all the frustration and negative emotion that he had for him, the Protector Guide still bailed him out?

Whatever. It didn't change the fact that Jonathan's prolonged absences got on his nerves.

"Don't you see?" Katarina actually had urgency in her voice. "Lockman is closing in on you and your friends! I saw even fewer cars outside than I did when I was here last time! Do you not see the ripples of your actions, Blue Aura? It isn't just you who gets penalized. The entirety of the estate's populace gets punished for the actions of a few!"

"You're right," said Jonah. "I'll tell that to Jael and Addington Vance."

"Who?" asked Katarina.

"Oh, no one important," said Jonah. "Just an Eleventh girl and her son. Both of them were being protected by some of those sazers that you think are so dangerous. Liz delivered Addington the night I rashly went to Dexter City, see."

Katarina's violet-blue eyes widened, which gave Jonah pause. So she didn't know that bit. Huh. But he went on.

"One of those sazers, girl named Autumn Rose, is Jael's biological sister," he said. "As I said, she and her friends—one of which is a dear friend of mine—were protecting her. And the vampires? They didn't come because I was being reckless. They came because a suuvus wanted to get initiated. He took his own life, and Creyton rewarded him by usurping his spirit."

Katarina looked stunned.

"Not finished just yet," said Jonah, "but almost. Lockman is a foul bastard. Yeah, his daughter was murdered by a Deadfallen disciple, but he's far from a saint. He bribed the officer up in Maryland who arrested me. Patience bailed me out, sure, but that was after Dace Cross left me there to the mercy of Tenth Law. Tell your beloved saviors that."

It cost him every ounce of resolve he had, but Jonah pulled his batons from his pocket, brought them to full size, and held them out to Katarina.

"Take 'em," he muttered. "And tell the Curaie, from me, that whatever happens to me now is on their heads."

Katarina took the batons, handling them reverently once more…or was it cautiously? "If only you knew the truth about these, Jonah," she said softly, "thenyou'd know why the Curaie is concerned about your raw emotion regarding everything."

That caught Jonah off guard. He recalled their first meeting, when Katarina had shamelessly gushed over his batons. She had been about to mention something about their previous owner before Jonathan cut her off. "What truth do you mean?" he demanded.

"I won't betray Jonathan," said Katarina flat-out. "Whatever my loyalties, he has always been kind and respectful to me, and I respect him. The Curaie offered him a position among them for Spirit Guidanceship. Did you know that? Back around the 60's or 70's, so I was told. But he declined. He opted to stay here and remain a Protector Guide, mentor, and Overseer of this estate. If he's had to deal with Elevenths like yourself, thenI can't even begin to conceive why he made such a choice."

That stung, but Jonah felt his upper lip curl into a sneer. Katarina walked to the door, opened it, and had one foot out of it before he had sufficient enough venom in his words to voice them.

"Yeah," he rasped, "because those sack-of-shit Spirit Guides are so much better."

He knew that someone like Katarina would consider that vicious and belligerent, but he didn't care. It was shock factor only.

And it had the desired effect. Katarina whirled around, looking as though Jonah had just slapped her. As expected, there were tears in her eyes, but they seemed to be more from indignation and not sensitivity.

"How dare you?" she whispered. "How... dare you! They are good people!"

"That's what you don't seem to grasp, Katarina!" snapped Jonah. "The Curaie ain't people, they're spirits. They are incapable of caring and feeling. Therein lay the problem."

Katarina glared at Jonah. Jonah glared right back. A person from afar might have thought that both of them wanted to kill each other from looks alone.

"Goodbye, Blue Aura," said Katarina, anger in her soft tone. "I pray we never see one another again."

"Couldn't have said it better myself," grumbled Jonah.

He closed the door in her face and turned away, once again attempting to lid his emotions. He'd had yet another sour experience with Katarina Ocean. He didn't need to see that woman again in life. Ever.

And on top of that, he was now without his batons.

Surely, things couldn't get any worse.

Then came another knock at the door. Like a fool, Jonah opened it without checking.

He was met by a sight that grated on his sanity even more than Katarina.

"Good morning, Rowe!" The unwelcome person's voice was as shrill as ever. "Can't say I'm surprised to see that you're embroiled in controversy."

Jonah couldn't believe she was here. It almost made him wish the Curaie would come back to confiscate something else. "What the hell are you doing here?" he whispered.

"Now, now," chided Reynolda Langford, "that's no way to greet a fellow LTSU alum! As for my purpose here," she pulled her face into an obnoxious grin, which was a sight made even more foolish due to the obscene amount of makeup on her face, "the *Rome's Ledger* wants interviews with you and your friends, so as to aid the Lockman Association!"

16

Reunions

Jonah heard Reynolda's words, but didn't believe them. No, scratch that. He did believe them. Why shouldn't this crap happen? It matched all the other luck he'd had lately.

Reynolda continued to smile. "Aren't you going to invite me in?"

Jonah's eyes narrowed at Reynolda's unabashed glee that he had no choice in the matter. It took him two deep breaths before he could bring himself to invite her in.

Reynolda steeped into the living room at the same time that several people emerged from their rooms, and Terrence and Reena came from the kitchen. Every single person looked at the new arrival in alarm. It was obvious that Reynolda didn't expect so many eyes on her at once, and her smugness faltered. It made Jonah smirk in spite of himself.

"Who the hell is this?" demanded Spader without hesitation.

Reynolda scoffed. Jonah glared at her.

"Spader, everybody," he announced, "this is Reynolda Langford. I know her from Kendall's Creative Writing class."

"Hmph." Reynolda's nervousness faded as contempt tightened her face. "That woman. She wouldn't even allow us to call her Professor Rayne. I suppose that that was testament to the fact that she had no place teaching a college course—"

Jonah saw the fire in Reena's face. Terrence's eyes darted her way as well. Reynolda was completely oblivious, and continued to dig herself into a hole.

"—and then she had the nerve to call my work sophomoric and pedantic, as if a professor younger than I am could ever tell me, a published author, anything at all—"

"Langford," said Jonah loudly, because she didn't deserve to get her head torn off despite her lack of people skills. "Do you see that woman there, next to the kitchen door? That's Reena. Kendall's girlfriend."

Reynolda regarded Reena's hardened face with genuine surprise. "You know, I'd heard that Kendall kicked on that side of the field," she said in an audible undertone to Jonah, "but I didn't believe it. I just thought she was confused—"

"Motherfucker!" Reena came Reynolda's way.

"Reena, no!"

Jonah abandoned Reynolda to restrain Reena. He couldn't allow violence to occur between the two of them. Reena was furious and lithe as a panther, while Reynolda was a dumpy soccer mom who happened to a journalist. Before the first strike, there was no question who'd win.

"Well, my word!" said Reynolda in shock.

"What the hell did you expect?" Reena snarled. "You were just insulting my girlfriend right in front of my face!"

"What the hell are you here for, anyway, Reynolda?" demanded Jonah from Reena's side. "Lockman said we had his undivided attention."

"Mr. Lockman is a busy man." Reynolda's voice was quite authoritative, as though she were the important one. "He is at his current office space conducting interviews with those that are affiliated with you people. And wouldn't you know it—" she turned deliberately to Reena, "—Mr. Lockman is interviewing Rayne this very moment. So it's be most unfortunate if I were to inform him that his current interviewee's ah—girlfriend— is one of the pack of freaks doing God knows what in this fancy house, wouldn't it?"

Jonah stopped Reena from jumping Reynolda again, but it was reluctant. So she wanted to play it that way, huh? She didn't even work for Lockman directly, and his influence had emboldened her. Jonah was ready to take the bitch's head off himself.

"Very questionable tactics, young lady." Daniel spoke the words from the threshold. "To come into a situation wholly alone, surrounded by unknown elements, and then proceed to bully a resident's loved one? Your behavior is bound to make your purpose here much more difficult to accomplish. What is that purpose, might I ask?"

Reynolda was taken aback by Daniel, which was a pleasurable sight to Jonah. Damn, if the man wasn't a menacing sight with that bow on his back!

"Um...hello there!" The pronounced cheeriness in Reynolda's was supposed to mask the fright that Daniel gave her. "Who might you be?"

"This is my home, woman," said Daniel. "You are the guest. I'll ask you who you might be."

Reynolda swallowed. Terrence snickered.

"I am Reynolda Langford," she announced. "I write for Rome's Ledger, and was sent here on behalf of Balthazar Lockman, whose association has been loaned the services of our paper's staffing."

That was quite a mouthful. Jonah might have been intimidated were it anyone else. But he knew full well that Reynolda memorized all that; she'd probably been coached to drop Lockman's name by the man himself. Unfortunately for her, the power of those credentials lay with the representatives of the Lockman Association. When that power was merely refracted, like it was with Reynolda right now, it just wasn't impressive. Daniel didn't look like he was impressed, at any rate.

"Cute description, albeit a posturing one," remarked Daniel. His voice was bored, but his eyes were alert. "But it still doesn't answer the question as to why you're here."

"I, um, was sent here to get a better understanding of you people," said Reynolda, who spoke the words as though she'd almost forgotten her purpose there. "See your daily living, habits...that sort of thing."

"Bullshit," muttered Jonah to Terrence and Reena. "She's here to soften us up for Lockman. I bet that he'd be here himself if he weren't in town, breaking folks down."

Daniel's expression changed very little. "Glean your information and whatever else you desire. I only ask that you bear in mind that you are a guest. I will guarantee our cooperation, but that expectation is a two-way street. What is given will be what is reciprocated."

Maxine whistled. Jonah raised his own eyebrows. Daniel showed neither fear nor concern about Reynolda's presence. He'd made it as clear as the sunny day outside that her bullying tactics would not be tolerated, nor would her backing provide her any leeway. Jonah had newfound respect for the archer. There was a harder edge to him that Jonah felt Jonathan could never achieve.

Then his eyes widened. Jonathan was there!

The Protector Guide, in transparent form, was behind Reena. He whispered, "Head downstairs. Do not make a spectacle of it."

Jonah blinked, and he was gone. It took him that long to realize that Daniel was still speaking.

"I'm Overseer of this home, and your unannounced arrival has caught all of my residents off guard," he told Reynolda. "I will give you a tour of the grounds, which are expansive enough to give them time to prepare themselves."

"With all due respect, Mr. Daniel," said Reynolda in a rather meek tone, "they seem to be prepared enough to me—"

"The grounds, Mrs. Langford," said Daniel. "I insist."

He hadn't raised his voice at all, but there was something about his tone that prompted Reynolda to roll with it. Sheepishly, she pulled a pen and pad out of her bag and cleared her throat.

"To the grounds we go!" she said in false brightness.

Daniel gave Jonah a meaningful look (as if to say that he knew that Jonathan was just there), and led Reynolda outside. Magdalena, Maxine, Spader, and Douglas all looked at each other. But Reena was the one who broke the silence.

"Daniel just bought us time!" she said in a loud whisper. "Use it to put away anything that's ethereal! Spader, get Bobby and Alvin out of the gym and fill them in. Maxine, do the same with Malcolm; he's in his wood shop."

"What about Trip?" said Liz. "And his posse?"

"They can take care of themselves," said Reena. "Now all of you hop to it! And Magdalena—"

"Way ahead of you, *hermana*," said Magdalena, who headed upstairs, undoubtedly to wake anyone still asleep and brief them about Langford. Jonah headed to the kitchen to get to the basement stairs. Terrence and Reena were right behind him.

"Jonathan appeared when Reena was about to rip Reynolda's face off," he explained as they descended. "He told me to meet him downstairs."

"What for?" asked Terrence.

"Couldn't tell you," said Jonah.

"Jonah, you might want to stash the batons somewhere—"

"They're an irrelevant matter, Reena." Jonah's voice was testy, and he didn't care. "Ocean was sent here by her leash holders to confiscate them."

"Say WHAT?" cried Terrence. "Why?"

"Oh, the usual," mumbled Jonah, "I'm a ticking time bomb who's barely evolved and irrational. Now, where is Jonathan?"

"I am right here." Jonathan stood near a familiar door.

"The armory!" said Reena, breathless. "Reynolda cannot see that! I completely forgot about it!"

Jonathan shook his head. "Do not worry yourself about it, Reena. The four of us right here are addressing the matter now."

"You're a lifesaver, Jonathan," said Terrence.

"Yeah," murmured Jonah. "Superb timing."

Jonathan's eyes narrowed. "I don't think I understand your meaning, Jonah."

"Really?" said Jonah. "Eh, it's nothing. The armory is a more pressing matter than anything on my mind, right?"

Jonathan looked at Jonah a moment longer, and then refocused on whatever the task was. First, he turned to Reena. "Reena, there is no possible way to relocate all of this ordinance, so for the time being, what we need is a small bit of inconvenience."

"Gotcha, sir." Reena flashed a comprehending smile.

Jonathan nodded at her. "You have been endowed."

Reena took the usual invigorated breath that accompanied spiritual endowment, then faced the door. Jonah thought he knew what was next, and braced himself, but it that wasn't necessary. Reena's cold-spot trick was minimal, and calculated in execution. They all heard the door contract due to the cold temperature. The action prompted Jonah to raise an eyebrow.

"What did you do that for?" he asked, puzzled. "If you wanted inconvenience, you ought to have made the door expand—"

"If the door got expanded, Jonah, then this next part would never work," said Jonathan. "Terrence, you have been endowed."

Terrence looked confused at this recent endowment, but then his face cleared.

"Oh, duh," he muttered, and grabbed the doorknob. One sharp yank later, and the door was perfectly jammed.

"One final touch," said Jonathan. "Jonah, you have been endowed."

Jonah felt the surge in his body, but the ethereality did nothing to assuage his confusion. "What is it exactly that you want me to do?" he asked Jonathan.

"The door has been damaged, contracted, and jammed," Jonathan explained. "If your friend up there is pesky enough to be persistent, she might suggest that the door could be opened with the proper amount of force. Dodging her at that point would arouse even further suspicion. But if the door was closed beyond repair…"

Jonathan's voice trailed off, allowing Jonah to fill in the blank. He nodded.

"Alright," he said, "I think. But it's been a while since I've done this."

"Makes no difference," guaranteed Jonathan. "You are an ethereal human. If it was possible for you then, it remains possible for you now."

Jonah focused on his right hand, willing it to have the necessary strength for the next part. Come on, he prodded, come on…

Slowly, blue essence engulfed his hand, like a skin-conforming glove of some kind. It gave his hand a sudden feeling of focused, intense strength that he hadn't ever felt there before, even when he lifted weights. Satisfied with its presence, Jonah wrapped his hand around the knob, much like Terrence had. But instead of pulling forward, Jonah wrenched up. With an unceremonious crunch, the knob parted from the door. Jonah completely ripped it off.

Finally, Jonathan looked satisfied. "Excellent work," he told them. "All of you."

"That was awfully elaborate," commented Jonah with a frown. "Couldn't you have just hidden it with Auric Shielding, or something?"

"No, Jonah," said Jonathan. "I couldn't have done that. You are well aware that it is imperative that we keep ethereality to a minimum, particularly now."

"Yeah? Well Creyton and his pack of fools didn't get that memo," said Jonah, who ignored Terrence's and Reena's attempts to catch his eye and stop him. "I mean, they've been flip-flopping into crows, even in front of Tenths. Why can't you make a damn shield—"

Jonah paused at Jonathan's look, in spite of himself.

"Reena, Terrence," said the Protector Guide, "leave us."

Reena chewed on her lip for a moment, then headed for the stairs. Terrence hesitated himself, but followed suit after a sharp eye from Reena. Jonathan watched them until the stairs curved out of sight, and then snapped his eyes to Jonah. Despite the blazing gray, the voice was serene.

"What is on your mind, Jonah?" he asked. "What is the root of the burgeoning mass of tension and disquiet within you?"

Jonah stared at Jonathan, but steadied his mind. The fact that he hit the nail on the head only annoyed him further. "Nothing much, sir…I mean, if there is nothing bothering you, why the hell should I worry?"

"Meaning?"

"Meaning," said Jonah in a rather sharp voice, "that we are being roughed up from all sides, like in a damn maelstrom, or something, and you are nowhere in sight! Lockman is interviewing people we know, and he's probably hardcore with his interrogation techniques. And Creyton? He could be threatening to topple everything in existence for all we know, and you, our so-called Guide and mentor, only bother to show up long enough to sabotage a damned door. I don't see the sense in that."

Jonathan's face was empty of emotion, but there was the faintest tightening around the eyes. "If you are implying that I am hiding, or that I'm afraid, you are mistaken."

"Then why are you M.I.A. all the time?"

"I am attempting to not make an already muddled situation further so—"

"So you're helping us with your absences?" demanded Jonah, who laughed with incredulity. "I'm sorry, I've had it wrong all this time! So you ignoring us, being gone for stretches on end, and showing up only for foolishness like door jamming is your way of looking out for us. I swear to God, Jonathan, if that's helping us, I hate to see what not helping us looks like. The way you come in here, give us tidbits of information, and then just leave…it must be what interacting with a drug dealer is like."

Jonathan closed his eyes, like that stung him. "Jonah, you do not understand—"

"Save it, man," mumbled Jonah. It was only by mumbling that he could prevent his voice from elevating again. "If you'll excuse me, I'm going to do my best to help my friends prevent the dismantling of everything you've built. It's too much to ask of you to do anything."

Jonah turned his back on his mentor. He didn't even wait to see if or when he vanished. Soon he was up the stairs, with his mind at work on new ways to throw Reynolda off of her game.

* * *

People tried hard, very hard, to go about things as they normally would. But the elephant in the room, or in this case, on the grounds, was at the forefront of every resident's mind. Jonah hoped that Reynolda didn't approach him first, because he hadn't cleared his mind of his frustration with Jonathan yet. His absences were meant to help them? Jonah wondered if Daniel shared that belief.

Reynolda spent several minutes conversing with Daniel. The archer wasn't actually rude or anything, but he made it clear that he wouldn't be kissing her ass because of her backing. Reynolda resumed some of her arrogance, but it was obvious that she was wary of that bow. Once Jonah rejoined Terrence and Reena, he found that Reena definitely viewed Reynolda as an enemy now, and it had zero to do with Lockman's cult investigations. The glare that his sister had trained on that woman when she moved from Daniel to Liz was reminiscent of a salivating lion scoping a wildebeest. It actually made Jonah laugh.

"Welcome to my opinion of Langford," he told Reena. "I've hated her since the day I met her. You didn't know Kendall then, but Reynolda was critical of her then, too."

"And I've known her longer than either of you," said Terrence with distaste. "Before she got that job with the Ledger, she was the president of the P.T.A. at the high school where I clean on Monday, Wednesday, and Friday."

"Was she an idiot to you and the other janitors?" asked Jonah.

"That woman was an idiot to the principal," scoffed Terrence. "So you know that everyone else on down was fair game."

Reena didn't seem to take in any of their words. "She could have bad-mouthed anyone," she whispered. "My father, my stupid mother…anyone but Kendall."

"Cool it, Reena," said Terrence, who attempted to pat her shoulder. "Righteous rage won't change her in a day."

"If she makes any further disparaging remarks about my girlfriend, I won't be changing her with rage," promised Reena.

Reynolda's thing seemed to be going well for the estate so far. It appeared that Daniel and Liz left the woman disappointed.

Then she reached Douglas.

Jonah frowned. For some reason, Douglas seemed to be a bundle of nerves when he saw Reynolda headed his way. He looked at Terrence, who shrugged.

"Hey, Doug!" she said as she extended a hand that Douglas hesitated before he took. It's been a while!"

Douglas cleared his throat. "Indeed it has, Mrs. Reynolda," he mumbled.

"You're in grad school, yes?" Unless Jonah was mistaken, there was nothing in Reynolda's voice but pure indifference when she asked that question.

"Yes I am," said Douglas. "Urban Planning."

"Urban?" Reynolda raised an eyebrow. "Why, then, do you live in the sticks, kiddo?"

"Because it ain't his plan to be here forever!" snapped Terrence.

Reynolda looked over at Terrence. "Doug can speak for himself," she said smoothly. "I mean…if he's a real man."

Douglas winced. Reena, who'd calmed somewhat, shook her head.

"I am a real man, thanks," grumbled Douglas.

" 'Course you are, puddin'!" said Reynolda. "So why are you mastering in that crazy city thing?"

Douglas closed his eyes. "What Terrence said." He sounded so reluctant that it wasn't even funny.

Reynolda flashed a smug grin, scribbled something, and then turned her attention to Spader. She wrinkled her nose, as though he caused her to itch.

"And what you think of this…place?" She didn't even bother to ask his name.

"Love it." Spader breathed heavily through his nose. "It's been good to me."

Reynolda chuckled softly. Jonah, who was far enough to be ignored but near enough to catch words, felt himself tense. She used to do that stupid chuckle back in their Creative Writing class, and it always preceded some type of trouble.

"You say that this fancy house is good to you, huh?" she asked Spader. "Because forgive me—and I mean no harm by saying this—but you look like the one who least belongs here."

"You have no idea, woman!" snapped Spader, instantly furious. "Jonathan saves plenty of lost souls!"

Every person within earshot snapped their heads to Spader and Reynolda. He gritted his teeth in disgust, while she raised an eyebrow.

"Jonathan?" The curiosity on Reynolda's face was almost ravenous. "Who is that?"

"I—I misspoke," said Spader. Unease had quickly unseated the anger in his tone of voice. "I meant to say Daniel's name."

"Did you really?" Reynolda scribbled some more. "You mistook the name Daniel for Jonathan? Why, I can't help but wonder?"

"I misspoke," repeated Spader, who looked furious with himself. "It just happened. A mistake, you know, like human beings make?"

Reynolda didn't look the least bit fooled by Spader's return to snarky tones. Her look resembled a greedy prospector who stumbled on something very valuable. Jonah really hated that look.

"Yes," she said at last. "A mistake, like humans make."

She turned to Daniel, who hadn't gone too far away.

"May I see the inside of the estate now, please?" she asked sweetly.

"If you wish," Daniel replied.

When they marched off to the porch, Terrence looked at Spader with fury.

"What the hell?" he demanded.

"It slipped!" snapped Spader, who looked guilty and defiant. "Sue me! I was pissed!"

"Pissed?" repeated Terrence. "I thought that you were supposed to be completely impassive. You know—impossible to read, but capable of reading everyone else!"

"Why did you have your hopes up so high, Terrence?" Liz joined the conversation, and appraised Spader with the usual negative emotions. "Spader has already proven that his ability to read people wasn't infallible once; why are you surprised that it's happened again?"

Spader looked furious. "Okay, so my game was off," he spat. "I'm back on top of things now!"

"See?" Liz actually got in Spader's face. "That's your problem! Everything is some depraved game with you! Why must you game everything? Why must you con everyone you know? You do yourself no favors when you show people just how conniving and skanky you really are!"

Spader took in a hard breath through his nostrils. "First of all, I'm not conniving," he grunted, "or skanky. And I'll tell you why everything is a con. Because the second you let someone in, they take advantage of you. It's either con, or get conned. I've made it this far because I'm good at it. Don't you dare judge me just because I have the initiative to do to other people what they wouldn't hesitate to do to me."

Liz shook her head. "Bless your heart," she said in a mocking tone. "If you were half as intelligent as you claim to be, you'd realize the folly in your words. Letting people in is a necessary risk, particularly when you forge bonds with loved ones."

Spader snorted right there in Liz's face. "Risk by yourself, toots," he said. "And don't come crying to me when someone rips your heart out and stomps that sucker flat."

"Watch how you speak to Liz, dude." Now Bobby was in the situation. "As a matter of fact, you just need to go ahead and shut up right now."

Spader shrugged. "I'm just being honest."

"Uh-huh," said Bobby. "And we all know that when people say they're bein' honest, it just an excuse to be an asshole. Drop it, man."

Liz frowned slightly at Bobby, as though she didn't quite appreciate his coming over to be Alpha Male like that. Jonah had to agree with her to an extent; she owned Spader quite decently before Bobby thundered to her defense. But Bobby didn't notice her expression because he turned his attention to Douglas.

"What was that about, man?" he asked him.

Douglas looked as incensed as Spader. "I remember that woman from around campus. I never liked her because she reminds me of Grandma 'Dine."

"Doug, you've gotta get over that!" Bobby exclaimed. "Why don't you address it? Why don't you stand up to your grandmother?"

Douglas roared, and flung the golf club he'd been holding. Everyone jumped when he did. This was more emotion from Douglas than anyone had ever seen.

"Stand up to Mrs. Decessio, Bobby," snapped Douglas. "If that goes well for you, then I'll give standing up to Grandma 'Dine a shot."

He stalked off. Everyone watched him.

"What did I say?" asked Bobby.

"That's a good question." The exchange temporarily distracted Terrence from Reynolda's presence on the grounds. "What did he say?"

"When will you men use your brains?" asked Reena. "It doesn't even matter what Bobby said, per se. It was how he said it. Doug probably thinks about standing up to his grandmother on a daily basis. And that bitch Reynolda playing him like that didn't help matters. He's probably sick of feeling emasculated and weak, particularly after what happened with Gamaliel Kaine."

Jonah looked away and scolded himself for forgetting that. The previous winter Gamaliel Kaine, the leader of another group of Eleventh Percenters, drove a blade through his own windpipe after having been coerced to do so by Jessica Hale via dark ethereal means. Douglas, who'd been in the wrong place at the wrong time, got framed for the murder. Gamaliel's band of Eleventh Percenters refused to listen to reason and threatened to besiege the estate is they didn't give Douglas up. Douglas' innocence was revealed a day after that, but apparently, he hadn't yet recovered from that experience.

"So that's why he was questioning his manhood," muttered Jonah.

"What?" said Terrence.

"Questioning his manhood?" Reena frowned. "Do I even want to hear this?"

"It's not what you think," said Jonah hastily. "But there is plenty of time to talk about it later."

Trip emerged from somewhere in the woods, Karin by his side. They both had Mason jars in their hands, which Jonah found odd. Wouldn't Trip, of all people, understand that his sound experiments counted as ethereality?

He and Karin paused when they saw so many people outside, and of course Trip had a sneer with Jonah's name on it.

"What's going on out here?" he demanded of the group. "You all comparing notes on laziness?"

Jonah was spared the retort by Reynolda's reappearance. She saw Trip, and took in a rather dramatic breath.

"Oh, my word," she breathed. "Titus Rivers?"

Jonah was stunned. Terrence, Reena, and the others seemed to be as well. Trip, on the other hand, was not. His eyes narrowed as he dropped the Mason jars to the ground.

"No," he grumbled. "That's my grandfather's name. My name is Trip."

"Uh, Trip," said Reena, "this is—"

"I know who she is," snapped Trip, without looking at Reena. "Reynolda Treadway."

"Oh," said Reynolda after a swallow. "It's Langford now."

"That so?" Trip's eyebrows rose. "That dumbass married you, after all?"

Reynolda turned red, and her mouth tightened. "I do not appreciate you speaking about my husband like that!"

"I don't give a shit," murmured Trip. "Now let me guess, Langford—you're here to write a piece on us savages?"

Reynolda still looked affronted, but seemed to exhibit some caution as she dealt with Trip. She certainly didn't have this reservation with anyone else, except maybe Daniel. "The staff at the Ledger has been loaned to Balthazar Lockman for the foreseeable future."

"Ah." Trip's eyes flashed. "So you're here buzzing around for gossip. Just like always."

Reynolda wiped a bead of sweat from her brow. Jonah glanced at Terrence, who shrugged to illustrate his own confusion.

"That last time was not my fault," she whispered. "And it has nothing to do with now. But I didn't know that you lived here! Would you give me a word about being around these people?"

"Yeah, I'll give you a word," whispered Trip. "I'll give you several words if you don't get out of my damned face."

Reynolda closed her eyes. "That last time was not my fault! Why can't you just find it in you to forgive me?"

"Forgiveness is nothing more than giving someone a carte blanche to screw up all over again," growled Trip. "So fuck forgiveness, and fuck you."

Reynolda paled. At that very moment, Daniel caught up with them. Even though he leered at the woman, his voice remained calm.

"Is there a problem, Mrs. Langford?" he questioned. "You only saw half of the estate."

Reynolda kept her eyes on Trip. "I think…I think I have all that I need. Mr. Lockman is going to have a field day with you people."

She practically ran to her car. Jonah slowly looked at Trip.

"You know Reynolda Langford?" he demanded. "How?"

Trip bent down, retrieved his Mason jars, and stood before he addressed Jonah. "Correct me if I'm wrong, but I think that I've already told you to mind your own business, Rowe," was Trip's response. "Karin, we're done here."

He walked off. Karin stared after Reynolda's car, and sighed. Jonah opened his mouth, but she shook her head.

"Don't even think about asking me." For once, her voice wasn't cold. She almost sounded sad. "You heard Trip. It's none of your business."

She followed behind Trip, and left behind a very confused group in the process. Terrence shook his head.

"What did we just witness, man?" he asked no one in particular. "So Trip knows Reynolda? And Reynolda is scared of him?"

"That wasn't scared," said Reena, "that was traumatized. Daniel, do you know anything?"

Daniel gave a smooth shrug. "Can't help you, Reena. You may need to ask Jonathan."

"No sense doing that." Jonah grimaced. "It'd be about as useless as a fur coat in August."

"Besides," said Liz, "we don't have the time to pry into Trip's personal life. That lady said that Lockman is going to have a field day. I hate the sound of that. Did she anything in there, Daniel?"

"Nothing," Daniel confirmed, though he seemed concerned about Reynolda's words as well. "She only got as far the basement, and seemed interested in the 'jammed door with no knob.' Then she abruptly said that she'd seen enough. But she witnessed nothing improper."

"Maybe she is going to go in on Trip, Spader, and Doug then," said Liz. "I sure didn't give her anything, but Spader—"

"Okay, okay." Spader's voice was sharp. "I messed up at a bad time. I got the point before you saw fit to repeat it."

"Believe it or not, Spader," said Bobby, whose irritation with him must have vanished, "I don't think your screw up was that big a deal. Anyone's, actually. I think that lady would have found a way to paint us negatively, no matter what anyone told her."

Jonah said nothing, but he knew that Bobby was probably right. Hell, there wasn't a "probably" about it. It seemed like Jonathan's genius plan failed; Reynolda still wound up suspicious of that damned door. And then Trip hadn't helped matters at all. He appeared to add fuel to a fire that already existed between himself and the reporter. Lockman scored quite a find when he assigned that woman to investigate. She knew so many of them and none of the interactions were pleasant or healthy.

Whoever said that reunions were beneficial ought to be shot.

"Well you know what?" said Terrence. "There ain't a thing in the worlds that we can do about it right now. It's Saturday afternoon, and we haven't had lunch. Let's eat."

Everyone seemed to diffuse somewhat while they consumed one of Terrence's stir-fry concoction. It allowed everyone to discuss the situation of the day with semi-clearer heads. Try as he might, though, Jonah couldn't get completely calm about it. Reynolda was so confident that they were already done for. What was that about? Had she noticed something Daniel had overlooked? Did she plan some spin some bullshit tale based on the less than stellar interactions with Trip, Douglas, and Spader? It was just the type of thing that Reynolda would do. Quintessential bitch, through and through.

Why did Katarina Ocean have to take his batons that day? Given what happened afterward, it was like a retroactive insult before injury. The Curaie were such a nuisance, and they were no closer to knowing what to do about Creyton than Jonah and his friends. Yet they still hid behind their veil of righteousness, and wanted to keep the pretense that Creyton's defiance regarding the laws of life didn't concern them. Didn't scare them. They wanted Jonah on ice, while Lockman, conversely, wanted to put all of them under fire.

Jonah didn't know how much more of this he could take.

"Uh, Jonah?" said Terrence. "I think that fork is done for."

"What? Oh."

He looked at his fork and realized that he bent it so much while in his contemplation mode that it resembled a stainless-steel noodle. His grasp must have tightened with each passing thought.

"Damn," he muttered. "Sorry about that."

Terrence shrugged. "No issue of mine! But you ain't gonna do anymore eating with that thing."

"Duly noted."

Jonah lowered the fork and rose from the table to get a new one. It was at that position where movement outside the window caught his eye.

"Reverend's Abbott's here!" he announced. "And—and Kendall's with him!"

A chair scraped across the floor, and Jonah didn't have to look behind him to know that it was Reena who was almost at the door before the new arrivals reached it.

"Kendall." Reena practically yanked her girlfriend into the kitchen and kissed her. "I've been worried out of my head! What—?"

"Reena, there is someone else at the door," chided Terrence.

"Oh, right," muttered Reena, who looked over at Reverend Abbott. "Sorry, sir."

"No offense taken, Reena," said Abbott as a laugh crept into his serious face. "I imagined that your girlfriend would take precedence over me."

Kendall closed her eyes. Clearly, she was in no mood to be humorous. "You guys can keep talking if you like," she said, "but I need to sit."

Jonah frowned at his former professor. She looked so tired and dejected, both of which were not her usual M.O. Ever since the first day he met Kendall, he'd come to regard her as one of the most strong-willed and resilient people he knew. The opinion of her colleagues and her relationship with Reena mandated she be bulletproof. She surely didn't look like that now.

"What did Lockman say to you?" he asked.

Kendall put her fingers to her brow. "That man is a shark," she answered. "Relentless. I've never seen anyone so blindly vindictive in my life, and that was my first time meeting him."

"What happened?" asked Reena.

"Well, I can't say it started off normally, because I didn't know what to expect," Kendall began. "He had asked some questions, and I suppose he was calm, but then his assistant came in and said he had an urgent message. It must have screwed up his day, because he was vicious after that."

"Oh, that bitch," said Malcolm suddenly, and several heads turned his way, surprised. "I was wondering what she was doing. Maxine had just come into the shop and filled me in about the Tenth snooping around here. When we left, Daniel was showing her the grounds, I guess. She had a pen and pad out, but she put that back and got out her phone. I assumed she was just being lazy, but now I know."

"Know what, exactly?" asked Jonah.

"Maxine told me how Langford pissed Reena off talking about Kendall," said Malcolm. "And how you, Jonah, said they were dating to shut her up. I'll bet you she texted Lockman's assistant, which prompted him to tear Kendall out a new one."

"Langford." Instantly, Kendall's face transformed. What once was fatigue was now fury. Even Reena took a step back from her. "That bitch could barely write her name, and she got a job with a paper. Now she's helping this man with his witch hunt. And now you're saying I got the third degree because of her?"

"Calm down, Kendall," said Reverend Abbott. "I've already told you once today that getting angry is one thing, but staying angry is another. This frame of mind won't help anything."

"How can you feel that way, Reverend?" asked Magdalena. "Look at what Lockman's schemes have done to the membership at the faith haven!"

"I'm not in this business to have the biggest and most powerful church, Magdalena," said Reverend Abbott. "The dealings of this very troubled man will not deter me from helping those who still call the faith haven their home church."

"You just wait," said Bobby in a cold tone. "Just wait. When this mess is over and Lockman gets owned, everybody who abandoned the faith haven will come crawling back."

"And I would gladly welcome them back," said Reverend Abbott. "Only God has the right to judge."

Bobby looked at the reverend incredulously. "Whatever, man. You're the preacher, not me."

"I'm curious," said Jonah. "How exactly did the two of you hook up today?"

"I was visiting the sick and shut-in around Rome today," explained Reverend Abbott. "I saw Kendall in the town square, looking like she needed some kind words. When I found out that she was on her way here, I decided to come too."

"I thank you for that, Reverend," said Kendall. "But I will say that it's a good thing I don't have a full understanding of the Eleventh Percent. I was no help to him at all. He was cold and evil because of that, too."

"What did he ask?" said Terrence.

Kendall shook her head. "Did you guys act 'holier than thou,' did you treat people like whatever path you lived on was the only way, did you do 'afterlife experiments,' or something—"

"Afterlife experiments?" said Jonah, aggravated. "My God, who does he think we are, some necrophilia zealots, or something? And he just happened to link up with the one paper in town that employs someone who hates both Kendall and me!"

"No," said Kendall.

Jonah looked at her. "No, what?"

"The Lockman Association linking up with the *Ledger* wasn't done at random," said Kendall. "I'm not supposed to know, but Mavis was gossiping about it some days ago."

"Mavis?" frowned Jonah. "What would that senile—" he glanced at the reverend and caught himself, "—um, what would Professor Mavis know about anything?"

Kendall pulled away from Reena and looked him in the face. It seemed as though she purposely focused her attention on Jonah alone. "Mavis never keeps her mouth shut. I've been around this woman the whole time I've taught at LTSU, and she has always gone one about her physical ailments, her inability to work a computer, how she hates her mom, and her friends."

"So what?" asked Jonah.

"So she was talking to Myra and Ferrus about how one of her closest friends was back in tow, and hadn't been here five minutes before she was interviewed by Lockman," said Kendall. "Not only was she helpful, but she suggested the Ledger. She said that the paper would have access to places that new-to-town investigators couldn't go."

Jonah shrugged. "Who would do that? Seems odd to me."

Kendall sighed. Jonah was missing something. "It's not odd at all when you think about it, Jonah. Now think; who would know Mavis, know me, know you, and know that Reynolda Langford hates us both, and has a job with Rome's Ledger? Moreover, who would use that knowledge to further some dark agenda, if what Reena has told me is accurate?"

Jonah's eyes bulged. Suddenly, it clicked. "Charlotte?" he croaked. "Charlotte Daynard is back in Rome?"

"What?" demanded Reena.

"That assistant who helped screw us?" asked Terrence.

"That lady that had Gamaliel Kaine's head all twisted?" said Douglas.

Kendall ignored all. She only nodded at Jonah.

"You aren't the only one who had a crappy reunion today, Jonah," she said quietly.

17

Hearts, Minds, and Duncan Hines

"I think you're wrong."

Jonah made an impatient noise as Felix repeated this for the third time that Sunday morning. He, Terrence, and Reena pretty much had the estate to themselves; most of the other residents went to the morning service at the faith haven to show support and solidarity to Reverend Abbott. But as much as they loved the man, Jonah, Terrence, and Reena weren't among them. Jonah hadn't had anything to do with church or religion since he'd lost his grandmother. Reena had confided to them a while back that her spiritual beliefs didn't require her to be "enclosed within a brick building every Sunday." Terrence just didn't trust himself not to nod off during the service.

Felix showed up unannounced that morning, but they didn't waste time being surprised about it, and chose to fill him in about what Kendall had said about Charlotte Daynard giving Lockman a hand up in demonizing them. But the vampire hunter flat-out refused to believe that Lockman's connection went further than it did.

"Are you kidding me right now?" said Jonah. "Why can't he be a suuvus?"

"Because the very notion would be a blatant contradiction to everything he stands for, Jonah," said Felix. "I've known Lockman a lot of years, and he would never be a suuvus. He hates all things that are set apart or even remotely clandestine. He'd categorize a suuvus as the occult without hesitation."

"So what?" said Reena. "Do you know how many hypocrites are in this world? Why can't Lockman be yet another one?"

Felix looked at them for a few moments, evidently deep in thought. But when he responded, it was calm and certain.

"He isn't in league with Creyton," he insisted. "Trust me on that."

The certainty in his voice prompted faint curiosity in Jonah, but Terrence beat him to it.

"You know something, don't you?" he asked point-blank.

"I know the man," said Felix. "I know how he works."

Unashamedly, both Jonah and Terrence looked at Reena, who wasn't wearing her dampener. She shook her head, disappointed. Felix laughed.

"Thought I was keeping you in the dark, huh?" he said. "I wouldn't. Not for something like that, anyway."

A sharp intake of breath from the stairs caught their attention, and they turned to see Maxine there. She had an Anime book of some sort, but she came to a stop on the stairs. Felix rose when he saw her.

"Maxine!" he said in a warm tone. "I was wondering if you could tell me something. I did come here for a reason, after all."

"Of course!" Maxine looked excited, and practically ripped her glasses off of her face. "Anything!"

"Where can I find Elizabeth?" asked Felix.

Maxine's face fell instantly. Terrence murmured, "Ouch." But Felix remained oblivious.

"She's…she's on the elliptical," she said in a soft voice. "I'll get her—"

She took a step lower, lost her footing, and fell down the stairs. They rushed to her , horrified, but luckily, she was fine. It hadn't been a far fall, and she hadn't hit her head or neck or anything.

"I'm good!" she cried before Terrence could ask. "I'm fine!"

Felix gave her a quick inspection, likely checking for blood or if anything looked out of whack. "You're completely fine?" he asked.

Maxine allowed Jonah and Terrence to pull her to her feet. It was clear that she was mightily embarrassed. "I am. The only thing hurt is my pride."

"Good," nodded Felix. "I'll find Elizabeth, then."

He headed to the kitchen, which led to the stairs that led to the fitness room. Reena left them for a second, grabbed something off the floor, and came back to Maxine.

"Keep these things on, Maxine," she snapped. "You could have broken your damn neck!"

Reluctantly, Maxine perched the thick glasses back on her face. "Thanks or helping me," she murmured. She then retrieved her Anime book, and headed back upstairs.

"I swear," said Reena, irritable.

"Give her a break," said Terrence. "Don't even act like you wouldn't get tripped up on the stairs if you had a crush on some guy!"

"Terrence, if I developed a crush on some guy, I'd throw myself down the stairs," said Reena.

Jonah laughed. Terrence rolled his eyes.

"You know what?" he shot at them. "Just for that, you're both helping me with Sunday dinner!"

Preparing food was enjoyable, and when people returned from the faith haven, no one had to wait. Their group was augmented by Mr. and Mrs. Decessio, Raymond, and June Mylteer. Felix said something about not wanting to take food out of anyone's mouth, but Mrs. Decessio pulled him down into a chair.

"What are you going to do?" she queried. "Go get some godawful chips or Krispy Kreme? You might be a sazer, but you don't need to be fouling up your insides like that."

"But I—"

Mrs. Decessio gave him a look. Felix fell silent and seated himself. "Yes, ma'am."

He reached for some baked chicken. Jonah smiled at Terrence.

"I love your mom," he said. "Did I ever tell you that?"

With a laugh, Terrence went to grab a second helping of something. Jonah made to follow, but two quick taps on his shoulder kept him in place. It was Mr. Decessio.

"Patience told me what the Curaie sent Katarina Ocean here for," he said.

Jonah's eyes narrowed. "Please don't tell me you agree, sir."

"Not at all, Jonah," said Mr. Decessio. "I think it's absurd. And kindly remember that lashing out at your supporters will leave you with none."

Jonah choked back a cynical comment, and chose to state the obvious instead. "I could have been the classic Southern Gentleman, and they still would've taken my batons."

"True," said Mr. Decessio, "but we can't even entertain that notion, because you weren't a Southern Gentleman. Was Ocean telling the truth? Did you really refer to the Curaie as sacks of shit?"

Jonah didn't answer. Mr. Decessio's nod made it clear that he didn't even need to.

"Jonah, I know that you aren't my son," he told him. "I have no right to act paternal toward you. But I am aware of how stressors can bring out the worst in people. I've been there."

Jonah took a deep breath, but said nothing.

"You aren't in the most wonderful position right now, and I understand that," Mr. Decessio continued. "But you have to think, not react. The Curaie's memory goes back a long way. Don't give them a reason to forever view you negatively, because that isn't who you are."

Jonah sighed, and nodded. "Yes, sir. I appreciate what you're telling me. I got you."

Mr. Decessio nodded, gave him a smile, and returned to his food. Jonah looked down at his chicken breast and potatoes. He had to stop acting out of emotion. But it wasn't his fault. Maybe his reactions could be more positive if just about every other facet of his life stopped reminding him of the negative.

"Got room for one more?" said a voice that pushed all the negative away.

"Vera!" squealed Liz, who hopped up and hugged her best friend. "Did you drive here?"

"I used the *Astralimes.* Jonathan gave me permission to after we spoke."

Jonah's smile faltered. Okay, some of the negative was back. "You talked to Jonathan?"

"Yeah," shrugged Vera. "He shows up all the time, just to give me a kind word and make sure things are peaceful at Colerain Place."

"I love Jonathan so much," said Liz. "It's such a blessing that he looks out for us."

Jonah wasn't so sure that he agreed with that. He hung out with Vera a lot during these past few months, and hadn't seen Jonathan one time when he was there. Was that just coincidence? Or had it been done by design? And what was this about Jonathan giving her "kind words?"

"Jonah?" said Vera.

He jumped slightly. Several folks had their eyes on him.

"Sorry," he said hastily. "The... the food got me really relaxed. What were you saying, Vera?"

"I was asking could I ride with you back to the city later today," said Vera.

"Oh," said Jonah. "Yeah, of course!"

With a smile, Vera sat at the table and joined in conversations. Jonah turned to Felix, hoping to distract himself.

"Prodigal and his friends," he said to him, "and Autumn Rose and Jael. How are they?"

Felix actually cracked a smile. "Patience got Jael back to her parents. Turned out they were worried sick about her, and were happy to welcome her back to their home, Addington in tow. Prodigal admitted that it was a smoother transition because Autumn Rose wasn't there. She hates them, and they aren't fond of her, either."

"I was curious," chimed in Bobby. "Were Jael and Autumn Rose adopted together?"

"No," scoffed Felix. "Just Jael. I think Prodigal said that she was six or seven at the time. Apparently, Autumn Rose kept her distance because she didn't want Jael to be tarred with the same brush."

"That was awfully considerate, looking out for her sister like that," said Terrence.

"As I've said before," said Felix, with a trace of irritation in his voice, "sazers could be functioning members of society if given the chance."

Jonah heard the tone change, as did Terrence and Reena, who cleared her throat.

"Okay," she said. "That covers Jael. "What about the rest of them?"

The distraction worked. Felix's featured loosened in contemplation.

"I put them up in a safehouse I have up in Dexter City," he answered. "Prodigal wanted to be prideful and stubborn, but I told him that there were too many of them to continue sneaking around the way they were. No more problems, and no more crashing in foreclosures."

Everyone around was pleased to hear that Prodigal and his friends were safe, and resumed different conversations. Some moments later, Felix rose, saying that he needed to stretch his legs. His departure gave Jonah a sudden inspiration.

"Be right back," he told those around him, and followed Felix. He knew exactly where he'd go, so it was no surprise to find him on the front porch, flicking his silver, *fleur-di-lis*-imprinted lighter on and off.

"This isn't stretching your legs," commented Jonah.

"You've got your definition, and I've got mine." Felix didn't look awkward at all. "Doesn't it ever get tiresome, Rowe?"

"It's what we do," said Jonah. "You're aware of that; you lived here in the past. Maybe you've just gotten used to being by yourself."

"Maybe you're right," murmured Felix, who looked away. "Did you want something?"

"Yeah, I did. What did you need Liz for?"

"I needed some insight on plant extracts and their effects," answered Felix. "I have some knowledge on the matter, but you can't beat the expertise of a Green Aura."

Felix's answer was prompt. There was no guilt, awkwardness, or discomfort. For that, Jonah was relieved.

"Oh," was all he said.

Felix raised an eyebrow. "What did you think?"

"Huh?" said Jonah without thinking.

Now Felix's eyes narrowed. He actually laughed, like Jonah had ensnared himself.

"What's funny?" asked Jonah.

"You are," responded Felix. "And Terrence, and Reena! Were you all thinking that I was going to make a pass at Elizabeth?"

Jonah cleared his throat loudly, because the action gave him a few seconds to think. "It wasn't like that, exactly! It's just that she's with Bobby and we were hoping that you knew that and no one wanted any controversy—"

"Jonah, stop." Felix raised a hand. "Just stop. Perhaps you were concerned about that somewhere in your mind, but that's not why you're here. You were concerned that I may have hurt Maxine's feelings."

Jonah's eyes widened. He'd expected...well, he didn't know. But it definitely wasn't that. "You noticed?"

"Jonah, I am a tracker and a bounty hunter," said Felix. "I can gauge when a lifeblood looter is about to commit murder. You think I wouldn't see when a girl has a crush on me?"

Jonah snorted. It wasn't like Maxine had been subtle about it. Maybe it was foolish to assume that Felix was oblivious.

"But she can keep her glasses on and stop near-killing herself," said Felix. "I got the point."

"So why are you letting her make a fool of herself?" asked Jonah.

"What's it matter to you?" asked Felix. "You trying to play matchmaker? You're Blue Cupid, now?"

"I—"

"Let me ask you something, Rowe, since you're so interested in sweeping around my door," said Felix. "Have you swept around your own? Are you and Vera still dancing around the point?"

Jonah felt his eye twitch. He'd almost forgotten Felix's occasional tendency to be caustic. "The fact that you went so far around the question tells me something, Felix. "Do you like Maxine back?"

Felix flicked the lighter on and off a couple more times. "I'm not what she's looking for, Jonah."

"What?"

"I'm not worth her hassle," said Felix in a cool tone. "She can do worlds better than me."

"What the hell makes you say that?" asked Jonah.

"First of all, Jonah, I'm poor," said Felix.

"Say what?" cried Jonah. "And they say that I'm a bad liar! You're a multi-millionaire, Felix—"

"You misunderstand me," interrupted Felix. "I'm poor in the regard that my money is all that I have. I haven't mixed well with people for a very long time. Why do you think I had to take a breather out here? Matter of fact, you'd better get back in there yourself, or you'll be missed."

"They'll be at that table eternally," dismissed Jonah. "Did you see all that food? But stop trying to change the subject. Why would you say that about yourself? Maxine seemed to see past it just fine!"

"Listen to me, Rowe," said Felix. "I'm a recovering alcoholic, I've got personality issues, my one redeeming quality is the fact that I'm damn good at killing vampires, and I'm on the wrong side of thirty-five. That girl is young, un-jaded, happy, and innocent. To saddle her with me, who is damaged goods, would be akin to a crime. End of story."

Jonah was flummoxed. Was Felix just being dramatic, or did he actually believe those things about himself?

"And oh yeah," Felix pocketed the lighter, "one more thing. As of right now, this conversation is buried. Now let's both get back inside. Mrs. Decessio scares me."

Felix could bury whatever he wanted, but Jonah told Terrence and Reena about their conversation the minute they had privacy. Terrence gave a shaky, incredulous laugh.

"So he does have a heart," he mumbled.

"Cool it, Terrence," said Reena. "All this proves is that he thought about it. Nothing more."

"And we already know he has a heart," said Jonah. "He can play the game just fine. I haven't forgotten those stupid crystallized roses he got Vera. He didn't have any misgivings then. I wonder what his dilemma is now."

"I think I know," said Reena. "Vera is a little tougher, a little harder in demeanor. She's not some hard-bitch by any means, but she's a long way from a sweet girl. Maxine...she's a nerdy comic-book lover from Asheville who'd rather make bracelets, read Anime, and watch reruns of *Star Trek* than paint the town red. Felix obviously picked up on that, and decided that they didn't mesh."

"You make Max sound like Katarina," said Jonah.

"Oh, God no," scoffed Reena. "We will not speak on that woman. She is a special case. I'm just saying that Felix thinks that Maxine is better off with another comic-con dork, like herself."

"There is never a dull moment," said Terrence, who shook his head. "They can clamp down on us, interrogate us left and right, and gut our resident numbers. And yet, there is still never a dull moment."

Having Vera for company on the drive back to the city was a welcome change from driving alone for Jonah. He usually spent the drives attempting to discern what the hell the lead singer of The Incline Down, Terrence's favorite alt-rock band, was saying. Some weeks before, Terrence lent Jonah some of their albums for night driving, with the promise that he'd never get drowsy. That much was true, but Terrence failed to mention that one couldn't drive for three hours with only the music of The Incline Down for company and not want to punch the first authority member you saw. Given Jonah's current state, that wasn't a great musical selection.

But there was no need for that music when he was with Vera. They had plenty to talk about just from the weekend alone. It was true for Vera as well as Jonah.

"Liz brought me up to speed on everything that happened," she said as Jonah moved to the middle lane on I-40. "I'm sorry that Ocean had to take your weapons."

Jonah glanced at the mile marker to prevent Vera from seeing the flash in his eyes. "Me too," was all he said.

"For what it's worth, Saturday wasn't great for me either," said Vera. "I almost got written up at The Stop."

"What for?" asked Jonah.

"I sort of—purposely spilled food on top of this guy," admitted Vera.

Jonah frowned. "What did you do that for?"

Now it was Vera's turn to contemplate mile markers. "For smacking my ass, and calling me Scarface."

Jonah's eyes widened in fury. "He did what?"

Vera actually laughed once she recovered from the annoying recollection. "Breathe, Jonah. I took care of it."

"Forgive me, Vera," said Jonah, "but he deserved more than spilled food—"

"It was fresh coffee." Vera's voice was devilish. "And fresh tomato soup."

A savage smile lit Jonah's face. "Nice."

"He's lucky," said Vera. "I was going to punch him, see. I was trying to think up how I'd talk myself out of punishment for doing that, but then Leliana called up an order of all these hot liquid things. Billy was going to write me up, but then I explained that I dropped that stuff because he smacked my ass. All thoughts of disciplining me were gone after that."

"You are bad," joked Jonah. "But it sounds like he deserved it. He sounds about as idiotic as my ex-girlfriend."

"Oh?" Now Vera had much more curiosity in her voice than Jonah had ever heard. "Who was she?"

"Priscilla Gaines," he answered. "On-and-off girlfriend through most of high school, and some of college. You talk about possessive, jealous, territorial...one time, she reduced this girl to tears in my dorm room, and she was just someone tutoring me in Economics. But anyway, she'd blow up about something, I stood up for myself, and we'd break up. Then we'd later have angry sex, make up...the pattern of our relationship was pretty set."

"Sounds glorious," said Vera with heavy sarcasm. "What was the final straw?"

Jonah sighed. "We'd had some argument over the phone about...something," he said. "The details escape me now. Anyway, she called me back and said that she wanted to make up, per usual. I said that was cool; we could meet up at this frat party I was going to that night. I waited for her to show up, and she didn't. Then, some three hours later, she butt-dialed me, and I overhear her with some other guy, telling him that I was a waste of time between kisses and all the damn heavy breathing..."

"Are you shitting me?" Vera looked angry for Jonah's sake. "Damn skank! Sorry that happened to you, Jonah."

"Eh," murmured Jonah, who, after some effort, stamped down the old anger for the long ago memory. "It's water over the damn. But I haven't had too many serious relationships since then. Can count 'em on one hand. How about you? Got a fair few past relationships?"

"Some," said Vera, staring ahead at the highway. "First was Martin, then James. Then there was Leah, and then Simone after that—"

"Leah? Simone?" Jonah raised an eyebrow. "You're into women, too?"

"Gender hasn't ever really been a factor for me, Jonah," said Vera. "To be honest, it's a lot like ethereality—you're most responsive with the essence and energy that meshes the best with you. For me, sometimes that mesh was with men, and other times, with women. Been with both, enjoyed my time with both. If I'm being real, remember that guy that Liz and Bobby set me up with a few years back? That was first guy I'd been with in a while."

"Huh," said Jonah, carefully considering his words. "He must have been amazing."

"He sucked, Jonah," was Vera's instant response. "Liz and Bobby sold me on a bill of goods, but he sputtered in every way. I'm not even ashamed to tell you this, but he said after our night together, he was enamored with me. That made *one* of us."

Jonah laughed. He couldn't help it. The fact of the matter was that the dude crashing and burning was hilarious. Vera laughed as well. That levity went a long way in getting his mind of abdicating his batons.

"Back to the idiot at the diner," he said after he caught his breath, "what gave you the idea to spill all of that hot crap on him?"

Some of Vera's mirth faded. "It's something that happens in *Snow and Fire*," she said.

Some of Jonah's mirth faded at those words, too. "Is Eden still on your case?"

"Not just Eden." Vera laughed, but it seemed a bit forced. "Now she's got our other friends on my case, too. Sydney, Alan, Ronald, Francesca…and several more."

"Sounds a little like harassment," opined Jonah.

Vera snorted. "It's not like that. They're only trying to sell me on the point that no one can be the lead in the play but me."

"Well, do you believe that?" asked Jonah.

Vera laid her head against the back of the seat. "Yes," she admitted. "Yes I do."

Somehow, Jonah knew that she would say that. But he didn't quite know how to feel about it, though. He didn't want her to go back to Seattle. He didn't. But he had no right to be a dream-killing bastard. They weren't in a relationship, after all. Eden Bristow had told Vera just that.

Man, Jonah hated that woman. How was it possible to hate someone that you didn't even know?

"What's on your mind, Jonah?" said Vera.

It wasn't even spoken like a question. She'd said it like it was a statement of fact. She may as well have told him to tell her what was on his mind.

"I—I don't know what to tell you, Vera," Jonah admitted. "I mean, the stage is what makes you happy. It's what in your heart."

"But that's just it." There was the tiniest trace of desperation in Vera's voice. "That's it right there! What if my heart and mind—what if they've changed?"

"Are you saying that you don't miss the stage now?" asked Jonah. "Because that contradicts what you just said two minutes ago."

"Of course I miss the stage," said Vera. "But I—it's not a simple matter of picking up my bag and leaving. There is you—I mean, there are all of you guys in my life now."

Jonah wasn't sure if Vera meant their friends at the estate. At least not at the start of that statement.

"I was practically alone when my mother passed into Spirit," Vera continued. "Then you came into my life, and I learned about the Eleventh Percent, learned about being an ethereal human…many things have changed. I'm not the same woman I was then."

"Of course you aren't," said Jonah. "You're a better woman. Stronger now. You're aware of why your mind didn't work the way your friends' did. And your mother is at peace now. That burden is no longer in your consciousness. If your mother is like most parents, she didn't care too much for being a shut-in."

Vera hung her head. "No, she didn't. But another thing has changed, Jonah. I'm scarred now. It's stuck with me. I was reminded of that just yesterday—"

"Fuck that guy!" snapped Jonah. "Vera, if you didn't have that scar on your jaw, the dude still might have found something wrong with you! Called you lazy, clumsy, or who knows whatever else. The scar on your face is meaningless. All the other ones that you have on your body are, too. I forget you even have it half the time. Forget that pig at The Stop. I'll bet everything I own that he was more disgusting than the food you dropped on him."

Jonah was breathing very hard, be he didn't care. All he wanted was for Vera to feel better. Scarface…that man, whoever he was, had some nerve.

He chanced a glance at Vera when he could. It was clear that the label bothered her, but she did look comforted, if only slightly.

"Jonah?" Her voice was quiet.

"Yeah?"

"You just drove past our exit."

"What?"

Jonah refocused on the road, and sure enough, their exit was about a mile back.

"Son of a—I'll get us right, Vera," he mumbled.

The blunder did the trick. Vera laughed.

Jonah dropped Vera off, went into Spectral Sight long enough to say hello to Wilhelmina the young spiritess, and then went home. He was asleep within minutes. He headed to S.T.R. the next morning, not even caring that it was Monday. After the weekend he'd had, Monday was actually welcome.

Jonah went straight inside the bookstore, and avoided looking into the other stores, especially the tattoo parlor. The most welcoming of smells met his nose when he walked inside.

"Mr. Steverson?" he called. "Sir?"

Jonah's boss appeared from around a bookshelf, a huge grin on his face.

"Good morning!" he said. "Made a little something for you guys for before the store opens!"

"Sure smells good," said Jonah. "What—?"

The door opened once more, signaling Harland and Amanda's arrivals. Amanda froze.

"Brownies." Her voice was longing. "Who's got brownies?"

Mr. Steverson laughed. "I made them, Amanda. For you all."

He revealed a large pile on one of the tables. They were baked to perfection.

"Really?" said Harland. "Why?"

"Because I appreciate all of you kids helping me get S.T.R. back up to snuff," replied Mr. Steverson. "And I love you all for it. Even you, Amanda."

Amanda barely even registered the jab. She and Mr. Steverson went on like that all the time, especially when it was time for her to look over the accounts.

Jonah picked up on her internal struggle, and winked at Harland. "Go ahead, Amanda," he said after he made his voice provocative. "Peer pressure…is it enough to sway you?"

Amanda blinked, then glared at Jonah. "You know I shouldn't. I'm trying to reclaim my figure!"

"Your progress won't be undone with a few brownies, dear," coaxed Mr. Steverson.

"Besides," said Harland, "you weren't worried about your figure when you were buying half of Panera the other day. I saw you, rolling your little boy in there, boldly as all get-out."

"Shut up," snapped Amanda as she took a brownie and stormed off. Mr. Steverson shook his head at Harland.

"You never contradict a woman on the subject of her weight, boy!" he chastised. "Haven't the men in your family ever told you that?"

Harland rolled his eyes. "And how well has that notion worked for you, sir?"

"Thirty-seven years, and counting!" said Mr. Steverson proudly.

Harland's smug expression faded, and there was a bit of scarlet in his face as he scooped up a couple of brownies into a napkin. "I guess I walked into that one."

He walked away to put his bag of lunch in the refrigerator. Jonah and Mr. Steverson shared a laugh.

"Did you really make these from scratch, Mr. Steverson?" he asked. "Did Ms. Christine help you?"

Mr. Steverson smiled devilishly. "It was me, but I'm gonna let you in on a little secret. They're Duncan Hines."

Jonah's jaw dropped. "No."

Mr. Steverson nodded.

"But you swear by homemade food!" said Jonah.

"Let me tell you something, son," said Mr. Steverson in that sage-like tone. "It doesn't matter where something comes from; it matters how it's done. Everything is store brand in some way, shape, or form, especially in this day and age. You couldn't even taste the difference."

Jonah smirked, and grabbed a couple. There weren't any irritating complexities here. No Creyton or his Deadfallen disciples, no cult busters, no absent Protector Guides who still managed to give kind words to everybody else, no confusion over feelings, and no confiscation of possessions by fairy-looking waifs. It was just books, buddies, and brownies.

With all the situations at the estate, maybe S.T.R. was Jonah's refuge.

He took a huge bite of a brownie. It was delicious. "You know, Mr. Steverson, I hope you and S.T.R. are here forever."

Mr. Steverson snorted. "Son, even I don't want that."

"Just humor me, sir." Jonah took another bite from his brownie. "Just humor me."

18

Locked

Jonah was grateful for the change of pace the S.T.R. provided. He never tired of Mr. Steverson's stories, Harland's presence, or Amanda continuously bringing her son to the bookstore to ask Mr. Steverson for pointers. He spent many lunches in the break room, poring over early editions of certain books, some of which Mr. Steverson simply gave him. The man wouldn't allow Jonah to pay for anything, which was generous and annoying at the same time. He was careful not to abuse that privilege, but he completely ignored it one day when he found a copy of *Time Games* in a box on the second level. He took advantage of Mr. Steverson's kindness in letting him keep it, and then dumped it into a barrel of weeks-old stagnant water. No one was experiencing that crap again. Not on his watch.

A twinge of guilt nagged Jonah after a couple of weeks, but it wasn't hard to figure out why. With all the time he'd spent at the bookstore, at his apartment, and with Vera, he hadn't once visited Nelson and Tamara. How could he forget one of his best friends during that hellish accounting job? His mind was saturated with Creyton and all the other crap surrounding the estate thanks to the Lockman Association. But that wasn't the strongest excuse. It couldn't be used as an excuse at all. He knew that if Nelson discovered that he'd been back in town since the summer, he wouldn't appreciate that. So when Jonah called him, he evasively said that he was back in town for the foreseeable future, and wanted to meet up. Nelson invited him to the house that very night.

"Oh," said Jonah rather awkwardly, "I'm supposed to hang out with my friend Vera tonight—"

"Not a problem," said Nelson. "Bring her too! I'm sure Tamara would appreciate the female company. See ya later!"

"But—"

Nelson hung up before Jonah could make further explanations. He stared at the phone hopelessly, then glanced at his watch. It was a couple minutes past one. Vera had just taken her lunch break. In five minutes, she'd probably head out to her car, grateful to play on her phone without interruptions, as well as avoid Zelda's and Leliana's attempts to make her eat The Stop's greasy food.

Jonah frowned. When had that happened? When had he memorized Vera's routine? When did he learn beyond a shadow of a doubt what she'd be doing at certain points in her workday?

He filed that away, and dialed her number. She answered on the second ring.

"What's up, Jonah?"

"Vera, um," Jonah's voice was quite tentative, "I got to tell you something about tonight—"

"You're not coming?" Vera almost sounded concerned.

"No, it's not that," said Jonah with haste. "I, um, just asked an old buddy of mine named Nelson if he wanted a visit, and he suggested tonight. I mentioned that I was supposed to be hanging out with you tonight, and wouldn't you know it, he suggested that I being you along to hang out with his wife."

Silence. Bothersome silence. Then—

"I'll do it," said Vera. "So long as I'm not expected to help anybody cook anything."

Jonah blinked. It was a good thing that Vera couldn't see his surprise. "You will?"

"Sure," answered Vera. "You never introduced me to Nelson and Tamara. It'd be nice to put names to faces."

Jonah was stunned. Vera had always been pretty easygoing, but changing up her plans at the last second? With no aggravation? "Okay, then," he told her. "See you after work!"

"See you then!" said Vera, and they hung up.

Jonah stared at the book he'd been reading, but didn't take in any of the words.

"Huh," he murmured to himself. "That went well."

But he couldn't help but feel a little suspicious. He was very glad that it went well; no doubt about that. But why?

Jonah picked Vera up for Colerain Place about an hour after she got off work, because she refused to meet new people while she was still a walking advertisement for The Stop, and desired to change her clothes. It was hard for him to focus when he saw the snug-fitting blouse she had on, and equally tight black jeans. It looked as though he'd have to center himself on the drive over. But, in no time, they were at Nelson and Tamara's home. Vera snorted when they parked.

"Oh look," she muttered. "They've even got a damned picket fence."

Jonah laughed at that. "I promise that they aren't like the Honeymooners, or anything. They enjoy married life, but they aren't cheesy about it."

Unless they've changed, he thought to himself.

But Jonah needn't have worried. Nelson and Tamara was the same awesome people they'd always been. Nelson treated Jonah like a sight for sore eyes, and Tamara and Vera hit it off nicely. The first part of the conversation was devoted to catching up. Jonah spoke on his summer road-tripping, being back at S.T.R., managing his weight, and the new beard, which Tamara thought fit him nicely. Since Nelson and Tamara didn't know Vera, everything she said about herself was fascinating; the usual things one would expect when dealing with new people. Even so, Jonah was thankful that Tamara wasn't like Liz, who gushed at every bit of new information. The conversation was going so well, until—

"So how long have you two been dating?" asked Nelson.

Both Jonah and Vera started. "We're uh—we're just friends."

Jonah had to work to keep his mouth from twisting. At that very moment, he discovered that he liked the designation even less than he did when Vera used it with Eden.

Now Nelson and Tamara looked at each other. Tamara grinned, which made her electric-blue eyes less intense by a fraction.

"Okay." It seemed like Tamara made a point to sound unconvinced. "Well, Vera, let's give the guys some privacy. I'll show you our house."

There was a shameless readiness in Vera when she rose from the table. She was just as eager to move on from the awkward moment as Jonah. Nelson smiled at the women.

"You two have fun," he said. "And trust me, Vera—you'll have more fun with Tam than you will with us. I have a lot to tell Jonah about Jessica."

Something stirred in Vera's face, but Jonah knew why. She hadn't gotten over the crow incident. He hadn't, either.

"Oh, right," said Nelson, taking Vera's expression for confusion. "Jessica Hale is this world class…um—"

"Skank whore," finished Tamara. "I'll say it for you."

"Right." Nelson grinned at his wife. "Jessica used to make Jonah's life hell, till he escaped. The only person who liked her was a guy named Ant Noble. He used to work with us all, but then he disappeared in February. God only knows what happened to him."

Jonah didn't dare look at Vera. They knew exactly what happened to Anthony, and Jonah, who'd seen it firsthand, still had occasional nightmares about it.

"Maybe Jessica bites the heads off of her old boyfriends," snorted Tamara. "But let's move on, Vera."

They left the room, and Jonah glimpsed Vera's attempts to clear her face of emotion after that exchange.

"That's done," said Nelson, who lowered his voice as he looked back at Jonah. "She's beautiful, man."

Jonah sighed. The relief that he felt to move on from conversation about Anthony fought the emotions that he felt concerning Vera's negative self-image. "She doesn't think so," he told Nelson. "She views herself as way too curvy, and she's also got a scar on her face—"

"I didn't see any scar—"

"You wouldn't have," Jonah explained. "She covers it by wearing her hair down, or covering it with fingers when she speaks. She always does that when she meets new people."

Nelson regarded Jonah. "Does she hide it from you?"

"Nope."

That rose Nelson's eyebrow. "Which means that you two have been around each other long enough for her to be comfortable with you," he said slowly.

Jonah gave Nelson a sideways look. "She's gotten comfortable with our entire clique of friends out in the sticks," he said. "I'm just one in the bundle."

Nelson snickered. "Thought so."

"You thought what?" asked Jonah. "There isn't anything to think!"

"Yeah." Nelson smirked. "Nothing at all."

Jonah sighed. Nelson whacked his shoulder.

"Why don't you just admit that you're in—"

"Nope!" said Jonah loudly. "Not going there! I'm certain that's not the case."

Nelson smiled. It was a very knowing smile that Jonah tried hard to ignore. He gritted his teeth, because curiosity got the better of him.

"For the sake of having the knowledge," he carefully worded, "and it's for future reference only—has no bearing on the current time—how will I know that—that's the case?"

Nelson looked at the refrigerator. There was a picture of him beaming with Tamara wrapped in his arms while they were on their honeymoon in the Poconos. He seemed to relish some memory before he turned his attention back to Jonah. "Well, nuances aren't universal for all guys; that much I know. But there is one thing that seems to hold true, no matter the man."

"And that would be?" asked Jonah.

"You know all the excuses that we make for being a bachelor?" asked Nelson. "Those things we say to justify being single for the long-term and all that? Well, they stop making sense."

Jonah frowned. "I'm not sure I follow."

"I'll use myself as an example," said Nelson. "I used to have all of these plans, Jonah. I wanted to travel the world, go to all these events in Madison Square Garden, road-trip across country—things like that. I wanted to be single when I did all that. It was a must. Who wants to have ties when they're flying free? Then Tam came along." Nelson laughed to himself. "I went into the store to buy new trainers, man. But I couldn't forget that pretty cashier with the intense blue eyes. Couldn't do it. I started making excuses to get a glimpse of her. I started eating lunch in the food court at the mall because it meant I'd get to see her when I left. Then I finally got the courage to talk to her, and by some miracle, she was interested. We got together, and I swear man, everything changed. It wasn't gradual, either. Everything that suited me for my entire life suddenly wasn't enough anymore. Life seemed out of whack if I didn't get to see Tamara, hear her voice at least. Every plan I had, everything that I thought I needed to be single to enjoy...they just seemed lonely without her. Not a single bit of it made sense if Tam wasn't there."

Jonah let all that sink in. Nelson was long-winded about it, but Jonah caught every word. So all the excuses that men made to be single stopped making sense. Did any of that apply to him? Did he feel that way about Vera?

Plans on life...he didn't have a plan. College and graduate school put a plan in his head, but he chafed the minute he got on the path. All he wanted to do was write books. And he still couldn't finish one. All the advice from a few people about keeping it up did nothing; he'd heard it before. Even from Nelson, Terrence, and Reena. But when Vera told him he needed to keep it up, it resonated. Her opinion mattered. He even saw it as a possibility after Vera praised his writing.

And all this time he'd known her at the estate. He had simply assumed that Vera was a part of the routine—a part of the pack, like Liz, Bobby, Doug, Magdalena, Maxine, and of course, Terrence and Reena. And when he was away from there, yeah, he missed them. But missing Vera was different. Hell, that thought was probably most prevalent in his mind when the Phasmastis Curaie dropped the hammer. And when he found out she would be back at Colerain Place, he'd been relieved. It made the glorified "exile" tolerable, knowing he could see Vera whenever he wanted.

Was it like Nelson described? Did his life make less sense if Vera wasn't there? He placed a hand to his temple.

"Nelson?" he said.

"Yeah?"

Jonah massaged his temple. "Can we talk about something else?"

Nelson snickered again. "Sure, Jonah."

"Thanks," he said. "How are things at Essa, Langton, and Bane?"

Now Nelson looked away, a cold sort of smirk on his face. "Before I tell you anything about the place, there is something I forgot to tell you. I'm leaving there soon. I'm going to open my own accounting firm."

Jonah's eyes bulged. "Seriously?" he demanded. "That's awesome, man!"

They fist bumped, and Nelson looked very pleased with himself. That relieved Jonah more than anything. If Nelson wasn't around Jessica, Jonah didn't have to worry about the bitch threatening his friend and his wife.

"It's easier to talk about the place now, because I won't be there much longer," marveled Nelson. "But let us proceed with the crazy. First and foremost, you haven't been there in a while. It's just *EB* now, for Essa and Bane. They changed it when Langton died."

"Really?" asked Jonah.

Nelson nodded. "It was a damn shame he died, but you know no one liked him. When they put the new sign up there, no one cared. But Jessica cared less."

Luckily, Jonah's hands were still over his eyes from the previous conversation, because they widened at Jessica's name again."That's odd," he said, playing dumb. "She was such an ass-kisser, and was always in his office."

"That's what we all thought," said Nelson. "She had been out of work, you remember, because of the stalker—"

"Yeah, I remember," interrupted Jonah, a little coldly. "Sorry—I mean, it wasn't a pleasant subject, stalking and all. But please, continue."

"So yeah, she was out of work, but she came back the day after Tony left," continued Nelson."She was pissed about something. She wasn't talking about it, but I assumed it had something to do with the stalker or whatever, because she had her arm in a sling."

Jonah smiled savagely. He knew why Jessica had gone to work pissed, and took great pleasure in breaking her arm.

"But after a few weeks, she was herself again," said Nelson. "Wardrobe, attitude, everything. People even asked her about Tony, but she said he had to go away. He was burned out, or something."

Jonah felt coldness in his stomach. That bitch-born skank.

"She wasn't sad at all," said Nelson. "I hate to say it, but a bunch of people started thinking she may have had something to do with Tony's disappearance."

Jonah looked at his friend, wide-eyed. Could it be? Had Jessica not pulled the wool over everyone's eyes? "Really?" was all he said.

"See, you weren't there, Jonah," said Nelson. "You didn't see it. She showed no concern, no sadness—nothing. We knew she was heartless, but she just went about her life, like she hadn't dated the guy for eight months. But hey, we could all be overreacting. Jessica's not that smart. What do you think?"

Jonah allowed himself a few seconds to take one or two deep breaths. He had to answer this question carefully. Nelson was going to open his own firm, but he hadn't left Jessica's presence yet. He was not putting Nelson, and by extension, Tamara, in danger. "People do some crazy things in this world," was as generic a response as he could muster. "But hey, man, you got Tamara to come home to, and that's all that matters."

Nelson nodded in agreement. "Very true. I am perfectly content with letting Jessica be our new supervisor's pet."

"What's her job description?" asked Jonah.

"Same as it was when you were there," Nelson replied.

"I didn't know what it was then," said Jonah.

"Neither did I!" replied Nelson.

Jonah looked at him, and they both burst out laughing. After such a conversation, it was good to laugh.

"So how long will you be in town?" asked Nelson, wiping his eyes.

"Like I said on the phone, friend," muttered Jonah, "I'm here for the foreseeable future. Now, let's check on the women."

"I'm glad that Tamara is a nice woman," Vera commented once they were back at Colerain Place. "Because if she was evil and laid those crazy blue eyes on me, I'd tuck tail and run."

Jonah laughed, in complete agreement."Yeah, you're right," he said. "If she gave Katarina one of those glares, the wimpy little girl would cry again. So what all did you guys talk about?"

"I told her about *Snow and Fire*," said Vera. "She was immediately in love with it. She told me she hasn't seen a play since high school, and ours sounded like it would definitely hold one's attention. She also said that Nelson looks up to you."

Jonah snorted."Can't imagine why," he said. "He's older, made smarter decisions, found the perfect woman for him in the mall, for God's sakes, and has more tolerance than I could ever scrounge. And oh yeah, he's about to leave that shithole and open his own accounting firm."

"Very impressive," said Vera, "but age means nothing, Jonah. And you could never fairly judge yourself against a Tenth Percenter. The decisions they make aren't like the ones we have to."

Jonah thought on it. Vera spoke the truth, but Elevenths weren't all that different from Tenths.

"What did you and Nelson talk about?" she asked.

No way was Jonah going to tell her the first part of their conversation, but unfortunately, that only left the other part. "He told me about how things are at the office," he said in a rush.

Vera was silent for a moment, then said in a soft but shrewd voice, "And by that, you mean he talked about Jessica the Psycho Whore."

Jonah sighed. "I didn't think you'd want to talk about her after the night she scared us shitless," he told her.

Vera actually chuckled. "It's not like ignoring her, or the rest of them, is going to make them less frightening, right?" she asked. "What did you find out now?"

Reluctantly, Jonah filled Vera in on what Nelson had told him. She winced at the lack of remorse, but took in Jonah's words just the same. When he got to the "cozying up to the new boss" part, she rolled her eyes.

"You said that she was good at that," she murmured while shaking her head.

"Yes, indeed," said Jonah. "I didn't know the devil existed 'til I got that job and met that woman. Or maybe I should say that the devil is Creyton, and she's the right hand. But you know the funny thing?"

Vera shook her head.

"You remember the lady I told you about who suggested the newspaper assist the Lockman Association? Charlotte Daynard?"

"Yeah."

"I think she is a little jealous of Jessica's role. It wasn't obvious, but it was there. I picked up on it that night."

He paused because Vera paled. She hadn't been keen on hearing the story Jonah recounted told when he described the Deadfallen disciples he remembered. He hurried on.

"The point is that I don't think that Charlotte appreciates the fact that Jessica is Inimicus. She must feel threatened."

Vera mouthed, "Huh."

"They are some sick people," said Jonah. "But Jessica…I can truly say I hate that bitch. I'm glad Nana isn't here to hear me say that, but it's the truth."

Vera nodded. "She's given you reasons to hate her."

"But you know what?" said Jonah suddenly. "Deadfallen disciples make for bad conversation. Wanna watch some Netflix?"

Vera shook her head. "I'm tired as hell, Jonah." She looked it, too. "I'm heading to bed. But it was great to meet your friends."

Jonah frowned slightly, but nodded. "You okay?" he asked, studying her face.

"Oh yeah," she said. "Just need to go to sleep."

"Alright then," he said. "I'll see myself out. It was a pleasure, Vera."

"Always a pleasure with you, Jonah," said Vera in a quiet tone.

Jonah paused, and regarded her with curiosity. She was already heading to her bedroom. Smiling slightly, he left.

* * *

Jonah unlocked his door, and carefully stepped over the threshold. Even though his doorway had been fixed to prevent a Threshold of Death, he still felt the need to be cautious. Maybe it was the conversation about Jessica that heightened his sense of anxiety. Flicking on his lights, he reached for the remote when something caught his eye.

There was a small note on his kitchen counter, rolled and sealed. Jonah picked it up with a frown. Why would this be here?

Then he remembered. He'd seen something like this before, when he and Terrence had been forced to flee the estate. This was a note sealed by a Guide. What had Terrence said? "*A message sealed by a Guide can only be broken by the addressee. Keeps the message from being intercepted.*"

So someone left him a note that they didn't want intercepted. And it was a Guide, obviously. Jonah wondered who it could have been. Jonathan certainly wouldn't bother with it nowadays. He ripped it open easily. Perching his reading glasses on his nose, he read the message written in neat, cursive writing.

Jonah,

It is imperative that you know this beforehand, because your recent episodes with anger will no doubt resurface if you were taken by surprise.

Balthazar Lockman means to interrogate you on Saturday morning, nine-thirty. He hopes to spring this upon you, and catch you off guard. Now you are aware. I implore you to remain of sound mind and of level temperament. You are to come to the estate tomorrow morning. Familiarize yourself with the changes. Miss Haliday will be alerted as well.

Jonathan

Jonah re-read the note. The aggravation remained the same with the new read.

So Lockman planned to spring it on him, huh? Wanted to catch him when he didn't have his wits about him. Jonathan figured that it was prudent to give him advance notice, because an impromptu announcement was sure to piss him off.

Unfortunately, that pissed him off.

Jonathan used jargon that made Jonah sound like a nutcase. That wasn't the truth. What was Jonah expected to do? Smile and grin like a buffoon while the ethereal world equated to an outhouse at the moment?

His recent episodes with anger…

Thanks, Jonathan, he thought. *Way to make me feel like shit in the purest form.*

He hadn't been angry in a while. As a matter of fact, he'd been a whole lot better since he'd left that damned estate—

Jonah paused. Did that just run across his mind? Was that how he felt now? The Grannison-Morris estate had been the haven. The place where he finally felt camaraderie. It infuriated him when he learned that he'd be uprooted. But, son of a bitch, the city had become the haven. It had S.T.R., where Jonah's only requirement was to be friendly. It had his apartment, where he didn't have to worry about dark ethereality. In this place, he was just one of many. With the exception of

Vera, no one here knew nor cared that he was not only an Eleventh Percenter, but the Blue Aura...

It had happened slowly. Jonah didn't know exactly when that time was, but it had happened.

And the revelation did Jonah no favors.

Did this mean he was a coward? Did this mean that he preferred to hide? To tuck himself away while the people he cared about struggled to keep their heads above water in the river of drama? It hadn't even been his fault that he had to relocate!

With painstaking effort, he shifted his focus to another matter that caught his attention in the note.

What did Jonathan mean when he said, "*Familiarize yourself with the changes*?" What had changed in a month? Surely Terrence and Reena would have informed him of anything crazy. He spoke to them every couple of days for updates...

Wait.

He hadn't done that lately. It was easier to just go about his routine of S.T.R., home, and hanging out with Vera. He hadn't spoken to Terrence and Reena, the two people who didn't need his blood in their veins to be considered his brother and sister, since the last time he'd been in Rome.

He closed his eyes, gritted his teeth, and spat a single swear word. At the same time, he came to a realization.

Jonathan could have easily told him all of that stuff himself. He left a damned note.

Maybe Jonah was wrong with his earlier thoughts. Maybe it wasn't so strange that the city had become the refuge.

Jonah hit the road the next morning a few minutes past eight. He'd already had words planned for Mr. Steverson, knowing that he'd never ask too many questions, but it turned out someone beat him to it.

"Why are you callin' me, son?" Mr. Steverson had genuine puzzlement in his voice when Jonah called him. "Your optometrist called me and told me about your appointments."

"Say wh—I mean, he did?" asked Jonah, eyebrows high.

"Yeah!" said Mr. Steverson. "You're good over here, boy. I know where you'll be. See you Monday!"

So Jonathan took care of every detail. He'd spared Jonah the need to lie.

"Oh, Jonathan," he said with mock pleasure. "You *should* have."

He quieted his mind as best he could while he drove down I-40, but remembered to keep a steady pace. After all, there were no Networkers around to get him out of a speeding ticket.

He had mixed feelings when he got off of Exit 81. It seemed like he had to put on a new mentality, like a hat, or something. He'd been cool, collected, and mostly carefree in the city. Unfortunately, in the land of Creyton, Lockman, and these soon to be discovered "changes," such an easygoing outlook wouldn't fly.

He turned onto the path that led to the estate, lowering his foot on the gas just a bit so as to hurry up and figure out the changes. Just the thought of some new crap had his mind busy at work again. Fifty feet down the drive, however, something occurred that made his mind instantly go blank.

An ash-grey, sheet-like thing appeared out of nowhere, and completely barred his path.

"WHOA!" Jonah slammed both feet on his brakes. Mercifully, the car came to a complete stop. Jonah stepped out, and gawked at the barrier.

It turned out that it was not a sheet, but a sort of ethereal barrier that gleamed ash grey. So this thing was powered by someone's aura. But who the hell was stupid enough to place it on the gravel driveway?

"What the hell is the deal?" said Jonah to himself.

Then a footfall drew his attention to his left.

"Hello, Blue Aura."

Jonah's eyes widened. "Cross?" he demanded.

Her nostrils flared. "It's Networker Cross to you, Blue Aura."

"No," Jonah shook his head. "You're not a Networker anymore. You're in Ethereamency, or whatever—"

"Indeed, I was," interjected Dace, "but thanks to you people, I'm back in the fold. Why do you think I'd be here?"

"I don't know," hissed Jonah. "You tell me!"

"I'm sure your buddies in there will fill you in," said Dace. "Now, accept your pass and go. It doesn't require a spiritual endowment."

She held out what looked like an inactive pager. Jonah stared at it.

"Why are you giving me a pager?" he asked her. "Those things went out of style with yo-yos and Gigapets."

Dace rolled her eyes. "It's not a pager, you dunce," she snapped. "It's a Tally. It lets us know how many Eleventh Percenters are on the grounds, as well as who they are. Now will you touch it?"

With a leveling breath, Jonah placed a finger to the ethereal contraption and then removed it. It glowed blue, made a clicking sound, and then returned to its original state.

"Now get in your car, and get out of my sight," grumbled Dace.

"Go fuck yourself," said Jonah as he lowered himself into his car. "It isn't like anyone else does."

"What did you say to me?" demanded Dace.

"You heard me just fine," Jonah replied.

The woman's nostrils flared once more. She gave Jonah the finger, then clapped her hands, and the ash grey barrier vanished. Jonah drove past her, eyes wide and mind racing.

What was the deal with that thing? And Dace Cross said "*us*." How many did that entail?

He was surprised to see Terrence and Reena seated out front. It was like they awaited him. His car was barely in park when he hopped out of it.

"WHAT THE—"

Reena silenced him with a slicing motion across her throat and mouthed, "*The studio.*"

She placed a hand on Jonah's back and guided him inside, Terrence in hot pursuit.

"Why aren't you guys at work?" Jonah demanded.

"Because none of us have been allowed to leave for four days," said Terrence. "They went around us, and made arrangements with our jobs and schools for whoever is a student. They wanted us all here to get Tallied."

The word "arrangements" caught Jonah's attention. "Why is the Curaie doing this?"

"Wait until we're in the studio," said Reena through clenched teeth.

They reached their destination not too long after that. Jonah and Terrence sat down, but Reena paced between a painted blade and a half-done painting of Piccadilly Circus.

"Why did we have to come down here?" asked Jonah. "I'm sorry that I haven't been calling, but—"

"It's a good thing that you haven't been calling us," said Terrence, who squeezed the side of his seat like the action calmed his nerves. "There is an S.P.G. practitioner out there named Farrow that's using Sunny Roots or some shit—"

"It's called Sonorusus," Reena corrected Terrence while still pacing. "It allows them to monitor our conversations, but Trip found a loophole."

"That right?"

"Mmm hmm," said Reena. "He's the sound whiz, after all. Apparently, Sonorusus works best on equal footing, because sound moves in waves. So when the waves flow above or below, ethereal reception is distorted. Something like that."

Jonah's eyes narrowed. "So we have to speak inhere?"

"Or the upstairs bedrooms," said Terrence.

"Swell," grumbled Jonah. "Now please tell me what they're doing here."

Reena finally ceased pacing. Terrence glanced at her, and she shrugged.

"Go for it," she told him.

"The Curaie think we're spreading chaos in the world," said Terrence.

Jonah began to tap his knee in anger. This song and dance got old a long time ago. "This wouldn't happen to have anything to do with Reynolda's article, would it?"

"It has everything to do with that article!" snarled Reena. "She twisted all of it! She made us look like wild freaks! Like nut jobs with a superiority fixation."

"What did she say? What was in it?"

Reena picked up a paintbrush, which her grasp snapped in two. "Trip's outburst was perverted into looking like he got completely belligerent when she asked him how we live here," started Reena.

"But that wasn't a fabrication," said Jonah. "Trip actually did get belligerent."

"You don't get it, Jonah," said Reena. "He got angry with her because they have a history, not because, as her article put it, *'an innocent query about the practices of the largely Bohemian residents was met with rage and belligerent behaviors from Titus Rivers III, son of Titus Rivers, Jr., an LTSU professor who was slain in a highly publicized murder in 1993.'*"

"Huh," said Jonah. "She threw in the old scandal to make people have grisly thoughts on top of everything else, did she?"

"Oh, it gets better," said Terrence. "Spader was described as a, '*vagrant; a Goth-looking vagabond prone to selective forgetfulness and changing his story in mid-sentence.*' I told him that wearing all those jeans with bondage straps would make somebody judge him the wrong way someday. But anyway, Doug got it, too. He was made to look like someone who is, '*slowly seeming to succumb to negative influences, which his youth and innocence only make that much simpler.*' "

That irritated Jonah something fierce, but then a prickle of worry hit him. "His grandma probably gave him grief for that," he muttered.

"She came here," said Reena. "She got one of Doug's brothers to drive her here, and then proceeded to tear him down just when the S.P.G. showed up."

Jonah sighed. Douglas couldn't win. He just couldn't. There was just no pleasing that grandmother of his.

"Langford also talked about Daniel and his 'menacing' bow," continued Reena. "And then…"

She closed her eyes and began to breathe slowly. Terrence eyed her with some concern, and then decided to assist.

"She brought up people's—um, ties to us," he said delicately.

Jonah's mouth dropped. He didn't need details. Reena was angry enough. "Sorry, Reena, but there is one thing I have to know," he said. "How bad did it blow back on Kendall?"

Reena's eyes moved to him slowly. "The good thing is that Kendall's and my relationship is our own," she said. "That Reynolda bitch didn't mention her name. She did, however, start a rumor around town that I go around corrupting women good Christian women."

"WHAT!"

"She wasn't even all that interested in Kendall's and Reena's relationship, Jonah," said Terrence. "Reynolda basically said that whoever has dealings with us is unsafe."

Jonah shook his head."That wasn't Reynolda talking," he grumbled.

"No, it wasn't," said Reena angrily. "But Lockman was in the article, too. His opinion was just strategically placed to be salient. He said, and I quote, that we, '*seem to flout rules, impede serenity, and live markedly hazardous lifestyles with unchecked ebullience.*' "

Terrence flung up his hands. "See, that's why I couldn't have conversations with this guy," he said. "I couldn't go five minutes without needing a dictionary!"

Reena sighed. "Ebullience means wild happiness, Terrence. Crazy zeal, a delight that's almost manic."

"Well, why didn't he just say that?"

"The point, Jonah," said Reena, "is that you needed to hear all that to understand why the Curaie sent their dogs here. They believe that we are making things dangerous for Eleventh Percenters as a whole. Those stories, however spurious and fabricated they are, risk exposure of the ethereal world. So now, we are being monitored."

"Like Sanctum?" asked Jonah.

Reena nodded."We've been Tallied. We have been given thirty endowments a month, which work on a declining balance. Any endowments we take, even for training, or day-to-day ethereality, count against that balance."

"But what about to protect our physical lives?" said Jonah.

"They say if our compliance remains within the parameters of their regulations, we should have no problems, because the professionals will be working in clear waters, or something," said Terrence. "That's straight from Engagah."

"You talked to Engagah?" Jonah asked.

"No, Jonathan did," said Reena. "You just missed him."

"Of freakin' course I did," he snapped. "You guys get a briefing, I get a damn note."

He told them about his surprising-but-not-really interview with Lockman on Saturday. Reena looked at him, urgency in her eyes.

"Jonathan was trying to help you, Jonah," she said. "He wouldn't have strayed too far from the estate—"

"He does it for Vera, and God knows who else—"

"They aren't you," Reena said simply. "But Jonathan would have had to send a rep. Meaning you'd need Spectral Sight. That's ethereality, and counts against the balance."

Jonah felt himself tapping his knee again. "What's the penalty for non-compliance?" he asked.

Terrence spoke up. "A mandatory thirty-day sentence on The Plane with No Name," he responded.

Jonah and Reena looked at him.

"Are you sure?" Reena asked, incredulous. "They bypassed Grounding?"

"Yeah, I'm sure," Terrence replied. "It was the last message Dad got from Patience before they started running wild with the Sunna-supasona—the sound shit."

Reena stared at him for a moment. Then, without warning, she punched a hole in the studio wall. Terrence and Jonah just about jumped out of their skins, and looked at her in alarm.

"What the hell?" exclaimed Terrence.

"I can't believe I used to have respect for those Guides!" she barked. "If they don't get with the program, we'll all wind up on the Other Side because of them!"

Jonah sat in his car, across the street from the building that Lockman had leased for his resident shop of horrors. He had been staring at the place for almost fifteen minutes, but still couldn't manage to pry his hands from the steering wheel.

He looked at his reflection in the rearview mirror, closely inspecting the bearded face and hazel eyes. Those eyes had seen a great deal, and based on present evidence, they were going to see a great deal more.

"This day will be wonderful," he affirmed. "This will be a great day. This meeting won't have a hitch, I'll be out in no time, and it will be a great day."

Strangely, this action didn't help matters much. It only reminded him that he hadn't done positive affirmations before going into a building since his accounting days.

"Damn it, Jonah," he said to himself. "Just go."

The building wasn't large; about the size of a rural doctor's office. It was set up much like one as well, with the huge desk up front and the offices behind several doors along the wall. The walls were painted a soothing taupe color, which was, given this place, the biggest oxymoron conceivable.

Wyatt Faulk, the guy at the desk, looked up at Jonah and grinned. He had been most disappointed when he barged onto the grounds, bold as could be, to announce Jonah's formal summons, because he did not receive the supplication and gasp of horror he expected. Jonah had been disappointed, too. Wyatt's car hadn't slammed into Dace's barrier.

"Go ahead," He gestured behind himself with his thumb. "He's waiting for you."

With a venomous half-smile, Jonah walked to the back door, which was ajar. So Lockman was waiting for him, probably glancing out every second. He didn't feel the need to knock.

The door opened easily, and Lockman sat at his desk, where he wrote on stationary with a sterling silver pen. Jonah stood there, hating everything about the man and trying very hard to comply with Jonathan's advice of keeping his cool…for his friends' sakes, at least.

"Sit down." Lockman didn't even look up from his writing.

Jonah did so. Lockman continued to write. This went on for five more minutes. Ten. Fifteen.

Jonah thought he knew what Lockman was up to. His goal was to make him impatient so that his cool and collected demeanor would falter. Oddly enough, it seemed that Lockman's own patience faded more and more with each passing minute. At the five-minute mark, his nostrils flared. At ten, his breathing became labored. At fifteen, he threw down the pen.

"How'd you do it?" he asked in a low, frigid voice.

Jonah frowned. "What?"

Lockman struggled to take even, measured breaths between each word. "How-did-you-do-it?"

Jonah looked at him, flabbergasted. "Do what?"

Lockman slowly curled his fingers around the pen as if he desired stabbing Jonah in the neck with it. "How did you get out of the charges in Dexter City, Rowe?" he demanded.

Jonah's eyes narrowed. "You're still hung up on that?" he asked. "It was bull—B.S., that's how."

"Who is Ovid Patience?"

"Hang on." Suspicion crept into Jonah's voice. "I thought this was about the estate."

"It is," said Lockman. "But what happened in Maryland let me know that you people's reach extends much farther than a tucked-away, palatial North Carolina estate. I have my sources, after all."

Jonah ran his tongue across his teeth. "Do you bribe all of them?" he asked quietly. "How much money was in that wad you gave Deputy Feldman, huh? Fifty? A hundred? A thousand?"

Lockman chuckled, though mirth didn't reach his eyes. "Do you feel that knowing that gives you power over me?" he asked. "Tell me, who do you think the populace would believe? An upstanding crusader, or a lapsed accountant who traipses with people who believe themselves ethereal humans?"

Miraculously, Jonah kept his face neutral, but his gut did a slight lurch. How the hell did Lockman know these things? But he wasn't going to be made a fool of, like last time. Maybe the offensive would help. "Why have you made this personal, Lockman?" he asked in a cold tone. "Why did you involve Langford? Why are you using half-truths to fuel your theories? Not a single one of us acts as though our way is the only way to redemption. That's a primary guideline for a cult, right?"

Lockman was silent for a moment. Maybe he didn't expect Jonah to know that. It was only by association. One could not be friends with Reena Katoa and not pick up stuff.

"I suppose you'd need to know the guidelines if you're going to defy them," said Lockman.

"I suppose you'd need to know the guidelines so you could use them as a sword," countered Jonah.

Lockman's jaw twisted. Jonah almost smiled. Lockman expected him to falter and crack like last time. It wasn't happening. Then—

"What's behind that jammed door in your basement?" he said suddenly.

"Huh?"

Damn.

Lockman smiled widely. "So you people are hiding something," he said, almost jubilant. "Who would have thought that you remain the weak link? You gave a good run, Rowe, but you stood no chance the minute your sordid activities came to light."

Jonah felt his breath coming laboriously. Weak link. "What's your beef, Lockman?" he snapped. "Why have you made it personal? I've asked you that already, and you conveniently didn't answer. Why do you hate us?"

"I don't hate you, Rowe," said Lockman quietly. "Any of you. And it's not personal. But I do not trust you people. People like you, who promise weak-willed individuals safety. Peace. But only if they conform to your way of thinking. My mistrust of you people is Brobdingnagian."

"Uh, what was that word?" murmured Jonah.

Lockman rolled his eyes, grumbling something that sounded like "backwater" and "yokel."

"That's your problem," snapped Jonah. "You can't see past your petty distastes and actually see reason. What would your daughter think?"

Jonah had gone too far. Lockman rose, a vicious blaze in his eyes. The sudden maneuver knocked half the things off his desk. He didn't seem to notice.

"Never mention my daughter," he whispered. "And I do mean never. That's a quick way to get your—"

Jonah took an involuntary intake of breath, which prompted Lockman to pause. That uncomfortable buzz was at the back of his skull again. He clutched it with his hand, gritting his teeth in frustration and concern. This could not be happening now…

Creyton stood in front of him. They were in that Godforsaken valley once more, and the spirits looked worse than ever. Creyton stepped on top of one of their backs, and the spirit cried out in pain. He paid no attention.

"Hello, Jonah," he said, a sly smile on his inhuman face. "You picked the wrong person to swoon in the presence of, didn't you?"

He moved closer. He and Jonah were now face to face. "I do not intend to keep you long," he said, the smile fading. "I just thought you should know that your borrowed time dwindles."

Creyton turned his heel, making the spirit cry out further. "You won't escape this time," he rasped. "I promise you that. Now, by all means, please resume your crashing and burning."

Jonah once again experienced the sensation of his consciousness slamming back into his body. His "borrowed time" dwindled? Creyton pulled everyone into a Mindscope to tell him that?

Wait. He had a bigger problem at the moment than far-off threats. He scrambled to his feet in a near panic. Lockman hadn't moved from where he stood, but his anger had faded. Now his features looked strangely gleeful.

"My, my, my," he said with triumph in his voice. "Suffering from substance withdrawal as well?"

19

Minnows and Whales

Jonah was cornered. He knew it. And a few seconds later, he was blocked on both sides: Wyatt was at the door, undoubtedly to investigate the sound made when he hit the floor.

Lockman now regarded Jonah with what looked like concern. It was evident in his expression, evenly mixed in with the contempt.

"Did we just see a withdrawal, Rowe?" he asked. "Or bad side effects?"

Jonah's eyes darted left and right. This must be what rats sinking in the water barrel felt like. "It—it wasn't what you think," he said lamely.

Lockman instantly snapped his eyes to Wyatt."What illicit substances cause such effects, Wyatt?"

"Barbiturates, sir," said Faulk readily. "Also inhalants. I wouldn't rule out cannabis, either."

"Cannabis is a plant that grows wild," dismissed Jonah, wincing at the dull ache in his head.

"So you admit to smoking it?" asked Faulk, fastening onto the phrase with swiftness.

"What? No! I'd never—"

"And most drugs are derived from plants, boy," snapped Lockman. "But apparently, you missed that school lesson."

Jonah looked at him suspiciously, then remembered what Reena had told him about Lockman's background in horticulture. There was something else, if Jonah paid attention to it. Something was in Lockman's voice: a knowing, a familiarity, like he'd just stumbled upon something he'd heard before. Experienced before. But the change in his voice hadn't occurred until he started assuming the usage of substances…

Jonah's eyes widened.

"No," he said in a low voice. "You think we're using drugs? Hallucinogens?"

Lockman smiled, and Jonah swallowed. Lucifer himself couldn't have hitched such an evil grin. "I never said that," he told Jonah. "But you just did."

Jonah stared at Lockman for a full seven seconds. He actually counted them. Then he ran, knocking Faulk out of his way.

"Hey!" shouted Faulk, but Lockman said very quickly, "Let him go. We're right behind him."

Jonah nearly wrenched the driver's side door off kilter, and threw himself into the car. He had to get back to the estate. This was bad. He had really fucked up this time. Damn Creyton and that Mindscope! He knew exactly what he had been doing. Damn him!

He was on the gravel drive before he knew it. He stopped before he reached Dace Cross' spectral grey sheet, and got out of the car. Jonah hoped that Dace had come to after the Mindscope. Else he'd have no way past the barrier.

"Cross!" he called. "Cross!"

"Will you shut up?" snapped a voice to his left, and he saw Dace Cross, who looked fine. Hell, she looked like a million bucks. "I have your Tally information, you really need to learn patience—"

"Let me through!" shouted Jonah. "We have a problem!"

"What are you talking about now?"

"Is everyone okay?" said Jonah.

"Why wouldn't they be?" Dace shot back.

"I don't have time for this! Is everyone alright from the Mindscope? Tell me!"

"What Mindscope?"

Jonah gritted his teeth. "The one that just happened, dumbass," he snapped. "Creyton put us in that ethereal desert again!"

"That was months ago," spat Dace. "Stop trying to incite a panic, dumbass."

Jonah looked at her, puzzled. Dace hadn't experienced the Mindscope? It hadn't been a blanket thing for all Eleventh Percenters, like the others?

But that meant... oh, hell...

Jonah snatched the Tally from Dace's hand. Dace, who hadn't expected the rash maneuver, let go of it.

"Stop!" she snarled. "You're making a mistake—"

Jonah shoved her away. She hadn't expected that, either, or she would have blocked it with her endowment. As it was, she stumbled into the hood of Jonah's car and butted her face against it before falling to the ground, enraged. Jonah barely registered the glare she gave him as he crossed the barrier and tossed the Tally on the ground.

"Daniel!" There wasn't time for all this calling people out! "Hey, Daniel!"

Suddenly, Daniel was there, which threw Jonah off guard. Bast was there as well.

"What's wrong, Rowe?" he asked, his solemn face pulled into concern.

"Daniel, get Bast to summon Jonathan," cried Jonah. "Creyton tricked me, and now there's a huge problem. I messed up, Daniel—"

"Damn right you have," growled a voice behind him.

Jonah turned, completely unprepared for the hands that grabbed him. He wondered why he was being restrained, but then Dace, livid, punched him in his face. Daniel roared, pulling his bow and an arrow from his quiver. He fired the arrow faster than thought at one of the people restraining Jonah. Dace had brought reinforcements.

She screamed in horror, but it was quickly revealed that injury was not Daniel's intent. The arrow's point missed the man's flesh entirely and pierced the collar of his jacket. The momentum of the thing sent him flying backward, and he crumpled in a heap on the lawn.

Daniel pointed the bow, loaded with another golden crackling arrow, at Dace and his shocked colleague, who still clung to Jonah's arms.

"No, your friend there isn't hurt," he directed at Jonah's captor, "but it was because that wasn't my plan. If you don't unhand that boy, that will change."

The man immediately released Jonah, and backed away. Two other Spectral Law practitioners did the same, leery of that bow. Dace stood her ground, angry. When she spoke, Jonah could see blood smeared across her teeth.

"You'll be sorry for that, Daniel," she promised. "And to think, you are a former Spirit Guide—"

"Protector Guide, Dace," corrected Daniel. "A title that I abdicated of my own volition. I seemed to recall the Curaie dismissed you from the Networkers because of your tendency for unnecessary force. Rehabilitated—look at this boy's face, and then dare to tell me your violence is in the past!"

"Him?" shouted Dace. "He practically threw me against his car! I didn't start—!"

"SILENCE!" roared a voice, and everyone turned.

It was Jonathan. He stood feet away, Bast at his side, his hands in the pockets of his slate grey duster. Though his hands were pocketed, Jonah could tell that they were fists.

"If you are done hiding behind your position, Cross," he growled, "you will leave this place."

"What is going on out here?" came Liz's voice from the porch. Soon, she was joined by the others residents who were just inside. Terrence and Reena moved to Jonah's side, while Trip, who tapped his ear with his index finger, frowned and looked at Jonathan. Dace caught none of this, as her hostile gaze remained on Jonah.

"Why do we have to leave, Jonathan?" she said through clenched, mildly scarlet teeth. "You didn't place us here, so you can't make us go anywhere!"

"We are about to have problems, bitch," snapped Trip. "Once again, Rowe here has subjected this estate to potential harm—"

"It wasn't like that!" snarled Jonah. "It was Creyton! He did another one of those overcharged Mindscopes, but it was only for me! He made me black out in front of Lockman!"

That elicited some shocked and surprised responses from the crowd, but Trip just shook his head.

"That's the thing, Rowe," he said. "You never do 'nothing.' If you continue with the nothing, soon we'll be on The Plane with No Name."

"Titus, there are bigger things going on right now than your personal issues," scolded Jonathan. He then looked to the group at large. "Balthazar Lockman is on his way here right now," he announced. "If any of you have anything remotely ethereal—"

Jonathan didn't need to finish his sentence. Everyone headed indoors at a breakneck pace. Liz pulled her hand from Bobby's grasp and looked at Jonathan fearfully.

"Sir, the armory," she said. "And the infirmary. I'd been doing experiments; there have been ten more cases of that mysterious illness—"

"Elizabeth, do not worry," said Jonathan hastily, glancing at Dace and her colleagues. "I'll take care of those places. Now go help your friends!"

Liz nodded quickly, and dashed up the steps. Terrence and Reena hadn't moved either. Jonathan fixed a stern gaze on Reena.

"Reena, you cannot be here," he said. "You acted as Jonah's legal counsel, and if Lockman sees you—"

"To hell with that!" said Reena, aghast. "I don't care about the ramifications of that ruse! If you think that I'm abandoning you all at a moment like this, you're insane!"

"Reena, it isn't abandonment, it's preservation," said Jonathan. "I do not want Tenth charges brought against you for impersonating an official."

"But I never said I was a lawyer, I said I was his legal counsel," argued Reena. "Anyone can be legal counsel—"

"Reena."

Jonathan hadn't raised his voice, but the tone couldn't have made things any clearer. Reena closed her eyes very slowly. Jonah and Terrence could both see that she was not pleased with hiding away, but her respect for Jonathan superseded her rebelliousness.

"Fine," she said. "I'm gone. Will you permit me to use the Astral-imes?"

"Granted," allowed Jonathan.

Reena swallowed down her frustration, and stepped into nothingness.

Dace took Daniel, Jonathan, Jonah, Terrence, and Bast all in one sweeping glare. She was clearly still seething about Jonah's attack. "We're gone, too," she said. "For the moment, at least. We'll let you cower in fear of a Tenth. The ignominy of that—" she shook her head in disgust. "But be aware of one thing. Whatever transpires here today is nothing—nothing—compared to what the Curaie will do when they find out about this defiance. You people were skating on thin ice as it was—one would think you would have learned to put your head down and keep it there, like Sanctum Arcist. But that's done now. Lockman and whatever he comes at you with is minnows compared to the whales you've got on your tail now."

She motioned to the S.P.G. members with her, and they all stepped into thin air and were gone. Terrence stared at the open air they'd vacated, breathing hard.

"Stupid assholes," he grumbled. "They wouldn't be worth the decals on their jackets if it weren't for the Curaie's backing—"

"Terrence, you have to prepare," said Jonathan sternly. "Dace's need to threaten has cost us precious time. Go help your friends. I'm thinking you have about fifteen more minutes."

Jonah, who'd been less talkative during these last few moments because his face was sore, looked at Jonathan with narrowed eyes. "And what will you be doing?" he asked.

Jonathan looked across the grounds, his face free of expression. "My job."

* * *

Jonathan was right. After fifteen minutes, Lockman showed up, complete with Faulk and the rest of the representatives of the Lockman Association. He had even gotten several deputies from the sheriff's department, who were either too stupid to realize they were Lockman's pass to do what he wanted, or simply bored with being useless and lazy.

"I didn't realize that there were this many deputies in the sheriff's department," commented Jonah.

"You wouldn't see 'em," said Bobby coldly. "Most of them spend their whole shifts pigging out at the Krispy Kreme across town."

Lockman and his posse barged in, saying little to nothing. They spread out amongst the rooms as if they knew the layout, but Jonah didn't bother with suspicion. They likely didn't know the layout; they simply invaded wherever they pleased. Magdalena and Malcolm sat down in the living room, Magdalena clutching hard at stress balls in both hands. Malcolm murmured something under his breath. Jonah didn't know if he was praying for assistance with maintaining his anger, or reminding himself that he couldn't fly off the handle because police were present. Alvin whispered the reason to Jonah and Terrence.

"Lockman sent some of his people to Malcolm's shop in the back," he confided. "They are rifling through everything, and you know how particular Malcolm is about his creations."

Liz had stashed away her healing satchel. She didn't even tell the other residents where she hid it. The infirmary was almost sparkling with how clean it was. Even so, her materials were overturned and roughly handled; they didn't even care when things were misplaced or dropped and damaged. Her favorite set of ethereal steel scales were sent crashing down to the floor, which immediately caused tears to spring up in her eyes. Bobby embraced her, and she sobbed shamelessly. It seemed that he deemed comforting his girlfriend a more beneficial action than assaulting the investigator.

Douglas was forcibly shoved away from a door that he'd inadvertently blocked, and he seemed to ding his elbow against the wall. Grabbing it in a rage, he took several purposeful steps toward the Lockman rep who'd shoved him, but the man gave him a slight smile and showed no fear.

"Go ahead, son," he prodded. "Please, do us a favor."

For a moment, Douglas looked as if punching the man would be the answer to his dreams. But he backed away. Lockman's guy nodded knowingly.

"Exactly what I thought," he grumbled. "Now go sit down, like a good little bitch."

Jonah tried very hard to keep his temper in check. These people had no respect for anything. Picking over everything. Breaking Liz's scales and scuffing Jonah's chessboard, which was a Christmas gift from Douglas. Terrence was ready to attack someone his own self when one of the deputies muttered, "Terrence?"

Terrence instantly recognized the pencil-thin guy, but it didn't seem to improve his temper at all. "Yeah, Breaker, it's me," he said.

Alvin looked up from the couch. "Breaker?"

The man turned, wide-eyed, to see another face he recognized. "Alvin? You're here, too?"

"Mmm hmm," said Alvin. "Bobby's upstairs. He just took his girlfriend up there to calm her down when those dudes broke her stuff."

"Who is this guy?" said Jonah, like the man wasn't there.

"Breaker Tanner here is a friend of the family," answered Alvin. "He was tight with Sterling; he's even had dinner in our house."

"Yep," said Terrence. "Dad's godson."

That caused Jonah's attention to sharpen, and Breaker's head to hang in shame.

"I'm so glad Mom ain't here to see you helping these idiots," said Terrence quietly. "She thought the world of you. What's next? You going to go in their house and tear up the place, too?"

Breaker looked at them, shaking his head. "I have a job to do here," he pleaded. "You know it's not personal."

"Is that a fact?" said Alvin, raising his eyebrows in mock surprise. "I don't think everyone present got that memo. How about you, Terrence?"

"Nope," said Terrence. "Not. At. All."

Breaker opened his mouth, undoubtedly about to voice even more supplicating words, but then the cold voice of Lockman was near.

"These people are well-versed in the art of manipulation, Deputy Tanner," he said sternly. "I warned you of this fact when I obtained the warrant here."

Jonah took a deep breath. Lockman kept his eyes on Breaker.

"I would advise you to leave them be, and refrain from talking to anyone else, particularly—" he pointed at Jonah without looking at him, "—this one."

"I have a name, Lockman," snapped Jonah.

"And a habit to match," said Lockman, still refusing to look his way.

"I AM NOT ON DRUGS!" shouted Jonah. "No one here is using substances of any kind!"

Now Lockman turned his gaze to Jonah and Terrence, grandeur and superiority in every inch of his tanned face. "Oh my word," he replied in a sarcastic, exaggerated Southern drawl. "Where is the Southern hospitality?"

"Southern— Maryland is the South, too!" cried Terrence. "You didn't discover that when you were researching necromancy and all that other bull?"

Lockman didn't answer, turning his attention back to Breaker. "Go out there and help my people with the case."

Working his jaw for a moment, Breaker went back outside. Terrence looked at Jonah, confused. Jonah wasn't doing much better.

"The case?" he asked. "What case?"

"Holy mother damn," said Spader from a window, and they joined him.

The case to which Lockman had been referring was carried by Breaker and three Lockman Association reps. It was about six feet long and had the width of a telephone pole. The case looked innocent enough, but its side boasted, in vivid red letters, *LOCKBREAKER.*

"That's a damn battering ram," said Magdalena in a hollow voice. "*Por dios...* He's going to—"

"Quiet!" said Malcolm hastily. A few of the investigators were nearby, eavesdropping with no shame.

Jonah knew what she had almost let slip. That battering ram was for the door that they'd fixed. The armory! He spat out a nasty word just as Lockman and his assistants returned. He looked at the crowd, who was now fearful.

"A wonderful reporter that I know—" he began, but Jonah cut him off.

"Reynolda Langford, the instigator," he grumbled.

Lockman looked at him coldly. Jonah leered right back. The defiance was a suitable mask over the fear and worry he felt. "Reynolda spoke to me at length about her findings here. She spoke of a lone door near a room of very subpar paintings—"

Jonah's eyebrows rose at that. If Reena had been here to hear that... Jonah decided he didn't even want to think about it. He refocused on Lockman.

"—that was the only door that seemed inaccessible. Why would that be?"

"Um, I don't know," said Alvin. "Maybe because this estate is old, and some things get forgotten?"

"Nice try, boy," snorted Lockman. "And it would have been halfway convincing if there weren't the aforementioned art studio right next to it, a fitness room, and a laundry room. There is no way such a place can be forgotten when it is near so many rooms that are used daily."

Alvin fell silent, looking like he'd been owned. It seemed that Reynolda did have a keen memory for detail. Too bad it concerned this.

"So I couldn't help but wonder why that one door, in this entire museum, was blocked," said Lockman. "And I could only come to one conclusion. You are hiding something."

No one said anything. Daniel looked at Lockman with pure hate.

"So, with my trusty friend here," Lockman indicated the case, "we will find out what Reynolda could not."

Jonah closed his eyes, ignoring some of the intakes of breath that people around him just took. Why, exactly, did Jonathan think warping the door would be enough?

"You are all welcome to follow," said Lockman in a sardonic manner. "But you cannot interfere, as that would be violation of the law. My friends here—" he indicated the police, "—will make sure you remain in accordance with that."

He nodded to his people, and they went through the kitchen and down the stairs. Worried as hell, some people simply sat and waited for the inevitable. Others, like Jonah, Liz, Terrence, and Bobby, followed them.

They all reached the basement quickly. It was almost as if Jonah was outside of his body, watching himself walking down the stairs. If Lockman saw the practice weapons, he'd run wild with it. If, by some chance, he got pictures, he'd team up with Reynolda again and probably make them look like—he didn't know—they were going to mercy kill themselves, or something. He thought of Bobby, Liz, Maxine, Magdalena. All of them. If they got branded as cultists, their lives were over. And Vera—she'd never realize her dream if she got tied to them. Lockman wouldn't think twice about it. He'd happily ruin every life here, and simply move on the next conquest.

Lockman milked it greedily. He wanted everyone's nerves on edge before he destroyed them. Jonah couldn't help but see the predatory look in his eyes as he let the tension build... all because Creyton caused him to black out in front of him.

Lockman could hesitate no longer. He gave his boys a signal and they began a five count, swinging the ram to and fro with each number. At one, they bashed it into the door. Jonathan's plan had failed. The icy bomb in Jonah's gut burst right along with that door as it came off of its hinges to reveal–

Nothing.

Jonah blinked, hard, and glanced over at Terrence. The exact same shock was on his face, but their eyes did not deceive them. There was absolutely nothing in that room.

Lockman breathed heavily, trying hard to contain his rage. His assistants stared stupidly, as if they couldn't comprehend what they saw.

Jonah almost laughed with relief. Daniel shook his head.

"Congratulations, Balthazar," he said. "You broke into an empty room."

Lockman moved his gaze to Daniel slowly. "Where is it?" he hissed. "Where is it?"

"Where is what?" demanded Daniel.

"Your lab!" Lockman shouted. "Your hidden cache of consciousness-altering substances!"

"Our what?" said Terrence. "Is that what you're on yourself? Looking for an invisible stash because you used up your own?"

"Don't disparage me, boy," he snarled. "Jonah Rowe had a blackout during our interview! I had merely inquired–"

"You had just threatened me," said Jonah. "I told you that I don't take drugs, and you came looking regardless!"

"Explain your blackout then!" said Lockman.

Jonah was at a loss, but before he could talk himself into another hole, Liz spoke up.

"Don't raise your voice anymore, Jonah," she said. "He's been experiencing stress-induced headaches for the past couple weeks. Environmental situations haven't been the best, having to travel to the city and back and not granting himself enough time to re-acclimate to varying climates. It must have hit him at the most inopportune time."

"And who are you, little girl?" Wyatt coolly appraised Liz. "Some sort of medical practitioner?"

"Yes, actually," Liz responded. "That's exactly what I am."

Wyatt looked stupid. Lockman shook his head wildly.

"That's a lie!" he exclaimed. "If it were merely a bad headache, why did he run?"

"I panicked!" said Jonah, loving this facade. His thoughts were much clearer now that the armory was empty. "It was crystal clear that you'd made up in your mind I was an addict, and I reacted. Not proud of it, but there it is."

Lockman looked as though his head was going to explode if he didn't calm down. "All of you are liars," he said in a dangerously calm voice. "There is something going on here, and I will wring it from you, so help me—"

"I have had enough of this," said Daniel, allowing a steely timber to seep into his voice. "You have ransacked our home, violated the sanctity of the place that these youths and I hold dear. Your invasion has proven fruitless, as it was always going to be, and now I want you gone."

Lockman ignored Daniel's last sentence. "My search was always going to be fruitless, was it?" he said. "You knew that, did you? Then why did all of you people follow us like puppies, watching our every move with bated breath?"

"You barged in on us like we were some kind of establishment of ill repute!" said Daniel, as though it should have been obvious. "You came unannounced, with a battering ram, no less! You even have a security team in the form of the local law enforcement! How many distasteful acts have gone unnoticed in town while they are here, catering to your whims like impressionable servants?"

"Now hold on there!" said one of the deputies, but Daniel gave him with a look.

"Prove me wrong, son," he said.

The deputy stared, clearly at a loss for words. Satisfied, Daniel turned back to Lockman.

"Now, I am asking with as much tact as I can muster after your rudeness. Depart, now."

Lockman had no choice. His impromptu invasion had failed. He had no legs to stand on. A vein twitched at his temple. "This is not over," he said quietly. "I will find out what is going on here, and when I do, you will all hang for it."

He went upstairs, the assistants and deputies followed him. People looked around, confused and hardly daring to believe that they'd dodged this particular bullet. Then everyone broke into shaky laughter, which quickly ceased when they remembered the mess upstairs.

"My heart was in my throat the whole time," said Magdalena. "What they did up there…"

"But what happened to the—" Alvin glanced upstairs, "—stuff?"

"Never you mind, son," said a deep voice behind them. "It's all back."

Everyone turned to see Jonathan inside the armory, along with every single weapon that the estate had. There should have been triumph in his eyes, but his expression was rather grim. Therefore, no one cheered, or wondered how Jonathan had done it. That look in his gray eyes seemed to chase away all traces of their pseudo-victory.

"Jonathan?" Daniel inquired, frowning at his expression. "What's the matter? Shouldn't you be pleased?"

"I am pleased," Jonathan replied. "Eluding Lockman for the moment was most pleasing. But I'm afraid it is to be short-lived."

"What do you—?" Daniel began, but then he stopped, frowned once more, and looked up the stairs. Jonathan was already looking in that direction. Jonah and his friends followed suit. He was about to question what they were supposed to be seeing when after a few seconds, a figure appeared at the top of the stairs, dressed quite sharply in what looked like a sixties-style business suit. The area was rather dark, but the spirit shone clearly, looking at Jonathan with a mixture of respect and, oddly, regret. Jonah glanced at Jonathan, whose face remained grim.

"Bernard," he said quietly. "Engagah sent you. Will this be a summons to them?"

The spirit looked away for a moment. "No, Jonathan," he said. "They are coming here."

There were gasps and intakes of breath from Jonah's friends, but he remained confused. "What's going on, Jonathan?" he asked. "Who is this spirit? And who are 'they?' "

"The Phasmastis Curaie," answered Jonathan. "They are coming here to the estate to evaluate my performance as Overseer of this House."

"And you know that how?" asked Terrence. "This spirit didn't say that."

"Because it's Bernard, boy," said Daniel. "He is only sent to Earthplane to alertProtector Guides, Guardians, and Elect and Very Elect Spirits of pending evaluations."

Jonah's blood ran cold. He imagined that the same thing was happening for his friends.

"When is this evaluation, Bernard?" asked Jonathan.

"Two and a half weeks from now," answered Bernard. "Thanksgiving Day."

Jonah felt a bit of confusion. Thanksgiving was that close? Had this whole saga with him jumping between the city and Rome been going on that long?

He'd had this thought a million times, and here a million and one: Whoever was in charge of time had a mean-spirited sense of humor.

"There are two other things," said Bernard quietly. "Engagah has requested that every Eleventh Percenter in the area attend."

"What for?" asked Maxine.

Daniel answered the question. "So everyone will know exactly what happened," he murmured. You kids can't go and paint the Curaie in a negative light. I swear, this is precisely one of the reasons why I embraced human life."

"Daniel, please," said Jonathan. "That doesn't help anything. So please stop talking. And the second thing, Bernard?"

Bernard almost faded from sight; he seemed that worried about speaking his next words. "It involved the presence of Jonah Rowe." The spirit's voice was delicate.

Many heads turned Jonah's way, but Jonah's eyes remained on Bernard.

"What about my presence?" he asked.

"Well," said Bernard, "it isn't allowed at the evaluation."

"What!" cried Jonah. "Why? What did I do?"

"You're doing it right now," said Trip.

Jonah ignored him. "I find it very difficult to believe that I'm the only Eleventh Percenter in the history of the world to have lost their temper," he snarled.

"Of course not," said Bernard. "It's simply because, well..."

"Well what?" demanded Jonah.

"It's because it's you," said the messenger spirit.

Jonah opened his mouth in a rage, but Jonathan said loudly, "This works perfectly, Jonah. It's obvious what the Curaie feels about you—and I know it's largely unwarranted." He added the last part before Jonah could say so. "This way, the heat involved will be entirely on me."

Jonah narrowed his eyes. "Heat?" he queried. "What heat? You haven't done anything, Jonathan."

"Except make the armory vanish," Terrence reminded him. "Can't forget that one."

Jonathan glanced at Terrence like he planned to say something, but must have decided against it. He looked at Bernard instead. "I understand, Bernard. Now please return to the Astral Plane before your form dissipates."

The spirit regarded Jonathan. He looked as if he sincerely regretted what he'd had to do and say. With a nod of farewell, he vanished.

Jonah looked at Daniel, who seemed ready shoot an arrow into someone. He looked at his friends, who seemed thunderstruck at what they'd just heard. Jonathan looked as though his mind were full of a million thoughts, and for once, he seemed to have trouble compartmentalizing them.

"All right, everyone," he said in a loud voice. "Disperse. The day is still young."

People complied rather awkwardly. How were they supposed to have a normal day now?

"We might want to tell Reena about this outside," Terrence said to Jonah.

"Why?" asked Jonah, still nettled.

"Because she doesn't have much to punch out there, you know?"

Thanksgiving Day descended so quickly that it almost felt like the preceding two weeks hadn't even occurred. The day itself brought a feeling of fear, apprehension, and anxiety. And, for Jonah personally, it also brought about a feeling of something like bereavement.

His past two Thanksgivings were grand affairs. So many family members and friends came, the food had been beautiful, and then most of the guys went to the family room for hours of football. Nella would laughingly teach Magdalena and Maxine guitar, and Reena would shamelessly criticize people for partaking in such gluttonous bliss.

That was not the case this Thanksgiving.

With the evaluation happening that evening, no one felt even remotely festive. Douglas was in the family room reading through one of his graduate course books. Spader kept to himself in the corner, wanting to be ignored, and getting his wish fulfilled. It wasn't like anyone spoke to him that much, anyway. Malcolm was in the wood shop. Magdalena and Maxine argued over who made for a better captain of the Enterprise, Kirk or Picard. Liz and Bobby's location was anyone's guess, and Alvin spent the morning in conversation with Mrs. Decessio about how Raymond had planned some road trip.

Jonah wasn't pleased with these things at all. Since he'd returned from the Outer Banks that summer, he felt as though an ongoing battle raged. And the lines were drawn distinctly—they had been for a while. There was Creyton, and his loyal Deadfallen disciples, who were getting stronger by the second. There was the Phasmastis Curaie, who blindly followed obsolete decrees and threw their weight around like nobody's business. Then there was Balthazar Lockman. Their solitary victory against him so far was too paltry a thing to celebrate. Lockman, in Jonah's eyes, functioned like a supersoldier: one bullet wouldn't kill him, it would just piss him off. He was determined, and had a laser-like fixation on the estate. And, last but not least, there was Jonathan, along with the residents of the estate. Jonah couldn't speak for Jonathan, because he was gone all the time, but he and his friends wanted to live normal physical lives so badly. But that was a hard thing to do when they were being hit from three different sides.

So it was no surprise that no one bothered to cook up any holiday food. Not even Terrence.

One thing of note that happened was when Nella showed up to keep Liz company. As Liz had disappeared with Bobby, Nella didn't have much to do. When Jonah finally dragged himself out of his room and saw her, he smiled. He wasn't a fan of Nella's changes in personality since dating that Dylan guy, but he decided not to think about that as he went in for an embrace. Nella complied, revealing something that dimmed Jonah's grin.

Oh, no she didn't.

"What's that on your arm?" he asked her.

Nella's eyes widened, while Jonah's narrowed. "Let me go find Liz."

She turned to leave him, but Jonah barred her path.

"You know Liz is with Bobby," he said. "It was one of the first things you found out when you got here. Now what is that on your arm?"

With a sigh of resignation, Nella extended her right arm, and Jonah pushed her sleeve up as far as it would go. On her arm was a vivid red rose. It started at the shoulder, and had been done to methodically stem around her bicep, ending at her elbow.

Jonah was in complete disbelief. "Are you kidding me right now?" he said in a loud whisper. "When did you get this, Nella?"

Nella swallowed. "Three weeks ago," she said. "Do you think it's nice, at least?"

"Does Sandrine know about it?" Jonah ignored that asinine question. "Your mom and dad?"

"Hmm?" asked Nella in an absent way, but not really.

Jonah gave her a cold chuckle. He invented feigning confusion in a tense situation. It felt like that, anyway. "I take it that you haven't told Liz about it, either," he murmured. "I was wondering about your recent obsession with dark, extra long-sleeved shirts."

Nella blinked rapidly. Jonah found it funny that she feared Liz's opinions more than Sandrine's or her parents. "I swear that I will tell them all very soon, Jonah." The girl tried hard not to wring her hands. "I'm just not ready yet."

"You aren't ready after three weeks?" demanded Jonah. "Three weeks, Nella? Wait…when you helped with the cleanup after Lockman's invasion, did you have that tattoo then?"

"Yeah," admitted Nella. "I kept my coat on the whole time, remember?"

Jonah took a deep breath. He didn't have the right to do this. He wasn't Nella's father, and he wasn't even old enough to act parental with her at all; he was barely a decade older than her. But it was obvious to everyone around that the girl had changed. She began to stray from herself the minute she got that little boyfriend of hers. She was so vastly different from the girl he'd met in Liz's garden nearly a year prior. He missed that girl. The braces. The precious pudginess. The occasional defiance when she felt wronged. What a difference a year made.

"This didn't have anything to do with Dylan, did it?" he asked her. "It wasn't his idea, was it?"

Nella was silent for a few seconds. A few more seconds. Half a minute. Long enough for Jonah to shake his head.

"What has happened to you, Nella?" he asked. "What happened to your opinions? What happened to your playing guitar? What happened to the interest in Valentania York? Anything this boy says goes? Is that it?"

"First of all," the sheepishness faded from Nella's face, "I haven't changed. I just got older. And smarter. My opinions are fine. I don't need that guitar; it's not like I was going anywhere in music, anyway. And Dylan is harmless. You have to face the fact that I'm growing up,

Jonah. I had to get out of the gardens one day. I am still a caring Green Aura. But life changes—"

"Girl, you're sixteen!" exclaimed Jonah.

"You're not my father, Jonah!" Nella shot back. "And you don't understand anything! If you grew up with Liz and Sandrine for sisters, you'd feel the need to get out from under that pressure too! I'm practically a woman now!"

"Practically a woman, huh?" said Jonah, shrewdness in his eyes. "Then why are you afraid of your parents and siblings discovering a tattoo you got because your boyfriend suggested it?"

The words stopped Nella cold. Something like a trace of her old self flashed in her eyes. Some part of her didn't want to admit that Jonah was right. "Are you going to tell Liz?" she asked quietly.

"No." Jonah shook his head. "I'm not a snitch, Nella. But I have to admit that I do not appreciate being put in this position. Liz is my friend, too."

There was gratitude in Nella's eyes, but her face remained set. "Thank you," was all she said before she left Jonah to go converse with Maxine and Magdalena, who'd finally ended the argument about Star Trek.

Jonah closed his eyes and just stood there. Things and people changed all the time. That was a fact of life. But with the rate that things changed nowadays, he wondered if there would be any remnants of his favorite estate routines when this was all over.

5:45 PM.

It was fifteen minutes before Jonathan's evaluation from the Phasmastis Curaie.

The one that Jonah was not permitted to see.

It pissed him off, but he kept a lid on it. Terrence was extremely helpful, for which he was grateful.

"Don't worry man," he told Jonah right before he went upstairs. "Jonathan is the best Protector Guide there is. This can only go one way—with him getting another win."

Reena tried to be supportive, but unfortunately, she was too irritated to put on a good show. "I'm just ready for them to speak their piece and get the hell on with their business," she'd confided in Jonah. To think, they just had to mar Thanksgiving for this shit?"

Jonah thought along those same lines while he watched his brother and sister leave. Both of them looked razor sharp; all residents were required to dress with "a sense of decorum that befitted the chief navigators of the Ethereal World." Or so Dace Cross had said. Jonah would have preferred to be right there with his friends in his Sunday best, but here he was, in an overstretched polo and faded jeans, on his way out of the estate while everyone else headed in.

He had half a mind to spend the next few hours at the Chuck Wagon, which, for whatever reason, was open regular hours, even though it was Thanksgiving Day. Then, he'd find somewhere to write. Something along those lines. The autumn evenings began so early, so he had to get things started now. He was near his car when a hard voice said, "Rowe."

Jonah turned his head in the direction of the voice. Coming his way, reluctantly it seemed, was Trip. He was dressed impeccably as well, sporting an olive vest, black shirt, and matching slacks. A snug, black watchcap shielded his bald head from the November chill, and he'd even added glasses to the ensemble. Jonah would have thought that he was a decent human being if he weren't such a prick.

"What do you want?" he demanded. "Shouldn't you be in there? I'm going to the Chuck Wagon."

"You are not," said Trip. "You're going to stay your ass right in that car, and wait."

"Says who?"

"Says Jonathan," replied Trip.

Without warning, he threw an old-fashioned radio Jonah's way. Reflexively, Jonah caught it and scowled at it.

"Great," he muttered. "First it's a glorified ethereal pager, and now I get a radio. I pass."

"The radio is but a conduit." Trip was impatient with his words. "This is a Deus Ex Machina."

"The Ghost in the Machine?" deadpanned Jonah. "That's cute. Now take it back."

"It's tuned to ethereality, shit for brains," snapped Trip. "Use the dial. The stations are conditioned to spiritual sensitivity. 101.3 will alert you of danger. 107.3 will alert you of spiritual activity, which is fait accompli here, so avoid it. 90.4 will allow you to listen to the proceedings."

That got Jonah's attention. "Why is Jonathan doing this for me?" he asked.

"I'm sure I don't care," said Trip, who turned and headed inside the estate.

"Bitch," muttered Jonah, but he seated himself in his car to be out of sight.

Not a moment too soon. People began to appear from the Astralimes, looking uncertain, confused, and fearful.

The Curaie requested the presence of every Eleventh Percenter around, and the request was granted. From his car, Jonah saw people he knew from the estate, but they had been displaced by the rash of messes in the past few months. People like Ben-Israel. Melvin. Benjamin. Noah. Barry. Countless others. And Jonah couldn't even speak to them.

Douglas had left for the afternoon and returned with his grandmother and a group of men who could only be his brothers and uncles. He had a stony look in his eyes, which was the usual expression he took on when he attempted to blow off his grandmother's criticisms. He saw the entire Decessio family, Sterling included. Terrence met them at the door, and they all went inside together. Jonah would have loved to have spoken to them, and he knew that Sterling was angry about sitting on the sidelines. He felt a kinship to the man for that reason. He saw June Mylteer. He saw Felix, who got many wary glances because people feared his potential Red Rage, but the vampire hunter handled it with an admirable amount of grace and class.

Jonah snorted. Felix had more money than everyone here combined; why should he care what they thought of him?

Then he saw Liz, Sandrine, Mrs. Manville, and Nella (Liz's dad was away on business, so he got a pass. Lucky dude). Judging by their interactions, Nella still hadn't told them about the tattoo. But Jonah didn't have the time or the concentration to dwell on that as his eyes moved past Reverend Abbott.

Vera was with the Manville family.

She was presentable and crisp, just like everyone else, but for several seconds, she was the only one that Jonah saw. She wore a burgundy shirt that seemed to carry a metallic sheen. The shirt met her waist and gave way to a black skirt that passed her knees and had a conservative slit on the side. On the whole, she was neatly put together, just like everyone else.

But her beauty was breathtaking.

Jonah lingered on Vera for so long that he almost missed the group that came next.

Eleventh representatives of the Curaie.

Jonah counted about twenty S.P.G. practitioners, six or seven Networkers, with Patience and Dace Cross among them. Dace looked excited, while Patience looked tense and worried.

And in their midst, ringed and protected it seemed, was Katarina Ocean. The Gate Linker. She was pretty, sharp, and timeless, but looked nervous as hell. Jonah mentally scolded himself because he had expected the Spirit Guides themselves to appear among them. After he saw Katarina, he knew their plan. Their grand, dramatic entrance would occur indoors somewhere, courtesy of a freshly linked Gate, courtesy of Ocean.

Jonah watched as Reverend Abbott lagged behind everyone. Once everyone was inside, the clergyman bowed his head, no doubt praying over the proceedings. Then he disappeared inside with everyone else.

There was a very odd feeling in Jonah's stomach after he saw all those people from his car. It was an unsettling thing. He felt like an outsider, a pariah in the highest degree. Like the family member that everyone liked and respected, but maintained a cordial distance from nonetheless.

Now that the grounds were empty, he wasted no time in turning the dial on Trip's radio (he refused to call it the Deus Ex Machina) to 90.4. After several seconds of white noise, he heard speech as clearly as if they were all in the car with him. He shoved his nerves down and listened.

"Jonathan," said Engagah's voice (man, Ocean worked quickly!), "we have convened here, in the presence of these Eleventh Percenters, spirits, spiritesses, heralds, and of course, one sazer, to conduct your evaluation."

Jonah frowned. One sazer. Did they have to point Felix out like that? He was glad that Autumn Rose wasn't there.

"You are aware of the format, Jonathan?" asked Engagah.

There was silence, then—

"Having participated in many of these, Engagah, I would say yes," said Jonathan.

"Be that as it may," said Engagah, "there are many present that may not be familiar with it. These next words are for them to hear. Four of us face Jonathan, the focal point, from the north, four from the west, and four from the south. Silver, our thirteenth, will have the side of the east."

Jonah remembered what Terrence told him way back when. There were thirteen Spirit Guides in the Phasmastis Curaie, so that decisions never ended in a tie. Fleetingly, he wondered what would happen if one of members opted to abstain. How badly would that suck?

"Very well," said Jonathan. "I am at your mercy. What is your point of contention?"

"Point?" said another voice, surprised. "You delude yourself into thinking that there is only one?"

"Truth be told, Silver, I don't see anything wrong at all," said Jonathan. "Whatever problems you have will be revelations."

"Revelations, you say," said a female voice. "So you desire to feign ignorance, then? Very well. Let us speak about your absurdly neglectful methods concerning your duties as Overseer of this House."

"I do not see what you mean, Vashti," said Jonathan, slight coldness in his words. "I have been nothing but vigilant and protective since the Vitasphera was passed into my hands."

"An action that did not occur until after you passed into Spirit, Jonathan," said another voice. "The Decimation happened despite your grooming and training."

"The Decimation happened because Thaine decided that we were too weak to remain on Earthplane with him," said Jonathan.

"You still choose to refer to Creyton by the name Thaine?" said Engagah. "He dispensed with all things that made him human when he chose to follow his murderous path of ambition."

"We called him Thaine from the minute his parents brought him on these grounds," said Jonathan flat-out. "Back when I considered him an ally. So in my consciousness, he will remain Thaine. That is just the way it is."

Jonah was confused until an unpleasant memory hit him. A long while back, Jonah was horrified to discover that his co-worker, Roger, was Creyton in disguise. At that time, he revealed his full name, Roger Thaine Cyril Creyton. To this day, he still couldn't believe that Creyton and Jonathan had ever been allies. Or, at the very least, civil enough for Jonathan to refer to him so informally.

"But those matters are beside the point," murmured Jonathan. "Reminiscing on the past won't help anything at all."

"They are relevant to today," snapped another Curaie member. "Creyton's betrayal must still seep through the walls that you've built around yourself. Could that be the reason that you are now hiding Offplane, having successfully swayed Daniel to your way of thinking?"

Jonah's eyes widened. Jonathan's absences angered him. They still did. But he never viewed him as a coward. He had to think that Jonathan didn't care for that one.

"For your information, I embraced ethereal life because my brother Broreamir did the same thing so as to become a Deadfallen disciple." Daniel sounded insulted and ice-cold. "As far as I'm concerned, the only ones hiding—"

"Daniel," said Jonathan warningly, "you are not the one under scrutiny here. I am. Please."

Jonah could almost feel the reluctant silence from Daniel through the radio. Jonathan returned to addressing the Curaie.

"My absences have been to protect my students from further roughhousing at the hands of Balthazar Lockman," he said. "His so-called crusade happened despite your efforts to keep everything from the Tenths. I sincerely hope that Lockman isn't looked upon as my blunder as well?"

Jonah whistled. That one took some balls.

"Refrain from insubordination, Jonathan," said a Curaie member. "One would think you're losing your touch."

"I'm afraid to say that I don't understand what you mean," said Jonathan.

"Well, there is your complete and total inability to control Jonah Rowe," said another member, who might have been the one named Silver.

Jonah felt warmth in his chest at those words that served to burn through some of his worry.

"Jonah is not my pet," said Jonathan. "He is young man experiencing troubles, and is finding new ways to adapt, much like everyone else."

"Everyone else does not rile the masses with their each and every action," said Engagah. "Rowe is increasingly unstable, and, from what we've gleaned, isn't very fond of your time away."

"That may very well be," replied Jonathan. "I do not know his mind. But Jonah is not a time bomb. He is a man."

"A man whom you are failing at training, Jonathan." Jonah remembered the voice from earlier. It was the Curaie member named Vashti. "You have you students playing vigilante. And not only that; they are also playing sleuths and doctors!"

Jonah thought of Ben-Israel and Liz, both of whom were in that room. He prayed that they didn't gasp or whimper, or anything. But then Jonathan spoke.

"The Green Auras to whom you are referring are named Elizabeth Manville and Ben-Israel Larver," he said. "They are wonderful healing auras, the both of them. And given whatever this mysterious illness entails, you need all the assistance that is available. They've made some breakthroughs that the Green Team may even benefit from hearing—"

"The Green Team does not need the inane experiments of amateurish children playing at real physical life," snapped a Curaie member whom Jonah hadn't yet heard. "Interference is second nature in this place, it seems."

"No, Eustace," said Jonathan, who sounded slightly aggravated now. "That would be Sanctum Arcist. I have never trained my students to be warriors."

"Yet they fight like dogs!" snapped that Vashti one. "Rowe assaulted a Networker after passing out in front of Balthazar Lockman. Then Daniel shot an arrow—"

"At a man's shirt," snarled Daniel. "Jonathan gave me the task of protecting this estate while Lockman lurks in the shadows! Instead of power plays, why don't you focus your attentions on Creyton and this strange illness? Not to mention getting Lockman off of our backs!"

There was a rather protracted silence, where Jonah distinctly heard Jonathan sigh.

"A former Protector Guide criticizing age old traditions and protocols," groused Engagah. "You need to listen to Jonathan, Daniel, and silence yourself, or you will be cooling your heels on The Plane with No Name."

Daniel scoffed. "Going to punish me for opening my eyes and playing offense?" he demanded. "I don't see the sense in hauling me off to The Plane with No Name while Broreamir makes a fool of you in far more prominent ways than I—"

"Endicott, Mero," said Engagah, "take Daniel away. Fifteen days and nights on The Plane with No Name. Let us see if you recall the code of honor that you flounced while there!"

Jonah's mouth dropped. They were going to arrest Daniel for telling the truth?

"No, don't!" said Jonathan. "Punish me. This is on me. Let Daniel continue what I've tasked him. Daniel simply wants matters resolved, and all issues addressed. Take me."

"You're now trying to justify the actions of your counterparts?" demanded a Curaie member. "Personally, I know everything that I need to know now. Vigilantism frequently going on around us. Hiding from a Tenth who brazenly barged into this place. And the inability to control pupils. Engagah, let us begin. Please grant us that."

Jonah's nerves took a turn. What the hell did that mean? What was about to happen?

"The vote commences," announced Engagah. "Vashti, spokespiritess for the Spirit Guides of the West, what is your vote?"

A few moments silence.

"No confidence," said Vashti.

"Mina Thyme, spokespiritess for the Spirit Guides of the South," said Engagah, "what say you?"

"No confidence," said the one named Mina Thyme with no hesitation.

There were gasps of fear. Jonah's grasp tightened on the radio.

"I, Engagah, Supreme Overmistress of the Phasmastis Curaie and spokespiritess for the Spirit Guides of the North, concur with the spirits and spiritesses of the West and South, Jonathan. No confidence. Silver, thirteenth, and sole Guide of the East, please conclude the vote. What say you?"

Silver had the audacity to let the silence spiral before saying before answering. "I conclude by concurring with all directions of Spirit. No confidence."

Jonah seemed to lose the feeling in his face. What had just happened?

"Very well," said Engagah. "As the vote of no confidence is unanimous, Jonathan, you are hereby relieved of your duties as Overseer of this Estate, as well as Protector Guide. The Vitasphera is officially stripped from your possession."

There were intakes of breath, Liz actually cried out in shock. Jonah would have done the same if he had enough breath.

"You're putting me out in the cold," said Jonathan with no emotion. "Are you going to put another Guide here?"

"No," said Engagah. "The issues at this estate are deeply-rooted and long-lasting, and this Lockman situation has only reiterated that it is time for us to step in. This will be resolved in the most advantageous way. Within ninety days, every resident here will be gone, and Daniel will be reassigned."

A chorus of "*What!*" and "*No!*" blasted through the radio; Jonah was surprised the thing didn't catch fire. What was the Curaie doing? Some of the estate residents had no place to go!

"You're displacing everyone?" Jonathan demanded. "Do you know how vulnerable that makes these people? Do you know how guilty abandoning this estate will make us look in Lockman's eyes?"

"Never you mind, Jonathan," said Engagah. "You are but a mere spirit now. And if you dare interfere with these matters from this moment on, you will be punished by forcible vanquishing to the Other Side."

There were louder protests. Jonathan called for silence. Jonah, who'd dropped the radio, retrieved it with frozen fingers.

"And Jonah?" Jonathan asked quietly. "What of him?"

Engagah took a pronounced breath. Jonah, clutching the radio, couldn't catch his own. "Jonah James Anderson Rowe is henceforth banished from the Grannison-Morris estate."

Jonah shouted loudly, and felt rawness in his throat. It didn't even register that his friends were screaming just as loudly.

"SILENCE!" shouted Engagah. "This disorganization ends now. Those of you with homes will return there. To those of you without homes, arrangements will be made for all of you over the course of ninety days. The Blue Aura will have no more fuel for his obvious rage issues, and professionals will take care of Creyton and his Deadfallen disciples, this ethereal illness, and of course, Balthazar Lockman. Adjourned."

Jonah stared at the radio. Jonathan had been canned. And he had just been thrown out of the Grannison-Morris estate. He was banished. Fucking banished. And in three months, all of his friends would be scattered.

The Curaie, those crackpot spirits and spiritesses, would pay for this. Jonah didn't know what to say, but words didn't matter. Violence was a universal language.

He reached for the door handle when the radio dial switched of its own accord to 101.1.

"Don't you do it, Jonah."

It was Jonathan's voice, through the radio. Jonah stared at it in awe. How in the hell?

"Yes, I can speak to the Curaie and speak to you through this radio at the same time," Jonathan continued. "I want you to stay right there, in the car. Don't worry about me. I don't want you sacrificing any further liberties on my behalf. I want you to protect yourself, son. At all times."

The radio shifted back to the frequency that allowed Jonah to hear the room where the Curaie just altered all of their destinies. He heard people in tears, arguments—but it was all noise. Pointless noise.

Jonah lowered his head to the steering wheel, and tightened his eyes to prevent further emotion.

"Damn you, Jonathan," he whispered.

Then a shrill sound tore his eyes open. Did he just imagine that?

But then he heard it again.

Hell no.

He raised his head from the steering wheel in pure disbelief.

There were crows. Three of them, all perched in a tree near the estate. They cawed again to one another, then took synchronized flight.

Jonah gazed hopelessly after them. The truth was clear. Those three Deadfallen disciples sat there in disguise, and heard the whole thing play out. Now, their birdcalls rang through the silent night, almost resembling laughter as they bulleted toward their Transcendent with the physical life-altering news.

20

Straight and Narrow

Jonah was tired of spirits.

He wasn't ashamed of that fact, either. He was sick of spirits.

He had gone for so long as an Eleventh Percenter with little to no exposure to the official side of things, or—call it what it was—the political side of things. And he wished that he could have stayed ignorant of it. It had been so much better when the Curaie had just been Spirit Guides somewhere in the ethereal world.

But now, he never wanted to deal with them again.

After he had been banished, and saw those cursed crows fly off to wherever Creyton was, he sat numbly in his car. He couldn't feel his fingers. But what he did feel was stubbornness. He was not going back into the estate to collect what few belongings he had there. They were meaningless, anyway. He couldn't face them. Not even Reena or Terrence. Not even Vera.

Not any of them.

So, using his cold, numb fingers, he started his ignition and simply left.

He hadn't planned on any stops, but the call of nature, coupled with the need for gas, mandated that he do so. And it was at the gas station that the first call came. It was from Terrence.

He pushed IGNORE.

Reena.

IGNORE.

Liz.

IGNORE.

Bobby, followed by Alvin.

IGNORE to both of them.

Then Vera called him.

Jonah hesitated. How many times had he and Vera had each other's backs? How many times had they laughed about patrons at The Stop? How many times had he spent the night on her couch? When one of them was stressed, the other sought to give aid. This time was no different.

This time was completely different.

Angry at himself, he pushed IGNORE for her call as well.

He was back on the road after a little while. Traffic was like a dream. Everyone was at home with their families and loved ones eating, or watching either football or the inexplicable reruns of *The Wizard of Oz*. He never quite understood the reason why they showed that movie on Thanksgiving. Maybe it was the whole "no place like home" thing.

But he wasn't thinking about family. Or home. Or any of that shit.

He was back at his apartment in no time. For some strange reason, he felt the need to bring that stupid radio with him, and he placed it on the kitchen counter. He didn't think it would be of any use, but he didn't want some passerby to bash in his window and try to steal it. Yeah, it was older than dirt, but people did crazy things in this world.

He lowered himself in his recliner, but had no interest in television. His phone had been vibrating nonstop for almost four straight hours. When he looked at it, he saw twenty-six missed calls, the same amount of voicemails, and about forty text messages.

He deleted all of it.

"Doesn't matter," he said to the phone. "I'm not one of you anymore."

And he wasn't. The Curaie saw to that. He closed his eyes and sighed. This was how it was now. He wasn't one of them any longer. And if he practiced thinking and saying it enough, maybe he'd start to believe it, too.

Maybe.

"Jonah!" said Mr. Steverson on Monday morning. "How did the eye exam go?"

"The wh—oh yeah," muttered Jonah. "It went fine."

"And how was Thanksgiving?"

"Eh," Jonah managed.

Mr. Steverson gave him a curious look, but didn't pry. Jonah loved him for that. The man never pried.

But five minutes later, he broke his own rule.

As Jonah got a cup of water, Mr. Steverson beckoned him to the back office. Confused, Jonah followed. Mr. Steverson closed the door, and invited Jonah to sit. The man waited until Jonah was comfortable before he spoke.

"Jonah," he said slowly, "you look as if you've seen a ghost."

Jonah's eyes narrowed. He'd been banking on Mr. Steverson's proclivity to mind his own business. But he chose now to be nosy?

And Jonah had just praised his respect for privacy.

It was time for a desperate measure. Maybe scaring Mr. Steverson off might do the trick.

"What if I told you that I had, sir?" he muttered, fully prepared for the matter to be awkwardly dropped.

Mr. Steverson looked at him strangely. Jonah waited. Any minute now…

But then Mr. Steverson nailed him again. "I would say that it explains a lot of things," he said.

Jonah frowned. What did that mean? "I'm not sure that I follow your meaning, sir."

"Listen to me, son." Mr. Steverson was dead serious. "I need not bore you with any more Vietnam stories. You've heard them all at least twice—"

"I wouldn't mind hearing one now, sir," attempted Jonah. "Wouldn't mind it at all, actually."

"Your keenness to change the subject only makes my point, son," said Mr. Steverson. "Now, please listen to me. When I got back Stateside, I suppose that you could say that I fared better than some of my brothers-in-arms. But let me tell you right now...I wasn't as 'normal' as the so-called professionals thought I was."

Jonah didn't know what to say, but he also didn't know what to think. On the one hand, he didn't know the point of this. On the other hand, he felt like Mr. Steverson really needed to get something off of his chest. As callous as it sounded, Jonah hoped that the man wasn't looking for a shoulder to lean on. He didn't feel up to the task on top of everything else.

"I learned to play the game, Jonah," continued Mr. Steverson. "That's what I had a talent for. Therapy wasn't going to do anything for me; I wanted a good book and my family. So I played the game. And I started S.T.R. Been blessed. But I had friends that weren't so lucky."

Jonah still didn't know what to say, so he settled for, "Huh."

Mr. Steverson grinned. "What I mean to say is that many people that have been through things like war don't do so well with normalcy, Jonah. It's like—like acting. You have iconic actors who lose themselves in roles. Then you have actors who look like no more than someone playing a character. The same is true with people who have experienced strife in the world. Or possibly have more to them than meets the eye."

He gave Jonah a shrewd look. Jonah looked at the man in awe. Mr. Steverson was a man with twelfth grade education, and went straight to the military after that. Yet he was more intelligent and observant than some of Jonah's college professors. What exactly had he said to this man, without actually saying anything?

"So you think I'm a person who is remarkable in some way, and is playing normal?" he asked.

"No," said Mr. Steverson. "I know it for a fact."

Jonah actually smiled in spite of himself. For some reason, this was helpful.

"So is that how you're remarkable, then?" asked Mr. Steverson. "You see ghosts?"

Jonah considered this. He was comfortable confiding a bit. Maybe it would help assuage some of the negativity in him. "I prefer the term spirits, sir," he said. "And it's not always. It's just from time to time."

"How long has it been happening?" asked Mr. Steverson.

"Pretty much all my life," Hey, it was the truth. Wasn't necessary to share all the nuances that went along with it.

Mr. Steverson nodded slowly. "I thought there was something about you that you didn't want the rest of us to know."

"It's not that I didn't trust you, Amanda, and Harland, sir," said Jonah hastily. "I just...prefer to keep myself to myself, is all."

"I can understand that, son," said Mr. Steverson. "But I have to know; does your ability to see spirits affect your everyday life?"

Yow. Of course Mr. Steverson asked that question. Of course! Did he have it in him to put all that baggage on Mr. Steverson? "You know what, sir? Work's a-calling—"

"Stay right in that chair, Jonah." Mr. Steverson's voice was stern.

Jonah complied out of respect for his boss. But he still had no inclination to answer that question. It must have been written all over his face, because Mr. Steverson nodded.

"Your silence tells me everything," he said. "Do you care to share anything, or maybe I ought to say is there anything you feel comfortable sharing? And if I'm prying, please let me know. I can be a nosy old man when I want to be."

The funny thing about it was, Jonah didn't think that it was prying anymore. This was actually helpful. Since he no longer had permission to be an Eleventh Percenter, it was nice to have someone to speak to. The question of how much to reveal was the only issue."I can tell you that something bad has happened, and I can't do anything about it," he conceded. "At all. I'm completely alone. I'm not whining, or anything; I was a loner for many years. But now, I'm alone again. It was rather sudden, and a little jarring."

Mr. Steverson looked understanding, but not piteous. For that, Jonah was very grateful."First of all, son, there is always a way out, of any problem," he began. "And I don't doubt you have a past as a loner. But that was the case at one time. It's not the case now. You've found camaraderie somewhere, I know it. That whole loner thing could very well have flown at one time, but it's not the truth now. I know that you have great friends; I've had the pleasure of meeting some of them. Did you have a falling out, or something?"

Jonah sighed. If he were a smoker, he'd have lit one up. "No, we didn't," he confessed. "But after—the problem, I didn't think it was a good idea for them to be burdened by me. So I took the option out of their hands. I have to re-learn how to function by myself again."

"Bad plan, Jonah." Mr. Steverson seemed poised to perch himself on his soapbox. "Your first mistake was assuming that you didn't need your friends, and that they didn't need you. You took the option out of their hands. Did it ever occur to you that they might not have been pleased with that?"

"It'll take some time, but—"

"No, it won't," said Mr. Steverson, who actually rose from the chair. "Thing about life, Jonah, is that bad things—like whatever just went down in your life—happen. They happen, son. I may not understand what your particular dilemma is, but I know that much. And you have friends that I have no doubt are willing to be there for you. And that's just because no matter what you're going through, you're still showing yourself to be a fine young man. And whatever it is, Jonah, you need your friends on this path."

Now Jonah felt like he needed to make Mr. Steverson understand, which was weird in itself, because Mr. Steverson didn't even know the issue. "I can't let them do that, sir," he said. "It's got to be on me—"

"That ain't true either," said Mr. Steverson in a louder voice than Jonah's. " 'Straight is the gate, and narrow is the path.' You ever hear that one before?"

Jonah shook his head.

"It's in the New Testament," said Mr. Steverson. "Basically, it means that the path ahead of you is the right one. The one that is guaranteed to make you stronger. The one you'll appreciate more when you're done with it. As challenging, and as hard as hell as it might be, it's right. The right way is straight and narrow. Any other path is a detour, and sometimes, the stuff you encounter on the detour is worse than the stuff you meet on the straight path."

Jonah stared, stunned. What Mr. Steverson said was profound; there was no doubt about that. But it was also crazy how his words were so similar to what Jonathan said told Gamaliel Kaine so many years ago: "You'll always know when you're on the right track, because that will be the one with all the obstacles." When a Protector Guide and a middle-aged Tenth Percenter sounded just alike and had never met each other, it got his attention. Finally, he nodded.

"I think I got the message, sir." Jonah meant it when he said it. "And I thank you for it. But I'm almost certain that we need to get to work. Amanda and Harland will probably be calling us lazy by now—"

"They're not here, Jonah," laughed Mr. Steverson.

"What? But it's M—"

Then Jonah remembered. He wasn't supposed to be there. Business at S.T.R. had been booming lately. So much so that Mr. Steverson declared the Monday after Thanksgiving an off-day, and told them to consider it an early Christmas present. He'd been so wrapped up in Jonathan's evaluation that he hadn't given the free day another thought. Like an idiot, he had shown up to work on his day off.

"Don't judge yourself so harshly, son," said Mr. Steverson. "It was an honest mistake, especially since you had your mind occupied. How else did you think I knew something was up with you?"

"Yes, sir," mumbled Jonah. "I bet—wait, why are you here, sir?"

"I came in long enough to water Amanda's plants," answered Mr. Steverson. "But when I saw you show up, ready to work, I figured you needed to talk."

* * *

Mr. Steverson's words were still in Jonah's head on Thursday evening, when he returned from S.T.R. The owner of that tattoo place still looked as though he was afraid of Jonah, but he was no longer worried about that. Maybe the guy was just a bitch.

He heard Mr. Steverson. His words got through. But he still hadn't returned anyone's calls. He just didn't know what to say. Reena was probably pissed at him, and Terrence was probably more pissed with the Curaie than he was with Jonah. And he hadn't even told them about the crows that took the news to Creyton.

And then there were the calls he hadn't returned from Vera. Which was a totally different story.

He shook his head. He awaited a delivery from Pizza Hut because he hadn't eaten all day. Maybe after a full stomach, he might have a clearer mind. Then he'd try to return the calls.

He wondered what exactly this banishment entailed. In the time since Thanksgiving, he actually hadn't thought about it; he'd been too busy with mental excoriations against the Curaie. And Lockman, too. But the crusader could wait. To be on the safe side, he hadn't gone into Spectral Sight, conversed with any spirits, or taken any endowments. He had already used a fair bit of his declining balance that the Curaie granted before his banishment, so he didn't want to risk anything now. Last thing he needed was to do some random ethereality, and then have the S.P.G. or even the Networkers show up at his door. He had no batons, and was vulnerable because of that, but he'd be damned if he went quietly.

He rested in his chair. Vulnerability against Spectral Law also meant vulnerability against Creyton. He was bound to know the entire story by now, compliments of his shape-shifting avian lackeys. In all honesty, Jonah was surprised that Creyton hadn't attacked him already. Because of the Curaie, he was a sitting duck. With his luck, he just might suffer another Mindscope and fall prey to that illness. How pissed off would Creyton be if he missed his chance to kill Jonah?

A knock at his door made him jump. A second later he snorted at his anxiety. Creyton wouldn't have bothered to knock, first of all. Second, unless the pizza delivery guy suddenly developed homicidal tendencies because he desired a higher tip, Jonah had nothing to worry about. He grabbed his wallet, went to the door, and opened it.

It wasn't the pizza guy.

It was Reena.

Jonah's eyes widened. With the look on Reena's face, she may as well have been Creyton.

She stepped into Jonah's apartment without even blinking her eyes. Jonah didn't know how to play this at all. Where the hell was Terrence? He excelled at damage control.

"Reena—"

She shut him up by holding up one hand. When she spoke, her voice was barely above a whisper.

"For all we knew," she said, "you could have wrapped your car around a tree. You could have broken your neck. You could have been rotting in a ditch somewhere, Creyton having murdered you at long last."

Reena's eyes were frosty, yet also looked as if they could catch fire. Jonah was really missing his batons right now. He was started to think he'd need them.

"You just left, Jonah," she continued. "You didn't feel like talking at that time, and I get that. But to just leave? You didn't even tell us you'd see us later! Not to me? Not to Terrence? Liz? Vera?"

That made Jonah think. If this was how Reena reacted, then how would Vera react? God, if his reticence played a part in her return to Seattle…

For some reason, Reena's eyes flashed."Really?" she demanded. "You get hung up on how it affects Vera, but not your brother and sister?"

Jonah's mouth twisted. *Damn* Reena and her ability to read essence! "Reena, there actually is an explanation—"

"I don't need your explanation," snapped Reena. "You heard from Trip's radio contraption that the Curaie banished you, got worked up, and viewed it as your friends were in, and you were out. As such, you took it upon yourself to shut us out, become an island, and crawl into an abyss of anger and confusion."

Jonah stared. How did she do that?

"I know the male ego is fragile, Jonah, but let me tell you this right here and now." It was at that point that Reena's voice began to elevate. "You don't get to take decisions out of our hands. You don't get to shut us out. You don't get to be an island. And you don't get to make us insane with worry."

At that point, Reena's anger broke. She wrapped Jonah in hug that was more like an anaconda's squeeze. All the oxygen Jonah thought he owned flew out of him.

"Reena—" he gasped, "can't—crushing me—"

"Ride it out." Reena's voice made it clear that she didn't give a damn.

Jonah fell silent, but it wasn't quite voluntary; he didn't have the breath to spare. Then Reena released him. She turned away from him and tried and failed to be surreptitious when she wiped tears of relief from her eyes. It was then that Jonah realized just how badly he'd screwed up when he abandoned his friends like that. Mr. Steverson was right. That lone wolf shtick didn't fly anymore.

"I apologize, Reena," he said as he rubbed his arms.

"Forget about it," said Reena. "You've got more to do. You know that, right?"

"Yeah," Jonah muttered. "So where's—?"

Terrence appeared, holding two large pizza boxes.

"Met the delivery guy in the hall," he announced. "Took care of the payment, and gave him a nice tip. Way I see it, you split these pizzas with me, and we're good. Deal?"

Jonah glanced at Reena, whose eyes were on the pizza boxes with scorn. It made him laugh. Finally.

"Deal."

21

Green and Red

Jonah wondered where Jonathan was, and what he was up to. But every time his mind ventured there, it brought up the emotions that he tried so hard to purge. So he did what he always did when his frustration got the best of him: distract himself with life.

In the days after Jonah made good with Terrence and Reena, he went about making amends with some other people he'd ignored for weeks and weeks. Bobby was glad that he hadn't been taken by Deadfallen disciples. Liz tried to stay angry, but it just wasn't in her nature, so after she sternly told Jonah off, she revealed that her family had plans to work something out with the Decessios for a big Christmas get-together. She also told him that his refusal to participate in it was not an option. Jonah hadn't planned to decline at all, but he was concerned a bit about room and space. The estate wasn't ever crowded. Jonah still didn't know the reason for that, but he always forgot to ask. But whatever the reasons, he was sure that Mr. and Mrs. Decessio's house wouldn't comfortably accommodate so many people.

But it'd be fun to try.

Jonah's apology to Vera was interesting.

He went to The Stop, and parked near her car so that there was no way that she wouldn't see him. He didn't dare text her; that'd just be tacky at this point. When Vera came out for her break and saw him, her hazel eyes blazed as she stormed his way.

"Vera—" he began for damage control purposes, but Vera cut him off with a finger to his chest.

"Jonah James Anderson Rowe," she said in a murderous whisper, "don't you ever, in your physical lifetime, ignore my calls again. I was frightened out of my mind! I didn't know what could have happened to you! You could have been so pissed that you wrecked your car that night! It was a holiday, after all; people are crazy on holidays! You could have been wide open and easy picking for anyone, especially Deadfallen disciples! What in hell's name were you thinking, leaving me hanging like that—"

"Vera!" said Jonah. "I know. I know. I screwed up. I didn't do right by any of you guys. But you've been so great, being up here with me and hanging out and all that, and I—I was just stupid. I'm sorry."

Vera took a deep breath as relief and anger fought each other in her expression. "You're going to atone for what you did," she said.

"Huh?" said Jonah. "How?"

"You're coming to my house tonight and watching *Cinema Paradiso* with me."

"Wait, what?" said Jonah. "Isn't that the one that makes everyone so emotional?"

"Uh-huh," said Vera. "The very same."

Jonah sighed. So much for keeping level emotions. "Fine. Done."

Vera calmed after Jonah acquiesced, and stood next to him. After several moments of silence, she sighed and spoke some more. "For what it's worth, I would have wanted to hide away, too."

"Really?" said Jonah.

"Duh," said Vera. "But see, Jonah... you're you. You just can't disappear willy-nilly like that. Mess like that gets folks in an uproar."

Jonah shook his head. He knew that he'd messed up, and he had no right to be angry at his friends for being angry with him. Decisions really sucked when one didn't think things through. "You're right," he said. "I apologize. Are we cool?"

Vera looked up at the steel gray sky. "After you watch *Cinema Paradiso* with me tonight, we're square," she said. "But I'm glad that nothing happened to you during the time you wouldn't speak to any of us."

"Yeah," said Jonah, ready to move on from that. "Are you worried about Lockman? The Curaie closing the estate down? And of course, Jonathan being gone?"

With her index finger, Vera traced her facial scar. It meant she was pensive. Jonah didn't even know when he began to pick up on Vera's quirks. Maybe it was when he accidentally memorized her routine. "Of course I don't want the estate to close down," she said at last. "The Curaie are self-righteous pricks, and they prove that every time they open their mouths. As far as Jonathan...I prefer to just trust him."

Jonah frowned slightly. "Trust Jonathan."

"Yeah," said Vera. "That guy—spirit, I mean—helped me to control my ethereality. Jonathan always scrapes out a win, no matter how bleak things are. Liz told me about what he did to the armory when Lockman came and inspected the estate. I haven't forgotten everything we've been through, Jonah. And even though I know you listened to it all on a radio, you weren't there to see Jonathan. He was pissed, of course, but he was so calm about it. He didn't shout and protest like the rest of us did. It was almost like he had a plan already. So I've decided to trust him. It makes me feel a whole lot more comfortable to trust him, wherever he is, than to trust the damned Curaie."

Jonah agreed with the last part, but had mixed feelings about some of the other things that Vera said. He wasn't high on Jonathan at the moment, and wasn't too fond of the former Protector Guide's track record as of late, and he didn't even want to count the absences. But he didn't hate him. Jonathan had done too much for him for that. Maybe Vera was on to something. Maybe so much had gone wrong that he had a willingness to grab any lifeline there was. "I would like to hope that you're right," he said at last, "because we might have bigger issues."

"How do you mean?" frowned Vera.

Jonah told her about the Deadfallen disciples in crow form that heard the entire evaluation, then flew off to inform Creyton. Vera tapped her arm for a few seconds.

"What did Reena have to say about that?" she asked.

"She immediately told Daniel," said Jonah. "And after what happened with Jonathan, he's ready to shoot anything that moves. But he's got to be careful, of course, with the S.P.G. still at the estate on sentry duty and all. But you know what? Let's just talk about something else. The Curaie puts me in the wrong mood. What are your Christmas plans?"

"Liz's house." Vera answered so readily that it was clear she was ready for a change of subject as well. "Did you know that everyone will be celebrating the holiday elsewhere this year?"

Jonah prevented the sneer at his lip. Yeah, he knew that. It made him hate this mess all the more.

"Liz is worried about Nella," said Vera. "She says that she's been changing over these past few months."

Jonah nodded. So Liz still didn't know about that tattoo. If she had, she'd have told Vera about it. Nella was heading for trouble, fast. She was either going to get her feelings hurt, or get her boyfriend hurt. One or the other.

But at that moment, Jonah realized that Vera hadn't said anything further. Her eyes were in the direction of two parked cars, but she probably looked at them without seeing them. And Jonah understood where her mind went.

"Vera, no," he said. "Nella would never make that drastic a change. Liz would slap her down like nobody's business. She wouldn't become wild like…like your sister Madison."

It didn't seem like Vera cared much for saying Madison's name, so Jonah did it for her. She seemed to appreciate it. "She better not," Vera replied at last. "But thank you for apologizing to me, Jonah. I'll see you later tonight. Bring Kleenexes; you'll need them."

Jonah had to admit that there were moments where he reconsidered his decision to become social with his estate friends. He got texts and emails almost daily now. No one wanted him to feel isolated or forgotten. But he kept Mr. Steverson's words in the forefront of his mind, and welcomed the deluge, however overwhelming it could be sometimes.

As it was, he had plenty of distractions. Christmas season was upon them. That fact was more prevalent at S.T.R. than just about anywhere else. Between patrons coming in for Christmas-themed merchandise and Mr. Steverson's exuberance in regards to his grandchildren's presents, Jonah was able to push down his issues as far as they would go. He knew Felix wouldn't approve of him burying things, but hey, it was the holidays. Reena helped a lot, making a point to call at least once a day, even if the call was two minutes. Terrence preferred texting, but he checked in as often as he could. No one spoke on the elephants in the room, i.e.; Jonathan, and the impending closure of the estate.

But there was one thing that Jonah couldn't ignore.

He emailed Liz and Ben-Israel about the mysterious illness that had been present for the past couple months (which Elevenths had come to refer to as the Mindscope Illness) the minute he had time to do so, which was about two weeks before Christmas. Something about it bothered him, and he couldn't put a finger on it. He figured that if he decided to be proactive, he would figure out what that was before it was too late.

Ben-Israel's email was to the point, or at least it was at the beginning. Then the dam broke:

Hey Jonah. I hope that this message finds you well.

The cases have increased, and the Tenth doctors are out of their minds with worry. MAN, how I wish I could tell them that there was nothing they could do, but obviously, I cannot do so, 1) Because of Lockman, and 2) It would reiterate the fact that I can't see a fix for it myself yet. I've consulted every Green Aura that I know, and have even reached out to some buddies I have on the Green Team. Nothing.

If you want to know how stumped I feel with this, check this out: I caught myself trying to pray last night. I thought perhaps faith might trump ethereal science.

Jonah blinked at the screen. Ben-Israel was an atheist. He wasn't as outspoken and militant about it as Trip was, but he'd tell anyone who asked him that as a Green Aura and ethereal scientist, faith and religion just didn't make sense to him. But he just said that he caught himself trying to pray. Damn.

Liz didn't fare much better, but at least she was void of Ben-Israel's doom and gloom:

Jonah! Hey, big brother! I can't wait to see you on Christmas!

It's clear that the Tenths are incapable of assisting, which is entirely not their fault. The Green Team, so I've found, have been going into hospitals from Emerald Isle all the way to Blowing Rock, posing as CDC and bringing people to Spirits of Vitality and Peace (that's the largest Eleventh healing haven in the southern United States, and it's in Concord). I heard that they are strict there, but it's a far cry from the little shop of horrors under the Old Lange Sign.

Jonah actually laughed. Liz was one of the most objective people that he knew, especially when it came to practicing healing. But he wasn't stupid. He knew that her only beef with the healing den under the Old Lange Sign was the fact that it was a favorite of the residents of Sanctum Arcist. He read on:

The Green Team has also been tasked with an extra burden. You have to understand, Jonah—some of these people weren't aware that they were Eleventh Percenters. I've done research, experiments, and troubleshooting. Haven't gotten a break. A few people are in a terrible state, and my heart goes out to their families. But Creyton hasn't done any more Mindscopes lately. I guess that's a plus.

One more thing. Ben-Israel and I learned something from our Green Aura friend, Akshara. She discovered that all the people who fell victim to this Mindscope Illness seemed... rebellious in some way, shape, or form. All between fifteen and thirty-five. Other than that, there is no connection between the people whatsoever.

I hope that this gets fixed quickly. And I hope that the Green Team isn't as stupid as the Curaie who backs them.

I love you, big bro. Again, can't wait to see you at Christmas!

Lizzie

Jonah looked away from the screen, so as to rest his eyes from staring at the computer. Liz and Ben-Israel were both on the same case, but along different tracks of thought. He knew next to nothing about the Green Team, other than the fact that they were the Green Auras tasked with going into Tenth hospitals to find people with ethereal maladies. It was another branch of the Curaie, but that didn't mean they were all pricks. And Liz said that that all the people were between fifteen and thirty-five. And rebellious? The age gap was too broad to mean anything, but the rebellious piece? What did Akshara mean when she told Liz and Ben-Israel that?

Jonah was no Green Aura. And he had no medical training or expertise at all.

So why did he feel, in every fiber of his being, that there was something the Green Auras were missing?

Jonah was busy at work helping Harland shelve newly rehabbed books at S.T.R. the next day. Amanda helped around the place with a questionable vigor, but Mr. Steverson confided in them that her son was going through colic, and she considered S.T.R. a reprieve. She hadn't even complained when she looked over Mr. Steverson's books.

When Jonah returned from lunch, Mr. Steverson was in a passionate conversation about something with another middle-aged guy.

"I just don't understand why people have to mark themselves up," Mr. Steverson was saying. "I mean, isn't that what paper is for? And there is man two or three doors down from me, Bryce something-or-other, who lets me keep his keys after he closes—"

"Huh?" Jonah wasn't even ashamed of his nosiness. The other man glared at him, and Mr. Steverson didn't look too thrilled about the interruption, either.

"What, Jonah?"

"Did you say Bryce Tysinger lets you keep his keys at closing?" he asked.

"Yeah, he does," said Mr. Steverson. "He drops 'em off here every night."

"Huh," murmured Harland, who'd also heard the exchange. "That's more than a little paranoid, don't you think?"

"Might very well be," said Mr. Steverson. "Maybe he's afraid of something being found in his little parlor."

Jonah's eyes narrowed.

"I don't mean like drugs or anything," said Mr. Steverson hastily. "I mean like...maybe he keeps his money there. Stashes them flash drives you young people always use. Maybe he has stuff he's not comfortable keeping at his house."

Jonah's eyes remained narrowed after he turned from his boss. Every time he saw that Bryce guy, he always looked as though he would piss his pants. Was that the reason? Was he afraid that Jonah would rob his establishment? Or was he afraid of everyone, and Jonah was the one who happened to discover that?

But Jonah didn't have time to dwell on it. He had work, and later on, presents to buy.

Jonah hated the mall year-round, but at Christmas, it was nothing short of torture. How was it that the holidays brought out the absolute worst in everybody? And since he'd been on edge these past few months, he had to be careful amongst the Christmas shoppers.

He passed by a woman trying her damnedest to calm her two toddler sons. She was nearly in tears with frustration. He pitied her, and stretched some of his balancing ethereality her way. He didn't know how well it would work, as he wasn't spiritually endowed (that and the fact that balance hadn't worked too well for him recently), but he thought he would at least try. He saw another man on his way out of a cutlery store. He looked very pleased with himself as he clutched a gorgeously wrapped box. Three seconds later, the bottom gave way and spilled all the contents. The frazzled employee must have wrapped the box upside down.

The most entertaining thing of all for Jonah was when he passed a couple having what resembled a game-time discussion. The man looked at the woman, nervousness and determination in his eyes.

"Alright, Bridgette, we are on a budget," he said. "You know the rules. No Victoria's Secret until after Christmas sales. The laptops work fine; we are not buying new ones. And when we get to the Pottery Barn, you will not gravitate to the most expensive items because you suddenly need them."

"Fine," said the woman, "but only if those same rules apply to you regarding F.Y.E., Gamestop, and that mahogany brown recliner that you've been ogling for three months."

The man's jaw dropped. It was all Jonah could do to keep from laughing out loud.

But on to business.

He'd already taken care of Bobby and Alvin. For Terrence, he got a neat little money clip. The guy had enough Duke University merchandise. For Reena, it had to be something artsy all the way. That particular one might not fly at the mall. He might have to look at Hobby Lobby or Dick Blick.

Then there was Vera. What to do for her? He'd already gotten her merchandise from *Wicked*. Though the initial presentation was ruined by Felix, Vera later said she adored the gifts, and even explained why she gushed over Felix's. The Christmas after that one, he'd gotten her an anthology of female playwrights. Vera might have been angry with Jonah at the time, but she loved that one, too. So what could he get her now?

Someone bumped into him from behind, and Jonah stumbled several inches forward. Jonah rounded on him, prepared to snap at him like everyone else was in this overpopulated place, but he stopped when he saw the guy.

The man looked disheveled, woebegone, and bone-tired. He hadn't actually bumped into Jonah at all; he'd lost his footing in an attempt to handle a very large package.

"I'm sorry, sir," he mumbled. "I didn't mean to do that."

"I see that now," said Jonah, calm now. "Are you alright?"

"I would be if I could get rid of this." The man surveyed his package with disdain. "Do you know that store back there kept me waiting fifteen minutes just to tell me that they didn't go for these kinds of things? I just wanted some extra money for Christmas! I've got twelve days, and I can't get this off of my back! I don't even like plays!"

That caught Jonah's attention. "Plays?" he asked him.

"Yeah." The man's voice was listless.

"Exactly what is it that you have there?" Jonah wanted to know.

"Some stupid poster of some play that's supposedly a big deal," the man muttered. "Less Miserable or something—"

"*Les Miserables?*" corrected Jonah. He kept his face emotionless, but internally he was on full alert. "And you want to sell it?"

"Yeah, I don't even care—" The guy paused once he realized that Jonah was interested. His entire demeanor changed from a despairing loser to a shrewd businessman. "—I mean, I was attempting to sell it…for sixty bucks."

Jonah very nearly laughed. It was obvious that that was pure bullshit. But Vera would love that present, he knew she would. He had to play this one intelligently. As such, he manufactured a frown. "Bye."

He about-faced and made to walk away. *Five…four…three…*he thought to himself.

Sure enough, the man caught up with Jonah, lugging his burden.

"Wait!" he cried. "Wait! How about fifty?"

"Twenty-five," countered Jonah.

The guy almost gagged. "Forty-five?"

Jonah laughed to himself. "Twenty-five," he repeated.

"Forty?"

Jonah snorted. The guy swallowed.

"But—aw, man—thirty-five?"

"Twenty-six," said Jonah randomly, "and that's as high as I'm going."

"Twenty-six dollars?" The man frowned. "That's an odd figure."

"Well, the holiday season is an odd time," Jonah replied with a shrug. "Take it or leave it."

The man made a face like he had just consumed something bitter, then said, "Done, dammit."

He extended his hand for the cash, but Jonah snorted again. He pointed at the box.

"Verify," he said.

With a scowl, the man lifted the poster out of the box. It was the genuine article. It was even framed, and autographed by a number of actors and actresses. Jonah could only imagine the look on Vera's face, but none of that showed on his face as he took it.

"Pleasure doing business with you," he said. "Merry Christmas."

The man grumbled something that Jonah didn't understand, took his cash, and walked off in a rather galumphing manner. Jonah left the mall, so thankful to be free from the crowd. No matter how many times he went there, when he left the mall, he felt reborn.

"Impeccable, Rowe," said a familiar voice as soon as he stepped out.

He turned to see Felix looking at him with an approving grin.

"Who would have guessed you were a haggler?" he asked him.

"Who would have guessed you came to places like this?" said Jonah, genuinely surprised. "Isn't it possible you could get riled in there?"

"The same is possible for anywhere," said Felix with a dismissive wave. "Especially during this season."

"Why are you here?" Jonah asked. "I thought you didn't care about holidays."

Felix cleared his throat. "I have my reasons," he said. "But since you're here, I have some information that you ought to know. I am going to tell Daniel, too, and I hope that he can make contact with Jonathan."

"Really?" said Jonah. "What's that?"

Felix took one of those centering breaths that made Jonah want to take a step back. "It concerns the sazer underground," he said. "Or what's left of it."

"What's left of it?" repeated Jonah.

"A great deal of sazers have been successfully seduced by Creyton's gifts," Felix replied. "The ones who refused to be swayed were forced to run, or not."

Felix let Jonah interpret that for himself.

"How are Prodigal, Autumn Rose, and the rest of them?" Jonah asked.

"Staying out of trouble, for the most part," said Felix. "Autumn Rose had to be sedated when she went into Red Rage after she heard about Jonathan."

"What would she care?"

"Everyone trusts Jonathan, Jonah," said Felix. "And he is one of the few who thinks sazers should be treated like equals."

Jonah looked away at that. Here was another endorsement for Jonathan. It was so funny how people could have so many opinions about one person. "How are sazers faring with this Mindscope Illness?" he asked.

Felix raised an eyebrow.

"It's what Liz and other Elevenths are calling it," Jonah supplied.

"Sazers react badly to it, Jonah," said Felix, doing his diaphragmatic breathing again. "Luckily, no one close to us has been affected. But the Curaie doesn't care about sazers. As far as some in the S.P.G. and Networkers are concerned, this was needed."

"What!" said Jonah. "What if it was one of them?"

"Word of advice, Jonah," said Felix. "There are two types of mentalities that it's pointless to try to understand—bullies, and bigots."

Jonah shook his head. "And there is still Lockman—" he began, but to his surprise, Felix scoffed, and waved a dismissive hand.

"Don't worry about that close-minded fuck," he said. "His shit will come back on him."

Jonah regarded Felix shrewdly. "You weren't singing that tune some months ago," he commented. "Do you know something?"

"I am a firm believer in karma," said Felix simply. "He bribes, manipulates, and coerces. It's going to hurt him one day. But anyway—"He walked past Jonah, headed for the mall entrance. "Nice haggling, and look out for yourself. I won't be surprised if we see a sudden upsurge in ambition." He pulled the door open.

"Felix?" Jonah called.

Felix looked back at him.

"You wouldn't happen to be shopping for Maxine, would you?"

Felix sniffed. "That subject is buried, Rowe. Recall that?"

* * *

Jonah awoke at a quarter past five on Christmas morning. He had a two hour, forty-six minute drive to the Decessio house, and, barring unforeseen circumstances, he'd get there right around eight. After he showered and trimmed his beard, he dressed and grabbed the handful of presents he was due to present when he reached his destination. He was heading out the door when he noticed the old radio. Trip had said one of the dials would alert him to danger. Should he bring it?

He answered himself just as quickly. No. Who would want bad news on Christmas?

Jonah had a hard time once he took Exit 81. He almost drove to the estate. It was like muscle memory. Then he remembered. He wasn't allowed there. And none of his friends were there, anyway. And, of course, in two month's time, the place would be closed, thanks to the Curaie.

With a mental shake that nearly caused his head to hurt, he drove on to the Decessio house, where he saw several cars he recognized, and one he didn't expect.

A Ford Escape. Douglas was there. And his grandmother wasn't with him, otherwise he'd be driving her Lincoln; she couldn't reach the Escape.

Christmas was looking better and better.

He kicked at the door, his arms laden with gifts, and was greeted by Terrence, who grinned.

"Just in time for Christmas breakfast!" he said, holding open the door to let Jonah in. "How was traffic?"

"Please," said Jonah. "The interstate was damn near empty."

Terrence led him to the family room, where he was greeted by most of the Decessio family. He hadn't seen Sterling since Jonathan's evaluation, and they hadn't even spoken then, so it was fun to catch up. Raymond and Mr. Decessio were outside at the chopping pile, hacking some extra wood so they wouldn't need to later. Alvin and Bobby struggled to give Mrs. Decessio their present first. Terrence had already explained that Reena spent the night with Kendall and would spend Christmas morning with her as well, so she'd show up around noon, which was the same time the Manvilles would show up with Vera. Jonah was grateful, but he was a bit impatient because he wanted Vera to see her present. But until that time, he had a hearty breakfast with the Decessios and exchanged presents with them. Mrs. Decessio made Jonah a cerulean blue quilt, which he took with surprise and gratitude. He never knew she had such a gift. "She doesn't do it much anymore. She spends more time gardening," explained Terrence.

Sterling got him a fountain pen, and Alvin got him a *Writing Fiction for Dummies* book ("You aren't a dummy, but it might have good stuff in there!"). Bobby got him a weight belt, which he knew he'd probably never use. That boy was a fanatic, but Jonah wouldn't have it any other way. Terrence had the audacity to get Jonah a hooded sweatshirt representing Duke. Jonah gave him a mock scowl.

"And to think, I got you a new set of steak knives," he grumbled, but wound up laughing. "You miserable little..."

Jonah asked after Douglas, and Mrs. Decessio laughed.

"He got here really early this morning," she said. "I let him sleep."

"Why so early?"

"Well, his house became...unpleasant," Mrs. Decessio explained. "He finally stood up to his grandmother."

Jonah nearly dropped his new sweatshirt. "No," he breathed. "On Christmas morning?"

"It was one comparison too many," said Mrs. Decessio with a sigh. "I had always hoped Maudine would give Doug a break, didn't happen. And the final straw was something petty—I think she said something about him needing to be a responsible man like his Uncle Lujack—and he snapped."

"Man." Jonah wondered when it would happen. As much as he hated to say it, Mrs. Chandler did have it coming. She was one of the most verbally abusive people he knew. And Douglas finally grew a set. In front of his entire family. On Christmas Day. Oops."Did she kick him out?"

"Nah, she didn't." Mrs. Decessio shook her head. "He left before things could escalate any further. I told him to sleep, and cool off. I hope it works."

"It did, Mrs. D.," said a weary voice.

Douglas was there with them. His eyes were a little red, but he was calm. "Now, I just want to open presents, eat, and be around folks that don't criticize me."

"The other half of the party's here!" announced Alvin, looking out of the window. "Sweet!"

Like clockwork, the Manvilles and Vera showed up, and Reena pulled in behind them. Bobby didn't even wait for Liz to reach the house; he went outside to greet her. At one time, Jonah would laugh about this with Terrence and Alvin. Nowadays, he felt more inclined to respect him. He wasn't quite sure when that had changed, but it reminded him of what Nelson told him.

Everyone came into the house, and Jonah finally got to meet Mr. Manville. He was dark-featured and reserved, both of which he had passed on to Sandrine. But he passed the dark eyes on to Nella. Liz didn't seem to have anything of him at all in her, but it was obvious she adored him, and for Jonah, that was enough.

He shook Jonah's hand and gave him a quick inspection, as though he aimed to gauge his abilities. Jonah hadn't ever cared for when older people did that; it made him feel like an apprehensive child again. Half the time he wanted to remind them that he was an adult as well.

"I feel like I know you already," said Mr. Manville, seemingly pleased with his gauge. "Liz and Nella speak very highly of you."

"I can say the same of you, sir," said Jonah respectfully.

With a quick nod, Mr. Manville moved on to Mr. and Mrs. Decessio. He'd found out what he wanted, deemed himself pleased, and rolled on. After the months of spying and nosiness they'd all experienced, it was quite refreshing.

"Merry Christmas, Jonah!" squealed Liz, throwing her arms around him with her usual beaming smile. "So glad to see you!"

Grinning, Jonah responded in kind, and caught a glance of Nella lugging some food that Mrs. Manville had made. He widened his eyes at her, asking without words if she'd revealed the tattoo. Looking aggravated, Nella mouthed, "*No!*"

Jonah felt a flicker of irritation, but quickly buried it when he saw Reena and Vera each holding beautiful items: Vera had what looked to be apple preserves in decorative bottles, while Reena held large brownies that were fashioned into Santa hats.

"Look at you!" he said, beckoning to Terrence and greeting them. "You letting your hair down for jolly ol' St. Nick?"

Reena made a wry face, but it was appearance only. "Kendall bought these and couldn't finish them," she said. "She knew you garbage disposals would destroy them."

"And you know what?" said Vera. "According to Mrs. Manville, the brownies go magically with these preserves. So guess what I'm trying after dinner!"

This was met with extreme enthusiasm, but Reena looked horrified. "All that sugar!" she cried. "It'll rot out your teeth!"

"That's the thing, Reena!" said Terrence. "Preserves never rot!"

Pretty soon, everyone was settled. To Jonah's delight, Vera loved his present, exhibiting a look of joy that he wished he could have bottled. He wouldn't see the allure in a million lifetimes, but Vera treasured it. That was plenty awesome for him.

Not long afterward, Terrence, Mrs. Decessio, and Mrs. Manville had the Christmas spread out for the taking. As there was glazed ham, Mrs. Decessio didn't put bacon in the mac and cheese, feeling it would be "entirely too much pork." Reena looked grateful as she prepared her plate, eschewing all meats except the turkey, but getting reasonable amounts of all the sides. Douglas, who still appeared mystified by his gumption earlier on, got a little bit of everything. Purposefully, Jonah, Terrence, Bobby, and Reena sat with him at the camp table erected next to the big table so as to accommodate the visitors.

"So what did it, Doug?" said Bobby.

Douglas scarfed down some ham, like he needed additional sustenance before recounting. "My uncle Lujack, who's Grandma 'Dine's second son, has recently gotten approved to buy a house," he began. "It's a blessing; he's wanted a house for his wife and kids for awhile. Grandma 'Dine, rather than accept it for the Christmas miracle it was, said that I should start taking charge and have initiative like that, and stop 'gallivantin' my life away in grad school.' I snapped."

"Man," said Alvin. "What did you say?"

"Don't remember half of it, but it was valid, and made sense when I said it," answered Douglas. "Everyone was so shocked, and Grandma 'Dine pulled the everything-I've-done-for-you card. I told her that she seems to work on a selective memory factor, and apparently wants me to do so as well. I do remember the great things she's done for me, but at the same time, I also remember the insults, heckling, and put-downs. I told her that. I couldn't focus on one, and block out the other. And after that, I left, and came here."

Bobby looked at him with newfound respect. "I gotta admit, Dougie, I never saw you doing that," he said.

"Me neither," admitted Doug. "Do you think I did wrong? Think I need to apologize? I mean, I meant what I said, but do you think I was out of line?"

"Not one bit." Reena's answer was instant, and she had so much conviction in her voice that even Sterling and Liz stared at her from the other table. "You know they say you can't judge family the same way you do other folks. That is B.S. Sometimes family needs to hear about themselves even more than other people. I applaud you for being a man, Douglas."

Douglas, unsurprisingly, didn't look entirely convinced, but the endorsement from Reena calmed some of his anxiety. He nodded.

Soon after, the conversations switched to random subjects and compliments of the savory foods. Jonah glanced at the other table, where everyone was in good spirits except for Nella. She popped an allergy pill and sniffed a couple times, but was also texting through the meal. Eventually she excused herself from the table, impatience in her face. Jonah saw Liz take a steadying breath, Sandrine's eyes flash, and Mrs. Manville's smile suddenly become mechanical. Feeling a vein twitch in his temple, he rose.

"Stretching my legs," he said to no one in particular.

Once he was out of the dining room, he found Nella near the back door, and overheard some of her conversation.

"Two days?" she was asking. "That's too long! I wish you could rescue me now."

"Really?" asked Jonah in a cold voice. "You need rescuing from friends and family now?"

Nella rounded on Jonah, murmured, "Let me call you back," and ended the call. "I don't need this, Jonah," she told him. "This is kid's stuff—"

"And you're so grown?" Jonah raised his eyebrows in mock surprise. "That's news to me."

"Leave me alone, Jonah. I hoped you wouldn't change on me, too—"

"Me?" demanded Jonah. "Changing? Nella, the only person who's changed is you!"

Nella laughed without mirth. "Let's take a close look, Jonah. I'm not as naive as you think. You punch out a suuvus in the Outer Banks, get sent away from the estate due to your anger issues, subject thirteen people to a vampire ambush 'cuz you were reckless, you assault a Networker, and then get banished. You're right—you haven't changed a lick."

Jonah's eyes narrowed. Before he could hurt Nella's feelings, as he was about to do, she blew her nose due to her allergies. The random act served to distract him. When Nella was done, she rolled her eyes.

"That's what I thought," she said, misinterpreting his silence. "You can't tell me a damn thing. Now if it's all the same to you, I'm ready to get this sappy shit over with."

Jonah spent three days at the Decessio house, where he, Reena, Terrence, Bobby, Alvin, and Douglas de-toxed from delicious food. Reena went for a run every morning, so it wasn't much of an issue for her. It had been fun, but the season was nearly over. There was an odd yet laughable envy between Terrence and Jonah: Jonah was jealous of all the days that Terrence had off from work, and Terrence was jealous that Jonah got to avoid the S.P.G. police-state that the estate had become. Jonah wished he could be there with them, but there was no point in voicing those words. Terrence and Reena already knew, and speaking it into being only made the reality of his situation that much sharper.

Douglas couldn't avoid his grandmother anymore, so when he left, they all wished him luck. Vera and the Manvilles left, with everyone having their own opinions about Nella's behavior. It got even crazier when, after they'd gotten home, Liz texted Bobby and told him that Nella left with Dylan before they'd even gotten all their presents into the house. Bobby, who'd wanted an excuse to hurt Dylan ever since Nella began to act differently, was ready to react, but Mr. and Mrs. Decessio said that interference might cause more harm than good, and it was the Manville family's right to handle her in their own way. Jonah had a very definite opinion on what to do about Nella, but he wanted so badly to respect her. But she made that harder and harder by the minute.

Before he knew it, it was time to go. He gave out hugs all around, and promised Mrs. Decessio he'd look out for himself. It was merely the routine; nothing of note had happened since he'd been banished. Maybe Creyton and the Deadfallen disciples didn't care about him now that he'd been exiled from his home.

"We'll be up there to visit you soon," promised Terrence when Jonah was feet away from his car.

Jonah laughed. "Terrence, I'll be fine."

"Tell that to Reena," countered Terrence, and they laughed.

"Point," said Jonah. "But I'll see you later man. And tell your mom that the food was excellent, as usual."

With a final wave, he was on the road.

It was at a stoplight that Jonah had a strong, inexplicable desire to drive past the estate. It hadn't exactly come from nowhere, because he did miss the place. He just didn't miss the people stationed on the grounds.

And how naked would the place be without Jonathan there?

But the feeling was so strong that it almost ached. It would be bad—very bad—if he didn't drive pass the estate. He didn't know how he knew that, but he was certain of the fact.

So instead of making the turn that would take him to the highway, he drove toward the Grannison-Morris estate.

Why was the feeling so strong? It was blaring, so much so that he nearly didn't register the large animal sprawled on the side of the road—

Jonah's blood turned to ice. As if on autopilot, he slowed, and pulled over to the shoulder. With hands that he barely felt, he turned off the car.

He hadn't passed by an animal.

He'd passed a person sprawled on the side of the road.

Jonah got out of his car, grabbing his flashlight as he did so. It had been two full minutes driving, so his backtrack would take a few moments.

He walked hurriedly but cautiously; the last thing he needed was to get tripped up or injured himself.

Twenty further steps, and Jonah's flashlight illuminated the goal. Once the light hit it, Jonah's eyes bulged.

It was indeed a person in a heap on the ground. And not just a random person.

It was Nella.

22

Re-Entry

An all-encompassing terror enveloped Jonah, and he would have shouted if his chest allowed him the necessary air. He nearly cracked the flashlight as he raced to the place where Nella lay.

"Please God, not Nella." The fact that this was the first time Jonah had prayed since he was eighteen didn't even compute to him. "Not her, please—she's just sixteen—"

He dropped down next to her, almost afraid to touch her. "Nella! NELLA!"

His body went colder and colder because he saw no signs of physical life whatsoever...

Nella coughed a dry, hacking cough and opened her eyes. "Jonah," she whispered.

"Nella..." Relief grasped him so strongly, his chest hurt. "What happened to you?"

"Jonah..." Even Nella's whispering was laborious. "Dylan. It was Dylan...he..."

Jonah's eyes widened. That boy was responsible for this? "What did he do? What did he do to you, Nella?"

"Hold me up, Jonah," whispered Nella. "My body hurts..."

Gripped by fear once more, Jonah sat on the ground, and cradled her in his arms. She seemed so frail and tiny; hardly the girl full of defiance and attitude she'd been in recent months.

"Thank you," she murmured. "But Jonah, you need to know... Dylan is a suuvus."

Jonah gaped. "What?"

"I've been so stupid," Nella scolded herself. "My God, I've been stupid—"

"You're not stupid, Nella," Jonah told her, tightening his embrace. "But Dylan is a suuvus? What did he do to you?"

"I—something's wrong with me," breathed Nella. "My body... I—I can't get it right."

Jonah insides went glacial. *Aw, shit.* "What's Dylan got to do with it?" he almost demanded.

Copious tears fell down Nella's pale face. "He said that Creyton would wipe out all of the undeserving scum," she said. "I was barely conscious. I've been feeling off for a while now, but I... I thought it was my seasonal allergies being extra crappy this year, or something. He... he told me that I was insignificant. Said, 'Roses are red, violets are blue, the Old Order is dead, and so are you.' Then he pushed me out. He stole my car, Jonah, and promised that no one would find me out here until it was too late." She let out a dry, hacking cough. "How—how did you find me?"

Jonah didn't answer. His mind was at work accommodating his internal change. The frigid fear that initially encompassed him now dissipated in the heat of the white-hot rage that burned his every fiber. But he had to take control. Nella had the Mindscope Illness. She needed help.

He rose, and lifted Nella into his arms. "Hold on, little sister," he said. "I've got you."

* * *

Jonah wanted the *Astralimes* so badly, but he remembered the monitoring. He wasn't aware of his restrictions, given his banishment and all. And any delay would be costly to Nella. So he sent a blanket text message, because he didn't have time to call:

I've got Nella. Need Green Auras ASAP.

He drove her to Terrence's house. Luckily, Reena hadn't left to spend the night with Kendall yet. Her tense face was the first one he saw, followed closely by Terrence and the others.

"Jonah, I am…strong enough to walk," protested Nella in a weak tone.

"Shut up," said Jonah, without venom or force.

He carried her into the house and all the way up to the guest bedroom, where Mrs. Decessio placed a cool cloth on her forehead.

"How did you find her?" she asked.

"It's a long, long story, ma'am," said Jonah. He needed to keep the incendiary information to himself long enough to see to it that help could be attained for Nella. He looked at Mr. Decessio. "The Spirits of Vitality and Peace. Are there any Green Auras there that you trust?"

"A few." Mr. Decessio had his phone in his hand almost immediately. "There are two for sure that I trust with my physical life, no matter what."

"That's great," said Jonah. "Now, Bobby—"

"WHERE IS SHE?" came a shrill scream from downstairs.

Bobby closed his eyes. "I'll do what I can—"

He never got the chance to intercept. The entire Manville family barreled into the tiny room, which instantly inconvenienced everyone. This wasn't the estate infirmary; they were bumper to bumper in this room.

"Oh my God oh my God oh my God," intoned Liz, who swooped on Nella along with her mother, "she's got it. She's got the Mindscope Illness!"

"Can you do anything, Elizabeth?" asked Mrs. Manville with desperation and worry in her voice.

"I don't know!" cried Liz. "I need help, I need help—"

"Ben-Israel just appeared in the yard," announced Sterling from outside the room. "Raymond contacted him. There are two other men, too—"

"That'd be Fuller and Malik." Mr. Decessio rose. "I'll brief them."

After some agonizing adjustments and rearrangements, the Decessio patriarch was out of the room.

"We need to leave this room," said Jonah, "so they can do their work."

"I'm not leaving my sister." Liz's voice was intractable.

"You've got to, Liz," said Jonah, "because there is something you need to know. At least for the moment, leave it to Ben-Israel and Mr. Decessio's Green Aura friends."

Jonah maneuvered out of the room and headed to the kitchen, hoping everyone would follow him. He heard pairs of feet behind him, but when everyone congregated, he saw that Mrs. Manville and Sandrine weren't among them. With a sigh, he just decided to roll with it.

"Where did you find my daughter?" demanded Mr. Manville.

Jonah sighed again. "Down on Hodges Road," he said.

"What?" Liz, whose eyes were on the floor, looked up. "But that's near the estate! How did you find her?"

"I'm not sure," admitted Jonah. "I just had this strong feeling—really, really strong feeling—that I needed to go that way. I found her down there, on the side of the road."

No one stared at him like he was crazy. They were all too full of gratitude to doubt him. But Mr. Manville was a powder keg.

"Did that boy have anything to do with it?" he asked.

Jonah's anger, which he'd successfully compartmentalized in favor of Nella's plight, was once again unchained. "Yes," he said bluntly. "That bastard is a suuvus. Nella was intended to be another victim."

Mr. Manville stood stationary for a second. Then he headed for the door. Liz's eyes widened in terror when she caught the look in his eye.

"Daddy—" she reached for his arm, but he jerked away. Mrs. Decessio blocked his path.

"You need to think, Karl," she said.

"Get out of the way, Connie," said Mr. Manville in a lifeless voice.

"You don't even know where to find him!"

"I'll hunt him down soon enough."

"So you've already made up your mind?"

"I'll sleep better tonight—"

"And what about Nellaina?" asked Mrs. Decessio.

"You can't understand, Connie!" snarled Mr. Manville. "And I wouldn't expect you to! All of your children are boys!"

"And how the hell does that make a difference?" snapped Mrs. Decessio. "Boys or girls, I'm still a parent! And, one parent to another, if your child is to get through this, she will need her family! All of her family! Imagine how she will feel if her father gets imprisoned in a Tenth cell because he favored his base-level wants over her!"

Mr. Manville stopped in his tracks. Liz touched her father's shoulder.

"Daddy, please."

Mr. Manville turned around. Humanity had returned to his eyes. "You're right, Connie," he said in quiet voice. "Nella is more important than vengeance."

"If vengeance is out of the question," said Terrence, savage pensiveness in his voice, "what about justice?"

Jonah was still too hot for much rational thought, despite the fact that Mrs. Decessio made a lot of sense. "What do you mean, man?"

"What I mean," said Terrence, "is that this isn't a Tenth matter anymore. That little puke is a suuvus, which means he has crossed into our world, and is therefore fair game."

"Fair game?" cried Mrs. Decessio. "Terrence, have you listened to anything I've said?"

"Relax, Mama," said Bobby. "He means for the Networkers. Maybe Patience can track him."

At that moment, Reena jumped, prompting everyone to stare at her. Her eyes gleamed with, bizarrely enough, triumph.

"Patience has got him!" she announced. "They're outside right now!"

The collective went outside, astounded. Sure enough, Patience stood there, next to Nella's car. There was a kneeling figure in front of him, with a bag over his head.

"Evening, ladies and gents," said Patience with no humor. "Don't worry; the bag on the boy's head is sound-guarded. He can't hear a thing we're saying. But let me save you all of the questions. I was just in the sheriff's department reviewing information—you know how people get speeding tickets this time of year—and I was looking for any joy riders that might be Eleventh Percenters. And then I discover that, due to an anonymous tip, an APB had been put out on Nella's car. I remembered her car because I was there when her dad gave her the keys to it. If her car was stolen, I imagine something ethereal was amiss, so I checked it out. Came across this boy in the parking lot of some bar. He tried to fight, but it was a damn joke."

Jonah frowned. An anonymous tip was put out for Nella's stolen car? Was there someone out there looking out for them in some small way? Jonathan, maybe?

"You are a blessing, Ovid," said Mrs. Decessio. "Arn's upstairs with Nella and three Greens. She's contracted the ethereal illness that's popping up here and there. This boy left her on the side of a road. If Jonah hadn't found her, she may very well have passed into Spirit."

Patience frowned. "What happened? Did she show signs of it in front of him? Did he panic, and steal her car?"

"No," growled Mr. Manville. "He is the *suuvus* who stole her car."

Patience's nostrils flared. "Oh, really."

"Question, sir," said Terrence. "Why'd you bring him here? Why didn't you take him to some Spectral Law facility?"

"Nella is family," said Patience. "And the Curaie's policy of ignorance at the moment is something that I am disinclined to roll with. This boy may need to be dealt with...off the record."

Jonah liked this boy's chances less and less. He'd picked the absolute wrong girl to fuck with.

"Take him to the shed," suggested Raymond. "He is not coming into our house."

Fifteen minutes later, the collective moved again. Patience made a few calls, and acquired some information through his Networker methods. Jonah didn't know what the man got, and didn't really want to ask. He was actually a bit distracted by Mrs. Decessio's strange request to Alvin for a pan of ice. Dylan was ethereally bound to a chair, courtesy of Reena. When he was secure, Jonah made to remove the bag, but Patience shook his head. The Networker walked to the shed's north wall, and placed two fingers there. A Spectral Illusion spread from his touch, and after about twenty seconds, the shed resembled a drab, long-neglected, adobe-type dwelling. It even included a rotting wooden door, a jagged window, and a bed that Jonah wouldn't sleep on even if it was the last bed on Earthplane.

Patience nodded at Jonah, and he removed the bag from the boy's head. It dawned on Jonah that he had never actually seen Dylan himself before. With his thick dark hair, build, and sarcastic features, he looked like every ne'er do well bad boy that all the teenage girls would clamor over. But the attributes that he'd certainly used to win over Nella were non-existent at the moment as he looked wildly around, anguished and terrified.

"What…what's going on?" he demanded.

"This, boy, is The Plane with No Name," said Patience in a menacing tone. "We've decided to interrogate you here. It's much easier."

"No." Dylan shook his head. "This isn't—that place. I'm a Tenth Percenter—"

"—who is a suuvus," Patience reminded him. "You forfeited every right you had as a Tenth when you started committing crimes in the ethereal arena. Due process, *habeas corpus*…they mean nothing here."

Dylan tried to look hardened, but his eyes betrayed him. "But—but I've got rights!" he protested. "What about my parents?"

"You have no parents, boy," said Patience. "You killed them, along with your landlord. I know all about you, Dylan Firewalker."

"Firewalker?" demanded Raymond, but Jonah's mind went elsewhere.

Nella had been with a killer? For months and months? Anything could have happened. Anything. But Jonah blocked the thoughts. Unimaginable things could have happened, but mercifully, they hadn't.

Until now.

Dylan began to realize his situation. "You can't hurt me," he attempted. "And you're lying! You wouldn't have a harmless middle-aged homemaker on The Plane with No Name. She don't even look like she can't hurt a gnat—"

Without warning, Mrs. Decessio punched Dylan across the face. She actually knocked over his chair. Jonah and all the Decessio boys stared at her, shocked.

"After everything that you told Mr. Manville," said Alvin, who shook his head.

Mrs. Decessio gave him a quelling look. The presence of the previously requested ice was explained as she plunged her hand into it. She'd planned to attack Dylan all along. "I'm a parent," she said to Alvin at last. "I can *be* a hypocrite."

"There you go," said Patience, who hoisted the chair back up and slapped Dylan's woozy face. "That was just one of us, boy. You see the people in this room? Nellaina Manville means something to each and every one of them. And that includes me. As I said, we aren't bound by Tenth justice here. So are you willing to cooperate now?"

"Wyndam O'Shea made me do it." Dylan said it without hesitation. "He said he'd kill me in the moonlight if I didn't. It hurt me to my heart—"

"You're a damn liar," snapped Jonah. " '*Roses are red, violets are blue, the Old Order is dead, and so are you.*' That ring a bell? Doesn't sound like you were so hurt to me."

Dylan blinked. He hadn't expected Jonah to know that. He tried a different tack. "I need protection from them. O'Shea, Charlotte, Inimicus, Darius—all of them'll come for me."

"You weren't thinking about that when you were corrupting my little girl with your lies," snarled Mr. Manville.

"Look man, it wasn't personal," promised Dylan. "I think I almost started to like Nella for real—"

Bobby and Raymond had to restrain Mr. Manville after those words. Jonah wanted them to release him so badly. He was trying so hard to keep from assaulting this boy himself. Reena and Terrence were behind him; they obviously didn't trust themselves to be any nearer.

"You had better talk, boy," said Patience. "Then, we'll see about protection."

Dylan swallowed. "All I know is what the Deadfallen disciples let me know," he said. "Something is supposed to happen that will shift the balance of power. The Transcendent has been working on it for months and months. Everyone involved is excited—they say it could very well be the Transcendent's magnum opus. The Curaie are scared out of their minds, and their efforts to contain the problem are failing because, so I heard, their efforts are only feeding the fire."

"And what is this event?" asked Patience.

"I don't know," shrugged Dylan. "All I know is that it's going to be bad. Like, biblically bad."

Everyone looked at Reena. Her neck was naked of the dampener. All she did was nod.

Now, no one knew what to say. All the Mindscopes, the cryptic warnings, the conversations with Creyton that only Jonah seemed to have—what were they leading to?

And Jonathan was nowhere to be found, stripped of everything by the Curaie.

Biblically bad.

Well, that just sucked.

"Thank you," said Patience. "We're done here."

Dylan blinked. "But I answered your questions!" he cried. "Nella didn't even die! I'll never be a minion now! So why don't you go ahead and get me out of this?"

"You were never going to be a minion, kid," said Raymond, looking at Dylan in disgust. "Creyton has no more use for them. He was just going to kill you and usurp your spirit. That would've been it. Poof."

"Plus, death isn't real," snapped Terrence.

"And I'm not letting you out," added Patience. "This Matt Harrill's territory. Remember that disciple? He hasn't killed anyone in so long. And what if he got wind that there was a defenseless Tenth stool pigeon in here, who has been singin' like a bird?"

Dylan's eyes bulged. Patience motioned to everyone, and they walked through the rotting wooden door. It was at that point that Dylan began to scream.

"WAIT! PLEASE! YOU HAVE TO LET ME OUT! NOW! COME ON! NO!"

When Jonah stepped out, he saw the exterior of the shed hadn't been disguised. When Patience shut the door, there was no sound of Dylan's screams.

"I'm gonna let him stay in there for a few hours," he explained. "It'll take the spunk out of him. He's a murderer; that'll be more than enough for the Tenth courts. He'll never be free a man again. He deserves worse than prison, but there you are."

Alvin looked at Patience in awe. "You are definitely the master," he marveled. "Can all Networkers do those illusions?"

Patience nodded his head. "They can. Acquiring the ability is the final piece to becoming a full-fledged Networker. But that's beside the point right now. Let's check on Nella."

Mrs. Decessio went to walk with Mr. Manville, Liz on his opposite side. Jonah fell back in step with Terrence and Reena.

"Little bitch," said Terrence. "I wish he were on The Plane with No Name, for real. He'd be eaten alive, and he'd deserve it."

Reena breathed heavily. "I couldn't say anything in there," she whispered. "If I had, I would've beaten him comatose, if I had managed to stop myself. So I stayed silent. I wouldn't assault a minor, no matter how much he deserved it."

Jonah didn't agree. He would have bashed that evil little bastard at any age, but his mind was on Nella.

They found Ben-Israel, Mr. Decessio and two men who could only be Fuller and Malik in the family room. Ben-Israel opened his mouth to speak, but Liz forestalled him with acid in her tone.

"You'd better tell me something good, Ben-Israel," she threatened. "Because my sister going into Spirit is not an option—"

"Liz, Liz," said Ben-Israel. "There is good news, and not so good news. Tell them what you told me, Mr. Fuller."

Jonah waited with labored breath.

"I don't know why it happened this way," said Fuller, "but over these past few months, I have seen thirty-eight of these cases. And of all of the strains, Nellaina has the least severe."

Yeah, there was relief. But Ben-Israel said there was some not-so-good news. They waited silently. Fuller took the hint.

"But it could mutate at any time," he went on. "Because of her less severe stage, Ben-Israel can administer a tonic that he's been working on for several weeks. It has to be administered every three hours."

They all stared. Every three hours? What if they missed one? Then what?

"What would you suggest?" said Mr. Manville.

"Let us take her to Spirits of Vitality and Peace," suggested Fuller. "I will personally vouch for her safety. It's a strict healing haven, but she'll be under the direct care of Malik and me. Ben-Israel can continue to assist us."

Liz and Mr. Manville looked at each other. An understanding passed between them.

"Only if I can assist as well," said Liz flat-out. "Make the arrangements. Make me an intern, or something."

"Don't you have enough on your plate with your studies?" asked Malik.

"Do you think that means more to me than my sister right now?" asked Liz.

Fuller nodded. "Done. No problem."

Liz looked at her father. "Do you agree, Daddy?" she asked.

Mr. Manville was one troubled man. He'd gone from horror and rage to discovering that his daughter had a lifeline. A lifeline that needed regular replenishing, but a lifeline nevertheless. "I wouldn't trust my little girl with anyone else than my other little girl," he said.

"Good deal," said Mr. Decessio. "Everything can be set up with the healing haven within a short while. We just wanted the entire family on board. She can be moved within the next half-hour."

Liz and Mr. Manville went upstairs with Ben-Israel. Bobby followed for moral support. Alvin simply sat. Ray and Sterling looked at Jonah.

"Looks like you're a hero, man," said Sterling.

"Not a hero, Sterling," said Jonah, instantly awkward. "I just got a powerful inclination at the right time."

Ray snorted. "Call it what you want, man," he said, "but you're a hero. I'm sure Nella would agree."

"They're right," said Terrence. "I think that in Liz's eyes, you can do no wrong now."

"I'm just glad she is away from that boy," said Jonah. "Dylan was such a terrible influence, and she liked him so much. Wouldn't hear a word against him."

"Well, that ain't the case anymore," said Terrence. "Do you want to crash here, Jonah?"

"Can't." Jonah shook his head. "Have to get back for work. Mr. Steverson's already thrown me so many bones that I don't want to abuse the privilege. But I want updates. As many as possible."

* * *

Four weeks passed. And Jonah called Terrence and Reena every single day. What he hoped to hear was that between Liz, Ben-Israel, Fuller, and Malik, they'd happened across a cure. But there had been no change. Nella still needed the replenishments, which had become a necessity in the extreme due to a brand new fear.

"They're hoping that Nella's strain doesn't develop a resistance to Ben-Israel's replenishment tonic," Terrence told Jonah over the phone. "Because if that happened, they'd have to resort to putting Nella into an ethereally-induced coma. Mr. and Mrs. Manville are vehemently against that; they won't be swayed. They flat-out shot down the notion of their daughter being made comatose."

Jonah was of two minds on the subject. He could never understand Mr. and Mrs. Manville's stance, because he was Nella's friend, not her parent. At the same time, all he wanted was for Nella to remain physically alive. Any way possible. So if it came to an ethereal-induced coma—if and only if it came to it—shouldn't it be considered?

He discussed it with Vera, and she, like him, didn't know what to think on the matter. Because she was best friends with Liz, she'd grown attached to Nella. She acknowledged that she couldn't fully relate, but she wanted her best friend's sister to be okay. Vera had a bone to pick as well.

"It's a good thing I wasn't there with you all," she grumbled during a dinner of Chinese food with Jonah. "I wouldn't have been like Mrs. Decessio and stopped with a sucker-punch. I'd have assaulted that boy to the point that Patience would have had to put me on The Plane with No Name. I would have for Nella's family's sake."

"We were all thinking along those same lines," said Jonah. "But Patience thought that the wisest course of action was for the boy to be brought to justice, sans the tooth that Mrs. D knocked out."

Terrence had also told Jonah that June Mylteer had been to the estate with disturbing news.

"June's sources said that Lockman is trying a different approach," he said. "June couldn't find out what that is exactly, but Lockman is confident that he'll have us all. I don't want the estate to shut down, but it looks like that is the only thing that will get him off of our backs."

Jonah closed his eyes at those words. "Felix said karma would bite Lockman," he revealed.

"Well, karma needs to pick up the pace," replied Terrence. "We're about to close, Daniel wants to assault someone, and Jonathan ain't here to do anything about it. With all that's happening, Lockman is just a roach in the pie right now."

Jonah frowned at the mental picture Terrence created as he hung up the phone. With all that was happening...he still hadn't forgotten those words from Dylan.

Biblically bad.

He tried to compartmentalize that, as well as Nella, on this particular day, which was February the Eleventh. It was time for grocery shopping, and he only did that at Wal-Mart or Aldi. As he volunteered to assist Mr. Steverson with rehabbing books for a time after work, going to Aldi would be cutting it close. So that left Wal-Mart, which required a mentality that couldn't already be stressed before you started.

He found himself doing positive affirmations before walking through the sliding doors nearest to the grocery area.

Jonah stuck to the walls as much as he could, remembering Reena's advice for grocery shopping: *Stick to the walls. Food's healthier. There are two things in the aisles and two things only; bad food and even worse people.*

Jonah did well, though. He only needed to brave two of the aisles; the one with the paper towels and the one that contained Red Baron Pizza, his cheat meal for the evening. Before he knew it, he was ready for checkout. The most accessible checkout line was one with a cashier of about twenty-one, who wore an expression that stated that she clearly didn't want to be there. Her nametag said "*CHLOE.*" Jonah decided to chance it.

Knowing that people responded better if people bothered to learn their names, he said in a kind voice, "Evening, Chloe."

Chloe responded in a bland voice. "Evening, Jonah Rowe."

Jonah frowned. "How did you know my name?"

"You're wearing a name badge, too," said Chloe, who was focused on ringing up Jonah's produce.

Jonah looked down and snorted. Indeed, he hadn't removed his removed his S.T.R name badge. "Man. I am tired."

He removed the badge and pocketed it. Chloe allowed herself a small smile.

"Busy night?" asked Jonah.

Chloe kind of shrugged. "So-so," she murmured. "But you at least bothered to speak to me, and not spend the whole time on your phone. I appreciate that."

"No problem," Jonah replied.

She priced the items, and Jonah handed over his battered debit card. It had seen better times for sure. Chloe swiped several times, but nothing happened. He frowned.

"Don't worry, don't worry," Chloe assured him as she reached behind the register for an empty bag. "This happens a lot."

She wrapped the card in the bag, then swiped it. Finally, it went through.

"There we go," she said with a full smile. "We're good!"

Jonah smiled, took his receipt, and lugged out his purchases. So an enjoyable experience at Wal-Mart was possible.

An uneventful trip later, and Jonah was back in the parking lot of the apartment complex. He had a lot of bags, but they were manageable. He had to put one or two on the ground so as to arrange the other ones in his hand. If ever there came a time to praise the inventor of elevators, it was now.

He gratefully plopped everything on the counter in his apartment, and snickered slightly when he found a small twig among the bags. It must have caught on one of them when he put the bags on the ground. He shrugged and tossed it in the direction of the trash can.

Jonah was ready to pre-heat the oven. A binge-watch of *Nikita, Arrow,* or *Supernatural* called his name, and he was more than ready for the Red Baron—

Then a faint sound caught his ears. It sounded like static; like the sound the TV made when the rabbit antennae was useless.

But his TV didn't have an antenna.

He followed the noise to the counter. It was the old radio that he'd never returned to Trip that made the sound.

"What the hell?"

Jonah grabbed it and looked at the dial. It had moved of its own accord to 101.3. What did the station indicate? Spiritual activity? Nah, that didn't sound right…

Then a growl froze Jonah in place. It was an unearthly, bone-chilling thing. It was almost as if he was under someone else's control as he turned in the direction of his trash can.

There was a Haunt there.

This one was more in the shape of a wolf than a dog. Its soot-black fur seemed glossy, and the red eyes were alight with murderous intent. It stood at the base of the twig he'd thrown at the trash can, muscles bunched and ready to attack.

For a moment, Jonah gaped. Then his mind unjammed a second before the Haunt leapt.

Jonah grabbed his dish rack from its place next to his sink to function as some sort of intercept. It was a desperate and rather pathetic move, but Jonah made a split-second decision. The Haunt slammed into the dishes. It was disoriented, but Jonah knew that that wouldn't last. Instinctively, he reached for his batons, but they weren't there. They hadn't been there in months.

Jonah couldn't fight.

But he could do a Mind Cage.

Felix said that once it was mastered, it could be done at any time.

He focused all of his energy on it and began to concentrate—wait.

He couldn't do a Mind Cage! His weapon of expression for the Mind Cage was an ethereal cage that sprung up from chthonic locations. If Jonah were outside, maybe it would have worked, but in his apartment, he was liable to gouge a hole in his floor, right into the apartment below. Other tenants couldn't be exposed to a Haunt. It'd be a bloodbath. Jonah had to stop it here.

But how?

The Haunt, who didn't share Jonah's mental qualms, lunged again. It actually collided with Jonah that time, but before it could clamp down on his throat, they toppled over the sofa. Luckily for Jonah, the momentum split them apart. The beast slid into boxes that Jonah had been too lazy to unpack, and he used that time to scramble to his feet and grab his computer chair as a blockade. The hellish dog came at him again, but Jonah batted it away with the chair. When he did so, he noticed that the thing's red eyes glowed, but that particular power was useless at the moment. With no ethereal human or vampire to interface with, the Haunt's Haunting power couldn't work. Jonah didn't have to contend with that.

But it was only a small comfort. A very small comfort, when Jonah remembered those ethereal steel claws and teeth.

How was he supposed to kill this thing? Anger was the tool, because as long as the fear was present, the Haunt was invulnerable. And right now, Jonah was scared as hell. He had no weapons—

Wait. Yes he did!

He chucked the computer chair at the Haunt, heard a distracted grunt, and fled to his bedroom, where he locked the door. It wouldn't hold, but Jonah needed some time to get what he was looking for, and hopefully, time to get mad.

He ran into his closet and upturned boxes and belongings. The inevitable banging at the door alerted him to hurry; it was a fight that the door would lose.

Think angry thoughts! he demanded of himself while he riffled through his possessions. *Think about Lockman! The Curaie! Think of Eden Bristow trying to poison and confuse Vera! Dylan hurting Nella! Damn twig—!*

Jonah's brain went quiet. Completely and totally quiet. It was like every racing thought in his mind desisted, making room for the sudden revelation.

That twig wasn't randomly picked up with the bags in the parking lot.

It was planted there. Surreptitiously placed within his groceries in a bag that came from behind the register, courtesy of the cashier that he'd been kind to.

Chloe. Another suuvus.

Jonah had been tricked. By a frickin' suuvus cashier from Wal-Mart.

That did it. No other thought was necessary. Chloe the suuvus was all the fuel he needed. The fear was gone.

Moreover, he'd found what he was looking for.

It was the ethereal steel-tipped arrow that Daniel gave him last summer, when the Curaie sent him back to the city in the first place.

The Haunt was nearly through the door, but Jonah was ready. He had the arrow in one hand and his old blanket (which he'd cast aside when he replaced it with Mrs. Decessio's new one) in the other. He readied the arrow and waited.

The Haunt finally succeeded, and burst through the door. It zeroed in on Jonah, clearly angry that its quarry had put up such a struggle. Jonah took a deep breath, cracked his neck muscles, and braced himself.

"Come on, bitch," he coaxed. "Hundred ninety-eight pounds of USDA beef right here!"

The Haunt threw an execrating snarl at Jonah. Claws and teeth bared, it charged, much more explosively than any normal animal would have—

—right into Jonah's old blanket, which he flung up at the last second. The Haunt's speed sent it blindly into Jonah's wall headfirst, and it crashed to the ground, hopelessly trapped in a mess of blankets. Jonah pressed his advantage and pounced, stabbing at the frenzied mound with the arrow. He stabbed again and again, allowing his anger to become an endowment in its own right. It was nice to have an object to take his anger out on, anyway, because it had been the one emotion that was prevalent all these months, and it gluttonously consumed the fuel that Jonah provided; Creyton, Deadfallen disciples, the stupid Curaie, what Dylan did to Nella, and now Chloe, Creyton's handpicked cashier from hell—

It took a few moments for Jonah to realize that he was bludgeoning an empty blanket. The Haunt had disintegrated into nothingness. Jonah wasn't sure exactly when that happened, but the thing was long gone.

Very slowly, he collapsed against his futon, momentarily thankful that his new quilt from Mrs. Decessio hadn't been touched. But the gratitude pretty much stopped there.

Someone had tried to kill him. Chloe had to have been working on someone's orders. But that didn't make sense. Creyton was a narcissistic, vain asshole; he'd devoted too much time to destroying Jonah.

As much as he spoke on wiping Jonah from Earthplane, a Haunt in a Wal-Mart bag just didn't seem like his style.

Was it possible that Jonah read Creyton wrong?

Hell, that was *very* possible.

But there was one thing that Jonah knew for certain. He wasn't safe here. And that meant that his neighbors weren't safe, either. And, despite himself, he'd grown comfortable in this forced arrangement. Slowly but surely, that had happened.

But that comfort was now gone. It had disintegrated just like that damn Haunt.

Jonah rose, slid the arrow into his belt, and then left the bedroom for his coat and keys. He was done with this pseudo-Tenth existence. If he was going to find answers, they would be found where he belonged.

He was going home. Come what may and consequences be damned, Jonah was going home.

23

Defenestration

The mass of emotions that Jonah felt began to ebb somewhat, which made for logic and reason. Once those damnable components started firing again, he realized the obvious truth.

He hadn't forgotten about the banishment, but he had forgotten about the Tally.

Dace Cross supervised that barrier at the estate, and it was utterly inaccessible unless the Tally was punched.

Suddenly, his epic return seemed a little misguided. He'd have remembered the Tally if he'd given the situation ten minutes thought.

Then his phone began to ring. He grabbed it without looking at the screen.

"Hello?"

"Jonah?" It was Terrence, which was a relief.

"Hey, man," said Jonah. "You have no idea the night I've had—" Wait. Terrence wasn't a caller; Reena did that. Terrence preferred to text. Why did he call? "What's wrong, man?" he asked bluntly.

"What? Nothing at all!" said Terrence, who actually snorted in disbelief. "I'm just sitting here eating tofu and sprouts for dinner."

Jonah frowned. "Tofu?" he repeated in a slow voice. "Sprouts?"

"Yeah, man!" That jovial note was still in Terrence's voice. "We're all healthy here; can't eat double cheeseburgers, pizza, and steak fries. That shit'll be the death of you!"

Now Jonah was alarmed. "Right," he said. "Where are you, um, eating this healthy stuff?"

"At the Strong Steak House, off Main Street," answered Terrence. "Everybody's trying to be health conscious now, so they have plenty of healthy options. Want to come? Gang's all here."

Now Jonah's eyes narrowed further. "Yeah. Thanks, Terrence. See you in a few."

"Sweet! Later, man!"

Jonah ended the call, and slowly lowered the phone into his cup holder.

Terrence never spoke in code. He always said exactly what was on his mind; it was one of the reasons why he and Reena were always at each other's throats. The tofu and sprouts... Terrence once told Jonah that if he caught him eating those foods, he had his express consent to kick him in the balls. Double cheeseburgers, steak fries, and pizza were all Terrence favorite go-to foods. Despite his ability to cook absolutely anything, he had one of those three things at least once every single week.

But it was when he said , "*That shit'll be the death of you,*" that Jonah actually felt fear. Death wasn't real, and the term was all but considered a swear word at the estate. All the residents had come to hate that word because it was a falsehood, and an insult to everything that life was. And Terrence said it like it was nothing.

And then there was the thing about the Strong Steakhouse. Terrence would never go to that overpriced place; he was just as frugal as Jonah was.

The gang's all here.

Jonah didn't quite get that one. Did it mean that Reena was with him? Or Reena, plus extra people?

But one thing was clear. Terrence was trying to get Jonah to run. And that made another thing clear.

After all this time, his brother didn't know him very well, did he?

Jonah drove on, his mind on his new destination.

Jonah parked a short distance away from the steakhouse. He didn't know what to expect, and wondered whether or not Terrence was trying to stay away as well. Was trouble near the place? Were the Deadfallen disciples out and about? Had Creyton done something himself? There were too many unknowns.

Then there was the question of defending himself. He didn't have his batons, and was leery of going into Spectral Sight due to the declining balance. So he didn't even know if there was a spirit or spiritess around to endow him. He still had the arrow, but goring a Haunt and stabbing a person...he'd just have to cross that bridge when he got to it.

He got out of his car and allowed blood to flow freely through his extremities. It was still winter, after all. Stiff muscles and winter air didn't mix.

The moment he let his guard down, he paid for it.

An arm wrapped around Jonah's neck like a sleeper hold, and the other arm crammed a dampened rag to his face, which smelled both pungent and sweet. Instinctively, Jonah's hands shot up the arm around his neck, but then another pair of hands clutched his hands to prevent his struggles. He couldn't think much as his mind went blank, but on the cusp of his consciousness, he scolded himself for thinking that parking away from the steakhouse had been a good thing, as being in plain sight would have prevented something like this. Seconds later, even that bit of information faded out, along with Jonah himself.

Ice-cold water forcibly brought him back to consciousness. He shook his head to get the water out of his nose, and immediately wished he hadn't. He had what felt like the grandfather of all headaches, and that rigorous activity only served to worsen the pain.

"What the hell?" he sputtered, and a figure above him snorted.

"Told you I did it right," said a voice that Jonah immediately recognized as Wyatt Faulk's.

"Hey, I didn't know," said another man from inches away. "I read that that stuff can induce cardiac arrest."

"Like I'd screw it up?" snapped Faulk. "What use would he be to Lockman if he's dead?"

"Death isn't real," grumbled Jonah.

"So you people keep saying," scoffed Faulk. "Now get up."

Jonah was roughly pulled to his feet, and was guided into what appeared to be the back of some type of office. He tried to get his bearings, but his headache was abominable. It took his entire focus just to walk with his captors.

He was shoved into the third door on the left of a hallway, and the door was slammed behind him. The room already had people in it, and Jonah tried hard to adjust to the light to figure out who they were. The need to do so, however, was nullified when a familiar but anguished voice said, "Aw, damn it, Jonah—you were supposed to run!"

"Terrence?" Jonah still battled his headache and blurred vision.

"Not just him," said Reena, who pulled black and scarlet strands from her face so Jonah could recognize her. "They got the both of us."

Now that Jonah could actually make them out, he stared at them in disbelief. "How did this happen?"

Terrence put two fingers in his mouth, which revealed blood on the tips when he inspected. "It was unprovoked, Jonah," he said in a savage voice. "Lockman and his bum grabbed me from the Chuck Wagon. Punched me in the mouth, and then tied my ass up."

"What the hell for?"

"Hell if I know," responded Terrence.

"Did he use knockout gas on you?" asked Jonah.

"You mean chloroform?" asked Reena. "That's what he did to you? Explains the slight burns on your face. But anyway, no. It was worse. Lockman didn't even attack me, like they did to Terrence. I had to stay late at the office, and Lockman's bastards showed up there. I would've fought, no problem, but they told me that if I lifted a finger, Lockman would make it so that Kendall would not only lose her job at LTSU, but she'd also be blacklisted from the field."

"And they told me, even after ganging up on me, that if I fought back, Lockman would create a 'scandalous link', or something, between Lloyd and me, and that he would also implicate Sterling in his investigation. They also said that if I tried anything, Bobby could forget about a career in football."

Jonah sat, ignoring the pain in his head as much as possible. "You guys got that, and I got the ether," he muttered.

"Chloroform," corrected Reena. "You probably feel hung over. Here—"

She moved next to him, and placed two fingers on the flesh between Jonah's thumb and index finger, and clamped there so tightly that he winced. Strangely though, the majority of the pain in his head faded. By no means was it completely gone, but it had downgraded from splitting agony to a dull nuisance.

"Better?" she asked.

Jonah nodded. Satisfied, Reena continued speaking.

"He didn't really have much to threaten you with, Jonah," she said. "Your attachments are to us, but since he already had us, that didn't mean much. So they just decided to level you. I'm truly certain that was the case."

"Why didn't you stay away?" demanded Terrence. "I know speaking in code ain't really my thing, but I dropped more than enough clues! You didn't pick them up?"

"I did, actually," said Jonah through gritted teeth. "I was quick on the uptake, interestingly enough. But there wasn't any way in hell I was staying away. Especially after the night I've had."

He told them about Chloe, the twig portal, and the wolfish Haunt. Terrence shook his head. Reena took a leveling breath.

"So I hit the road after that," said Jonah. "I spoke to Terrence, and then I got jumped. Is this Lockman's big plan you were telling me about?"

"I'd expect so," said Terrence.

"It couldn't have happened at a worse time," snapped Jonah. "Because I believe that something bad is going to happen tonight. Pardon the vagueness, but after Chloe slipped that twig in my bag, I've suspected something's going down."

"How exactly do you figure that?" asked Terrence.

Jonah rolled his eyes. "Because Creyton has made it clear that he wants to kill me," he answered in impatient tone. "Now he's got Chloe the Wal-Mart Psycho haunting up my groceries. First Jonathan, now this. A plan has to be coming to fruition."

Terrence looked worried, Reena looked doubtful. Jonah glared at her.

"What?"

Jonah, did it ever occur to you that that Chloe girl might have done that on her own?" asked Reena. "Maybe she wanted to speed up the process of becoming a minion by killing Jonah Rowe, the Blue Aura."

"Not buying that," said Jonah flatly. "If Chloe knowingly went over Creyton's head like that, she'd be lucky to *just* get killed. No, it was Creyton. And I bet it's got something to do with what Dylan said."

"What, the whole 'biblically bad' thing?" asked Terrence.

"That's the one," said Jonah. "Now if only—"

"Shut up," whispered Reena, suddenly alert. "They're coming!"

Sure enough, the door burst open, and four people were practically shoved in the room one after the other. Jonah, Terrence, and Reena looked at them in shock. It was Liz, Spader, Douglas, and Vera. Why were they here? All they had done in this Lockman mess was—

"—get quoted in Langford's article." Jonah finished his thought aloud. The information just kind of dropped in his head, and settled there, like an invasive insect. "But wait—where's Trip? He was in the article, too! And why are you here, Vera? You didn't actually get quoted; you weren't even there the day Reynolda came to the estate!"

Before Vera could answer, Lockman stepped in, a triumphant smile on his face.

"Vera wasn't there that day, it's true," he said, "but she was there tonight, when were innocently apprehending Elizabeth here."

"Innocently?" cried Liz, rounding on Lockman. "You grabbed me in the middle of the night!"

"It seemed as though you appeared there rather randomly," said Lockman. "And we weren't even expecting you until later tonight, when your usual schedule puts you at home at about nine p.m. What changed your routine tonight?"

Liz looked shocked. And Jonah knew exactly what she felt. So Lockman had been watching them. The more important question was how long he'd been at it.

"What changed tonight, Elizabeth?" repeated Lockman.

"Don't answer him, Liz," said Jonah sharply. He knew where Liz had been; she'd been with Nella at The Spirits of Vitality and Peace. Lockman couldn't know that. He already knew enough as it was. "We want to know why you have us here."

"Simple citizen's arrest," said Lockman with a chuckle.

Reena's eyes flashed. "You need to familiarize yourself with facts," she snapped. "First of all, not a single one of us have done anything. Second of all, the state of North Carolina has no statute for citizen's arrest!"

Lockman looked at Reena with a quiet rage. "Reena Katoa, Little Miss Legal Counsel, failed artist, and dead-end secretary, I have had it with your constant challenging and countering. So you picked up a book and happened across salient information? Good for you. But unfortunately, none of the beer-bellied farm hands down here would be aware of the lack of statutes, so you can't rely on that. As for not doing anything—" Peculiarly, he turned to Wyatt and the other man, who were still at the door and observed the whole thing like excited children. "Leave now," he told them.

"Sir?" Wyatt looked confused.

"Are you deaf?" snarled Lockman. "I said, GET OUT!"

Some people jumped. Jonah frowned at the man. The one-eighty was rather jarring. And by the looks on their faces, Wyatt and the other guy thought so as well.

"Yes sir," said Wyatt uncertainly, and left. Lockman checked the door, and then returned his gaze to the group.

There had been a transformation in his face. The triumph was replaced by something that was almost primal. It looked beyond anger, beyond even rage.

"As for you not doing anything," he rasped, "you have no idea how accurate that is, Katoa. But that is only half of you people's story. You run around, flouting the moral fabric of good, unsuspecting people. That's no problem. Your pulchritude is on full display when you do it."

Terrence looked at Jonah and mouthed, "*There he goes again with those crazy words!*" The action wasn't missed, and Lockman turned his glare to Terrence.

"Unfamiliar with that word, Aldercy?" he demanded. "Is it too *faincy?*"

He purposely mispronounced the word, once again in that exaggerated, buffoonish drawl. Terrence's face hardened. Lockman turned back to Jonah and Reena.

"You spout that life is forever, or some such nonsense," he continued as if there had been no interlude with Terrence. "That's no problem."

Then he completely ignored everyone except Jonah. That quickly, it became a conversation between just the two of them. His face changed again. It was now a rictus of rage, and something like...pain?

"But when an innocent eighteen year-old girl is killed by a Deadfallen disciple, you did nothing."

Liz gasped. Reena was utterly speechless. Vera actually sat back, looking at Lockman in disbelief. Jonah barely noticed them. He was too busy with being thunderstruck Lockman's words.

Lockman saw the effect that his words had caused, and straightened to his full height. "Yes, that's correct," he whispered. "I know all about Eleventh Percenters. Ethereal humans—whatever you choose to call yourself."

"How—?" Liz sounded desperate, breathless. "How can this be?"

Lockman checked the door once more. Satisfied, he turned back to them. Jonah couldn't understand how this man was so confident in the face of seven enemies. But then he realized that Lockman had the upper hand. His advantage was political and psychological. The threats against their families were an example of the former, while the revelation about his knowledge of the Eleventh Percent was merely the latest.

"How can it be, little girl?" he asked. "Because of the true master of that ostentatious dwelling place of yours. Jonathan."

"Jonathan?" said Jonah, puzzled. "What, did he appear to you or something?"

"Yes, he did," snarled Lockman. "That bastard spirit appeared to me and told me that I needed to pay more attention to my daughter, because she was on a bad path. Her boyfriend, Davis Powell, was a disciple of Creyton, and called himself a Deadfallen disciple. Then the next thing I know, she is dead. That son of a bitch slaughtered my baby girl. And then he conveniently disappeared and his home was burned to the ground. So very sloppy."

"Lockman, you're making a mistake," said Reena, wide-eyed. "It was made to look sloppy. Creyton sent another Deadfallen disciple to burn down that house. Powell was killed by Creyton himself—"

"Jonathan should have killed him!" snarled Lockman. "He should have wiped him off of the face of the earth, instead of finding me and giving me free advice on how to raise my daughter! He should have killed Powell before he even met my daughter!"

"That's not the way Jonathan does things, man!" said Jonah. "We aren't killers!"

"Then explain Davis Powell!" fired Lockman. "He must have missed that!"

"Davis Powell was a Deadfallen disciple!" protested Douglas. "We're nothing like—"

"Stop talking, you bitch idiot," snapped Lockman over him. "Jonathan did nothing. You sit there, peaceful and serene, while Creyton and his disciples do whatever they want. Know what that means? You're just as bad as the rest of them. So I swore—took a blood oath—to send all of you down in flames. All scum who corrupt and poison minds. All those who take innocent people and use and twist them to the point that they can't even think straight. My daughter is dead because of you people. My wife is, too. Died right after Samantha, from fever and grief."

Lockman's voice actually caught after those words. They all stared at him, horrified. When he turned his gaze to Jonah, his usual disposition was back.

"So when you people say life is everlasting... that death isn't real... it only makes me hate you more. When I think of Samantha, of Lucille, your whole ideology just enrages me. They were taken from me, and you people are to blame. All of you bastards."

Liz had become slightly teary-eyed after hearing about Lockman's family, and now sought to reason with him. "This isn't right," she pleaded. "There are people out there who actually twist people's minds. There are actually cults out there. But we are not a cult. We never have been! And the fact that you knew that all along could hurt you, too!"

"That's where you're wrong, stupid girl," said Lockman, who glared at Liz. "Who do you think these stupid people in this stupid town will believe? Balthazar Lockman, the morally upright patriotic crusader who persevered through loss and strife, or you people."

Jonah frowned as Lockman took them all in with a scathing glance.

"A woman who acts as though she is a man," Reena's nostrils flared, "an idiot who apparently doesn't know any words containing over two syllables," Terrence looked as though he swallowed a brick, "a delinquent bum who already has one foot in the penitentiary," Spader bristled, "a waif who couldn't solve her way out of a paper bag," Liz's eyes widened in shock and anger, "and Chandler—Jesus boy, you don't matter at all."

Douglas tightened his eyes and his fists. Lockman passed over Vera and looked at Jonah.

"And Jonah Rowe, the piece of trash whose parents didn't even want him."

Jonah was on his feet. The thing about it was the fact that he didn't actually register rising. His breathing was a bit labored, and he couldn't seem to center his mind. "Take that back, Lockman," he said in a very quiet voice.

Lockman contemplated Jonah scornfully, not the least bit afraid. "You can't touch me, boy," he said in all confidence.

Jonah barely heard him. "You don't know shit about me or my family," he whispered. "Take it back. I won't warn you again."

Lockman actually closed the gap between them. Jonah heard Vera take a sharp intake of breath, but he ignored it.

"You don't matter, boy," said Lockman. "Your every action stinks of failure. You fell off of the stupid tree and hit every branch on the way down. And since she didn't have any better since than to take you in, the same can be said for your grandmo—"

Jonah threw the single, most vicious punch he ever had into Lockman's nose. Blood sprayed from the point of impact, and it lifted Lockman off his feet. He landed rather awkwardly on one leg and crumpled near Vera's spot. Terrence punched the air, teeth bared.

"Yeah!" he exclaimed. "Old fuck had it coming."

"Hell yes, he did," grumbled Reena, who stared at the unconscious man with vitriol.

Jonah didn't regret what he had just done in the slightest, and his gaze on Lockman was so hard that eyes almost hurt.

"Jonah—" said Vera uncertainly, but Jonah raised a hand.

"I'm good," he said. "He just shouldn't have said anything against Nana. Fuckin' asshole."

Spader spat at Lockman's head, which made Liz cringe, despite everything. "I've got your delinquent, bitch," he snapped. "It's a shame you did that before I could, Jonah. I'd have liked that."

The door flew open; Faulk must have come to investigate the noise. He was overtaken by shock when he saw his boss in a heap on the floor. Jonah and everyone else froze right along with him. No one knew what to do.

All except Spader.

He bulleted past Jonah, and drove an elbow into Faulk's mouth. The force of it propelled Faulk out of the door against the hallway wall, where he slid down, out like a light. There were instant loud screams, and Spader ran into the thick of things, ready to fight Lockman's staff.

Terrence and Reena followed him without hesitation, but Jonah stayed back, looking at Vera, Liz, and Douglas.

"Vera—" he began, but Vera's eyes flashed.

"NO!" she shouted. "Doug will look after Liz!"

She pushed past Jonah, and ran out of the room. Jonah shrugged and followed her without another word.

The office space was a madhouse with fighting. Terrence struck some guy in the groin with his knee, and simply shoved him down to the ground, where he writhed in agony. Reena applied a sleeper hold to some woman who tried to hit her with a taser. She clawed at Reena's arms, but each attempt got feebler and feebler as her consciousness faded. Spader shoved a man over a desk, while Vera yanked a guy's shirt over his head and proceeded to punch any portion of his body she could reach. There didn't even look to be anything for Jonah to do himself until he heard a noise behind him and whirled around.

Lockman, who'd regained consciousness, stared at him with the utmost loathing. Due to his badly broken nose and blackened eyes, the expression was rather gruesome.

"Bastard..." he spat, "kill you..."

An object struck Lockman in the back of his head, and he immediately clutched it with a howl. Jonah moved to attack him, but Terrence beat him to it. He grabbed Lockman by the collar and launched him through the window of his office, where he landed in a heap on the front lawn.

"I do know them *faincy* words," snapped Terrence in a perfect impersonation of Lockman's exaggerated mocking drawl. "That one right there was a little something called defenestration!"

He noticed Reena looking him.

"Don't look at me like that," he said with defiance. "I got that word right. I know I did."

"No, it's not that," said Reena. "Did you think...don't you think that was a little overkill?"

"Nah," said Terrence. "I was responding in kind for him kidnapping us." He looked at the person who threw that object at Lockman's head, which turned out to be Douglas. "Doug, what prompted you to do that?"

Douglas looked angry as hell. "He just stood up," he muttered, "looked straight at Liz and me, and simply walked out! He just left, like we were a non-entity, or an afterthought ! That—that stuck in my craw."

"Forget all that!" cried Jonah, and everyone looked at him. "We need to get the hell out of here before they come to! And we all know the *Astralimes* is out of the question!"

"Um, Jonah?" said Vera. "It's seven of us. Getting the hell out of here might be a little difficult to accomplish."

"No, it won't." Spader said those words with a devilish smile. "I see three ways to accomplish it."

"What are you talking about, Spader?" said Liz with impatience.

Spader pointed at the gaping hole that Terrence had just made in Lockman's window. Jonah followed with his eyes, and saw three black vans with *Lockman Association* on the sides of them. He almost smiled himself.

"Haven't driven a van in years," he said to the group at large, "but you never forget how. Let's blaze."

24

Unlocked

Before anyone knew it, the seven of them were on the road in one of Lockman's vans. Everyone was conversing in a rapid fire fashion that was largely counterproductive, because no one could actually hear what the others were saying. It all ceased when Reena, who sat in the passenger seat next to Jonah, shouted, "QUIET!"

She closed her eyes for a moment, drinking in the silence, and then spoke in her normal voice. "We can't go home. Not right now, anyway. We're hot property; too hot. Damn Lockman. He knew that we weren't a cult the entire time!"

"He actually swore a blood oath against all Eleventh Percenters?" said Terrence, incredulous. "The entire ethereal population was to pay because one Deadfallen disciple killed his daughter? The man's a pothead. He's floating out past Saturn; he's freakin' gone!"

"I just wish that he hadn't allowed his anger to ruin him," said Liz, who was still shaken over Lockman's story. "Jonathan wanted to help him, and he misinterpreted that as Jonathan leaving him hanging. And he's let that define his entire life."

"Doesn't matter," snapped Spader. "The man is crazy. His grief is now demonizing innocent people."

"A term that must remain loose in regards to you," murmured Liz.

"Hey! What's your—?"

"Drop it, guys," said Vera. "Not right now. Please. We've got enough on our plate as it is."

"I hate to interrupt all of this," said Douglas, "but where exactly are we going?"

Everyone was silent once more. The dominant feeling a little while ago had been to put as much road between themselves and Lockman as they possibly could. Now that they'd done that, the feeling was rather aimless.

But Jonah had something in his head. An idea had steadily taken hold ever since he'd vanquished the Haunt.

"I think whatever Creyton is up to will happen soon," he announced to the group. "I've told Terrence and Reena already, and now I'll tell the rest of you."

He recounted the story of Chloe and the Haunt to them. Liz let out a small gasp, while Vera reached beyond his seat and clutched his shoulder.

"Well, shit," she said. "I'm glad you thought of that arrow."

"So you're thinking that that was some kind of event to set off some more hell, huh?" said Spader.

"Pretty much," said Jonah.

"Well, like Reena said, we can't go home, and Jonathan's not around," said Liz. "Who else is there to talk to?"

Jonah sighed. Time for his idea.

He told them, and wasn't the slightest bit surprised when his words elicited pure shock. Terrence actually laughed.

"Sorry," he chortled, "but for a minute there I thought you said—"

"He did," said Reena, stunned.

Terrence stopped laughing at once.

"Are you nuts?" he demanded.

"A little bit," admitted Jonah.

"Jonah," said Liz, and he could practically feel her eyes blazing into his back, "I thought that you were trying to avoid The Plane with No Name!"

"That's true, Liz," said Jonah. "That's exactly what I'm doing. Or trying to do, anyway."

"And that is your big plan to do so?" demanded Vera.

Jonah sighed. "I know where I stand there, Vera," he said. "And it's adversary. But I think that's fine, because making peace doesn't occur with your allies. It occurs with your adversaries."

Vera said nothing. Spader scoffed.

"Poetic much?" he muttered.

"I, for one, am game," said Douglas. "But do you know how to get there?"

Jonah's eyes widened. He didn't know where he was headed. The whole plan hinged on knowing the right location.

A location that he now realized that he did not have.

"I—"

Jonah fell silent. He was about to admit that he didn't know, but a mental burst flooded his entire mind. It seemed that having access to more than ten percent of his brain had more benefits than he thought.

"Are you going to say something, Jonah?" asked Reena.

Jonah pressed the gas a little more, keeping an eye out for the nearest exit to I-40 West. "Yeah, I am," he told her. "I know where to go."

"This is the place?" said Spader in total disbelief.

Jonah's internal navigation, or whatever it was, led them to a gorgeous suburban home. It was not ostentatious enough to stick out from its counterparts, yet it still wasn't quaint enough to blend in. Jonah guessed that it might be Carolina blue, but in the moonlight it simply looked white. There was a driveway shaped much like a crescent, but there was no car. Slightly untrimmed hedges framed the place, and at the current time, there was a light on inside.

"How are you going to play this, Jonah?" asked Reena, with true curiosity and not an ounce of sarcasm. "You're the quarterback here."

"Do you want to break into the house?" asked Spader.

"No!" hissed Liz. "Please tell me that's not the plan, Jonah!"

"Absolutely not!" said Jonah. "I want this to be peaceful."

"So what are you going to do?" asked Terrence.

Jonah swallowed. "I'm going to walk up to the front door, alone, and ask to be allowed inside."

"Bad plan," said Spader and Terrence at once.

"Psycho plan," said Vera.

"Definitely risky," said Liz.

"I think you can make it work," said Doug.

"It's going to take some balls for that to happen, though," said Reena.

Jonah hopped out of the van. He'd put nothing above his friends, but the deliberation was liable to drive him insane. With a final deep breath, he walked up to the door and knocked.

The quietness of the night allowed him to hear a stirring inside, followed by hurried steps to the door. Jonah readied himself.

The door opened a crack, still latched. Katarina Ocean looked at her visitor with a mixture of curiosity and welcome. Upon seeing who it was, however, her violet eyes widened in fear, and she made to slam the door.

"No, wait!" said Jonah.

"Get out of here!" cried Katarina. "How do you know where I live?"

"Long story—"

"Wrong answer, Rowe." She made to close the cracked door once more. "Now leave my doorstep, or I'll call Networkers—"

"Katarina, just wait!" said Jonah hastily. It was all he could do to try to ignore how terrible the look she gave him made him feel. "Just hold on. I just want to talk. Please just hear me out. I don't want any trouble. I swear it on my Nana's grave."

Katarina regarded him, and then swallowed. "You've got thirty seconds."

Jonah took another deep breath. "I think Creyton is about to pull the trigger on whatever he's been planning all these months. I was complying with my banishment—" his facial muscles worked double time to prevent the scowl, "—this whole time. Haven't done anything. I went for groceries tonight. The cashier that rang me up turned out to be a suuvus, and she put a twig in my grocery bag. A Haunt materialized in my apartment, and tried to kill me."

Katarina frowned. She seemed to forget the fact that she was timing Jonah. "Are you alright?" she asked with genuine concern.

"Fine, fine," Jonah rushed on. "It's over and done with now. But I think that that action might have been ordered by Creyton. Leads me to believe that it was done for a reason. I wanted to know if you've heard anything at all on your side."

Now, Katarina's eyes narrowed. "What would make you think that I know anything?"

"You're the Gate Linker to the Median for the Phasmastis Curaie," replied Jonah. "You always know more information than you share."

Katarina's eyebrows elevated at Jonah's words. What he said must have thrown her for a loop. He hoped that he hadn't gone too far, and he also hoped that his words weren't presumptuous. She stared at him for several more moments, and then closed the door long enough to unlatch it.

"I'll talk to you," she said after she'd opened the door wide.

Jonah hesitated. "It, um, it isn't just me," he told her. "I've got some friends with me. I thought it would be common courtesy to get your permission to—"

"I assumed that you wouldn't be alone," murmured Katarina. "They are welcome as well."

Jonah waved at the van, hoping that his friends would see him from the tree-lined street. Luckily, they did. He waited for them to join him. Terrence and Reena looked at him in an inquiring sort of fashion. He assured them with a nod.

"Make yourselves comfortable," said Katarina once they were all in her house. "I'll be right back."

She left them in her living room, where they took in all the sights. Katarina's home smelled as though she'd recently lit several scented candles. Jonah noticed that Liz, Vera, Reena, and Spader all had their eyes on what appeared to be interestingly designed wallpaper. Oddly enough, it only covered one portion of Katarina's wall. It consisted of innumerable tree designs, lakeside scenes, and mountain ranges. Those things, at least in Jonah's mind, shouldn't have gone together. But Katarina made them fit with one another seamlessly. It was quite a sight.

"I apologize for leaving you." Katarina had rejoined them. "My television is upstairs. I turned it off to conserve energy."

"Yeah?" said Spader. "What were you watching up there?"

Katarina frowned slightly at the boy's nosiness. "*Downton Abbey,*" she answered. "It's about the only thing worth watching, next to *Rosemary and Thyme.*"

Douglas' head snapped in Katarina's direction. Thankfully, she didn't notice.

"What is this wallpaper, Katarina?" asked Liz.

"It isn't wallpaper." Katarina's voice was soft again. "It's Kirie."

Jonah was clueless, as was Liz, but Reena nodded approvingly.

"Japanese paper-cutting," she clarified for everyone else. "How long have you been doing it?"

"Since my fingers were strong enough," said Katarina. "I also sing; Enya is one of my biggest inspirations. But the Kirie is my heart."

Jonah looked at the artwork again, noticing that there was a homemade label at the bottom of each work: Kirie by the Ocean.

"My God," whispered Douglas. "Skilled and beautiful, too."

Jonah glanced at Terrence, and knew that they were both the same mind. Out of nowhere, he wondered if he'd ever had such foolish thoughts about Vera. But then he remembered the situation, which successfully centered him.

Katarina invited everyone to sit, which they did. Jonah chose not to join them, which made the Purple Aura cast wary eyes on him.

"Why don't you sit down?" she said to him.

"I'd rather stand," said Jonah, "if it's all the same to you."

"Please, Blue Aura." There was a trace of supplication in Katarina's voice. "You standing there like that…it makes me nervous."

Jonah was about to protest, but Liz widened her eyes at him. It was ridiculous, but Jonah remembered that he had to remain calm, lest Katarina turn on the waterworks.

Douglas noticed her anxiety, and gave Jonah a scolding look. "Katarina, thank you for welcoming us like this," he said. "And I also want to say that the Kirie art is amazing."

"Kiss-ass," muttered Spader, which earned him a kick from Liz.

Katarina gave Douglas a small smile. "Thank you. I would like to do more with it, but the job at the Median is very demanding."

Her tone and face were wistful, and everyone caught it. Katarina noticed that fact, and her eyes widened, like she realized a mistake.

"Not that I'm complaining," she said in a hurried sort of way. "The Curaie takes very good care of me. This house is proof of that. But that isn't why you're here. What's going on, Blue Aura?"

She placed her entire focus on Jonah. It was almost like she disregarded everyone else. Her violet-blue eyes weren't intimidating at all, but Jonah still felt the need to be on his P's and Q's.

"My friends and I need to know whether or not you know anything about what Creyton might be doing," he said to her. "Like... like some knowledge that the Curaie has, but doesn't want us to know."

Katarina looked away. There was doubt in her eyes that Jonah didn't understand. "Why should I tell you anything, Blue Aura?" she asked softly. "Why should I trust you with anything?"

Jonah frowned. For one, that designation was tiresome. And second, Jonah had shown her kindness, so why did she feel the need to act like this?

"Katarina–" began Terrence with impatience in his voice, but Jonah saw Reena place a hand on his arm and shake her head.

As much as it frustrated Jonah, he knew what that action signified. He burned the bridge, so he had to mend it. He gritted his teeth.

"I will tell you why, Katarina," he said. "Because Creyton has an advantage at this time, and I'm tired of stabbing in the dark."

"Stabbing in the dark?" Katarina folded her arms. "You are a civilian, Blue Aura. Your rashness has gotten you permanently deferred."

Jonah choked on the response that nearly escaped him. "I'm aware of that, Katarina," he said, "and I was tolerating that as best I could. But then a Haunt tried to tear my throat out! I was complying with the Curaie, but Creyton and his disciples don't care about my being permanently deferred. Did you know that he had Deadfallen disciples perched near the estate, listening in on every word that was said during Jonathan's eval? They were in crow shape. I saw them fly off, no doubt to spill their guts."

The look on Katarina's face told him everything he needed to know.

"Yep, that's what I thought," he said to her. "There has to be a halfway meeting point somewhere, Katarina. My friends and I need your help. It's necessary—"

"Or you'll get angry again?" asked Katarina.

"Yes!" snarled Jonah without thinking, and he instantly regretted it.

His friends looked at him in disappointment; Terrence even sucked his teeth. That was unnecessary, because Jonah already knew that he'd blown it. Now that it was time for damage control, his mind failed him. It left a ringing silence as a result.

"That's precisely the point, Blue Aura," said Katarina, redness in her pale cheeks. "You've been this way since the moment we met. Do you want to know why I told you that I hoped we never saw each other again? Because I am afraid of you, Blue Aura! I have done nothing to incur your rage, yet I've been on the receiving end of it each time we've had an interaction. You've been nothing but a jerk to me since last summer! You don't deserve my help! You don't deserve anything from me!"

Jonah wanted so badly to be affronted. He wanted to be impatient. Furious. But he couldn't do it. Because Katarina had a point. Jonah had been a raw nerve these past several months. And since the people that were responsible hadn't been around him, he's taken out his anger on his friends. More than once. It was maddeningly ironic that the main people who were loyal to him, the main people walking through the fire with him, were the same ones who experienced his frustration. But he'd been especially foul to Katarina Ocean. All she had done was be in the wrong place at the wrong time. When Jonah thought of securing her assistance earlier, he thought she'd be cooperative after she'd heard his piece. Instant amends, like a sitcom where every issue was resolved in thirty minutes or less.

But that wasn't going to happen here. If he wanted Katarina's help, he was going to have to earn it.

"Katarina, you're right."

She looked at him, shocked. "I am?" she breathed. "You're—you're owning up to it?"

Jonah rose, choosing not to look at his friends. He maintained eye contact with Katarina, not wanting to make her nervous. "I am indeed owning up to it," he said. "I'm a better man than this; Nana taught me so much better than this. I shouldn't have treated you that way. You were never the one placing the checks and balances on our lives. You had a job to do, and you were simply doing it. You were absolutely right when you said I don't deserve anything from you, and you are well within your rights to kick us out of your house. But I hope that you can see past my anger and the mistakes I made while experiencing it. Katarina, from the bottom of my heart, I apologize."

He extended his hand. He knew it was cheesy and corny, but he had nothing else.

Katarina stared at his hand for a moment, and then swatted it aside and wrapped him in a hug.

Terrence and Spader stared at the two of them in shock, but their looks paled in comparison to how Jonah felt.

And to his horror, Katarina was in tears again.

"I am still mad at you, that won't just vanish," she murmured as she pulled away from Jonah, "but I forgive you. Taking responsibility for your mistakes like that took strength and class. I respect and appreciate that more than you know."

Not knowing a satisfactory response to that, Jonah merely nodded. Terrence cleared his throat.

"Does this mean that you'll share some info with us?" he asked Katarina.

She wiped her eyes and nodded. "I'll tell you as much as I can. Let me go get cleaned up. We need to go to the Median."

She went upstairs. Jonah looked at Reena, and was surprised to see a small smile on her face.

"You're pleased?" Jonah was instantly suspicious. "I thought you said that Katarina was overly sensitive, and set women back and all that."

"I stand by that," Reena assured him, "but there aren't a lot of men who would do what you just did to earn peace. I have newfound respect for you, Jonah."

"Because he showed kindness?" said Terrence, incredulous. "Reena, given the amount of emotion that you show, or lack thereof, I can't help but find your admiration confusing."

"Told you I was a complicated woman," shrugged Reena.

"My dear Lord," said Liz, who stared at the stairs and shook her head, "you guys tell me that I'm soft-hearted."

"Don't compare yourself to that submissive ass woman," said Vera. "I'm all for burying the hatchet and all that, but does she have to tear up with every emotion?"

"Everybody's different, Vera," said Douglas. "Sweetness doesn't equate weakness."

"Maybe not," said Jonah, 'but damn—what's wrong with you, Spader?"

Spader looked very bothered about something. His unshaven face didn't even look like this when he played poker. But before he could say anything, Katarina was back, dressed in a burgundy button-down and tan slacks.

Jonah frowned at her. She shrugged.

"You never know who will see," she said.

"Katarina, will anyone give a damn about your fashion at this time of night?" asked Jonah.

"There are many on the ethereal side of things who don't live in a nine-to-five world, Jonah," said Katarina. You simply never know—"

"I gotta ask you something, Ocean," interrupted Spader. "Something isn't adding up. You and Jonah here have had your issues, and he got you all scared and ticked off at the same time. I get that just fine. But before the fences were mended, you let us into your house. All of us. After you made it clear that your opinion of us wasn't a savory one."

Jonah's eyes widened. What was this little punk doing? "Just roll with it, Spader–"

"Hell no I won't," said Spader stubbornly. "I want to know. You're prepared to give us some information, despite not knowing what to think about us. It was just too easy. Even after Jonah laid himself bare, your willingness to cooperate was too easy. What's the deal?"

Jonah was ready to punch Spader. Katarina was on board. The hurdle had been crossed! And Spader chose this time to be observant? What if Katarina went back into her sensitive emotional box and threw them out of her house?

But Katarina surprised them by smiling, and nodding. "You're right, Royal," she said, "but it wasn't as easy as you may think. At one time, I didn't know what to think about any of you, and truth be told, I'm still dealing with that. But a friend that I've recently made has been working on me. Letting me know that you guys had hitherto unknown layers."

They all looked at each other, confused.

"Who is this friend?" asked Vera.

"She's waiting for us in the Median," answered Katarina.

She walked to her front door and palmed it. It glowed purple for several seconds, and then returned to its normal state.

"Gate's ready," she told them. "Let's proceed."

They followed her through the door, and walked into the Median. As Jonah had used the *Astralimes* with Jonathan to get there the last time, so simply walking through Katarina's gate was pretty cool.

He took a few moments to re-familiarize himself with the points of interest there, which included the lights that functioned with no power source, the furniture that accommodated any body type, and the mahogany doors that didn't actually have rooms behind them. Vera, Liz,

Douglas, and Spader looked around in wonder. Terrence sampled one of the couches, while Reena focused her attention on Katarina, who was on her way to her desk.

"Where is this friend who has been waiting on us?" she asked.

"Go into Spectral Sight," instructed Katarina.

Jonah was iffy about ethereality for obvious reasons, but his curiosity won this round. He closed his eyes, took a deep breath, and willed the curtain to rise, and the stage actors to perform. When he opened his eyes again, there was one addition among them.

The spiritess was a few inches taller than Liz, with straight auburn hair that fell to her shoulders. There was a peppering of freckles on her face, and her expression was one of warmth and welcome. Jonah looked her over with interest.

"Jonah Rowe," she said kindly. "It's a pleasure."

Jonah glanced at Katarina, and then back at the spiritess. To refer to him as alarmed just didn't cut it. "I'm sorry, spiritess," he said, "but you have me at a disadvantage. I don't know who you are."

"You wouldn't," said the spiritess. "This is our first time meeting. My name is Samantha."

Jonah gaped at her. He had, after all, heard that name mere hours ago.

"Samantha?" he repeated. "As in—?"

"Samantha Lockman?" she finished for him. "The very same, Jonah. I am the daughter of Balthazar Lockman."

Everyone looked at the spiritess, thunderstruck. Funnily enough, now that Samantha had identified herself, Jonah could see the family lineage. She had her father's look of determination in her eye, as well as the look and air of leadership. But where Lockman's features were hardwired for only the most contemptuous of glares, Samantha showed warmth and friendliness. It made Jonah wonder how she might have turned out if she were still physically alive.

"Why exactly are you here, Samantha?" asked Reena. "One would think you'd be near your father, attempting to assist him with recovering from your passing into Spirit."

"Well, I'm not," said Samantha simply. "I'm here with all of you."

"Samantha approached me right after Jonathan's evaluation, when I was dissolving the Gates between the estate and the Median," Katarina explained. "She said that we needed to talk."

"About what?" asked Jonah.

"Everything," said Samantha. "But the things that are relevant to you guys are all that matter right at this time."

Jonah glanced at Terrence. "She's really mysterious," he commented.

"Most spirits are," shrugged Terrence. "But I already like her more than her damn father."

"I don't mean no harm by saying this," said Spader, "but how do we know we can trust you, Samantha?"

"Easy," said Samantha. "I've helped you already."

"You have?" asked Liz. "How?"

Samantha turned her attention to Liz. "I'm the reason Jonah had the inclination to drive down Hodges Road to find your sister," she revealed to her. "I'm also the one who tipped the law about Nella's stolen car when Patience came digging. Then she turned her eyes to Jonah. "I am also the reason why you suddenly knew how to reach Katarina's house when you decided that you wanted her help. I'd like to think that I've done far more for you than my father has."

"So that's how you found out where I lived," said Katarina. "That was a major creepy factor for a minute or two. Now, I'm fine with it."

It took a minute or two for them to digest that information, but Liz came closer to Samantha and hugged her.

"Thank you," was all she said.

"You're more than welcome," said the spiritess. "Don't even mention it."

Jonah glanced at Terrence. "She's very mysterious."

"Most spirits are," shrugged Terrence. "But I already like her ten times more than her damn father."

Jonah agreed, but didn't voice it. "Okay, Katarina, Samantha," he said. "What have you got for us?"

Katarina moved to a file cabinet and clutched the handle of the top one. It gleamed purple, and then she pulled it open.

"You had to link up a Gate for files?" asked Douglas.

"Of course," said Katarina. "Do you think Curaie files would be stored in simple file cabinets? No. They are…elsewhere. That's all you get from me."

She brought out some files that were baby blue in color, and spread them across her desk. Jonah and the others crowded around to take a look.

"What are these exactly?" asked Vera. "Are these files from the Curaie's chambers?"

"You wish you were so lucky," murmured Katarina. "These are reports from the Very Elect Spirits, who get their information from the Elect Spirits. This is the material on which their messages are recorded; simple paper from wood is useless on the Astral Plane."

"Useless," said Spader, pensive. "One could say the same thing about third party information."

"True," said Katarina, "but Samantha said that there was something interesting here concerning the Mindscope Illness."

That caught Liz's attention. "Let me see."

She grabbed a certain group of files, but Katarina put her hands on them with a frown.

"No one could make heads or tails of those particular ones," she said. "They're medical related. You'd need a Green Aura for those."

"Guilty," said Liz with sarcasm.

She sat down next to Katarina and began to thumb through pages with her. Jonah figured that they'd need privacy, so he grabbed some other files and took them to his other friends. They left Liz, Katarina, and Samantha at the desk while they took over some of the sofas. Jonah looked at Reena.

"I've got to ask you two," he said. "One of you is an essence reader, and the other is a poker player, and therefore a great reader of people. Do you trust this? Katarina's help?"

"She is sincere." Reena's response was instant. "There isn't a trace of duplicity in her essence. Katarina's actions are not sudden at all; that would have been suspicious. But she is frightened out of her mind, and that's after conversations with Samantha Lockman."

"Reena's right," said Spader, the poker player and astute reader of people. "It took her growing a massive set just to get this far. I was iffy at first, but now I'm on board. She's one hundred percent-real."

"I had no doubts of that," said Douglas.

No one responded to him.

"Look at this." Jonah held out a page for everyone to see. "They've been following odd activities since the activation of the Inimicus card. Just how much have they been hiding from us on account of our being civilian Elevenths?"

"There is something here about disappearances over the past few months," said Vera with a frown. "A few Tenths, but mostly Elevenths. It says here that the Curaie instructed Spectral Law practitioners to tell the families that they were making hopeful strides."

"Would have been wonderful if it weren't a damn lie," said Jonah, who pushed his reading glasses further up his nose. "A recurring theme in their bullshit is that the so- called qualified Elevenths were taking care of the Eighth Chapter crimes. But apparently, Matt Harrill is the only Deadfallen disciple they've caught during this mess, and who was responsible for that, I wonder?"

"Good point," said Douglas, clearly anxious to contribute something other than his infatuation with Katarina. "They must be proud of the Deadfallen disciples they've already caught. Pity that those ones were on The Plane with No Name before Creyton achieved Praeterletum. Makes them kind of beside the point, no?"

"It says here that Patience got written up a couple times," said Jonah, irritated. "They were recommended by Dace Cross. Little bitch."

"Saw that coming," said Reena. "He was too helpful to us and Jonathan. I'm surprised they haven't tried anything with June Myl-teer or Mr. Decessio."

"Oh, they're simply civilian Elevenths, too," muttered Terrence. "They probably view them as not worth—"

A loud, unnerving gasp tore Jonah and his friends from their thoughts. They turned to Katarina's desk, where the Gate Linker looked at Liz's snow-white face in total confusion. Samantha stood nearby, looking as though they'd found what she desired them to.

"Liz?" said Jonah, who went to her side. "What's up? What have you found?"

Liz said nothing. Her gaze was transfixed on the page in her hands. Katarina gently took it from her, and frowned at it.

"I don't see anything of note," she said slowly. "I've been over this page a million times my own self, and I don't understand what's entailed here."

Jonah didn't need to be persistent, but Liz looked paralyzed. He rounded the table, turned her chair in his direction, and grabbed her shoulders. "What is wrong, Liz?" he asked again.

Liz met his eyes. There was terror there that Jonah hadn't ever seen. "Jonah..." her voice matched her expression, "Nella...my God...it's worse than we thought..."

"What is?"

"It's a plague, Jonah," whispered Liz. "The Mindscope Illness...it's a plague."

"What!" cried Katarina, who looked at the paper again. "How did you make that out? I told you that I read and re-read this page—"

"You also said that only a Green Aura could make the connections," said Liz, whose eyes remained wide. She'd even broken into a light sweat. "Creyton is planning for all the infected people to pass into Spirit at once. They are a beacon...some sick sort of beacon. That ethereal illness will leave their bodies as soon as they pass into Spirit, and spread."

Everyone looked around at each other. Even Spader had no comeback.

"Is that why those spirits and spiritesses looked so weak?" demanded Jonah. "On the desert of the Ethereal?"

Liz nodded. "I think so. I also think that that's where Creyton created the illness. I can't even begin to imagine everything that's in it, but I bet that at least two of the ingredients are spiritual essences that he's usurped, and toxic feedback that's spawned when essence is not allowed to naturally progress. I wouldn't be surprised if there is some sort of diseased lifeblood involved, too."

Reena clamped the desk tightly. "When the—when the illness is released, what will be its range?"

Jonah knew that Reena didn't want to say, "When the infected people pass into Spirit," because that number included Nella.

Liz looked at Reena. It was obvious that sweat wasn't the only moisture on her face when she did so. "Every Eleventh Percenter who had those blanket Mindscope dreams," she whispered.

Spader looked at Liz like she'd spoken in a different language. Terrence made a choking sound, Reena closed her eyes, and Vera look deflated. Jonah couldn't feel the bottom part of his face.

"All of those Elevenths," he croaked. "Us..."

He rounded on Samantha. "There's got to be something. Every known Eleventh Percenter had those dreams, which had to have also included the Deadfallen disciples. Creyton would have inoculated them. He would have them immune, if no one else."

"My thoughts exactly," said the spiritess. "But I have no information on that. No spirit or spiritess would get close enough to Creyton to learn his plans, because the threat that they will be usurped is too strong."

Jonah turned to Katarina, who hadn't recovered from her own shock. "Katarina, please," he said with desperation, "do you know anything at all about this? Have the Curaie mentioned anything about where a cure might be? Have they let anything slip at all?"

Katarina looked so afraid. She'd already compromised many of her beliefs by helping them as much she had up to now. But to divulge information that she ought not to know...she probably felt like was a step too far. "Blue Aura, I—I can't," she said. "If Engagah found out—"

"Katarina," said Samantha, "you are still a physical being, so I understand your fear, and desire for self-preservation. But if what Elizabeth said is true, then there is much more at risk than your little job. Take it from a spiritess, no job is worth your physical life."

Katarina stared at Samantha. Jonah had no idea what was on her mind at that time, but he knew that her fear was clouding her judgment. If only he had a spiritual endowment so that he could help to balance her!

Then again, he had no right to impose. He already felt like a bully around her anyway, so there was no need to reiterate that with ethereality.

It would have to come from her.

So he waited.

"All I can tell you," she whispered at last, "is that all the infected had one thing in common."

"We already know that," said Liz. "They were all rebellious."

"No," said Katarina. "Not that. They all had body art. Tattoos."

A current of horror coursed through Jonah. There was no way in hell. "Son of a bitch," he breathed. "That was the link. That was the reason they were considered rebellious. The tattoos."

Everyone looked Jonah's way.

"What are you saying, Jonah?" asked Reena.

But Jonah ignored her and turned to Liz. "Liz, I'm sorry," he said, "but there is something that you never knew. Nella got a tattoo, at Dylan's request."

"She did what?" Liz's eyes flashed. "Jonah, why didn't you tell me?"

"I wanted her to do it," said Jonah defensively. "But she got sick before she could. She got sick from that damn tattoo. And I know where she got it."

"You do?" asked Reena.

"I do," said Jonah. "Blood Oaths Tattoos by Bryce Tysinger. It's the tattoo place near S.T.R."

"I'll be damned," said Terrence. "That's probably why the guy always looked scared when he saw you. He thought you'd figure out that he worked for Creyton."

"And he always gives his keys to Mr. Steverson for safekeeping," said Jonah. "He was afraid of getting mugged, so he said. But Mr. Steverson was under the impression that he was hiding something. Now, I know what the deal is. He would be punished if someone broke in and accidentally tampered with Creyton's work, or something. He knew that Mr. Steverson could be trusted, so he gave him the keys every night."

"Dear God," said Liz. "The man probably put the illness strain in the tattoo ink!"

"I bet you that little shit Dylan was supposed to check in by now," said Vera. "He was probably supposed to charm or persuade more people to go there!"

"And I'll bet anything I've got that if the Mindscope Illness started there, then the means to end it are there as well," said Jonah. He looked at Terrence and Reena. "We've got to do this ourselves," he told them. "All for one and one for all—"

"Say what?" said Spader, eyebrows raised. "I'm aboard this train, too!"

Jonah regarded the kid with unmasked scorn. "Spader, if you think for one second I'm trusting you—"

"Look." Sincerity crept into Spader's features again. "I've messed up sometimes, okay? I never forgot about the fuckup with Sanctum; I don't need to be reminded of it. Let me fix that. Let me come along."

Jonah didn't like it. At all. Reena was of the same mind, and Terrence looked stone-faced.

"What if you come across locks?" persisted Spader.

"I can pick a damn lock," dismissed Jonah.

"What if you come across one that a cute little hairpin won't budge, huh?" said Spader. "What then? You need me. Deal with it."

Jonah had nothing. Spader, whatever his faults, was far from useless. With a resigned sigh, he nodded once. Unfortunately, that nod prodded Vera to speak.

"If you're taking Rat Boy, you're taking me," she said.

"Rat Boy—!" began Spader, but Jonah interrupted him.

"Vera—"

"I told you a long time ago that you don't tell me what to do, Jonah," she told him. "I'm a part of this, whether you like it or not."

"Me too," said Douglas.

Those two words turned every head in the room.

"No," said Jonah.

"Yes," said Douglas right back.

"Go back home, Doug," said Terrence. "Go watch that Downtown thing or whatever it is—"

"It's Downton, and I'm not going home," said Douglas. "You're my friends, and I want to contribute an extra set of hands."

Reena approached the man with a serious look in her eye. "This could be really serious trouble, Doug," she said.

"Yeah," said Spader. "You might get blood on your chinos. Or that merino wool sweater."

Douglas scowled at Spader. "To hell with my clothing. I really do not care."

Jonah ran a hand across his face with impatience. "Whatever! Now—"

"You've forgotten about me," said Liz.

Jonah raised his hands in frustration, but Liz fixed a cold, determined look on him before he uttered a single word.

"Save your anger, Jonah," she murmured. "It means nothing to me. In case you've forgotten, my baby sister is bedbound in a healing haven, getting a tonic shot into her blood every few hours. She will not pass into Spirit, nor will she be a catalyst to infect God knows how many more Elevenths. The other tattooed people won't be, either. And on top of that, why exactly would you go into a situation that is largely medical in nature, and leave behind the Green Aura?"

Jonah's frustration melted. Truly, it faded away. Lizzie had a point, after all.

Spader began to laugh, out of the blue. Liz gave him a salty look.

"What's so funny?" she demanded.

"You can't come," he giggled. "You don't have Bobby's permission. He has to green-light your every move, doesn't he?"

In the blink of an eye, Liz rounded the table and poked Spader's neck. Spader was about to laugh at the action, but then his eyes widened, his body did a sort of twitch, and he fell to the ground in discomfort and pain.

Jonah looked at her, stunned. "What did you do?"

"Not important," spat Liz, who had scornful eyes on Spader's quivering form. "But Spader's gonna feel like his body has one big Charley Horse until he apologizes for what he said."

Spader was in pain. It was evident in his face and movements. It would have been laughable, but precious time was wasting.

"Liz," Jonah tried not to sound impatient, "we have to go."

But Liz stepped back, and folded her arms. "The little creep is going to apologize."

"Will you apologize to her, please?" Douglas demanded.

Spader tried unsuccessfully to look defiant. But what Liz had done must have been brutal.

"Fine," he gasped. "Fine."

Liz was unimpressed. "You heard what I said."

"I...I'm sorry, damn it," croaked Spader.

Still scowling, Liz knelt and pressed the same spot she tapped in the first place. Spader sighed in relief.

"We might need to defend ourselves," said Reena. "But I don't—"

"You have been endowed," said Samantha. "All of you."

Jonah felt the invigorating surge throughout his body that he thought would never happen again. It was almost righteous.

"Katarina, please link up a Gate to their armory," requested Samantha. "As well as the infirmary. Elizabeth may need her healing satchel."

After a timid swallow, Katarina did as she was asked. Thankfully, Jonah's friends didn't waste time marveling at the admittedly cool ethereality, and they hurried into the armory. Liz hopped into her room to grab her satchel.

"I have to go," said Samantha. "I'll muddy the waters for Dad, because he'll want your head now. Maybe literally."

"Wait," said Jonah, really curious of the spiritess. "Why are you going against your dad like this?"

Samantha sighed. "Dad has to be stopped. The father that I knew, loved, and cherished came into Spirit with me and my mother. Don't think that I don't still love my father, because I do, eternally. But I could no longer stand by and watch these vengeance-filled witch hunts continue. Peace and blessings, Jonah."

She vanished, leaving Jonah still a bit confused. He heard his friends moving carefully around their respective areas so as not to rouse anyone or alert the S.P.G. watchers that were outside the estate. A sniff caught his attention, and he turned to see that Katarina had tears in her eyes once again.

"What's the matter?" he asked, alarmed. "I didn't hurt your feelings again, did I?"

Katarina ignored the question and focused on Jonah. "Are you really who you say you are?" she asked him. "Are you really a good person?"

Jonah was caught off-guard by the question. Where had that come from? "I would like to say that I am," he said. "I hate when bad things happen to good people, like right now. I'm nowhere near perfect, and accept that fact, but...but I would like to say that yeah, I'm an alright guy."

Katarina looked at the two Gates still in use, and seemed to struggle with herself over something. Finally, she closed her eyes and whispered, "Damn it."

She took Jonah by the hand and pulled him to an undesignated door. With her free hand, she touched the doorknob, waited for it to gleam purple, and then opened it.

What Jonah saw defied space. It was a vast...vault. That was the best description of it. There were safe deposit boxes as far as the eye could see. There was no way that a place like this could fit in this room. Then again, the room wasn't even there five seconds ago.

Katarina pulled him along a row all this time, and stopped at a safe deposit box numbered 92708. Steeling herself once more, she placed two fingers on it, and it swung open. She pulled out a box, removed its contents from within, and held them up in Jonah's face.

They were his batons.

"Take them," she said.

Jonah was stunned. He slowly pulled them from Katarina's grasp, and felt a pleasant sense of security and comfort when the batons touched his skin and gleamed blue once again. He'd missed them so much, but he regarded Katarina.

"Why are you defying the Curaie like this?" he asked. "I'm grateful and all, but why are you doing it?"

Katarina closed the deposit box. "You were wrong about me," she said. "I *do* feel. You're not some sadistic bully; I see that now. You're a good man. Good luck…Jonah."

25

Sins of the Son

Katarina had one final gift to give. Since the Astralimes remained out of the question, she deactivated the three gates she'd made, and created a new one that linked them the business complex where S.T.R and Blood Oaths Tattoos were located. Jonah was last in line out of the door, and he paused for a few seconds, looking at Katarina.

"Thank you," he told the Gate Linker. "I'm glad that we were able to begin again."

"You're welcome," said Katarina. "And I'm glad we were, as well."

She closed the door, and Jonah and his friends were in an alley. Liz looked slightly confused.

"Where exactly are we?" she asked.

"Katarina did us a favor," Jonah explained. "She didn't put the gate in front of either store; we'd probably have scared the hell out of some people. She put it here, between the thrift store and the taxidermy. We're directly across the street from where we're going. Look."

He pointed. Both S.T.R. and Blood Oaths Tattoos were in plain sight from their vantage. Douglas shook his head.

"Katarina is an extraordinary woman," he said fondly.

"Task at hand, Dougie," said Terrence. "So what are we doing, Jonah?"

"You are going to wait for me for a few minutes," said Jonah. "Just long enough for me to go into S.T.R. and back. I called Mr. Steverson while you guys were getting weapons and everything."

"You did?" said Reena, surprised. "Did you convince him to give you the keys to the tattoo parlor?"

"Nope," said Jonah with gratefulness in his voice. "Turns out that Mr. Steverson was worried about that guy. When I told him that we might be able to help him, he was all for it. No convincing necessary."

"You told Mr. Steverson that we were helping a suuvus?" said Vera.

"All I had to tell him was that it dealt with the spirits thing," Jonah clarified. "It was all he needed to hear. Now you guys watch the tattoo place. I'll be right back."

Jonah hurried across the street, and used his key to unlock S.T.R.'s door. It was late, so Jonah knew that Mr. Steverson was at home. He hated having to call so late, but Mr. Steverson got out of bed and left the keys in a visible spot. Jonah grabbed them so fast that he barely noticed the note next to them. He was ready to get back to his friends, but something—either instinct or conscience— prompted him to read the note. He put his reading glasses on, brought out a baton, and let the blue gleaming object illuminate the paper:

Jonah,

Whatever it is that you're doing,

please be safe. I hope that you succeed in helping that man. I also hope that the spirits that you have contact with prove to be a blessing. But you're a great young man, so I have faith that you'll get things done. Like I said, be safe, and remember that you are not alone. Not now, not ever.

Mr. S

Jonah closed his eyes, and snorted to himself. Mr. Steverson was the best. No nosing around, and no scorn. Just a desire for Jonah to stay safe. He made an instant decision right then and there; when this was all over, he was going to surprise Mr. Steverson and his family with dinner, or something like that. Just a gesture to be nice and respectful. Maybe he could get Harland and Amanda to come, too.

He pocketed the note and the baton, left S.T.R. and locked it back, and then rejoined his friends.

"Got the keys," he announced. "Have you guys seen anything?"

"Jonah," said Reena, who looked puzzled, "Bryce is in there."

Jonah frowned. "He's in the store right now? He's locked inside?"

"No clue," said Reena, "but there is definitely someone in the place. We just saw a man look out of the window and then retreat somewhere within."

"He must be out of his mind now that it's been almost a month since Dylan brought in anyone new," said Liz with venom. "Let's get in there and deal with him. See if he has an answer."

As a tight collective, they crossed the street to the tattoo parlor, where Jonah wasted no time unlocking the door. After walking past the place so many times, it was a rather surreal experience for him to actually walk inside. He didn't know what to expect.

The first thing to notice was the walls, which were completely covered in artistic capabilities, or simply put, graffiti. Jonah didn't know what he should see in the establishment, so the mats, vinyl, boxes of latex gloves, body art supplies, bottles of antiseptic, and lubricants may very well have been the norm. Despite that, he was not comforted by the look of normalcy at all. There seemed to be an undercurrent of tension and fear, or maybe even some dark anticipation. It made a chill run down his spine.

"I used to want a tattoo," murmured Spader, "but that desire is fading more and more with each passing second."

"Good to hear, Royal," said Liz, who, too, took in their location. "You're skanky enough as it is."

Spader opened his mouth angrily, but then decided to remain silent. Jonah assumed that the boy must have recalled Liz's nerve tweak and had no desire to experience it again. Smart boy.

Once they reached the small compartments which were meant to shield patrons from view, Reena raised a hand.

"Time to be more careful," she whispered. "Just in case anyone is hiding back there."

"Listen!" Vera's hiss was sudden. "What is that?"

Jonah listened, and clearly heard someone—

"Choking?" he said aloud.

Reena stiffened, wide-eyed, and raced for the bathroom. Jonah and the others followed suit.

Reena nearly bashed the door in. A man with an expression so cold that would have made Trip cringe looked up in surprise. They'd interrupted what was clearly meant to be a murder; the guy was strangling Bryce with long, determined fingers. Upon seeing that his grisly deed now had an audience, he abandoned Bryce and attempted to climb through the bathroom window.

"No!" shouted Reena, who hurried forward and grabbed a leg. Jonah was right behind her as he grabbed the other leg so Reena wouldn't get kicked. Together they yanked him back. Neither of them was concerned with the rather rough way he hit the ground.

The man must have made himself oblivious to the pain he felt when he hit the ground, because he whipped around fast, and Jonah swung a baton at him. He ducked with an almost dancer's grace and produced a weapon of his own, which gleamed black when he held it aloft.

"Deadfallen!" shouted Terrence.

He attempted to help, but the restroom couldn't accommodate anyone else. Reena caught the hand that wielded the weapon before the Deadfallen disciple could do any damage with it, and Jonah, willing the air around them to bend to his will, dropped his baton and flexed his fingers.

"Let him go, Reena!" he cried.

Reena released him, and Jonah allowed his wind ethereality to take over, and aimed a specific amount at the attacker. The force of the air threw the man so high upwards that he slammed into the ceiling and cracked it before he slammed face down on the floor. He didn't pop up that time.

"Any lingering doubts that we're in the wrong place?" he asked Reena with a rather dry humor.

Reena didn't laugh. "We need to restrain him. But it's not like we have any rope, and the process of conjuring ethereal fetters takes a minute or two—"

"Here." Liz handed over thin but very strong rope from her healing satchel.

"Um," Spader looked at her with elevated eyebrows, "why exactly do you have rope in that bag of yours?"

"Most Green Auras have rope," Liz explained. "There are occasions where patients need to be restrained to prevent thrashing during healing procedures."

Reena tightly bound the Deadfallen disciple from his upper arms to his ankles, then set him up in the one remaining stall that hadn't been smashed. Jonah grabbed Bryce and brought him to standing while he took loud gasps of air.

"We're going to have a little chit-chat," he told him. "And if you plan on lying to us about anything, don't. Just…don't."

He forced the tattoo artist down in a chair that Douglas pulled from the door. Jonah noticed that Liz's green eyes looked ferocious; her mind was clearly with Nella. Even though Jonah wanted some answers, a small part of him wished that Bryce would lie once. Or twice.

But then, the man threw them completely for a loop.

"Are you Elevenths my masters now?" he asked.

Terrence's brow creased. "Say what?"

"You just beat Asa Brooks," said Bryce. "He was the main one ordering me around. I've been afraid you'd come in here and shoot us down for months, Jonah Rowe. Are you going to own me now? I don't want anyone else to get hurt."

"Anyone else?" cried Liz, who pushed past Jonah and grabbed the man's shirt. "You tried to kill my sister! And God knows who else! You suuvi are a piece of work. Why Nella? Why did you have to include my sister in your filthy schemes?"

"I'm innocent!" said Bryce, horrified. "I only follow orders! I'm not a suuvus!"

"You're lying!" snarled Liz. "Tell us the truth!"

"It's in your best interests to listen to her," said Jonah with an icy tone.

"I am." Supplication laced Bryce's voice. "I'm not the suuvus. My son is."

His words were met with silence. Reena took in an incredulous breath.

"No way," she whispered. "No fucking way!"

"Um, no way what?" said Terrence.

"You are not Dylan's father!" said Reena. "You can't be! Patience said that Dylan killed his family, along with his landlord!"

Jonah shook his head. What? And poor Liz was so stunned that her grip slackened on the man's shirt.

Bryce looked deeply saddened. "I can't be a suuvus, because I'm an Eleventh, just like all of you. You may have seen that the wall over there says Bryce Tysinger, but that's not my name. My name is Bryce Firewalker."

Jonah stared at the heavily-inked man, flabbergasted. Douglas gave a shaky laugh. It was as if he experienced any more reeling events, he'd probably call it a night soon.

"You're an Eleventh," said Jonah. "And Dylan was a Tenth."

"Yeah," said Bryce. "He was full of hatred and jealousy from the moment he realized what ethereality was all about. It drove him crazy that he wasn't an ethereal human. So he shot his mother and me in a rage when he was sixteen. I lived."

"Wait, wait," said Liz. "When he was sixteen? But he is sixteen right now!"

"That is not true, girl." Bryce met Liz's eyes. "My son is twenty-one."

Liz looked as though she'd been punched. Vera slowly brought an arm around shoulder, looking angry but shaken. Reena and Douglas looked about the same, and even Spader seemed discomfited. Terrence had a look on his face that showcased his fury, but Jonah just felt cold again. He thought of Samantha Lockman, an innocent victim of the Deadfallen disciples. Nella could have gone the same way, and on top of that, the boy lied about his age. Jonah prayed that he never saw that boy again. Because he knew, beyond a shadow of a doubt, that if they did, he wouldn't bother trying to control himself.

"C-Continue your story," he stammered to Bryce. "Just—just talk. How are you still physically alive?"

"Pure dumb luck," sighed Bryce. "Dylan's bullet didn't quite snuff the physical life out of me like it did Priscilla. I survived, and I ran. I made it as far as Arizona, and thought that it was something that I could hide from. Had a tattoo place there. But then, last spring, Dylan found me. He came to my house in the middle of the night, with some girl named Chloe—"

Now it was Jonah's turn to be off-balance. "Chloe?"

"Yeah," said Bryce. "His girlfriend. He said he had friends in wicked places, and he needed me to come back to North Carolina. He said that he would lure female Elevenths, and Chloe would lure males. If I wanted to stay physically alive, he told me, all I had to do was give 'em tattoos with a special ink. If I refused, well…" his voice trailed off.

"You weren't alone out there in Arizona," said Spader in a shrewd tone. "You actually moved on with your life. Got a new family."

Slowly, Bryce nodded. "No one will ever replace Priscilla," he said, some certainty back in his voice, "but you're right, boy. I moved on enough in my heart to try again. All was well, until Dylan came back into my life."

Liz sighed. "I'm sorry. You're just as much a victim as my sister. But you're son wronged us as well."

"Did you kill him?" asked Bryce.

"No, we didn't," answered Jonah. "We aren't Creyton, or his disciples. And Bryce, we are *not* your masters."

Bryce looked so relieved. Somehow, Jonah felt that the relief was more about his freedom, not about his son's continued physical life. It was truly messed up that he had no love for his own son, but Dylan was sick. He was a killer. Maybe a different set of rules applied there concerning affection.

"Bryce, listen," said Jonah. "Creyton had Dylan put some kind of ethereal disease in the tattoo ink you've been using. It only affects

Elevenths. Chloe and Dylan brought you Elevenths to ink up, and, consequently, infect them. They've become carriers, or, as it's been put to us, beacons. If their physical lives end before they are cured, the illness will leave their bodies and infect every Eleventh Percenter who experienced those blanket Mindscopes."

Bryce looked at him, terrified. "Illness…no…what have I done?"

"Dylan had a proverbial gun to your head, with bullets provided by Creyton," said Reena. "But you can help us stop it. We want to find a cure, and it's got to be here."

Bryce stood up. "If what you're looking for is on the premises, then I have no idea where it might be."

"You don't know the ins and outs of your own premises?" Douglas didn't even mask his own suspicion.

"Not entirely," said Bryce. "They picked this place, not me. This tattoo parlor was already set up when Dylan came to get me and threatened my new family."

"That can only mean one thing." Reena rose. "The dirty work isn't done in plain sight. There must be a secret spot somewhere. Somewhere that Creyton has probably had for a long while."

"And it just happened to be near Jonah's new place of work?" mused Liz. "That's just a tad bit odd, no?"

Jonah agreed, but really couldn't think about the coincidence right now. "We need to find a secret entrance of some kind," he said.

"How exactly do we do that?" asked Douglas.

"Simple," said Jonah. "We'll use the same principle that Terrence and I used when we found the secret entrance back at the Abbott grave. Remember that, Terrence?"

"Oh yeah." Terrence snickered. "We all need to look for something that shouldn't be here."

Douglas still looked puzzled, as did Vera, but everyone split up and began to search, Bryce included. They looked over all the nooks and crannies with fine-toothed combs. Jonah looked near the mirrors, around the autoclave, and even in the ruined bathroom, wondering if there might a trapdoor there, or something. He even checked the stall with the unconscious Deadfallen disciple. No luck.

Frustration building, he left the bathroom and grimaced at a funky collage on one of the walls—

And froze. A prickling on his neck got his attention. Jonathan told him a while back that it was wise to trust that feeling.

He looked at the collage, which depicted some of everything. There were body types of all kinds, with tattoos over every inch of their bodies. Some of their outfits were absurd, some risqué, and some oddly conservative, yet they all had tattoos galore. But what was odd about it? What shouldn't have been there?

Then Jonah saw it. There was a rounded, friendly face with a deer-in-headlights expression. She had a tattoo of a scorpion on her forehead...but no body. Of all the faces on the collage, this one was the only one with no body attached to it. If that wasn't something that shouldn't be there, he didn't know what was.

Overtaken by anticipation, he put his hands on either side of the face so that he wouldn't lose track of it. "Guys, I got something!" he called.

He didn't take his eyes off of the face, and let his ears tell him when everyone joined him.

"What is it?" asked Terrence.

"We're finding out together," murmured Jonah, who took a deep breath, placed his hands against the painted face and pushed.

A wide portion of the wall retreated about ten feet, then slid to the left. The hole revealed an antechamber of some sort, with glimmering bits of something in the walls. Momentarily distracted by all this, Jonah barely registered Vera's voice.

"That's ethereal steel!" exclaimed Vera. "Jonah, try this with me—"

She covered several protrusions with her hand. Jonah did the same. The white of her aura joined with Jonah's blue and illuminated every bit of metal down the walls. The endowment-powered lights ended at a dark opening that led to a large set of steps.

"Okay." Jonah took a deep breath. "Doug, Liz, Spader, Vera...this is the last chance to go back."

None of them moved. At this point, Jonah didn't expect them to. But he looked at Bryce.

"What's your new wife's name?" he asked.

"Daphne," answered the tattoo artist.

"Get Daphne, get any money you saved up, and blaze," Jonah told him. "You can even go back to Arizona, if you want. Dylan and Chloe will never bother you again."

Bryce looked hopeful, but leery. "Are you sure about that?"

"I guarantee it." Jonah didn't feel the need to go into details. They didn't really matter.

Bryce gave him a swift nod. "Thank you all for everything," he murmured, and stepped through the *Astralimes* and was gone.

Jonah looked down those stairs. "Straight is the way, and narrow is the path," he mumbled to himself.

"What was that, Jonah?" asked Reena.

"Nothing, nothing."

They descended the stairs. The walls were so wide that they didn't even have to be in a perfect single file. But then the stairs stopped at a large wooden door, with the most ancient lock that Jonah had ever seen. Spader clucked his tongue.

"Your little hairpin ain't getting through that," he said unnecessarily. "Back up, please. And don't stare directly into the awesome."

"If Jonah can't pick it, what makes you think that you can?" demanded Liz.

Spader gave her an uncharacteristically cold look. "I've never picked a lock in my life."

Liz's eyes narrowed. "You expect me to believe that?"

"Believe what you want," muttered Spader, who had refocused on the door. "It's a free country."

Spader splayed his fingers, and, rather dramatically, slapped one hand against the door. Everyone looked at each other, baffled, but then the place where Spader's hand was located began to glow with the red of his aura.

"I'm gonna let y'all in on a little secret," he announced while he placed his other hand on the door. "Nature doesn't like to be perverted and violated by human beings. Wood, for example, doesn't like being turned into doors."

His other hand began to glow at that particular area of the door, and he began to bring his hands closer together.

"Nature has a life of its own, and a spirit of its own to go with it," continued Spader. "Life never ends for us, and the same is true of nature, since it's a living thing. As such, there is always a trace of nature's life force that remains in it even after it's been converted into toys and objects for mankind. And that lingering life force is never pleased with that treatment."

He closed his red-glowing hands at the doorknob and lock. After a few seconds, the lock began to tremble. A few seconds after that, the entire thing—knob, lock, everything—fell out of the door, and clattered to the ground. Smug, Spader rose.

"So with proper concentration and skill, anyone looking to get through a door can use that lingering life force to their advantage."

Jonah was impressed. He wasn't even ashamed to admit it. Terrence raised his eyebrows, while Reena shook her head in wonder.

"You're good," commented Vera. "That's bad, but you're good."

Liz tried hard not to look impressed. "I never knew that was the case," she said in a small voice.

"Well, that's what you get for judging me," replied Spader.

Liz hung her head somewhat. Jonah took over the awkward moment.

"Alright guys," he said, "I'll lead the way,"

They began the slow descent. Jonah tried hard not to think of what he and his friends were getting into. He attempted positive affirmations, and tried focusing on elevated thoughts, such as successfully preventing the mass plague before it began,and Nella receiving a cure for the Mindscope illness. But negative emotions continued to permeate any walls he tried to build, and fear was the most prevalent.

Halfway down the steps, the gleaming ethereal steel fragments embedded in the walls began to dim.

"Jonah," said Vera.

"Way ahead of you," said Jonah.

Jonah put a hand to the wall again, as did Vera. The path was illuminated once again. Once that happened, he caught a glimpse of Vera's face and saw trepidation there as well. For some reason, it gave him a small sense of comfort. Vera's opinion had always mattered to him, and if he saw that she was worried, too, it took a bit of the weight off of his shoulders.

Because of his mental distractions, he hadn't even realized that the steps had ended and he was on level ground once more.

"What the hell?" said Spader.

In front of them were metallic gurneys. There were about forty of them. They all moved to them with caution. Jonah found them eerie, despite the fact that there wasn't anything on them.

"I suppose we should be thankful no people are actually strapped to the gurneys," he said.

"I'm not worried about now," said Liz, "I'm worried about what's happened on them before. Reena, can you read essence from this?"

She pointed to drops of blood on a gurney near her. Reena extended her hands over it, and her fingers gleamed with the yellow of her aura. After a few moments, she frowned and shook her head.

"It's too old," she said. "Whatever essence and life force there was has long since faded."

"Question," said Douglas. "What exactly are we looking for down here? Because that whole 'shouldn't be here' approach applies to a lot of things down here."

"If the disease was created down here, then the antidote, or at least the breakdown of it, should be down here as well," said Liz. "So we'll be looking for file cabinets, sample records—those sorts of things."

"Seriously?" said Spader.

"Yes, seriously," said Liz. "They wouldn't unleash an illness, especially an ethereal one, out into the world if they couldn't shut it back down if they needed to. From an ethereal and medical standpoint, it's completely reckless, illogical, and unsound."

"With all due respect, Liz," said Terrence, "we ain't dealing with the most logical and sound people here."

"They're sound enough to want to protect their own asses from the illness, if nothing else," countered Liz.

Terrence thought on it. "Point," he conceded.

"What about these drawers here?" asked Vera from several feet away.

There was a collection of rusty drawers pushed flush against the wall. Everyone walked to them, and discovered that every single one of them was locked.

"Hang on," said Spader, who placed his hands on two separate drawers at the same time.

"Your party trick is useless now, Spader," scoffed Liz. "This isn't wood—"

Liz was silenced by the locks clicking in surrender. Spader looked at her with smugness in every inch of his face.

"Metal comes from nature too, Lizzie-Beth," he said. "Surely they taught you that at LTSU."

Liz's eyes narrowed, but she made no comeback. Her thoughts must have gone to Nella. She remained silent as she went through papers. Spader unlocked the other drawers, and Jonah and the rest of them began to help Liz out. Douglas opened a drawer and immediately recoiled.

"Oh, God." He sounded revolted. "This one's full of syringes, gauzes, and surgical equipment."

"What?" said Jonah. "But I thought that this illness was cultivated from spirits and spiritesses."

"It was," said Liz.

"So that blood over there was lifeblood?"

"I'm thinking so." Reena that time.

"How can that be?" demanded Vera. "Surgical equipment? You can't operate on spirits!"

"Creyton and the Deadfallen disciples could if they were made tangible," said Liz in a slow voice. "If that were the case, then the sky was the limit."

Jonah whistled. "That would void a spirit. Emaciate them of their essence. But if that was the case, why did Creyton need the beacons?"

"What are you saying, Jonah?" said Douglas.

"I'm saying that if they went to this length, why bother with the middlemen?" said Jonah.

"That's a great question, Jonah." Liz frowned as she looked at another file. "But there is something strange about these experiments—Douglas?"

Douglas ignored her. His eyes were in the direction of the gurneys.

"Doug, what do you see?"

Jonah looked in the same direction. He didn't see anything—until his eyes adjusted.

A single crow was perched on one of the bloodstained gurneys. It looked austere, almost majestic. But Jonah knew better. That bird was the disguise of a vile murderer. And Jonah thought he knew which one.

"Go ahead," he muttered. "Vera and I already know, but let the rest of them see."

The crow cawed loudly, and Jonah imagined that he heard laughter within it. Then the form began to change before their eyes. The black, glossy plumage as the form expanded in size. The beady black eyes gave way to a frigid blue, while the pointed face gave way and rounded and smoothed out to reveal a human face, engulfed by the formerly strawberry blonde, but now brunette hair. She could do it in the blink of an eye, but Jonah knew that she decided to milk it for shock value.

Jessica Hale sat where the crow had been. Surprisingly, she wore pants, but they were so skin-tight that Jonah couldn't believe she could breathe. Her propensity for skanky outfits was nauseating.

"There is something that the Transcendent teaches us," she said quietly. "He says that when you know the nature of your prey, you can read their thoughts. And when you know their thoughts, so, too, will you know their decisions. And he was right, as he always is. You decided, all on your own, to come here and die, Rowe. And you even brought people to die with you."

26

The Push

Jonah heard his friends' reactions behind his back. Terrence swore; no surprise there. Liz backed into something, murmuring, "Oh, my God." Douglas let out something between a choke and a gasp. He didn't know what Reena was thinking, Spader either. But he did wonder about Vera. She, like him, had seen Jessica's transformation before, and he knew it terrified her. He couldn't imagine what seeing it again would do to her from a mental standpoint.

"Jessica," he said slowly, "your beef is with me. Not my friends. Let them walk."

"I refuse," said Reena before Jessica could respond, and stood next to him while elongating her javelin to a yellow-gleaming slender weapon.

"I'm with you come hell or high water, Jonah," said Terrence, who stood at his other side.

Jonah's other friends moved forward as well. So they weren't going anywhere. Swell.

As irritated as Jonah felt, though, there was relief that his friends were unwilling to abandon him. Like Mr. Steverson said, being a loner didn't fly anymore.

Jessica watched all of this and chuckled. "Bravery," she whispered. "Loyalty. Admirable traits, apart from the fact that those who exhibit them always wind up dead. I applaud it regardless. I wasn't going to let any of you go anyway, but I still applaud it."

Jonah looked at her with scorn. "Since when have you cared about admirable traits?"

Jessica raised her hands. "What, I can't have layers?"

Jonah sneered. "Bitch, you don't even wear layers."

Jessica licked her lips. "Touche, Jonah dear. Touche."

"Plus you seem to be missing something, Jess," said Jonah. "There are seven of us, and one of you. And I've been waiting to get you back ever since you broke my jaw. So what makes you think you can stop us?"

Jessica tapped her throat with two French-tipped nailed fingers and uttered , "*Per Mortem, Vitam.*" About a dozen other crows came into view, all clutching twigs in their beaks. Seconds after that, they shifted into other Deadfallen disciples.

Jonah saw faces that he recognized, like India Drew, Charlotte Daynard, Dell Rankin, and Wyndham O'Shea among them. He didn't know the other ones, but that hardly mattered.

He felt a hand clutch his arm. It was Vera. Jessica noticed that action and grinned.

"You were saying, Rowe?" she asked sweetly as she finally hopped off the table. "Don't kid yourself. Your situation is hopeless. You can even put your little rainbow-colored weapons away. And oh yeah—Spader, was it?"

Spader twitched, surprised by the acknowledgement.

"Smooth move with the door," complimented Jessica. "Smooth as velvet. But unfortunately—"

She snapped her fingers, and the way to the stairs was barred by a door that contained the same types of locks the one that Spader disabled had. Spader's mouth dropped in shock.

"Now then," said Jessica, who beckoned her comrades forward as she neared Jonah's group, "this is what's going to happen, Rowe. Your little green-eyed friend there is going to return every file she just lifted.

Their deaths will be quick. Or quick enough, I should say. Sadly, we have to be nice to you, at least for now."

"Oh, don't give me that shit," snapped Jonah. "Had this been earlier tonight, I might have believed that. But then Creyton got his suuvus flunky to throw a twig in my groceries—"

"No, Rowe," said O'Shea, and he and the other disciples looked annoyed for some reason. "Chloe Spears did that on her own. She wanted revenge for her boyfriend, Dylan. You got him caught, after all. In her anger, she went over the Transcendent's head. And the stupid little bitch paid for that."

Jonah blinked, floored. "She…she tried to kill me on her own? And then you killed her?"

"Sadly, no," said O'Shea. "India and Dell did."

"I'd like to say that she didn't feel a thing," said Dell in a voice that contradicted that statement, "but India always gets carried away."

"Quick and painless weren't our orders," murmured India. "Besides, I just did some Ungifted job hunter a favor. That Wal-Mart branch has a job opening now."

Liz made a sound in horror. Jonah knew how she felt. Chloe and her boyfriend were both scum, but to hear India Drew speak about murdering Chloe like it was a kindness was just sick. He had to get his friends away from these people.

"I thought that Creyton loved having people to torture and lord his power over," he ventured. "Why does he want to kill over half the ethereal world?"

Jessica snorted, and looked at her fellow disciples. They all seemed to be amused about something. "See, Jonah? This is what happens when the children overhear grown folks' conversations. You attempt to understand things that you can't even begin to, and then you try to influence matters far too progressed for you to stop them. Now tell that girl to put the files back."

Jonah couldn't allow that to happen. They seemed to have a mad-on for those files, which led him to believe that the means for a cure to the Mindscope Illness lay within.

"Perhaps tonight?" said Jessica, slightly impatient.

"Liz, put those papers in your satchel," said Jonah. "You'll be needing them."

Charlotte shook her head. "Jonah, please don't attempt to grow a brain, darlin,"' she said in that meditative voice of hers. "Your very essence stinks of fear. Don't be courageous. Else you'll make it so your buddies die slowly tonight."

"No, Charlotte, let him," said O'Shea, who pulled out knuckle apparatuses similar to Terrence's, except they were tipped with a razor's edge. "Let him make things worse for them all. Let him treat them like dust in the wind."

Ding! That was it. Wind. That might assist here. But there was no way to regulate it. He'd have to hit everyone. How could he get his friends to brace themselves?

"Douglas?" said Charlotte suddenly. "What are you doing here, son? You are a way over your head!"

Douglas cleared his throat. "I'm right where I belong," he said in a steady tone.

Charlotte laughed out loud."With a hammer, darlin?"

Jonah frowned. He knew what Terrence and Reena would have, and he knew that Vera never parted with the dagger that Reena gave her when they first met. But he didn't pay much attention to what Liz, Spader, and Douglas would have. He glanced over, and sure enough, Douglas wielded a hammer, the head of which gleamed silver with his aura. Really?

Then he realized that he'd just agreed with a Deadfallen disciple. That made him feel a little sick. He returned to the plan forming in his mind.

"Charlotte, why exactly did you help Lockman demonize us?" he asked her. "Doesn't putting us on the spot muck up Creyton's plans, whatever they are?"

Charlotte grinned. "Sweetie, that was just fun," she told him. "The Transcendent enjoyed watching y'all flail around and try to maintain an image in the eyes of that dumb lil' town. As for mucking things up, the Transcendent's plans are never altered, least of all by a rage-blinded, Ungifted crusader."

Charlotte must have loved the sound of her own voice. That was good, though. Jonah had gathered enough force, and was just about ready to unleash it. He hoped that his friends would understand, and let him off the hook for what he was about to do.

"Put the files back, little girl," said Jessica, "or I'll kill your spirit before I kill you."

"What?" said Liz, baffled. "What do you mean?"

"Tell me something, Wyndham," said Jessica, who made her voice provocative. "Are you up for a trip to Concord?"

Liz whimpered. Vera's hand, which hadn't left Jonah's arm, tightened.

"I'm up for anything, so long as death is involved," replied O'Shea. "Why?"

"I want you to go to the Spirits of Vitality and Peace," said Jessica as she inspected one of her nails. "The girl's youngest sister—the one that Dylan was screwing—is there, being kept away from death by a mere tonic. I want you to go there and kill her in the most delicious way possible, unless of course, Rowe here can convince this girl here to return those files—"

Jonah unleashed his power, freeing all the gathered air. Most everything was knocked astray, including cabinets, several gurneys, files, equipment, Deadfallen disciples, but also him and his friends. He landed on his back, but kept a vice grip on his batons. Looking up, he saw that Jessica blocked being windswept by using ethereality of her own, but strangely, she didn't attack. She ran to some door practically threw herself through it. Weird.

But it was immaterial at the moment, seeing as how they had to get past several angry Deadfallen disciples.

"Jessica barred the way out!" Jonah scrambled to his feet. "We need to find another one!"

Jonah was glad that his friends adapted quickly. Liz, who had a tight clutch on the files, stuffed them into her satchel and got up to run.

Unfortunately, the Deadfallen disciples had recovered as well. One of them did some dark ethereality maneuver, which unleashed more hell. It felt like Jonah's own wind trick hit him from behind, but the air was hot against his back and felt like a whip. He actually crashed onto a gurney and rolled about two feet before the thing collapsed at sent him back to the floor. He saw a disciple reach for Vera, only to have her knife raked across his wrist. He grunted in pain, and Vera rolled away from him. Someone grabbed for Jonah's throat, but he blindly swung a baton and freed himself.

"HIT 'EM AGAIN, DECLAN!" roared O'Shea.

"NO!" shouted Jonah.

But the heated winds swept through the area again. This time Jonah got knocked into a door, which was blasted off of its hinges. He still had momentum, so he rolled a few more feet before coming to a halt.

His head spun and it felt like he'd busted his lip, but he was otherwise alright.

He rose to his knees, and saw Reena slowly coming to her own feet nearby. Inches away from her, Douglas clutched his forehead, groaning in disorientation.

"What was that?" he demanded when he saw Jonah and Reena. "You think they have the strength to do that again?"

Jonah ignored the question and looked around. Reena and Douglas were the only ones near him. No one else was in sight. Panic began to rise within him.

"Where is everyone else?" he demanded.

Reena started, and looked around herself. "God, no," she whispered. "I'm hoping that they reached one of those other doors. I saw a couple doors before those essence blasts. I think they reached them."

"How can you be sure?" cried Jonah.

Reena closed her eyes. "Because they better have," she said.

Jonah wanted to have her faith. He truly did. But fear and worry began to take his mind to the darkest of places. "I'm going back out there." He retrieved both batons. "I'm not even entertaining the notion of leaving this place until—"

Jonah got tackled from the rear. As his eyes had been on Reena, he'd missed the entire thing. He saw Reena get rushed as well; he saw a flash of white hair. India Drew. So who the hell had nearly knocked him out of his socks just now?

"Neat little move, Rowe," said a hard voice that Jonah recognized to be Dell Rankin. "Try your foolishness now!"

He produced a crescent-shaped weapon, which gleamed black the second he touched it. Without thought, Jonah attempted to intercept with a baton, but Rankin dodged it, then expertly flicked the weapon out of Jonah's hand.

"Cute try, dumbass," snapped Rankin.

He doubled his efforts, and Jonah was at a clear disadvantage.

Then the horrible creaking sound of old metal made them both look up.

Douglas did a flying—something—from some platform near the wall. Jonah didn't know what the hell he'd been trying to do, but the outcome can't have been the plan.

He landed on both Rankin and Jonah, which caused all them to fall. It was the third time that Jonah had gotten knocked to the ground.

And it pissed him off.

Rankin lost the crescent-shaped thing when he hit the ground, which Jonah supposed was something, but was already looking around for it. He spotted the thing before Jonah managed to untangle himself from Douglas, and reached for it with a smug grin. But Douglas pounced over, hand extended, and slammed down twice with the hammer, which crushed Rankin's hand. Rankin's smug look faded, and he screamed in agony.

While admittedly impressed, Jonah didn't waste too much time with it. He rose, got his other baton, and crowned a howling Rankin in the face. He hit the Deadfallen disciple so hard that he actually rolled over on the floor from the impact.

Now Jonah regarded Douglas. "That was…impressive, Doug—"

"A LITTLE HELP!" shouted Reena.

Both men wheeled around to see her still battling India Drew. Douglas bounded forward before Jonah could stop him, and India caught the movement. With no hesitation, she reached into her pocket and flung something at his face. Whatever it was made a rather loud thump when it connected, and Douglas about-faced on one heel, dropped his hammer, and collapsed.

"DOUG!" screamed Jonah, but then—

"Jonah!" cried Reena. "The outlet!"

Jonah looked around, confused, but then he saw what she meant. There was an electrical outlet on the wall. His endowment allowed him to sense that the wiring followed the length of the wall—right to where India and Reena stood. Jonah wondered how Reena noticed it, but then came to the only logical conclusion: It must be some sort of torture area, using electricity through ethereal means. Reena must have picked up on the collective essence of victims past.

Reena managed to put some space between her and India by kicking India against the wall. "Do it, Jonah!" she yelled.

But before Jonah could even move, India reached forward and clutched Reena's arm.

"If you activate the device, you blast her too!" warned India. "What do you say to that, Blue Boy?"

Jonah pulled his hand back and swore. Reena attempted hard to free herself, but India would not be denied. He wondered why India hadn't stepped from the wall, but then saw that her foot was stuck in the floor. He truly didn't know what to do. And he was worried about Douglas. Hell, he was worried about his missing friends. But he needed to do something about this present situation…

Reena gritted her teeth. "Do it, Jonah," she told him.

India looked at her like she was insane. Jonah actually did the same.

"Hell no!" he answered.

"DO IT!" roared Reena. "ZAP THIS BITCH!"

Cursing himself, Jonah touched the exposed outlet. A flash of blue fired along the length of the wall and hit both women. He winced when he saw both bodies spike due to voltage; he didn't even know Reena was capable of such a shrill scream.

Then it was done. India collapsed, and Jonah heard a sickening pop from where her weight came down on her awkwardly-lodged ankle. Reena fell to her knees, and just kind of slumped over to her side.

Jonah looked at her, and then at Douglas. Roaring in frustration, he went to Reena first, whose clothes were actually steaming.

"Reena!" he cried. "Reena, wake up! Wake up!"

Reena cleared her throat and stirred. Jonah was so relieved that he was almost light-headed.

"Zeus...has nothing...on you," she murmured.

Jonah almost laughed, but was instantly serious. "Are you alright?"

He helped Reena to her feet. She stretched, but was still groggy.

"Wonderful," she mumbled. "Did you know that stimulating...stimulating muscles with electricity...makes them stronger?"

Jonah raised an eyebrow. "No, Reena, I didn't know that," he said. "But I'm glad you're alright."

"Not that it matters," mumbled a thick voice nearby, "but I'm here, too."

Douglas was on his haunches, and Jonah winced. Whatever India pitched at him had badly broken his nose. The sight of it served to further center Reena, and both she and Jonah helped him to his feet. Reena appeared more composed, but still had some trouble focusing. To Jonah, it seemed like she wanted to ignore what had just happened to her.

"Hold still, Doug," she commanded. "I'm going to straighten your nose. When we get out of here, I'm sure Liz can set it and fix it entirely. And put those teeth in your pocket. They can be put back in as well."

"Teeth?" asked Jonah, but then he saw four teeth in Douglas' palm. "What did that bitch hit you with?"

Douglas ignored Jonah, but only because Reena was working on his nose. It seemed to be far from a pleasant experience.

"Reena...ow, damn it...OW!"

"You're a man, Doug," snapped Reena. "Will you act as such, or is that too much to ask?"

"It has nothing to do masculinity!" protested Douglas. "It just hurts!"

"I just got fried like bad pork, Doug," Reena reminded him. "Now shut up and let me work!"

With a final cracking sound, Reena was done. Enough. Douglas remained quite a sight, though. His left eye was blackened, his nose clearly needed further assistance, and Jonah saw swelling near his jaw, presumably where he'd lost those teeth. But now that his nose was straighter, he seemed to be in better spirits.

"I guess Terrence was right," he mumbled, looking down at his shirt. "I did get blood on my merino wool polo."

"Let's get out of this room," said Jonah. Hearing Liz and Terrence's names reminded him that his friends were still around here somewhere.

"Sounds like a good idea," said Reena. "I don't want to be around here when those two wake up."

"I hate to be pessimistic," said Jonah, "but there are plenty more where they came from. Doug, get your damn hammer. Reena, the javelin might hinder you, but—"

"Good point." Reena miniaturized the weapon, and dropped it in her pocket. "But that might work."

She grabbed a socket wrench from a nearby table. It gleamed yellow in her hands, revealing it to be ethereal steel.

"Who are these people?" asked Douglas. "Why would Deadfallen disciples need ethereal steel socket wrenches?"

"Don't know, don't care," said Reena. "Let's go."

Because of Rankin's blasts, the door was no issue; Jonah, Douglas, and Reena simply walked through the hole. The main room with the gurneys had been completely deserted, which gave Jonah prickle of anxiety.

"Reena said that maybe they tried some of these doors," said Douglas in an attempt to calm the mood. "Let's try some ourselves."

"Can't hurt," said Reena. "Let's see what's behind door number one."

Weapons aloft, they tried the room. Empty.

"On to the next," muttered Jonah.

The next room was empty, as were the two next to it. When they reached the fifth door, Jonah was so eager to see someone else that he didn't even care if they were Deadfallen disciples that they'd have to fight. Unfortunately, that room was empty, too.

"Shit!" he snarled. "Where is everyone?"

He made to slam the door, but Reena blocked it with her foot.

"Wait!"

She pushed it open, frowning as she walked to some type of drawing board. Jonah couldn't see anything at all, so now he had to deal with being impatient as well as confused.

"Jonah, fire us up," commanded Reena.

Jonah did so, which illuminated a diagram of a familiar dwelling. Jonah's eyes narrowed.

"What—is that—what is that?" he sputtered.

"This is the estate!" exclaimed Reena. "They have a depiction of every room! I couldn't have drawn a better one! And look—there is one of Sanctum Arcist! And that one there—" she pointed, "—is the Spirits of Vitality and Peace! Why would Creyton have these?"

"Do you think that it's possible—" Douglas was forced to pause in order to wipe blood from his nose, "—that these places are the primary ones they want to see get devastated by the Mindscope Illness?"

Jonah sighed. He hadn't thought of that. They had to find a cure. But for that, they needed Liz. "We need to—"

Someone charged in, and collided with Reena in the process. The person struggled and let out a cry that they all recognized.

"Liz!" said Reena quickly. "Liz, it's me! It's Reena!"

The struggles ceased, and Liz looked around. "Thank God! You're still physically alive!"

Jonah noticed that Liz looked rough. Her dirty blonde hair was dirty for real, there was blood at her mouth, and her eyes were bloodshot.

She seemed to realize something, and her eyes widened. "Where are Terrence and Vera?"

"What?" said Jonah. "You—you don't know?"

"Wait," said Douglas, "what about Spader?"

"To hell with Spader!" Liz snarled. "I got knocked into the gurneys right next to him after that second blast. We ran away from two Deadfallen—I think I managed to crack a case of vials over a guy's head, but he didn't even stop running—and we got to one of the rooms. Spader actually did something useful and stabbed the guy, and I nervestruck the other disciple with him, but not before he punched me in the mouth. Once we had breathing room, Spader told me that this wasn't going to work, and used the Astralimes! The rat bastard left me by myself!"

Jonah growled in his throat. To think, he saved that boy from punishment last winter after he nearly got them all killed. He actually gave Spader a chance. He thought the kid wanted to atone. Wanted to change. But after all those proclamations, he was still a piece of shit. "Fuck him," he said, readying his batons. "I hope that the Networkers that the Curaie have monitoring the Astralimes caught him when he got to wherever he was going. We need to find Terrence and Vera, but let's get out of this room before we're cornered. Liz, we need to keep that satchel safe. More importantly, we need to keep you safe, too."

They slowly made their way out to the main area, just to regroup. Before Jonah could say another word, that painful buzz at the back of his skull flared again. He dropped his batons and clutched his head; his friends clutched their own as well. There couldn't be any more visions—what would be the point of them now?

But then, the pain ended. It didn't even last two seconds. What the hell?

"That one was different," said Douglas. "No vision came with it. No desert, no spirits."

"Why did it happen?" asked Liz. "I thought they were meant to mark us for the Mindscope Illness!"

"I thought that..." Jonah's voice trailed off. Everyone looked at him.

True, the Mindscopes were meant to trigger everyone. But that had been occurring for the past several months. Before then, the Mindscopes had another purpose—

"We need to run," he told them. "That Mindscope was meant to look for us!"

"Not look for," said Reena quietly. "Find."

They were surrounded by Deadfallen disciples. There were more than before; they must have called for reinforcements. Even Rankin and India were among them. Rankin's jaw was practically hanging off, and his right hand was useless, but the left one was fine, as was the weapon in it. After the shock treatment, India had a sort of Bride-of-Frankenstein-thing going on, and she favored her ankle as she moved. But she looked doubly murderous because of those things. All the disciples had black-gleaming weapons trained on Jonah and his friends. Jessica wasn't with them, but that was hardly important right now. Charlotte, who wielded a short bat with black-gleaming spikes at the end of it, came forward.

"Drop your weapons." Some of the musical quality in her voice was gone. "Now."

Swearing, Jonah did so. Reena dropped the wrench, and Douglas relinquished the hammer. Liz, who only had the satchel, raised her hands.

"Got a little surprise for you," said Charlotte. "Francis!"

A Deadfallen disciple positioned outside the ring they'd made flung two figures into the circle. It was Terrence and Vera. Terrence's head was bleeding, and he looked furious. Vera had blood at her nose and under her nails.

"One's missin,'" said a disciple. "That Spader boy."

"The punk abandoned us," grumbled Jonah. "You got cheated out of one victim 'cuz he was a fuckin' coward."

"Language, Rowe," chided Charlotte. "But it's immaterial. He'll get gotten to soon enough. Now Rowe, you need to pay attention. Guys, do it."

All around them, the Deadfallen disciples dipped their weapons downward. Jonah frowned at the curious action, but then he saw that they all dripped with something too dark to be blood. His mouth hung open.

"Ah," said Charlotte, satisfied, "you're gettin' the picture. For the dumber ones among you, that is tainted tattoo ink. Bryce had been unwittingly using it for about a year. We'll have to thank him when we find him."

Jonah hoped that Bryce had gotten his wife, and they were long gone. But he pulled himself back to the present situation.

"There are now six of you," Charlotte went on. "That's six opportunities. Rowe, you will get the Manville girl to toss over the files, right now. Each refusal with result in one of your buddies here being infected. Or killed; I'm good either way. But, as I said, you have six opportunities."

Jonah looked at Liz's frightened, but defiant, face. He looked at Reena, who looked as though she wanted to kill something. Douglas, Vera, Terrence. He knew they wouldn't abandon him, even now. Loyal family to the end.

Christ, if he ever saw Spader again...

"What's the holdup, Rowe?" asked Charlotte. "There will be no more miracles. That ship's done sailed. You have no more ethereal tricks up your sleeves. There is no escape. The Transcendent won this game before it even started—"

Claudette fell silent when a large Deadfallen disciple took a sharp intake of breath. She gave him a cold look.

"What, Jud?" she snapped.

Jud blinked at her, as though confused, then he fell flat on his face. An arrow was lodged in his back, with the final traces of gold fading from it.

"Finally, damn it." The voice was familiar, and its owner stepped out of the darkness. It was Daniel, with a quiver of arrows, another gold-gleaming one already aimed to shoot. "I finally got to shoot a physically living target!"

India snarled at Daniel, and threw one of the same objects at him that she'd struck Douglas with earlier. Daniel calmly shot three arrows, rapid fire style. The first intercepted the object, the second hit India in her already damaged ankle, and the third hit her in the shoulder. Her cries were of pain and surprise as she fell. Not even paying her any attention, Daniel looked straight at Jonah and the others.

"Get down!" he commanded.

Jonah was puzzled, but obeyed without question. His friends did as well.

Not a moment too soon.

The barrier that Jessica rigged earlier blew off of its frame. Felix entered, wielding two ethereal weapons that gleamed the color of his aura. He was followed by June Mylteer, Patience, Raymond, and two other people that made Jonah do a double take: Sterling, and Spader.

"Hey, Reenie!" shouted Sterling. "It's hot as hell down here! Mind cooling us off?"

Reena rose, fury in her features. "With pleasure."

She clapped her hands, and the whole scene was icy in seconds. Jars of nearby liquid cracked, while others burst entirely. The Deadfallen disciples screamed in protest and dispersed, but now they had to fight. Spader ducked down, and made a beeline for Jonah and the others.

"You guys okay?" he asked.

"Fine," said Jonah, who eyed him steadily.

"What?" Spader questioned when he noticed the look.

"We... we thought you..." Liz attempted, but her voice failed her.

"Let me guess," said Spader. "You thought I bitched out, and ran?"

Completely humbled, Liz could only nod.

"I only left so I could get help," Spader looked more serious than he ever had. "I ain't a coward, Lizzie. There're a lot of things that I freely admit to being, but I ain't a coward."

"I hate to break up this NBC moment," said Terrence, "but grab something and fight!"

They all got their weapons and joined the fray. Spader pulled out a pouch of leather, shook it like a drink, and a switchblade lowered from it, which instantly gleamed red. He joined Terrence in engaging one of the larger Deadfallen disciples.

Jonah wanted to fight, but instinct made him want to protect Liz. Surprisingly, she would have none of it.

"Thanks, but no thanks!" she snapped. "I'm not a great fighter, but I know where to strike, remember?"

As if to accentuate that point, she ran up behind an unsuspecting Deadfallen disciple and grabbed her near her left shoulder blade. The woman yelped in pain and fell to the floor.

She ran to aid Vera, who was tangled with another disciple. Then Jonah was distracted by Reena, who struggled with Charlotte.

"Unhand me, you abomination!" snarled Charlotte.

"Suck it, bitch!" roared Reena. "I'll show you what happens when you fuck with my girlfriend!"

Jonah almost laughed; he remembered the bone that Reena had to pick with Charlotte.

But his distraction cost him.

What felt like hot wire wrapped both of his wrists, and he dropped both batons in surprise. Wyndam O'Shea was responsible for it.

"Not so dangerous without your chopsticks, are you, Rowe?" he rasped. "I've dreamed of beating the shit out of you ever since you pitched me out of that window to break your damn fall!"

"You dreamed about me?" murmured Jonah. "I'm flattered, but I don't kick on that side of the field!"

O'Shea roared and threw a punch with one of those razor-edged knuckles. Jonah barely got out of the way in time, but felt one slice across his left shoulder. He cursed because his hands were bound. Eventually, O'Shea would get a shot in. If only he could free his hands—

O'Shea threw another punch that Jonah actually blocked, but the only offense he could manage with his bound hands wash to give him a hard shove. O'Shea staggered back, but laughed with no mirth.

"Pathetic," he snapped. "And you're supposed to be a hero—"

WHAM.

There was a sickening thump, and O'Shea bellowed in pain. Jonah looked, and saw Terrence. He'd hit the Deadfallen disciple with a metal folding chair.

He gave O'Shea another chair strike. The lunatic collapsed to a knee, but was still conscious.

"Are you kidding me?" snapped Terrence.

He swung the chair a third time, aiming for O'Shea's head. With a spray of blood and a strangled shriek, the psycho crashed on his back, out cold.

"Thank you!" spat Terrence, who threw down the chair and unbound Jonah's hands. "He didn't slice you too bad with those things, did he, Jonah?"

"No," scowled Jonah. "I didn't give him the satisFACTION!"

He finished the sentence with a stiff kick to O'Shea's side. As the man was already unconscious, there was no reaction. Jonah didn't even give a damn.

"Moon-loving bitch," he grumbled. "I'd push him out of another window if I had the chance."

Terrence smiled. Together, they looked over the scene.

Several Deadfallen disciples were on their knees, with their hands ethereally bound behind their backs. Patience and Sterling used materials they'd scrounged from the cabinets to wrap the tattoo ink-laced weapons. India was swearing so much that June Mylteer gagged her mouth after murmuring, "Do you kiss your mom with that mouth?" Neither Charlotte nor Jessica were anywhere in sight. Damn.

He was momentarily distracted by Vera. There was a look on her face that he couldn't place. Jonah approached her, concerned.

"Everything alright, Vera?" he asked.

Vera swallowed. "Jessica didn't get caught," she murmured. "That crazy bitch got away."

Jonah sighed, understanding. Jessica was probably the Deadfallen disciple that unnerved Vera the most out of the bunch. Jonah couldn't very well blame her for feeling that way; how could you expect someone to react after they saw someone who'd threatened them shape-shift into a damn bird? "I noticed that too," he said, placing a hand on her arm. "But don't worry about her. That bitch won't get far. One day, and one day soon, I'm gonna drop her myself. And if you feel that strongly about it, maybe you'll be able to watch me take her down whenever that happens."

Vera sort of smiled, but it didn't last long. That was fine, though. Jonah would personally help her through her concerns. It was the least he could do.

"Liz needs to get back to the infirmary at home," said Douglas to the group of rescuers and friends. "She has a set of papers that might cure the illness."

Felix looked at Douglas with respect. "Look at you," he marveled. "Badass preppie, with battle scars to boot!"

Reena and Terrence clapped Douglas on his back. Liz regarded Spader.

"I'm sorry that I called you a rat bastard," she mumbled.

Spader frowned. "You called me a rat bastard?"

Liz's eyes widened. She'd forgotten that Spader hadn't been present when she'd called him that. "Um, no, I didn't. I said no such thing."

Jonah almost chuckled, but then frowned. A feeling of fear gripped him. It was almost primal in strength. He couldn't imagine where it had come from, but it was sudden and all-engulfing.

"Jonah?" said Terrence. "What's up?"

Jonah ignored him. Almost as if he received a beckoning of some kind, he turned his back on the group and left them. He barely heard the voices that attempted to call him back.

He ran to the same door that Jessica disappeared through earlier, flung it open, and ran up a flight of stairs. What began as a power walk became a jog, and then a full-out run, and then a race against time. The fear was so strong. What he was afraid of was at the end of the hall. Get there…he had to get there…

He reached the end of the hall, where there was one final door, already ajar. He had the sudden feeling that it had been left open for him. Batons ready, he pushed the door wide.

It was a wide, cavernous room, with dim lights that gave everything a feeble glow. But he didn't need that much illumination to see.

Jessica Hale stood there, calmly filing a nail. When she saw Jonah, she gave him a radiant grin.

"Very good, Rowe!" she said. "You followed that trail of fear so beautifully! So your phobia remains true. Isn't it so sexy how emotions can be used and twisted?"

Jonah's eyes narrowed. He wasn't afraid of Jessica. At least, not to the point of the near-debilitation he just felt. What was the deal? "You didn't have to play ethereal games, Jess," he told her. "I'd have come to you one-on-one all on my own—"

"Save it, Rowe," said Jessica, bored. "The fear was very real, Jonah. You just don't know why you felt it. Yet."

"I ain't afraid of you, Jess," said Jonah. "I might be afraid of the lengths I'll go to in order to get you back for all that you've done, but that's where it stops."

"You should be afraid of me," whispered Jessica. "You should also be of the lengths I'll go to myself."

She walked out of the light; her shoes made snapping sounds on the wood. Jonah frowned after her, but kept his batons ready. He had no clue what Jessica had in mind, but he hadn't forgotten that fear.

Jessica returned to the light, but she wasn't alone. She had a hostage, bound and gagged.

It was Mr. Steverson.

Jonah's mouth fell open in shock and terror. All the breath in his lungs escaped.

Jessica opened an old-fashioned straight razor, which gleamed black in her hands. Then she stood behind Mr. Steverson and placed it at his throat.

"No bravado, Jonah?" she asked. "No icy wit? Where are those balls of ethereal steel now?"

Jonah couldn't think. Fear and confusion had a stranglehold on his mind that left no room for rational thought. How did she get Mr. Steverson? Why wasn't he home in bed? "Jessica, if you hurt him—"

"Don't threaten me, Jonah," warned Jessica. "Just... don't. Especially right now."

Jonah swallowed hard. Now, fear fought anger. He just couldn't understand why Mr. Steverson was there. But he didn't deserve to be in this situation. He shouldn't have been anywhere near this place. "Let him go, Jessica. You want a victim, take me. Please, let him go—"

"That's right, Jonah." Jessica sounded hungry; almost like she got some rise out of this. "Beg. I want you to beg me. Grovel. Get on your knees."

At that moment, Mr. Steverson began to scream through his gag. Jonah's eyes widened. What was wrong? Had Jessica already injured him?

Jessica lowered the gag with a smirk. "What is it, Gramps?"

Mr. Steverson laser-focused on Jonah. "Don't kneel, boy!" he said with conviction. "Don't do it! Not for this! Not for her!"

Jonah shook his head vigorously. "Now's not the time, Mr. Steverson!" he cried. "You can't have that pride right now! She'll kill you!"

"Let me die, then!" roared Mr. Steverson. "I'd rather die on my feet than watch you grovel on your knees!"

"No!" protested Jonah. "Jessica, lower the razor! I'll do anything!"

"Don't let this woman—!"

Jessica scoffed and returned the gag to Mr. Steverson's mouth. "I swear, I'm the toughest man here, and I'm a woman," she murmured. "Now then... Rowe, you know my demands. Kneel, or the old man dies."

Jonah had no choice. Mr. Steverson's eyes blazed; his disagreement was etched in every trace of them. But Jonah didn't care. Jessica wasn't killing Mr. Steverson.

He knelt. Jessica's eye gleamed.

"So nice," she said. "So obedient. Well, I've got good news for you, Rowe."

She lowered the razor from Mr. Steverson's neck. Jonah waited. He was going to kick her ass the second he had an opening—

"Remember the trace of scarlet in the Vitasphera, which signified that someone close to you was going to die?" she asked suddenly. "Well, it's still there—but the good news is that it was never ever meant for your little sazer friend."

She elevated the razor. Jonah's eyes widened in horror.

"DON'T!" he screamed, but it was too late.

With a look of ecstasy, Jessica lowered the razor, its blade now vividly scarlet. So scarlet that it masked the black gleam of her endowment. Mr. Steverson took a few clumsy steps forward, his eyes on Jonah, and then fell to the floor, physically lifeless.

27

Brink

Jonah stared at Mr. Steverson, begging himself—pleading with himself—to wake up from this nightmare. It hadn't happened. It hadn't. There was no way.

Jessica began to laugh. "Are you going to cry, Rowe?" she asked. "Did I just destroy a bromance here?"

Jonah felt his stinging eyes rise to Jessica's grinning face. He gripped the batons so tightly that it probably would have hurt were he able to feel pain right now. But all he felt was rage. "I'LL KILL YOU!"

He charged her. His only goal was to permanently wipe that grin off of her face. Unfortunately, Jessica was ready. She blocked his first attack in such a fashion that it knocked both of his weapons away. She still had the razor, but Jonah didn't even care.

"THAT WAS MY FRIEND!" he bellowed. "HE HAD A WIFE! FOUR DAUGHTERS!"

Jessica parried another strike, still smug. "Tell it to someone who gives a shit."

"YOU LITTLE—!"

Jonah got through Jessica's defense and punched her across the face, and she fell to the floor. She touched at her lip, and then raised a shocked face to him. Finally, the grin was gone.

"Motherfucker!" she growled. "That's your *ass*!"

Jessica shot to her feet faster than Jonah expected, and tagged him in the gut. She followed that with a knee lift to his chest, and then she grabbed him by the shirt and slammed him to the floor. It took him by surprise, and hurt like two kinds of hell.

"Yeah, Blue Man!" she taunted. "You want revenge, yes? Why are you on the ground?"

She aimed a kick at his face, but, unthinkingly, Jonah grabbed her foot and pushed it back. She lost her balance and he smacked her two good times before kicking her away. She spat on the floor, and regarded him with rage. Jonah threw a punch, but Jessica blocked it and looped his arm, hitting two facial strikes of her own. Jonah shook them off and attempted to jerk himself free, but the bitch held him fast. She attempted a knife-edged thrust to his throat, but Jonah used his free hand to catch hers and wrench back her fingers. She yelled in pain, and Jonah forearmed her, finally freeing himself. He wrung Jessica's arm behind her back, intending to slam her into the west wall, but she blocked the goal by getting a foot up against the wall. She then put her weight into it to push them both to the floor. Jonah's landing was awkward, and knocked some of the breath out of him. Jessica, on the other hand, used the momentum to keep rolling, and made it to her hands and knees. It was at that point that she retrieved the razor that she'd dropped.

At that moment, Jonah's ethereality must have balanced him, at least in some small way. Just like in the numerous trainings, he began to see the little details; take inventory of the little emotions. Jessica was good. Better than good, actually—Creyton had taught her well. But Jonah's fuel was base-level, and purer because of that. It included the indignity of the great man who lay in a pool of his own blood mere feet away. That was the thing that made Jonah block Jessica's swipe with the razor, despite being unarmed. What made him block her again, and dodge the next blow. And it was the thing that let him know that as good as Jessica was, she was too sure of herself. Too cocky, and too assured of victory. If he hung on for just few more moments, her hubris would cost her.

And it did.

She made a slice at Jonah's heart, and he flung his arm upward and knocked her swing astray. The mistake left her open on the left side. Jonah made to exploit that when she shouted, "ENOUGH!"

Jonah's body defied all his desires and commands, and froze at her will. Jessica had used her secret ethereal weapon…the C.P.V. She'd stopped him in his tracks.

Jessica wiped blood from her mouth and then smoothed out her shirt. "Now you understand why it is stupid to ever fight me," she told him. "One would have thought you'd have learned that after what I did to Tony. But then again, you're a dumbass."

She wiped the razor off on her sleeve as the smug smile returned to her face. "You're hurting. I get it. But I have the perfect solution for your grief. I will give you the opportunity to join the old man down there."

She came into Jonah's personal space. "Look at me," she said in that dark, provocative tone.

Cursing, Jonah looked her in the eye. He felt such hatred that his eyes were almost burning.

"Now, take this razor," commanded Jessica.

She extended it, and Jonah took it, all his struggles ineffective.

"Now, the beautiful part." Jessica's voice was laden with pleasure. "Put the razor on the right side of your neck, and slice into your carotid artery. Do it slowly. I am in no hurry."

Growling, Jonah raised the razor to his neck. He had no control over the action. He struggled, but Jessica's ethereality was too strong.

The blade began to piece his neck several seconds later. He was going to kill himself, right here in front of Jessica, who smiled as though this was a rapturous experience.

Was this how his physical life was going to end? In complete and utter failure? He'd defied Mr. Steverson's final request of him in order to save his life, and Jessica killed him anyway. Now Jonah was going to join him, no more able to defend himself than his dear friend had been.

But then something began to happen. Thinking anew about Mr. Steverson's murder instigated renewed rage within Jonah. It was powerful; blinding. Jessica had taken the man away from his wife. His daughters. From the patrons of S.T.R., who loved his stories. She'd taken him away from Harland and Amanda. From Jonah himself. It made his blood boil, and his throat began to burn with bilious heat. And he was supposed to just give up? He was supposed to allow Mr. Steverson's murder to mean nothing?

"NO!"

He ripped the razor away from his throat. Whatever ethereal yoke Jessica had over him was gone. He'd broken her control.

Jessica stumbled back, as if she'd physically been pushed away when Jonah broke her hold. She stared at him, dumbfounded. "How did you—? How—?"

Jonah rushed her. She was too stunned to defend herself. Without conscious thought, he restrained her on the floor. One of her arms was underneath her, and consequently pinned under both of their weights. Jonah had her other arm gripped above her head. The razor, which she'd stupidly handed to him, was now at her throat.

"Jonah, you can't do this," said Jessica, fearful. "You don't have it in you—"

"Shut up." Jonah's barely heard his lifeless, guttural voice over the blood in his ears. "Don't say another fucking word."

Jessica's breathing was rapid; it was obvious that she grasped for mental straws. But she came up with nothing.

Somewhere on the cusp of Jonah's hearing, there were footsteps in another part of the room. It was white noise. Meaningless. Then he heard voices.

"Oh my God! That's Jonah's boss!"

That was Terrence. Then, his sister spoke.

"Jonah, it's Reena," was her tense statement. "She is not worth it. You don't want to do this."

"I've never wanted anything more!" barked Jonah. "She deserves to die!"

"Death isn't real, Jonah—"

"LOOK AT MR. STEVERSON!" Jonah shouted. "TAKE A GOOD LONG LOOK! DON'T GIVE ME THAT BULLSHIT ABOUT DEATH BEING FALSE! HE IS DEAD, AND THIS BITCH IS DEAD WITH HIM!"

There were more footsteps. The rest of his friends must have turned up, because Reena cried out, "Wait! Don't say anything!"

The new arrivals seemed to spark a brainwave in Jessica. "You can't kill me, Jonah," she repeated.

"Why can't I?" rasped Jonah. "Please enlighten me."

"Your girlfriend wouldn't like it."

That made Jonah blink. He heard a sharp intake of breath from someone, but ignored it. Was Jessica talking about Vera? That was rather random. "What the fuck does that mean?"

"She could never look at you the same way again," said Jessica. "Not if you murdered her sister."

Jonah gaped. From afar, Spader exclaimed, "SAY WHAT!"

"You're lying," he told her. "You're lying to save your worthless life!"

"I swear it's true, Jonah—"

"Vera's sister's name is Madison!"

Something flashed in Jessica's eyes. "That's my middle name," she revealed. "Jessica Madison Hale. Did she tell you that her name was Altivera Haliday, or some such bullshit? No, it's Altivera Hale. We grew up in a seven-room house; the address is 810 Colerain Place. We even shared the same bedroom. My bed was at the wall, and Altivera's bed was near the door because she had a fear about sleeping near windows. Tell him, Altivera!"

Jonah's entire world was burning. He was surprised not to see real-life embers raining down around him. It was a lie. It had to be a lie.

Numbly (but still maintaining his grasp on Jessica), he turned his head, but saw none of his friends. He had a self-imposed tunnel vision that was completely directed at Vera.

"Vera." Jonah's voice, previously inhuman, was now supplicating. "She's lying. Please... tell me she's lying!"

Vera fell to her knees, and began to sob. This behavior was so out of character that it threw Jonah off guard. Liz infringed on his tunnel vision and embraced Vera's shoulders.

For some stupid reason, Jonah still clung to some last desperate hope that it was a lie, because Vera hadn't actually said anything.

"I think that's confirmation enough," said Jessica. "Therefore, you can't kill me in front of my sister."

Jonah turned his focus back to Jessica, and pressed the blade further on her neck. Her eyes widened.

"What the hell are you doing?" Jessica squeaked. "Now you have proof that—"

"It was you," whispered Jonah. "You were the one that was born evil. You were the one who threw Vera through that coffee table and scarred her. You're the reason why she doesn't think she's beautiful; the reason she has trust issues. You would have watched her get killed tonight, and had no problem with it. You only revealed that to save your life. But all you did was tell me that Vera is the way she is because of you."

Jessica made to respond, but Jonah elevated the razor far up to her throat that the thing was indented in her flesh.

"Stop talking," he said. "I'm no expert on killing, but I'm pretty sure that move your mouth too much more, flesh will get cut. But it doesn't matter, slut. It doesn't matter."

Jonah didn't hear his friends' protests. He blocked them out.

But then another presence emerged in the room. Jonah was so steeped in rage and hatred that he barely registered it.

"Very good, Rowe," said an inhuman voice.

It was Creyton. But Jonah still didn't care.

"I never imagined that you had it in you," Creyton continued. "I am pleasantly surprised."

Jessica half-smiled. She knew that she was saved.

But then—

"Do it, Rowe. Kill her."

She hadn't expected that. The glee faded from her face.

"Hear that, Inimicus?" Now it was Jonah who had the cold smirk. "Your beloved Transcendent doesn't give two shits what happens to you. He just gave me permission to end you."

"Seriously, Jonah?" said Terrence from afar. "You're gonna listen to Creyton now?"

"Ignore him, Rowe," snapped Creyton. "He doesn't understand. Now kill her. She is guilty of more than you know."

Jonah's hand began to tremble. It would be so easy…so easy to kill her, to avenge Mr. Steverson…not even Creyton would miss her…

"Jonah."

Jonah's eyes widened. The last time he'd heard that voice, it had come out of an outdated radio, warning him not to lose his cool.

"Jonathan." Creyton was cold. "This matter has nothing at all to do with you. This boy has experienced loss, and now he had earned the right to vengeance."

"As though you care about what he's going through," grumbled Jonathan. He returned his focus to Jonah. "Jonah, this is not who you are. You are not now—nor have you ever been—a harbinger of vengeance. Drop the blade, son."

"Do you see Mr. Steverson?" Now Jonah's voice cracked. "You see him, Jonathan? This bitch here did that….she killed my friend. She deserves nothing less."

"That's right, Rowe," said Creyton.

"It's not right," said Jonathan. "Not in the slightest!"

"This is who you've become, Rowe!" Creyton's voice was full of fervor. "All roads have led to this! Southern Shores. The Curaie's strong-arming of you, and displacing you. Not to mention all that Lockman has put you through. And now this. You've changed, Rowe. Accept the man that you've been hardened into. Light is past. Dark is now."

Dark is now…

Those words had a curious effect on Jonah. A wrong effect. The words just didn't mesh well with his spirit.

"What would you have me do, Jonathan?" asked Jonah in a quiet voice. "Mr. Steverson was close to me, which means that I'll never speak to him again. What do you think he'd say if I let her up from here?"

"He wouldn't want you betraying yourself." Jonathan's response was instant. "He would say that you are better than soiling your spirit with blood spilled through premeditated murder. Drop the blade, son."

Jonah looked down at Jessica, who stared back at him in unbridled terror. A damn coward. Dangerous and conniving, but once the power and control were out of her hands, she punked out. She was just another coward.

A coward not worth the decision he was about to make. Tears breached his eyes. They didn't fall until now.

Jonah had dug into Jessica's flesh until a surface-level slit formed at her throat. A thin line of blood saw open air because of that fact.

"Now you've got a scar just like your sister," he whispered.

Then he tossed the razor aside, and shrank away from Jessica.

He heard sighs of relief, and a low "Thank God" from Liz. But he felt none of their feelings. He didn't feel anything.

Creyton roared in fury. "You weak, pathetic fool!" he snarled. "You couldn't even perform a simple murder! Even when it was justified! You are a disgrace, boy. Let me show you how it's done. It shall be your last sensation."

He extracted a short, jagged spike from his wooden staff and made to plunge it through Jonah's chest.

Then, what felt like the world's most powerful vacuum pulled at Jonah's back, and he felt himself get yanked from the danger zone. He was pulled until he was in his friends' midst. Reena and Terrence grabbed at him and pulled him into a standing position. He didn't acknowledge them, but only because he searched for the source of that ethereality.

It was Jonathan who was responsible. His hand was still aimed at Jonah. Creyton looked at him in shock and fury.

"Leave the kids alone, Thaine." There was a ringing chord in Jonathan's voice. "If you want a victim, here I am. Take me, if you can."

Creyton's eyebrows rose. "You cannot interfere, Jonathan," he said slowly. "You couldn't do so as a Protector Guide, and you can do even less than that now. The Curaie would have your lifeblood."

"To hell with the Curaie, Thaine," Jonathan shot back. "I don't give a damn what they do to me anymore; truly I don't. Your carnage and manipulation will not hurt my students."

"Do not call me Thaine," snarled Creyton. "That man died when his supposed allies left him in the cold."

"You lost your mind!" said Jonathan. "You wanted us to pervert the very essence of life! You were the betrayer, not us!"

"Tearing oneself from obscurity is not betrayal, Jonathan!" barked Creyton. "If you had acknowledged my superiority then, perhaps you wouldn't have died that night!"

"YOU WERE THE MOST GIFTED OF US, THAINE!" Jonathan shouted. "Why could you never see that? Why did you have to embark in darkness?"

"I have no time for this," muttered Creyton. "Disciples, destroy him. Whoever succeeds can have his spirit."

Several Deadfallen disciples came into view, dropping twigs at their feet. Jonah's friends raised their weapons, but Jonathan shook his head.

"The fight is mine," he told them. "Stay out of it." Then he faced the disciples between him and Creyton. "One chance, Thaine. Tell them to back off. We will be face to face, regardless of your choice."

Jonathan began to walk to Creyton. A disciple chucked a meat hook at him. He swatted it aside, and with hands that glowed gold, sent the man flying across the room without even touching him. Another man raised a full-on sword, but Jonathan rendered it useless by causing it to splinter and crack with his ethereal power. That guy got knocked backward as well. Jonathan barely even broke stride.

The Deadfallen disciple nearest to Creyton pulled a bow smaller than Daniel's and let an arrow fly.

"Jonathan!" screamed Reena, but she needn't have.

Jonathan caught the arrow, literally caught it, turned in a full circle so as to gain more momentum, and jabbed it into the man's upper chest. With a howl of pain, he fell.

Creyton was stunned. "I thought you found practitioners of violence abhorrent," he murmured. "Thought you were honorable."

"I am mostly a peaceable spirit by choice," said Jonathan, "but violence is the only language you'll understand."

Creyton shrugged. "Pick a weapon, then."

Jonathan raised his golden-glowing hands. "I have everything I need right here."

Creyton grimaced, and swung his staff. Jonathan blocked that with sparks of gold, and shoved Creyton back. With a snarl, Creyton grabbed Jessica and shoved her roughly aside, dispensing with his jacket as he did so. Jonathan also threw away his duster. Jonah hadn't ever seen him without it, but that was beside the point.

Creyton flung down a twig and disappeared, but re-appeared near Jonathan seconds later. Unfortunately for him, Jonathan blocked his strike by grabbing his arm at the wrist.

"Evade and overtake?" demanded Jonathan. "I taught you that maneuver, Thaine!"

"Here's something new," growled Creyton.

His hand darkened, and what looked like smoke flew from there into Jonathan's face. Jonathan grunted in surprise, and swatted the stuff away. It was then that Creyton smashed him across his face with a forearm, which knocked Jonathan back. Creyton attempted to use the tip of his staff to vanquish Jonathan, but the spirit dodged left, and spat lifeblood into Creyton's face. The psychotic Spirit Reaper roared, and rubbed at his eyes.

Jonah heard his friends gasp in surprise, and he was right there along with them. Unless his eyes betrayed him, his dear mentor had just fought dirty to get an advantage. But he was far from repulsed. It was quite a pleasant surprise to know that the Jonathan was no paragon.

"Damn you!" snarled Creyton, who still rubbed at his eyes.

"Being damned yourself blinds you more than my lifeblood ever could," growled Jonathan.

Creyton relinquished the essence of a spirit he'd usurped and guided it at Jonathan, but Jonathan calmly raised his hands and dissipated it, hopefully giving the spirit peace. But this turned out to be a distraction, as Creyton raised a hand and caused an unconscious Deadfallen disciple to levitate into the air. Jonathan's eyes widened.

"No, Thaine!" he cried. "Don't do it! You'll break his neck!"

Creyton couldn't have cared less as he pointed to fingers and sent the man flying Jonathan's way. Jonathan ducked, but as soon as the man flew over his head, he caught him at the beltline, which probably saved the man's physical life. Opportunistic as ever, Creyton charged with his staff forward, aiming to stab Jonathan in the back and finally vanquish him.

"NO!" shouted Jonah.

But at the last second, Jonathan lost all of his substance and went transparent and weightless. Creyton stabbed empty air, and then Jonathan regained form, snatched the staff from Creyton's hands, and whacked him across the chest with it.

Creyton flew onto a table, but continued to roll when he got there, graceful as a cat. He landed on his feet, and his eyes were aflame with anger as he eyed Jonathan. He took an inhumanly deep breath, raised his hands, and splayed all of his fingers. The fingers turned the darkest shade of black that Jonah had ever seen. Then Creyton knelt down and placed his fingertips on the floor. A wave of black began to spread from his fingers like living water.

Jonathan made an exclamation of horror, which Jonah didn't like. As if panicked, Jonathan placed his own fingertips on the floor, and the same effect took place, only Jonathan's wave was gold.

The colors met, and the room began to quake.

"Transcendent!" screamed Jessica. "What's happening?"

"Shut up, girl!" barked Creyton.

He growled in frustration, while Jonathan bared his teeth.

"The bitch had a good question!" said Terrence. "What is Creyton trying to do? While we're at it, what's Jonathan doing himself?"

"I don't know!" answered Reena. "This is ethereality that I have never seen!"

The room shook violently, which actually knocked Liz and Douglas to the floor. They were about to get back to their feet when Spader caught Jonathan rigorously shaking his head no, and got everyone's attention.

"Protect yourselves, kids!" Jonathan shouted. "Protect each other!"

It seemed as though everyone took the hint. They moved away and then joined together. Jonah realized that his arm was wrapped in Vera's. He glanced at her, but her eyes were tightly shut. He didn't know if she was braced for impact or preventing herself from shedding further tears. He decided not to think about it right now.

Then there was a vicious, yet oddly muffled explosion that knocked everyone down to the floor. The room rocked, jostled, teetered...and then it was done.

Jonah opened his eyes and winced.

All around them, they were dazzled by gold. It was quite a sight, but what lay beyond was pure disaster.

It seemed that Creyton had tried to collapse the room. That dark essence had the function to make the room cave in on itself. Jonathan's golden protection must have saved them. Jonah, his friends, Jonathan himself, and Mr. Steverson's body were all that were present. Jessica, the other Deadfallen disciples, and Creyton were nowhere in sight. Jonathan stood at the center of the room with one hand still outstretched.

"Are all of you alright?" he demanded.

"Yeah," said Reena, "we're good, sir. Thanks to you."

"Glad to hear it," said Jonathan, pleased.

"Did Creyton blow himself up?" asked Spader. "Is that too much to hope for?"

"I'm afraid so, Royal," grumbled Jonathan. "He grabbed Jessica and used a twig portal to flee. He knew that I wouldn't chase him because my focus was on protecting all of you. The other disciples…he abandoned them. I couldn't save them."

No one was too upset about that, which Jonathan frowned at.

"All life is precious, people," he said in a stern tone. "Now, then," a portion of the gold faded, which exposed the gaping hole that had once been the door, "return to the main chamber. This sordid adventure is nearly over, but there are a few more details to iron out. Elizabeth, take these."

Jonathan used his free hand to extract three vials from his pocket, which then floated of their own accord to Liz's hands. Every vial was full of milky liquid.

"I want you to use the *Astralimes* to go to the Spirits of Vitality and Peace," he commanded. "One vial is for Nellaina, the other two are to be replicated, and used for mass production. Give them to Fuller and Malik. No one else. And Elizabeth, make sure Nellaina drinks that directly. No water afterward."

"This is the cure to the Mindscope Illness?" Liz cradled the vials as though they were rare jewels. "How did you get it?"

"Not important," said Jonathan, but he didn't sound short or irritated. "The point is that this illness ends now."

"Does this mean that the plague has been averted?" Liz sounded so hopeful.

Jonathan contemplated something. "Short answer, yes," he said at last. "But we will talk more later, when we're all back at the estate. Vera, you and I will have private conversation as well. But never mind that now. Go on, everyone."

Vera swallowed. Douglas attempted to place a hand on her shoulder, but she shrugged him away. Everyone turned to leave, but Jonah remained unmoved, staring at Mr. Steverson. Terrence grabbed his shoulder.

"Come on, man," he said, but Jonah refused.

"What about…about…" Jonah couldn't bring himself to refer to Mr. Steverson as "the body."

"I will take care of it, Jonah," said Jonathan in voice of understanding. "And, unlike with the Curaie, you can rest assured that my words will not ring hollow when I say them. Now, please go."

Reluctantly, Jonah allowed Terrence to guide him away. He didn't want to see Mr. Steverson like that anyway.

When they returned to the main chamber, it was much more populated than it had been when Jonah ran out of it. There were several more Networkers and Spectral Law practitioners. The apprehended Deadfallen disciples were ethereally chained in a single-file line, and all of their twigs had been confiscated and broken. Jonah saw that India Drew's mouth was still covered.

Felix stood apart from everyone else, deep in conversation with...Samantha Lockman. Maybe conversation was a bit of a stretch, because Felix was doing more nodding and writing than anything else. Jonah might have given the matter further thought, but he couldn't find it within himself to care. Everything going on—everything—was insignificant in comparison to Mr. Steverson's murder.

Patience spoke with Dace Cross, who then looked at Jonah and had the audacity to nod with approval. The hell with that bitch. Jonah sought only his friends, who sat near the wall where the Deadfallen disciples' initial heat blast had occurred. He and Terrence joined them.

"So what are we doing?" asked Terrence.

"Couldn't really tell you," said Reena. "Felix just told us to sit here and look worse for wear. Which isn't hard."

'What for?" mumbled Jonah.

"All he said was that it would help matters once all these Elevenths were cleared out," said Douglas. "God only knows what that means."

"Sterling and Raymond went back to the Decessio house," Liz told Terrence. "Once everything was well in hand, I mean. Sterling was so glad to finally feel helpful that he didn't even care. They didn't wait for you because...well, I'm sure they figured that your place was here. I told them to tell Mrs. Decessio that you were fine."

"Damn, Lizzie," said Terrence, "you just know me so well!"

Patience was all business, so he didn't say anything to them. He did, however, acknowledge them with a short, respectful nod. The he refocused on the task, nodding at Cross. The woman made a hand motion, which chained the Deadfallen disciples' hands to their feet as well.

"Full speed ahead, folks," said Patience. "We've got a very busy day ahead."

In about two minutes, everyone had used the *Astralimes* to leave. The place was much quieter as a result. Jonah welcomed that. Cross and all the other Networkers who showed up after the fact were all pleased with the haul. They were as excited as kids. And Jonah couldn't give less of a damn. The "impressive" haul didn't even matter to him. They took credit for something they hadn't done. The only one of them that had done anything was Patience, yet they were going to treat it as a team effort, and skate over the fact that others were responsible. Assholes.

Felix walked to their group after Samantha disappeared. "You guys look like you have been through hell and back," he commented. "That's good. It's gonna help things immensely."

"Felix," said Reena. "It's late. Please stop being mysterious. Why is our current disposition a good thing?"

"I'm sorry for all the mystery, "said Felix. "But it will all make sense right about—"

A roar of rage on the stairs made them all jump. Felix smiled in anticipation.

"—now," he finished. The smile on his face faded, and he adopted a somber expression.

Balthazar Lockman stormed into the chamber, flanked by his people as well as several police. He looked terrible; his nose was smashed, courtesy of Jonah, and there was a knot at the back of his head, compliments of Douglas. The other members of The Lockman Association looked rough themselves, but not as bad as their boss.

Spader snickered at him, but the anger-crazed man paid him no attention.

"Here they are, officers!" Lockman bellowed. "The ones that that assaulted us! They are members of a known cult that refer to themselves as Eleventh Percenters. It's a fancy name for subversive activities meant to inhibit innocent people's thinking. Arrest them right now!"

"Officers," said Felix, "I hope to resolves this calmly. My friends and I have been through a hard night."

"Duscere?" Lockman looked surprised. "What the hell are you doing here?"

"Hoping to end your reign of terror once and for all." Felix did it well; he even added urgency to his voice. "Officers, I apologize that this man has summoned you here under false pretenses, but he is the true charlatan."

Everyone looked around, confused. One of the officers stepped forward.

"Son, this is Balthazar Lockman," he said, puzzled. "This man has neutralized cults all over the country—"

"Sorry, officer," interrupted Felix, "but he's done no such thing."

Terrence, Reena, and everyone else hung on to Felix's every word. Jonah, despite everything, even found himself interested.

"Where did Duscere get dirt on Lockman?" Douglas whispered to Spader.

"No idea," said Spader, "but I'm anxious to hear it."

"Balthazar Lockman hasn't neutralized a single cult over his entire career," Felix went on. "His entire rep is a front designed to bolster support and secure backing."

Lockman laughed with derision. "That is a very serious accusation, Duscere. You would do well to move along while you still can. Perhaps this is due to the grudge you hold against me after New Orleans."

"Funny that you mention New Orleans," said Felix. "Outing that necromancer cult was your breakthrough success, no? Well, I worked the files of everyone whose lives you ruined during those months, and found something very interesting."

Lockman gave Felix a dirty look as the sazer pulled notes from his pocket.

"Turns out they all happened to have ergot in their systems throughout the entire investigation," revealed Felix.

Reena's mouth dropped. Spader blinked. Jonah gaped at Lockman. He'd seen the man's demeanor crack before, but it hadn't ever been due to fear.

"You did the thing well, man," conceded Felix. "I grant you that. You even made sure that the files were sealed. But after I found that little piece of info, I did a little more digging, and discovered that the so-called necromancer cult were no more than tourists who wanted to see the cemeteries. They weren't trying to escape at all. They were trying to leave town. People were more inclined to believe your lies, though, because you were who you were, and they pitied you."

Even some of Lockman's own people looked at him with confusion. Lockman's eyes flashed.

"This is utter absurdity," he snapped. "You have no proof of this garbage!"

"Actually," Felix flashed a rare smile, "I do. You rent out office space everywhere you investigate. It's only inspected by you, isn't that right? Well, I inspected your office space in Rome near the Grannison-Morris estate, and found evidence of a hallucinogen designed to flow through the vents. God only knows how many interviewees you had that said insane thoughts about the estate."

"Foolish," said Wyatt readily. "If you knew there were hallucinogens in the air in those offices, why weren't we affected?"

"Simple," responded Felix. "Lockman has put the idea of self-fulfilling prophecy into all of your heads, right? And doesn't he always toast to a job well done before your investigations actually commence? With Chateau, I believe?"

They looked at Felix, stunned. Jonah did as well. How did he know all this?

"There is a nullifying agent in the Chateau," Felix told Wyatt. "Lockman has been drugging all of you for years; I'm surprised your bodies never developed a resistance to the antidote. But go get checked out. Your blood's probably teeming with the crap."

"We get blood work done yearly!" protested another Lockman Association employee. "It's a requirement for our job!"

"I imagine that it is," replied Felix, "but aren't your physicals always done by Lockman's personal medical team? Didn't that seem a tad bit odd?"

The woman fell silent, looking stunned and betrayed. Terrence whistled.

"This is an outrage!" spat Lockman, but all eyes remained on Felix.

"I have evidence dating back to the whole thing in New Orleans that Balthazar Lockman has manufactured every event that made him noteworthy," he told them all. "He has leaned heavily on his background in horticulture to implement the proper tools to twist the minds and bodies of people. The Lockman Association is a sham."

Jonah thought back to Lockman's accusations of substance abuse; how he'd jumped to that conclusion so readily. It was because he was guilty of that very thing himself. It seemed that the man abandoned his morals and conscience entirely after he lost his family.

The officer who'd spoken up earlier now looked awkward. "But Mr. Lockman said that these kids assaulted him."

"These people were held against their will in Lockman's office space," said Felix. "They were probably capable of any unspeakable acts while they were trapped there, breathing in his illicit airborne drugs. Believe me, officer—you're not here for them. You're here for Lockman."

Lockman looked crazed, and without warning, lunged at Felix. "You son of a BITCH! I'll kill you! I'll—!"

Felix crowned Lockman in his already damaged face, knocking him back a few inches. The man landed in a heap, out like a light.

Felix adopted an alarmed look. "I—I had no choice, officers," he murmured. "I just reacted; it was self-defense. I had no choice."

"Calm down, son," said the officer, who looked down on Lockman with spite and disdain. "We were right here. The man threatened to kill you. It was justifiable. But for the record—I'm glad you're not a fighter, son. You just about knocked him out of his pants...you don't know your own strength."

Felix gave the man a sheepish shrug, and took a couple steps back.

The other members of the Lockman Association looked like they didn't know what to do. Jonah would have pitied them if he didn't hate every single one of them.

"Look man," Wyatt said to Felix, "I'm sorry. We didn't know—"

"Save it, Faulk." Felix's words were short. "I'm going to have to take a rain check on you sucking up to me. Keep your words for the police. The next couple of months won't be pretty for any of you, I imagine."

Felix turned his back on them, and returned to Jonah and the rest of them. As the Lockman Association people surrendered themselves to the police, one officer looked at Felix with a frown.

"Two questions," he said. "First of all, who are you? And second of all, why did Lockman bring us here? What is this place?"

"I'm Felix Duscere," answered Felix. "I'm a Private Investigator, and have my license to do that right here if you desire to check my credentials. As for your second question...it's my understanding that when my friends here escaped Lockman's office, he gave chase. They eluded him and came to the city here, where my friends Jonah and Vera reside. Why they chose to stop at a tattoo parlor is anyone's guess, seeing as how they've got Lockman's drugs in their system. Unfortunately, Lockman found them because they escaped in one of his vans. I'm thinking there must have been a tracker on it. But if it's all the same to you, I think it's time to carry Lockman and his people away. I want to give my friends here the chance to collect themselves and rest."

The police officer shook his head, neither looking puzzled nor suspicious anymore. Two of them picked up Lockman's unconscious form, and the other officers escorted the other members of the Lockman Association up the stairs. When they were gone, both Jonathan and Samantha reappeared.

"That was the performance of a lifetime, Felix," praised Jonathan.

"Lockman's crimes did half of the work for me," said Felix with a grimace." That was two percent performance, ninety-eight percent truth. This man has destroyed lives and deserves worse…no offense, Samantha."

"None taken," said the spiritess. "And Jonah, Terrence, Reena, all of you—I am so sorry that my father put you through all of this. He has done such unspeakable things in my 'honor.' You deserve more than an apology, but that is all I can do."

"That is far from true," said Reena. "You led Jonah to find Liz's sister. I'm sure she'd damn near worship you if she hadn't already used the *Astralimes* to the Spirits of Vitality and Peace to cure Nella. You also helped us conclude that this was the place where we might get to the bottom of this entire mess. I think I can safely speak for all us when I say that you have nothing to apologize for."

Samantha closed her eyes and nodded. Jonathan placed a hand on her shoulder.

"You've made very difficult decisions," he remarked. "What will you do now?"

"My father compromised everything he believed in when I passed into Spirit, followed so quickly by mom," said Samantha. "I have a feeling that he will have a lot of time to contemplate all he's done. Maybe I can help him. Kind inspirations, warm words in dreams…anything to let him know that he never had to lose himself for me."

Jonathan nodded. "I wish the greatest success in that, Samantha," he said. "You are one of the bravest and most dedicated spiritesses I have ever encountered. Peace and blessings to you and your father. Now and forever."

He embraced the spiritess, and she clung tight to him, as if she knew that she had her work cut out for her. Then, with a quick smile to everyone, she vanished.

"Now, Jonathan," said Felix, "is there anything else—?"

"No, Felix," said Jonathan. "You get to work sanitizing this scene, as well as improvising a vaccine for the sazers. I hope that the materials I gave you will help."

"They will," said Felix. "I'm sure of it."

Jonathan turned to Jonah and his friends. "I want you all to go home and rest," he said. "We will all speak later. And I do mean all of us. But right now, go home."

"So we can use the *Astralimes* freely again?" asked Reena.

"No," said Jonathan. "You will activate the Tally, and I'll be damned if you all get arrested after everything you've done."

"What are we going to do, then?" Jonah's voice was so hollow and flat that he didn't even recognize it.

Jonathan struggled with something, and then walked to one of the doors. "Come here, all of you."

"Um, Jonathan?" said Douglas. "What are you doing?"

"Something I thought I'd never do again," murmured Jonathan. "Make a Threshold of Life."

Jonathan wrenched the door open, and pressed the threshold with his hand five times. It flashed gold each time. "You will walk across this threshold, one by one," he instructed. it will place each of you into your own bedrooms. I will join you soon."

"What are you gonna do, sir?" asked Spader.

"Meeting with the Curaie," answered Jonathan. "I will request my job back, along with their blessing to return to the estate. If they don't grant those things, then I will take my job back, and return home anyway. But as I said, you will be deposited into your own bedrooms. I want you all to get some sleep, even if it's only five minutes."

Jonah grimaced. He didn't think he'd ever achieve sleep again.

"You first, Jonah," said Jonathan. "I think you've earned the right."

Jonah glanced at his friends, who all looked to be in agreement. Except for Vera. Her eyes remained on her feet.

Jonah closed his eyes and stepped across the threshold, ignoring the shifting ground underneath his feet.

28

Reality

Sure enough, Jonah stepped into his room. It was pretty much the way he'd left it. It was so late; the clock read 4:48 A.M.

But he didn't go to bed, though. He was wide awake.

Instant grief descended on him, and before he knew it, hot tears fell down his face.

"I'm sorry, Mr. Steverson." The guilt was heavier than a barbell. "I'm so sorry. Wherever you are, please forgive me—"

His voice caught. He didn't deserve forgiveness. He was the one who had failed. Mr. Steverson told him not to kneel, but he defied him in an effort to save his life. But Jessica killed him despite the defiance. Jonah failed to save him.

He looked outside. It was still dark, but the sky was bursting with stars. It pissed him off. The bright stars enraged him.

The sky shouldn't be so brightly lit when Mr. Steverson was gone. The world should be dark. Nothing great or wonderful should even exist. Nothing joyous. It was an insult.

Jonah wiped his tears. The sadness was shuffled to the back, and now there was only numbness. Just like the night when his grandmother passed into Spirit, he removed his shirt, and lay, barebacked, on the floor. It was still winter, and the floor was freezing, but that was the point. As long as he could feel the cold, it meant that he at least felt something.

This was wrong. Terribly wrong. Mr. Steverson was one of the kindest, most selfless people Jonah had ever met. He had persevered as a young black man through the racism and bigotry of the Jim Crow south. He went to Vietnam and survived. He'd even earned a Purple Heart. He came back stateside, started a family, and opened S.T.R. He gave Jonah a job in good faith. It had been a gamble, because Jonah was an out-of-work accountant who had zero experience working in a bookstore. Jonah had even confided, at least partially, his true identity as an ethereal human to Mr. Steverson, and the man hadn't judged him. Hadn't called him crazy.

The man had lived through all of that to be murdered by a Deadfallen disciple. Who got to keep her physical life. Jonah's vengeance had been prevented.

Where was the fairness in that?

He'd had the razor. He'd broken through Jessica's power. She was stupid enough to hand him her razor, because she had that much confidence in her ethereality. But Jonah had broken through it. The bitch's physical life had been in his hands, and all he was able to do was scar her at the base of her throat. Jessica was now scarred, just like her sister—

Jonah closed his eyes tightly. He would not think of that. No way in hell.

A stiff breeze shocked his shirtless body, but he didn't bother to open his eyes. He knew who was there.

"You may as well leave," he muttered. "Nothing you say will make a damn bit of difference."

"I will not leave, Jonah," said Jonathan. "We have things to discuss, and then I need everyone here to convene—"

"I'm not going anywhere, Jonathan," Jonah told him. "You need to leave me alone."

"We need to talk, Jonah—"

"You had months to talk to me, man." Jonah's coldness was unveiled. "You should've done it then. Now, I don't feel like talking."

"Let me try to help you, Jonah," said Jonathan.

At this, Jonah rose to a sitting position and draped his arms across his knees. "Let me save you the trouble, Jonathan." His voiced matched the hardness of his gaze. "I will tell you all of the bullshit that you want to tell me, and I will even do you the pleasure of telling you why it's bullshit. First thing you'll say is that you know exactly how I feel. That's a lie, because you don't know my heart, and if you're under the assumption that you know what's in my mind, I promise you that you'll be wrong one hundred percent of the time. Second thing you will say is this, too, shall pass. Well, seeing as how we all grieve differently, those words don't help a damn thing. Third thing you will say is that Mr. Steverson is in a better place. No he's not, dammit. The only better place he could be is home with his family!" Jonah threw himself back down to the floor. "And I couldn't even avenge his murder," he growled. "You wouldn't even let me kill Jessica."

"You're damn right I didn't," said Jonathan in a hard voice. "You have no idea how great a thing it is that you didn't kill that woman."

"Yeah? Why?"

"Because you're a good person, Jonah," said Jonathan. "A just, upright man who does the Blue Aura proud!"

Jonah was up on his feet faster than lightning. Jonathan didn't flinch or twitch, but he did look wary as Jonah yanked a baton from his pocket, flicked the bottom switch, and watched the blue essence engulf it.

But he had no intention of attacking Jonathan.

He looked at the blue gleam with irritation and anger. It was the blue that supposedly made him a big deal. The blue that made him stand out.

The blue that did nothing in the world to save Mr. Steverson.

"I never wanted this, Jonathan," he said, eyes still on the baton. "None of it. I'm sure that I didn't have a sudden burst of clarity in my mother's womb and decide to be the Blue Aura. Creyton supposedly sees me as a threat, is that right? The man has probably screwed up my life in ways that I don't even see. Because I'm the Blue Aura. I'm tired of it, Jonathan. I'm sick, and I'm tired! I have no sense of self!

No identity! Hell, the Phasmastis Curaie doesn't even bother to call me by my name! Katarina used my name once, and that just happened tonight! I didn't ask to carry anyone's lives. I didn't ask to be a beacon, or any of that other shit. It was slapped upon me, because of this."

Jonah waved the blue baton in Jonathan's face. For whatever reason, there was a hint of pride in the Protector Guide's eyes. It didn't go unnoticed by Jonah, and it filled him with more anger. Did Jonathan not hear him? Not take him seriously?

"This makes you happy?" he demanded. "Why is that? Because I'm a so-called savior? Because this is blue? In case you didn't hear me the first time, I don't want this shit, Jonathan! Do you know how many times I wished that this baton would gleam some other color? Green, yellow, white—hell, even bloodred, like Trip! But it's blue. It's always blue. For BALANCE? I can't even balance a checkbook, let alone my damn life! And people have got their hopes riding on me? Get them to place their hopes elsewhere; they'll be better off. Mr. Steverson had faith in me—" his voice cracked, but he continued on, "and it got him killed. He got killed because of me. Because of this—fucking—AURA!"

He flung the baton to the floor. The blue light went to a dim spark and then faded. Jonah didn't even look at it, though Jonathan did.

"The least I could have done for him was avenge him," he whispered. "But you didn't let me. Would it have been so bad?"

At that, Jonathan's eyes shot to Jonah, serious, focused, and stern. "It would have been the single most catastrophic action you could have ever performed. If you had done so, you would have destroyed countless lives."

Jonah frowned. That didn't sound like the cryptic, roundabout guidance that Jonathan usually dispensed. It sounded like cold, hard fact. And truth be told, Jonah was scared by it. "How exactly do you figure that?" he asked.

"Come downstairs," said Jonathan, who headed for the bedroom door. "I will explain everything, but everyone else needs to hear it as well."

Jonah grabbed his shirt from the floor, but realized that it bloody and filthy, so he grabbed another one and followed Jonathan downstairs, through the kitchen, and into the family room. It already contained all of his friends. Even some that he hadn't seen in a long while. Of course Trip and the rest of the undesirables were present. Grayson looked at Jonah and gave him a slight nod, which Jonah returned despite himself. A part of him still wondered why Trip hadn't been accosted like everyone else who had been mentioned in Reynolda's article. But after everything that had happened, Jonah realized that it didn't even matter. Besides, he'd already been in perilous situations with Trip once or twice, and they hadn't been great experiences. So no harm, no foul.

Liz had returned, and was in Bobby's arms. But as Jonah looked her over, it seemed as though she wasn't there because she needed Bobby's protection. She was simply there because she loved her boyfriend's grasp. It made him look for Vera, but she'd set herself apart from everyone else. She looked in the opposite direction, and purposefully avoided his eyes. Jonah didn't know what to think of it. She was still his friend, right? Still the same woman he'd confided in, dined with, crashed with, and watched all those Netflix binges with, wasn't she? Should his opinion of her change, simply because her older sister was Jessica Hale?

He tightly shut his eyes. His brain continued to shut down at that notion.

No, not the notion. The fact.

He seated himself next to Terrence and Reena. Jonathan looked over at Vera and shook his head.

"No, Vera," he said. "You will sit among us, not apart."

"It's not a big deal, Jonathan," said Vera in a terse tone.

"It is a big deal, as are you," said Jonathan. "I refuse to allow you to sit apart."

"You know something, Vera?" said Alvin. "You can pick your nose, but you can't pick your family. We say that all the time in our house, usually regarding Aunt Monica."

"Most uncouth, Alvin," commented Liz, "but I think Vera got the gist."

Vera sighed, rose, and sat next to Liz and Bobby. Jonathan waited until she was settled, and then nodded.

"The time has come to tell you the truths that are unknown to you," he announced. "That goes for Jonah as well as everyone else. But before I do that, there are two bits of information that will benefit our moods and our knowledge. Daniel will be here in—now."

The wind picked up, and Daniel stepped into being. Jonathan looked at him.

"Well?"

"You were successful, sir," he said. "The Tally has been disabled, and the sentries that the Curaie had around the estate have all been reassigned. The Deadfallen disciples that were captured tonight are on The Plane with No Name. And Jonathan—"

Jonathan's eyes narrowed, and Daniel stepped up to him to speak in his ear. Jonathan's expression didn't change, but it was clear that what Daniel told him wasn't good. Jonah looked at Reena, who wasn't wearing her dampener, but to his surprise, she performed the cutthroat sign and mouthed, "*Nothing.*"

That surprised him. She didn't glean anything at all?

Daniel left Jonathan's side, and Jonathan seemed to give himself a mental shake.

"Very well," he murmured. "The Curaie's pincers have loosened, and are gone. That's the first piece. The second piece comes from Elizabeth."

Liz stood. She had teared up, but Jonah sensed no sadness. "They administered your tonic to Nella," she said, "and it took hold almost immediately!"

Jonathan smiled hugely. Most everyone was so relieved. Jonah knew that he was.

"She no longer has any need of Ben-Israel's replenishments," continued Liz. "Ben-Israel is still at the Spirits of Vitality and Peace, helping to make huge batches of your cure. He texted me a few minutes ago to update me, and said that Mr. Decessio's Green Aura friends told him that everyone who was introduced to the Mindscope Illness through the tattoo ink will be cured within the hour! Nella will be moved here in about a week. Creyton's plague was averted before it even began."

There were further ripples of relief around the room, but they all ceased when everyone saw Jonathan's face. Very slowly, he closed his eyes.

"As I said," he murmured, "it's time for everyone to know all. The first thing that you should all know is that there was never going to be a plague."

The room was silent. Even Trip was surprised. Jonah's eyes narrowed.

"What are you talking about?" he asked. "What about what happened to Nella? The other people who got infected? The tainted tattoo ink?"

"It was all theater," said Jonathan. "Well, theater in the regard that it performed its function of getting you involved, Jonah."

Jonah wondered, but Reena shook her head.

"Wait, that can't be," she said. "That's just not true. This illness has been wreaking havoc all over. Liz and I looked over the symptoms, and Ben-Israel did the same thing from afar. Then there were the Mindscopes that made us all vulnerable. We had them all at the same time—"

"Think of it like this, Reena," said Jonathan, his voice quiet. "Say that you have information that could potentially change the course of the known world. Better yet, since we are talking about this fake plague, say that there is a disease, and you claim to have the only cure. The meek and the innocent don't believe at first, so you make an example by infecting small groups. Here and there, of course; it has to look random. You only infect a small group, because you have to leave a group large enough to frighten. The masses get so afraid, they are willing to do anything for that cure. Including scheming, self-preservation, worrying—all the components of the survival instinct. When people are surviving, they become blind to truths that stare them right in their faces. Theater. And the Mindscope Illness was just that. The people who had been tattooed with the tainted inks were the small group designed to convince everyone. The universal Mindscopes were meant to frighten you all. And when you were all finally convinced—and frightened and worried because of that fact—Creyton got what he wanted, which was free rein to implement his true scheme."

"Which was what?" demanded Jonah.

Jonathan focused on Jonah in such an intense manner that it made him feel a little awkward. "To push you over the brink, Jonah. Creyton played the role of a gaslighter."

Many confused eyes looked between Jonathan and Jonah. Jonah's confused eyes stayed right where they were.

"Gaslighter?" Jonah repeated. "What the hell does that mean?"

"It's the term for a specific kind of mental abuse," began Jonathan, "in which information is corrupted and spun about, usually to aid the abuser in some way, shape, or form. Events and situations are manipulated with the sole intent of making an innocent victim question their own thoughts, perceptions, and sanity. Creyton has been doing this for months, with a rather…unique twist to it. He didn't gaslight you, he gaslit the ethereal world, as well as many Tenths. They were full of false, convoluted information about you, as well as the rest of us. When the perception of you changed, you changed right along with it. It was what Creyton wanted. If you paint someone as unhinged, human nature tends to make them come to act that way. Creyton also took masterful advantage of the Curaie's actions against you."

Jonah frowned. That just sounded so sick. And at the same time, it sounded so…Creyton. "Okay, so he was…gaslighting, or whatever…making people believe lies about me, about all of us, knowing how we would react. Why did he want to push me to the brink?"

Jonathan's mouth twitched. "Before I continue, Jonah, there is something else that you have to know. Something that you all need to know. Because the truth of things won't make sense if you do not."

Jonathan looked at Daniel, who sighed, and stood. The archer sounded so resigned.

Jonathan nodded, and Daniel took an arrow and pricked his own forefinger. Jonathan removed something from his duster pocket, which Jonah recognized as the sharp object that Creyton aimed to stab him with earlier. At that moment, Jonathan's fingers began to glow gold. He held the blade out for everyone to see. With his own look of resignation, he uttered, "Lifeblood, illuminate the truth."

The blade began to gleam black, as though Creyton himself were there, still wielding it. Everyone gaped. Trip rolled his eyes.

"Put your tongues back in your mouths, children," he mumbled. "We Elevenths don't need fingerprint dusting equipment. That is an ethereal tactic to show the aura of the weapon's previous owner."

"Shut up, Titus," snapped Daniel. "No one likes a...what did Terrence call it? Smartass."

Trip's fists tightened. Terrence grinned, but it faded just as soon as it had come. Jonah shrugged.

"So it's Creyton's weapon," he said. "It's the one you took earlier tonight during your fight. It gleams black. What else is new?"

"Keep watching," said Jonathan without looking at him.

Jonah scoffed, but did as he was asked. As everyone watched, the black seemed to lighten somewhat...take on a different color...

"Not black," said Jonathan with a sigh. "Midnight blue."

Jonah heard, but didn't believe. Douglas' mouth fell open. Most everyone else looked at Creyton's weapon like it was toxic.

"I believe that Reena told you once that you were the eighth Blue Aura in history, Jonah," mumbled Jonathan. "That was not the truth. You were not the eighth, but the ninth."

Numbly, Jonah looked at the weapon, and then back at Jonathan. "Creyton is a Blue Aura, too?" he whispered.

He willed Jonathan to say no.

But it didn't happen.

"Indeed he is," said the spirit.

"Wait," said Spader, "hang on. I ain't color-blind. That is black. Creyton is a black aura."

"There is no black aura, Royal," said Jonathan. "All the colors of the spectrum make black. There couldn't be an Eleventh Percenter with a black aura. Creyton's aura is blue. It appears black because it has…turned dark."

"It's turned dark?" cried Jonah. "What the hell does that mean?"

"I plan to explain it to you," said Jonathan sternly, "provided you calm down and listen."

Jonah sat there, breathing heavily. Then he gave a terse nod.

"Thaine was the eighth Blue Aura," said Jonathan. "Treated like a huge deal from the very start. He was ambitious, highly intellectual, and sadly, ruthless. I need not go into his history once again. But when he enacted the Decimation, his aura turned dark, along with his spirit. Then you were born into this world, Jonah. Another Blue Aura, but vastly different from Creyton. You are a good man, plain and simple. Light Blue. It's one of the reasons that Creyton bade you walk away when the two of you first met."

"He warned me to walk away because I was a Blue Aura like him?" Jonah demanded. "Are you joking?"

Jonathan took a slow breath. "He wanted you to walk away because he was afraid of what you represented, Jonah. He still is, actually."

"That I can believe," said Terrence, but Jonah ignored the words.

"Bullshit," he said. "I am no match for Creyton."

"You've beat him already," Liz reminded him.

"Because I took a volatile endowment from a bunch of psychotic spirits!" said Jonah. "A feat made possible only by the fact that my aura balanced it!"

"A win is a win," said Spader.

"That win is water under the bridge now," said Jonah, feeling his impatience elevate again. "Creyton achieved Praeterletum. He came back from the grave."

"Which brings us back to the reason he wanted to push you over the edge," said Jonathan.

"And what is that reason?" demanded Jonah. "What was the point?"

Jonathan looked at the flames in the fireplace. The way the flames danced in his eyes made him look as eerie as Creyton. Through all the negativity, Jonah briefly felt thankful that Jonathan was on their side. "Creyton's plan goes all the way back to the trip you took last summer," he began. "When that suuvus at the diner, influenced by India Drew, made you look guilty of things you hadn't done. That occurred after the first blanket Mindscope, which was something that Creyton hadn't been able to do until after he achieved Praeterletum. It was the one where the Deadfallen disciples siphoned essence off of you all."

"Was that a lie, too?" asked Terrence. "Because Daniel is here! And all of us felt that!"

"Yes and no," said Jonathan. "That very first one, where Daniel rescued you all from the Deadfallen's colored stings? That one was real. But the subsequent ones were not. They were show. A subdued mind, like when a subject is asleep, is quite vulnerable."

"So the Desert of the Ethereal wasn't real, either?" asked Jonah.

Jonathan's eyes darkened. "It's very real," he grumbled. "A place of tortured spirits and spiritesses should not exist, but yes, that's a real Astral place. You've just never seen its actual location; as I said, all the Mindscopes after the first one were for show."

"I'm going back to that sleep vulnerability thing," said Jonah, still not entirely convinced. "We were all awake the other times we had Mindscopes!"

"It was like a Haunting, son," said Jonathan. "Once the affliction was planted, it could be forcibly flared up at any time. But I want you to understand something, Jonah. Everything that has happened—the suuvus getting to you, Lockman, the Mindscope illness, the gaslighting, everything—was to push you overboard."

"But how was that illness going to push me?" asked Jonah. "I wasn't even involved until Nella!"

"Bingo." Daniel had left all the explanations to Jonathan up to that point. "A personal connection. One that gave you the desire to get involved."

Jonah looked at the both of them. He didn't like where this was going. Truth be told, he hated it. "And how was this supposed to end? What was I supposed to do once I was pushed over the edge?"

Concern colored Jonathan's face again. "It was to end with you committing murder."

There was another tangible silence in the room. Jonah felt like he was going to be sick. The thought of murder made him sick. Just the thought of it.

"Wait," he said suddenly. "Jessica…she was supposed to kill Mr. Steverson all along? Was that the act supposed to push me over the edge?"

"Yes," sighed Jonathan. "When that trace of scarlet appeared in the Vitasphera, it was meant for him, not Prodigal. Anyone who knows you knows you would go to save Prodigal if you could; the hunkered down sazers with him were merely an added bonus. It was merely another step in the plan to get you worked up. Of course the good fortune that came out of it, which included the rescuing of the sazers and the welcoming of new life, were not a part of the plan. But Creyton adapted, and worked it into the context of his plans."

Jonah buried his face into his hands, willing any remaining anger to keep the tears at bay. That was a fail. "I never had a chance to save him," he whispered. "I could have prevented this whole thing had I known."

"That is unfair, Jonah," said Reena. "There isn't anything you could have done, especially since you were in the dark with the rest of us."

"Why was Mr. Steverson there?" Jonah asked Jonathan. "Why wasn't he at home?"

"He was worried about you, son," answered Jonathan. "You messaged him for Bryce's keys, but after giving the matter some thought, he felt that leaving the keys wasn't enough. His time as a soldier may have long since passed, but he still retained the code to leave no man behind. He was your friend, and in many ways, viewed you as a son. So in his eyes, he couldn't just drop off the keys and go home. So he came back with the goal of assisting you in any way possible." Jonathan shook his head. "That was when he fell into the clutches of Jessica

Hale. The final piece of the puzzle was in. All she had to do at that point was manipulate your emotions to the proper level, and...you know the rest."

Jonah was unable to stem the tears after Jonathan's words. Mr. Steverson had come to help him. He didn't know how to help, but he came to help anyway. A loyal soldier to the end. Little did he know that the enemy expected his sense of honor and loyalty to lure him to the tattoo parlor. It was just like a deer prancing into a trap. His good qualities cost him his physical life. That had been the plan all along.

"There is something I don't understand," said Magdalena. "How would Creyton know enough to tell Jessica that Jonah and his boss were so close?"

"Because about two years ago, Creyton worked with us, disguised as Roger," mumbled Jonah. "He'd used someone else's likeness and essence to disguise himself, remember how I told all of you that? He knew that we were all tight. I was stupid to think that he'd forget what he learned about us back in the old bookstore."

Bobby sneered. "And he passed all that information over to Jessica, who exploited it."

"Deceitful, skank twat," growled Reena.

Vera rose from her seat, impatiently wiping her face.

"Sit down, Vera," said Jonathan.

"Jonathan—"

"No, Vera." The Protector Guide was stern. Intractable. "Do not think me heartless, but you are one of us. And unfortunately, truth doesn't cease to be truth just because you distance yourself from it."

Vera bit her bottom lip, and sat back down. She still wouldn't look at Jonah.

Trip snorted. Jonah was on his feet before he knew it, closely followed by Terrence, Reena, and Spader of all people. Trip rose and beckoned to them.

"Bring it," he said. "Fuckin' bleeding hearts."

"Sit down," commanded Jonathan. "And Titus, get out."

Trip's smugness faded. "Excuse me?"

"Get out," repeated Jonathan.

"What the hell for?"

"Because you don't seem to understand the finer points of decency at the moment," said Jonathan. "Now, go."

Trip rose, belligerent. "That woman there is the younger sister of the devil's slut, and you say she is one of us. I, on the other hand, have been here longer than anyone in this room, and I have to leave?"

"Yes, you do." Jonathan's voice was sharp. "Leave. We will have words later."

Trip stared at Jonathan like he wanted to attack him. "If my name was Felix, you wouldn't have a problem."

"If your name was Felix, you wouldn't be a problem," snapped Daniel. "Now do what Jonathan asked you to do, unless you require assistance with it."

Trip stormed out of the front door, slamming it so viciously that things came off of the wall. Jonathan stared at the door for several moments, and then returned his eyes to the other residents.

"We have strayed," he said unnecessarily, "but Mr. Steverson's murder was to be the final straw for you. You were to kill Jessica, which would have made Creyton's plan complete."

"That's something I don't get," said Douglas. "Surely Jessica didn't volunteer to lay down her physical life, did she?"

"Oh no," muttered Jonah. "She was just as surprised as I was when Creyton told me to kill her. He was willing to sacrifice his most loyal disciple just to drive me crazy. But Jonathan, I don't understand—why would turning me to the dark side help Creyton?"

Jonathan regarded the fireplace again, but then looked Jonah in the face. "Jonah, you are the Light Blue Aura," he said. "Forgive the pressure I am about to place onto you, but you are the best hope for causing Creyton's irrevocable defeat. Creyton is the Dark Blue Aura. He has been that since he turned his spirit to the shadows. I don't have to tell you that Light is a threat to dark, no matter the scenario. As long as you are a beacon of Light, Creyton has reason to fear. And if you had killed that woman, you would have embraced the darker aspects of your spirit as well, thereby becoming a dark Blue Aura yourself. You've seen the effect that one dark Blue Aura had on the ethereal world. But two..." Jonathan actually looked afraid. There was no filter, and no masking it. It was genuine fear. "It would have been as if the ethereal world had gotten diagnosed with two terminal illnesses simultaneously. Creyton would no longer have been the primary threat, because if you had turned dark, the Curaie would have to neutralize you, too. Patience told me what Dylan Firewalker told you that evening in the Decessio shed. Something along the lines of Creyton planning something biblically bad? He was right, but he wasn't referring to that infernal plague ruse. It entailed turning you dark. Making you a target; a murderer, just like Creyton."

"Jonathan," said Terrence suddenly, "Dylan said something else that night. He said that the Curaie was trying to stop something, but their efforts were making things worse."

"And they have been, son," said Jonathan. "I think that Jonah knows how their plans have backfired."

"Sending me away from the estate," said Jonah, whose eyes were now on the ceiling. "Clamping down on my decisions...on everyone's decisions. The checks and balances, that damn Tally, taking my batons—and capping all that off with the banishment."

Then Jonah shot up from his seat, startling some of the others. But he paid them no attention. It was Jonathan only.

"Jonah?" said the Protector Guide. "What—?"

"That's why you cut across Katarina that day in the Median," he said. "That's why you stopped her. It's also the reason why she had such an internal struggle concerning giving me my batons back."

He could feel the confusion of his friends, but Jonathan hadn't moved. Daniel murmured, "Bright kid. Too bright."

"Um," murmured Spader, "what is the bright kid talking about?"

"The previous owner of my batons was Creyton," said Jonah. "Katarina was going to tell me that that day."

"Yes," said Jonathan. "That's true."

Jonah had centered himself for the most part, but he felt his emotions flare up again. "That means the Curaie knew what Creyton was trying to do! They knew he was trying to make me unstable, and they didn't tell me? *You* didn't tell me, Jonathan?"

"I cannot speak for the actions of the Curaie, Jonah," said Jonathan. "They make their own decisions. But I am guilty of hiding things from you as well. I was trying to protect you. I was trying not to put more weight on you. And you know as well as I do that if you knew Creyton's master plan, you would have dug deeper in an attempt to prevent it, which would have only made things worse."

Jonah felt his eye twitch. "I don't know how much more of this I can take, man," he warned.

"It's high time you learn," said Daniel.

Jonathan gave Daniel a quelling look. "You're on the hook now, Jonah," he said. "And this is the part that includes all of you."

"What are you talking about, now?" asked Jonah.

"In my absences," began Jonathan, "I did my best to remain involved in everyone's safety. Daniel was my proxy. Lockman was aware of my existence, but everyone else would have been crazed if they discovered that spirits still walked Earthplane. I spoke to everyone when I could, excluding you, Jonah, because I couldn't influence you. Your path was and is your own, and I had faith that the goodness within you would eventually win out. Though I did occasionally tell you that you needed to rein in your temper. My faith in you was not misplaced. I helped you, Terrence, and Reena fix the door—"

"And why was that important, sir?" asked Reena. "Fixing the door was pointless. You emptied the room."

"No, Reena," said Jonathan. "Katarina Ocean did."

"What?" piped up Douglas. "Katarina did that?"

"Indeed," said Jonathan. "She has been assisting me periodically throughout these tumultuous months. Though she had loyalty to the Curaie, she trusts me and disapproved of Lockman. It was one of the reasons Samantha approached her. I got her to tinker with Gate linkages, so that the door would attach to an empty room. I knew that

Lockman would barge in here eventually, and I wanted you all to be protected. But the door had to be damaged; otherwise the Gate might have switched back over to its original state once Lockman hit it with the battering ram. Katarina followed my instructions superbly, and is a most extraordinary woman."

Douglas looked to be in full agreement of that. Jonah felt stupid once again. He'd given Jonathan such hell over that elaborate door thing, and all the while it had been to help them. Liz stood up, actually raising her hand as she did so.

"I have to know, sir," she said, "if the plague was a lie, why were the Deadfallen so hell-bent on getting the files back?"

Jonathan and Daniel looked at each other. Jonah really hated when they did that.

"The files you took outlined not only the false plague, but an event that the Curaie has feared, and attempted to prevent, since my days as a physically living being," said Jonathan.

"Which is what?"

Jonathan looked over them all. "Omega," he said.

The word hung there. It was amazing how Jonathan made that word sound so sinister.

"What's Omega?" asked Bobby.

"The ethereal endgame," answered Jonathan. "The goal is to wipe out an opposing side. It was something Creyton discovered after he was cast out of the estate. When he brought about the Decimation, Omega was his goal. Despite the heavy losses, however, his plan failed."

"Why?" Jonah wasn't sure he wanted to know, but he asked the question anyway.

"Because Omega isn't just about war," Jonathan told him. "Creyton thought that wiping out an opposing side was all there was to it. But that is not the case. There is a spiritual side to Omega. It is about destroying a way of life, not just life itself. And to do that, the target has to include a beacon. A center of hope. Like the Light Blue Aura."

Jonah felt the stirrings of nausea once more. This was too much. Entirely too much. But Jonathan wasn't done.

"That's what the Decimation lacked," he revealed to everyone. "But it's what's present now. Creyton was willing to do it, but only as a last resort. If he had succeeded in turning Jonah to the dark side, the need for Omega would have been negated. But Jonah proved himself honorable, and Creyton failed in making you something that you are not. Now the lines are truly drawn, and Omega is coming. It's light versus dark, and a Blue Aura will fall."

Jonah felt many eyes on him as he turned to look at his mentor. He felt like he had a bad head cold, or something. Was this a nightmare? Or maybe he needed to stop asking that question. Whenever he did, the reality always exceeded it in spades. "How can you be so sure, Jonathan?" he asked in a hoarse voice.

Jonathan joined his hands. "Remember the crow dream you had when you first got here, Jonah?" he asked. "That's how."

"What?" said Jonah. "I've tried to block that out."

"Liar," said Jonathan. "But I don't blame you. That crow dream foretold events to come. The first crow in your dream was your defeat of Creyton at the gravesite of the Covington House. The second crow was the 49er bringing Jessica—Inimicus—into play, which brought us to the third crow, and that was Creyton's unprecedented Praeterletum."

Jonah's eyes narrowed. "You knew what those crows in my dream meant all along?" he asked with heat.

"That'd be a bit of a stretch," said Jonathan. "I knew they foretold something, but I had no idea what that could be. And never in a billion lifetimes would I have foreseen Creyton returning from the grave. That, as we have already said, was unprecedented. But that was the third crow. And only with the third crow could the fourth one ever come to pass."

Jonah stared. "The fourth crow being Omega?"

"Yes." Jonathan's voice was quiet once more. "The largest crow from your dream; the one that never landed. Creyton will land it soon."

* * *

The next couple of weeks were uneventful, at least in comparison to the past few months. Lockman's exposure as a charlatan sent ripples all across the nation, but in the little, tucked-away town of Rome, North Carolina, all the citizens now swore that they knew something was off about Balthazar Lockman. And suddenly, everyone couldn't be nicer to the estate residents, their families, and Reverend Abbott, who saw the membership at the faith haven swell to new heights. When asked by Terrence why he had welcomed them back, the reverend contemplated him sternly.

"This is a platform of faith, Terrence," he said. "All are welcome, even the shifty and the frivolous. What kind of clergyman would I be if I excluded them?"

"Just like all the rest of them," answered Terrence under his breath.

"What was that?" questioned Reverend Abbott.

"Not a thing, sir," said Terrence. "Not a thing."

No one spoke about Jonathan's revelations, but they were on everyone's mind. Jonathan insisted that Creyton would take his precious time, because he'd never pull the trigger on a half-cocked plan, so people allowed Omega to be the thing they let hang there. It could stay that way, at least for a while.

Jonah and Vera didn't speak. He wanted to so badly, but he didn't know what to say to her. What could he say? Jessica was her sister. And her sister had fucked up his life on more than one occasion, the latest of which with the murder of his friend.

But he tried not to think about that on a Friday evening at the beginning of March, when he burst into the infirmary and heard, "JONAH!"

There was Nella, the picture of perfect health. Liz, seated at nearby desk, was as bubbly as a child. Nella laughed when Jonah wrapped his arms around her. He welcomed the change from the defiant, scowling girl she'd been before Dylan showed his true colors.

"You look wonderful!" he observed.

"I feel wonderful!" gushed Nella. "Jonathan's cure started working almost as soon as it got into my blood! Liz is keeping me here just a little while longer just to make sure all is well, but I can leave tomorrow!"

"Great." Jonah meant it, too. He was so happy to see the girl healthy and whole that he almost didn't want to speak. But then, Nella's smile faded.

"Jonah, I am so sorry that I was such a stupid bitch," she told him.

"Nella," said Liz in a rebuking voice.

"I'm just being honest, Lizzie," said Nella. "But Jonah—I was so blind and dumb. I thought I was in love. I thought he was—" she shook her head. "But I've learned my lesson. I'm never dating again."

As much as the fraternal protector in Jonah loved to hear Nella say that, he knew he couldn't just leave it there. He let out a reluctant sigh. "Nella, there are some guys out there that are garbage," he told her. "Seriously, there are. Some are worth it, though. There is no need to close off your heart. At the same time, though, there is no hurry. You'll meet someone someday, who will be everything that you want and need, and he won't be a suuvus."

Nella, who looked somber, actually snickered. That was the teenage Green Aura Jonah loved.

"You've got plenty of time," he assured her. "You've got Green Aura skills to hone, maybe more trips to Valentania York, and you've got something else, too."

He stepped out of the infirmary long enough to grab the surprise he left at the door. It was Nella's guitar. She took it reverently, properly placed it, and began to play some seventies rock song. She was a genuinely gifted guitarist.

"I'm gonna miss teaching Vera," said Nella wistfully.

Liz dropped something behind them. Jonah didn't pay much attention.

"What do you mean?" he asked.

"I'm gonna miss Vera," said Nella, whose eyes were still on the guitar strings. "Her house on Colerain Place sold sometime last week, I think? Jonathan helped with that, I am sure of it. But she's leaving tonight and moving in with Eden in Seattle until she gets her own place. But of course you already knew that, right?"

She looked up from the guitar, saw Jonah's face, and paled. Her skin resembled the state it was in when he'd found her on the side of Hodges Road.

"You—You didn't know?" she whispered.

Jonah stared at Nella for ten straight seconds, and then about-faced, and headed out of the infirmary.

"Jonah!" called Liz. "JONAH!"

"Mind your business, Liz!" Jonah threw over his shoulder.

He bounded the stairs faster than breathing, and was at Vera's room in what felt like seconds. He opened her door, fighting every urge not to call her name. Vera whipped around, dropping her coat on the floor in the process. Clearly, her plan was to use the *Astralimes* straight from her room, but Jonah wrecked that.

They stared at each other, but for several moments, didn't say a word.

Jonah looked around Vera's room. Her bed was made, but her belongings were all gone. No doubt Jonathan had already used ethereal means to make sure her luggage preceded her. Jonah couldn't help but feel a pang at how—*empty* her room was. But he felt another pang when he noticed Vera's outfit. She was wearing the same silvery shirt and black skirt she'd worn on their first date. Plus, the sweet scent of rose oil hit him. God, that was wrong. But he had to brave it. Deal with it.

"There is no point in trying to stop me, Jonah." Vera broke the silence in a voice that was steady only by a bit. "My mind is made up, the house on Colerain Place is sold, and I've already got everything worked out with Eden."

Jonah took a steadying breath. "Can we at least talk before you leave?"

Vera tried to look suspicious, but she just wasn't up to it. She seated herself on the bed.

"Thank you." Jonah seated himself next to her. "Were you really not going to say goodbye, Vera?"

"I've said goodbye to everyone, Jonah," murmured Vera.

"Everyone is not me, Vera," countered Jonah.

"What do we have to talk about, Jonah?" said Vera in a louder voice. "Huh? You know my deepest and darkest secret. Now you can hate me, too."

"I don't hate you, Vera!" said Jonah. "It just wouldn't be right if you left here without us talking! We can have a mature conversation, can't we? We're friends, right?"

Vera looked away from him. It seemed like the wall was the most interesting thing in the world to her. Jonah had no issue waiting. If he didn't get every detail, he at least wanted something. Finally, she obliged him.

"I didn't know that we were Eleventh Percenters, obviously," she began quietly. "I was unfamiliar with that term until I met you guys. I thought Madi—" she sighed, "Jessica and I were just weird girls. Maybe it came from Dad, because our mother was normal. Frail. She and Jessica butted heads for as long as I can remember. Dad was no bargain, because he worked ninety-hour weeks. Hardly ever saw him. If I had a dollar for every time I had to referee shouting matches between my mom and Jessica, I'd be richer than Felix right now. Like I told you before, Jessica did any and everything, with any and everybody. That's probably what drove our mother to smoke a pack of cigarettes a day. Then Dad passed into Spirit, and she went up to three packs a day. No one was surprised when the cancer diagnosis came. Then came that night…I already told you about that night. Jessica disappeared, and I was scarred up. She didn't even come to Mom's funeral. She was probably with Creyton by that point—I don't know, and I don't care. But the day she no-showed Mom's funeral was the day I cut her out of my life. I changed my name shortly thereafter."

She resumed silence. Jonah said nothing for a bit.

"So that was why you had that look on your face when I told everyone that Jessica was Inimicus," he said eventually. "Was that night at that Italian restaurant—?"

"—the first time I'd seen her since the night we beat the hell out of each other?" Vera finished for him. "Yeah, it was."

"That's also why she was so stunned to see us together that night," said Jonah.

"And why I was frightened as hell," said Vera. "It's not every day you see your estranged sister ,whom you hate beyond all reason. Not to mention seeing her shape shift into a damn crow and fly off."

Jonah shook his head. "The night that she revealed herself as Inimicus, Creyton said that she was an aimless woman when he found her," he told Vera. "Do you think she felt bad about your mother's passing into Spirit?"

"Couldn't tell you," shrugged Vera. "Jessica only ever cared about herself, so I really don't know."

"Is that why you're leaving?" Jonah cut right to the chase. "Because we all know?"

"What if it is, Jonah?" asked Vera. "What if I said yes? Could you blame me? How would you feel if you were, as Trip put it, the younger sister of Creyton's slut?"

"Are you really making decisions about your future because of a comment made by *Trip*?" demanded Jonah. "What about me?"

"This has nothing to do with you, Jonah!" Vera rose to her feet, heat in her voice. "Or Trip! This is my life! I have to look out for myself, because I haven't done that in a very long time! And why are you so worried about it? You've already said that Jessica and everything associated with her was evil. Remember that?"

"I didn't know that that included you, Vera!" protested Jonah.

"And that's supposed to improve the situation?" Vera shot back. "Say I stayed here, Jonah. Could you be in a relationship with me? Could you honestly be with a woman who carries the same blood in her veins as the bitch who killed one of your closest friends?"

Jonah felt blindsided by that. "That's an unfair question, Vera."

"It's a valid question, Jonah," said Vera. "But if you could bring yourself down from your damn high horse, you'd see that it doesn't matter anyway."

"What?" blinked Jonah, taken aback. "What the hell does that mean?"

Vera narrowed her eyes, scrutiny in every inch of her features. "Why are you doing this, Jonah? Why are you trying to stop me?"

"Because—because I don't want you to leave!" said Jonah. It was lame as hell, but he didn't have anything else at the moment.

"Why not?" demanded Vera. "Why do you want me to stay here? For you? I'm supposed to sit here until you're ready? We've had this more-than-friends-but-less-than-lovers situation for a while now, Jonah. And now you know who my sister is, which confuses things even further. Jessica putting everything out there like that has returned all that past shit to the forefront of my mind, and I don't know how to push it back just yet. But you want me to stay, and haven't given any thought to what I need to do. Now I ask you—is it fair to me to stay here, remaining unfulfilled and stewing in raw emotions, just so I can accommodate the time you take making up your mind?"

Jonah didn't answer. He couldn't. Vera had asked him some hard, brutal questions. They hit him like bricks. And damn it all, he had nothing for her.

"Yeah," said Vera. "I didn't think so, either. I need to do what's best for me, and you need to do what's best for you. So this is what will happen. We go our separate ways, now, before any true strings were attached. Go forth, be a hero, write books—take the reins on your life. I will go to my friends and get *Snow and Fire* into motion. Hopefully, we'll be successful, and the sky will be the limit. Anyway, you'll be living your life, and I'll be living mine."

She took a step back to put more space between the two of them. Jonah didn't move. Once again, he didn't know what to say to her.

"In time you'll forget about me, Jonah, and I want you to." Vera almost managed to sound matter-of-fact. "You could even link up with Rheadne again. I'm sure she'd be more than willing to—"

Jonah closed the space between them and kissed her. Vera's lips were so soft; they felt good against his. The second he made contact, he was angry with himself. After all those dinners, all those Netflix nights, and all those conversations at The Stop, he'd never kissed her. Why hadn't he done it sooner? Why hadn't he done it any time before now?

Jonah broke away from her. Vera looked stunned.

"I hope that wasn't too forward," he said quietly. "I just didn't want to say that I'd never done that. But I'll let you go now. No strings attached, just like you wanted."

He turned to leave the room, but Vera grabbed his arm and whipped him back around.

"What–?"

Vera kissed Jonah with fervor that she'd never exhibited. The intensity of her kiss took him by surprise, but he was quick to recover.

It didn't take long to realize how the night would end. But Jonah didn't mind that at all. Clearly, Vera didn't, either.

Vera broke away from Jonah long enough to tug his T-Shirt over his head. He gave her the same treatment, relieving her of the silvery blouse. She lost her bra next, then allowed him to lower her onto the bed. It was at that moment that Vera stopped him, and they looked into each other's eyes, hazel to identical hazel.

"This doesn't change anything, Jonah," she breathed. "I'm still going to Seattle."

"Not right now, you're not," said Jonah, tugging at her skirt.

"No, not right now," Vera agreed. "Jesus, not right now."

Jonah had no words for it. Yeah, he'd had sex before, and enjoyed each time. But none of those previous encounters—none of them—were like the one with Vera. Both of them were spiritually endowed, and both were also as intense and rigorous as the other. He touched every curve, kissed every scar, and reveled in every sound. Every bit of it was perfection. Remarkably, that was only part of what made it beyond words. During the time he was with Vera, there was nothing wrong. He hadn't spent the last several months fighting for his sanity. His enemies were nonexistent, and there was no danger at all. Omega was simply a character in the Greek alphabet that had been dusted off by fraternities and sororities nationwide. The only thing that mattered was the matchless phenomenon of how perfectly and seamlessly he and Vera fit together. It was almost criminally blissful. And when Vera cried out in ecstasy for the final time and collapsed on top of him, it was very much like waking from a dream where Creyton, Deadfallen disciples, and uncertain futures didn't exist. And with wakefulness came reality, and reality came...everything.

But Jonah fought those thoughts back. They wouldn't mar him.

Not right now.

Jonah woke up alone the next morning.

Vera had left in the night. The only trace of her presence was the faint scent of rose oil.

Jonah couldn't say that he was surprised. It only made sense, and Vera hadn't ever been one for prolonged goodbyes.

But it was still a blow to wake up and not feel her there.

He placed one hand at his brow and the other in the empty space at his side. He felt something there that made him frown.

It was a note. Because he didn't have his reading glasses, Jonah had to bring it up close to his face to read it. With mixed emotions, he lowered it.

Vera wrote:

Jonah.

We got it out of our systems. It was magnificent. My God, it was magnificent. And I don't regret it.

But we got it out of our systems.

Now you can forget about me, and go about your way. No confusion, no disorganized emotions.

You're free, and I'm free. Now, do me one favor.

Live. Please, just live.

I will do the same.

Vera

Jonah looked at the ceiling. Short and sweet. That was the note. And that was that.

Yeah, right.

We got it out of our systems. Those were Vera's words.

"Says you, Vera," Jonah said to the ceiling. "Says you."

29

The Spirit of it All

Jonah stood at the cash register of S.T.R. His key, and its copy, were in his hand.

Mr. Steverson's funeral had already come and gone, but Jonah's appearance there was brief; just the duration of the service itself. Harland had obliged small talk, but that was about it. Amanda was in tears the entire time, and looked to be seconds away from bawling if anyone spoke to her, but that was no bother. It wasn't like Jonah had much to say.

He purposely avoided Mr. Steverson's family. He didn't have it in him to face them. Yeah, Mr. Steverson's murder had been in Creyton's plan all along, but that only made matters worse. The whole game had been about Jonah. It had been about him losing his grip on his sanity. His boss, secondary mentor, and friend had been collateral damage in a plot to turn Jonah into a vengeance-seeking murderer. Either way, all roads led back to him.

The guilt was settled into his very flesh; it was like a damn tick. He wondered if it would ever go away. It wasn't as toxic as the guilt he still has for Nana's passing, but it was close. Quite close.

Mr. Steverson's family had decided to close down S.T.R. They thought that trying to continue the bookstore without him just wasn't right, and would be too painful. Harland had already dropped off his keys, and had been kind enough to drop off Amanda's as well, since she couldn't bring herself to set foot in the store again. Now it was Jonah's turn.

And it was hard as all hell to part with them.

The simple matter of placing them on the counter and walking out wasn't so simple, it seemed. His eyes kept wandering to different locations in the store, and the memories they held. There was the storeroom, where Harland had confided that he'd gotten Mr. Steverson a watch as a late birthday present only to discover that the man already had one just like it. There was the couch near the True Crime section, where Amanda had deliberated at length about baby names before Zach was born and had to put on a forced smile when Mr. Steverson declared that the name Zebedee would be a better name than Zachary. And there was the section of entirely rehabbed books where Mr. Steverson had told Jonah that S.T.R. would always be his home.

Such great times.

That would never happen again.

There was a moment where Jonah, only for that moment, hated being close to Mr. Steverson. Eleventh Percenters couldn't see the spirits of other Eleventh Percenters, nor the spirits of Tenths that were close to them. If only he hadn't considered Bernard Steverson a dear friend, he just might be able to see his spirit right now. Then again, would it have been as important to him if the two of them had not been close? And what if Mr. Steverson decided to just cross over the Other Side? Was he angry with Jonah for defying his final wish and humiliating himself in an attempt to save his physical life? Was he angry that Jonah hadn't avenged him and slit Jessica's throat?

Jonah had even attempted Spectral Sight in order to see if the spirits of Mr. Steverson's Vietnam buddies were still around, but they were nowhere in sight. The door was entirely closed, leaving more questions than answers.

Hell, there were no answers.

Finally, he laid the keys down on the counter next to Harland's and Amanda's.

"I'm sorry, Mr. Steverson," Jonah said aloud for the hundredth time. "Please know that. As long as I walk this earth as a physical being, I am sorry."

"It wasn't your fault."

Jonah's eyes flew open, and he turned around. There was a woman standing behind him. She was shorter than him, and her eyes were slightly red. Jonah seemed to remember her from the funeral, and there was something familiar about the facial features and the general air of warmth and friendliness.

"You're one of Mr. Steverson's daughters," he guessed.

"Mya," she nodded. "The oldest. And you must be Jonah."

"Yeah, that's me."

"I know it wasn't your fault, Jonah." Mya stepped closer to him. "Daddy loved you guys, but he was the proudest of you."

Jonah closed his eyes. "He shouldn't have been," he muttered. "The worst day of his life was when he met me."

"Knowing my Daddy the way I did, he would have disagreed," said Mya. "He talked about you all the time. And you weren't the one that hurt him."

Once again, the guilt began to rise like lava in Jonah's chest. She just had to say that, didn't she? "Listen, Mya—"

"Jonah, Daddy always said that a soul never left a body unless it was ready to leave," Mya interrupted. "He used to say that that belief was the thing that kept him sane in Vietnam, next to the reading books. I never thought too much of it myself, with things like murder and war and all that, but now it's the main thing helping me through this. Daddy must have been ready. He must have felt that he'd done all that he needed to do, and was ready for whatever comes next. So, if that is the case, then it couldn't have been your fault."

She hugged him. Jonah hugged her back. The guilt hadn't faded very much, but he appreciated the words hugely.

"You take care, Jonah," said Mya, and he could hear in her voice that she wasn't as strong as she let on. "I hope that when Daddy looks down on us from time to time, he will do the same for you."

Jonah spent the next couple of days in his room at the estate. He didn't talk very much to anyone, but thankfully, everyone gave him his space. The only person that he sought out for conversation was Reena.

And it had nothing to do with Mr. Steverson.

"Did you know, Reena?" he asked her point-blank. "Did you know that Vera was Jessica's sister?"

Reena closed her eyes and sighed. "Yes."

Jonah wanted to be angry, but he'd had far too much experience with that emotion lately. It was exhausting. Still, he asked, "Why didn't you tell me?"

"It wasn't mine to tell, Jonah," Reena replied. "You may view that as a lame or cheap answer, but it's true. Clearly, Vera took some massive strides to distance herself from her past. I wasn't about to open the wound back up for her."

Jonah ran his tongue across his teeth. "That explains your advice from last year. Don't prod, don't pry, just support."

"Pretty much," nodded Reena. "From the minute that it was revealed that Jessica was Inimicus, Vera was in a state of panic concerning whether or not any of us would find out. Jonathan found it out soon enough—he's Jonathan—but I can't speak for him. I can only speak for me. And what I felt was that Vera needed friends more than she needed to outline her family lineage."

Jonah didn't really know what to say to that, so he let it pass. He decided to ask Reena another question. "You can read the essence of your friends, no matter where they are. Is she happy, Reena?"

Reena raised her eyes to Jonah. "Would that information benefit you at this point, Jonah?"

"She's my friend, and I care about her well-being—"

"You're a bundle of emotions because she fucked your brains out, and then left you in bed," said Reena.

Jonah stared at Reena, but Reena shrugged.

"Jonah, one of the reasons that you consider me your sister is because I'm real with you," she said. "I don't sugarcoat things any more than you do. If you can't stand the heat, then get the hell out of the kitchen."

He shook his head. Classic Reena. "Is she happy, Reena?" he repeated.

Reena took a deep breath, regarded a painting for several seconds, and then returned her gaze to Jonah. "She's where she wants to be, Jonah. That's all that matters."

Jonah took a drive that turned into a four-day break. He considered it "Mental Health Time," and even turned off his phone during those days. When he returned from the trip on a Saturday at nearly three in the afternoon, he wondered why no one was outside. They weren't being spied on anymore, so Jonah figured that the place would be peopled once again. After all, he was the only one with a reason to be sad.

He walked into the family room, and saw that everyone was there. Daniel, Bast and the other heralds, Terrence, Reena, Douglas, Liz, Spader, Malcolm, Maxine, Magdalena, Ben-Israel, Akshara—everyone. They were huddled into the family room, and looked afraid. Scratch that. They looked terrified.

"What the hell is wrong in here?" he asked them.

They all looked at him, but Reena was the one who answered. "When you were on the road, the Curaie sent that rep of theirs to summon Jonathan," she said.

Jonah's eyes narrowed. "What for?" he asked slowly.

"For that night," answered Reena. "The night he fought Creyton and saved us all."

"What was wrong with that?" questioned Jonah.

"Don't you remember, Jonah?" said Liz. "Jonathan was stripped of his Guidanceship, and forbidden to do anything that interfered. What he did for us was not allowed."

Jonah blinked. With all that had happened, he had forgotten about that decision. He hadn't given it another thought. "So Jonathan preserved physical lives, and that's a bad thing?"

"He directly interfered after his rights and rank had been revoked, Jonah," said Spader. "He practically gave the Curaie permission to hand him his ass."

"Hand him his—?" Jonah shook his head. "So what are they going to do? Surely they can't put a spirit on The Plane with No Name!"

Terrence answered this time. "No, they can't, man. They might—they just might vanquish him. Force him to the Other Side."

"That cannot happen!" Jonah cried. "We've—we've got to stop it! Daniel!" He looked at the archer, who was near the kitchen door. "You know them, dude! Appeal to them! You were a Protector Guide for years and years!"

Daniel shook his head, tightly gripping his bow as he did so. "No can do, son," he murmured. "I'm not one of their favorite people because I turned my back on my rank. Since I became a physically living being to help Jonathan, any influence on my part might make things worse."

"That's a different tune than the one you were singing about playing offense!" protested Jonah.

"If I do anything, boy, not only will they possibly vanquish Jonathan, but they'll detain me, too." It was at this point that Daniel looked angry. "Besides, Jonathan ordered me to remain where I am. I don't love the idea, but I listened."

Jonah gaped. "So no one's going to do anything?"

"Haven't you been listening, Rowe?" said June Mylteer, whom Jonah hadn't even noticed up to that point. "There is nothing we can do."

Jonah stared at him for several moments. Then he made his decision.

He dropped his bag and jacket right there on the floor, which surprised everyone.

"What are you doing?" asked Spader.

"Sorry, June," said Jonah, ignoring Spader, "but that's the wrong answer."

He braced himself to use the *Astralimes.* Many of his friends rose in disagreement.

"This ain't the time to be a badass, man," said Terrence.

"Not my goal, Terrence," said Jonah.

"Jonah, please—"

"You aren't deterring me, Liz."

"Jonah, wait—" began Reena, but when Jonah heard her voice, he turned around.

"Save it, Reena," he told her. "You were right. I do love you and consider you my sister because you're real with me. But you love me as your brother because I'm real with you, too. And that realness stretches to everyone."

He turned and took the two-step trip through the *Astralimes* into the Median.

Someone jumped, startled, and Jonah was unsurprised to see that it was Katarina.

"Jonah?" she said. "What are you doing here?"

Jonah frowned. "Why aren't you at your desk?"

"I—"

"You know what, it doesn't matter," said Jonah, but then he quickly added, "I don't say that to disregard you. I'm just here for a reason, and time is of the essence. Can you link me to the Gate where Jonathan is?"

Katarina looked awkward, and strangely apologetic. "I can't make those links anymore," she revealed. "There is a new purple aura here. A new Gate Linker."

Jonah's eyes widened. They canned Katarina? Because she did the right thing?

Now he was really pissed.

His eye caught something, and he looked at the doors. Something was different.

They were alike in every way, even down to the symmetry. But the doorknobs were dissimilar. Whereas a dozen or so were the color of steel, one carried a sheen.

A purple sheen.

"Ding," grumbled Jonah, and he hurried for it. Katarina cried in out in fear.

"Jonah, no! They'll punish you! You'll be sorry!"

"I'm already sorry, Katarina," said Jonah, cognizant of her sensitivity and therefore careful with his voice level. "I'm sorry that I didn't do this sooner."

He put his eyes back on the door and banged it open.

Every eye in the tribunal turned to him in surprise, and it wasn't a pleasant surprise, either. Jonah wasn't nervous in the slightest, but he looked at the new Gate Linker and immediately felt disapproval. Katarina was a natural; with her timeless features, she blended right in with the whole shtick. But this new woman looked out of place, vacuous, and dopey. Jonah disregarded her, and looked at the Phasmastis Curaie.

All thirteen of them were there, so this meant that Jonathan was on trial. He stood in front of them, not unlike someone in front of a firing line. But his eyes were on Jonah as well, and they had a bizarre mixture of pride and concern.

"Jonah," his voice was tense. "Of all the presumptuous actions—"

"You saved me, Jonathan," said Jonah. "Now I'm here to return the favor."

"Blue Aura," said Engagah none too kindly, "this is a most impertinent—"

"Stop." Jonah faced the Overmistress. "First of all, that whole Blue Aura thing? It's tired. My name is Jonah Rowe. I'd like very much for you to refer to me by my damn name, seeing as how I'm not the only Blue Aura in the world."

The members of the Curaie looked at each other nervously.

"But we'll get back to that in a minute," Jonah went on. "This whole thing about Jonathan being on trial for saving all of us from being victims of Creyton and the Deadfallen disciples? It's bullshit in the purest form."

Katarina, who'd chased Jonah into the tribunal, gasped sharply, as did the new Gate Linker.

"This spirit right here," Jonah pointed to Jonathan, "this Protector Guide, has been working tirelessly against Creyton ever since he achieved Praeterletum. Ever since he has re-activated every Deadfallen disciple he has. I didn't agree with all of his methods, but you aren't ever gonna agree with people you love all the time. Instead of matching him in effort, what have you been doing? Clamping down on us. Calling us vigilantes. And having an especially strong vitriol for me."

Katarina whimpered. Jonathan's face was calm. Jonah replenished his lungs with a few breaths, and then continued.

"It would do you well to learn the consequences of civil war," he said. "I've got a perfect example. The mess between us and Sanctum Arcist last year. A completely hellish situation brought on by Creyton using his people to manipulate prejudices between Gamaliel Kaine and Jonathan. Creyton hadn't even come back to physical life yet, and he still held all the strings. As a result, civil war almost happened between two groups of Eleventh Percenters. What stopped it? Luck. And how did you respond to Creyton's resurrection? By making Sanctum damn near useless, and then you turned around and did the same to us. You banished me, and took my weapons. All in the name of making me docile. You claimed that your qualified professionals would take care of the situation. Forgive me, but how the hell was that supposed to happen when you were using the Networkers and the S.P.G. to Tally us, and keep us under lock and key?"

Katarina's mouth fell open.

"You are speaking like a barely matured child—" began the Spirit Guide named Silver, but Jonah shook his head.

"Shut up, I ain't finished," he said. "I'm sure that by now you are well aware that your banishment helped nothing. And it's funny you mentioned children. Let's run with that for a bit, alright? Most children look to their elders to explain how to get through this thing called life, right? But some elders, like yourselves, see fit with not bothering to show the way. Yet you have the audacity to blame us for being lost."

"Stop," whispered Katarina. "Jonah, you have to stop!"

"I will not stop, Katarina," said Jonah. "They need to know."

Katarina looked as though she feared for Jonah's physical life now. It was just refreshing to see her not afraid of him. But that was another matter.

"Your disdain for sazers almost caused the murders of a dozen of them, as well as an Eleventh girl and her newborn son. Another Eleventh girl, Nella Manville, was seduced by a suuvus, and nearly passed into Spirit from an ethereal disease that was also a part of Creyton's big ruse. A great man—" Jonah's voice nearly broke, but he continued on, "—lost his physical life as part of Creyton's plan to drive me to the brink, and make me a Dark Blue Aura like him. I would have been another target of your qualified professionals, so-called. And recently, I discovered that you all knew Creyton's intentions. And your solution was to put me on ice. Creyton used your own checks, statutes, and balances in a way that has turned this whole thing into one of the biggest clusterfucks of all time."

To say that the looks Jonah got were steely would have been a woeful understatement. But Jonah didn't care. He just didn't care.

"You want to know the sad thing?" he asked them. "You Guides are barely hearing anything that I'm saying. You're just chomping at the bit to vanquish Jonathan, and punish me. But if that happens, it proves that I'm right. You can't hear the truth about yourselves. Punishing me was the first thing on your minds when I walked in here, and don't you dare look me in the face and say it wasn't."

He looked at Jonathan, and was surprised to see that all the concern had faded from his expression, leaving only the respect. Katarina still looked like she feared that the Curaie would smite Jonah. The new girl was just…there. He sighed.

"But you're not going to punish me," he said. "You aren't going to punish anyone. And I'll tell you why. Because we are on the same side."

Katarina's eyes widened. Engagah and the other Spirit Guides looked surprised as well. Jonah wasn't concerned with these reactions. He wasn't doing a one-eighty at all. He simply needed to expel all the venom before he could speak his piece.

"You can't punish Jonathan, because you need him," he said. "We need him. We are going to need each other. All of us. I know that you are acting out of fear. You are afraid of Creyton. You are afraid of the fact that he's come back to life. He's changed things. And you're afraid of Omega. These things scare the hell out of you. Guess what? They scare the hell out of me, too."

He had picked up a spiritual endowment from a sweet spiritess while he was on the road, and was glad of that fact now. He raised his hand, and willed the ethereality to make his fingers gleam blue.

"It's methat's been marked, after all," he said. "Light Blue versus Dark Blue. One Blue will rise, and one Blue will fall. Yeah, it scares me. I hadn't said it out loud yet, but there it is. I'm cool with my fear, though. The friend that I just lost threw a bit of Bible at me that stuck. Straight is the gate, and narrow is the path. I'm on that path. No detours, because the detour could be worse than the path itself. No more of this bullying and throwing weight around. If Creyton is going to be stopped, all hands need to be on deck. Even if those hands include sazers. Look at the thirteen of you. All of you have taken forms that represent a great many ethnicities in this world. Black, white, Asian, Latina, Middle Eastern, Native American, Pacific Islander—just look at yourselves! It makes no sense to illustrate such diversity if you're going to engage in exclusivist practices concerning Creyton. His team is an elite fighting unit. We ain't that. Not by a long shot. We need to work together, or at the very least, be civil and cooperative. You need to let Jonathan off the hook. He is a hero. That's not a crime. Give Sanctum Arcist some breathing room. Gabriel Kaine can thrive; he might just exceed his father and brother. If we don't all get on the same page, now, Creyton will plow right through us. Do these things before it's too late. You take stuff for granted, and wind up waiting too long—"

Jonah paused. That was another story. This matter had nothing to do with Vera.

"We need to at least be allies," he said. "But we need everyone. And that includes Jonathan."

Finally, Jonah fell silent. He didn't know what it was like for someone's tongue to be tired until that moment.

Members of the Phasmastis Curaie regarded him, while others looked at Jonathan. Engagah steepled her hands.

"Pardon us," she murmured, and they all faded from view.

Jonah gaped at the empty seats. "What—?"

"Shh!" said both Jonathan and Katarina.

And then the Spirit Guides reappeared. Jonah actually started.

"That was fast," he commented.

"Time doesn't exist where we are," said Engagah. "Now, Rowe, please be silent. You have spoken your piece; it is now our turn."

Jonah held his tongue. Finally.

"Jonathan, we summoned you here to hold you accountable for disregarding our ruling with your personal interference and brazenly resuming your role at the Grannison-Morris estate without our permission," said Engagah. "We have deliberated amongst ourselves, and have come to a decision."

Jonah closed his eyes. Shit.

"We have unanimously voted to indefinitely suspend your punishment," announced Engagah.

Jonah's eyes flew open. What did she say?

"As insolent and insubordinate as the approach may have been, there was something to what the boy has said," she continued with a grudging note in her voice. "These divisions have proven costly in various ways. There are many details that need to be ironed out, Rowe, but civility is a reasonable goal."

Jonah glanced at Katarina, who was just as stunned as he was. The Curaie had just let both he and Jonathan off the hook!

Just then, several Spectral Law practitioners burst into the door, no doubt taking advantage of the still active Gate. They looked murderous when they saw Jonah, but Engagah raised her hands.

"Force is neither necessary nor tolerated here," she told them. "We have reached an accord." She turned to Jonathan. "Jonathan, would you mind remaining here while these people leave the tribunal? As your punishment has been suspended, we now need to discuss many things going forward. It would be copacetic for these discussions to occur sooner rather than later."

Jonathan regarded the Spirit Guide, and then nodded. "It would be my pleasure, Engagah."

Engagah turned to Jonah, Katarina, and the S.P.G. officers. "Leave us. And Katarina, we wish you the absolute best in your future plans."

Katarina swallowed, and nodded rapidly. "Thank you, Engagah."

They all turned to leave.

"Jonah."

He turned back to Engagah. "Yes?"

"For your blatant disregard of the protocol of the tribunal, you are ethereally grounded for a period of two months."

Jonah stood there, breathing in and out. All eyes were on him, not knowing what to expect.

"Fine," he said at last. "Got it."

"But your banishment from the Grannison-Morris estate is now lifted," Engagah added, her tone begrudging once again. "We will handle the breaking of your lease in the city, and you will not incur fees or penalties. The estate is once again your sole residence. You may go."

Seconds later, they were back in the Median. Jonah was so thankful to be away from the Curaie that he didn't know what to do. He had no idea where the courage to do that had come from, but it had achieved something.

And he got a punishment. But he deserved that one. For once.

"Jonah?" Katarina's soft voice broke through his thoughts. "Can we talk?"

Frowning slightly, Jonah followed her to a nearby sofa and sat down. She sat opposite him, and placed her fingers on her knees. Jonah was surprised to see her nails were painted the color of her aura. "What's up?"

Katarina sighed. "Bernard Steverson was a dear friend of yours, wasn't he?"

Jonah's eyes narrowed. "Yeah, he was."

Katarina nodded. "When he passed into Spirit, he chose to stay behind—"

Jonah's eyes bulged. He opened his mouth to blast Katarina with questions, but she shook her head.

"Let me finish," she said. "He chose to stay behind long enough to give me a message for you. Then he asked me to dissolve a portion of the boundary to the Other Side, so that he could cross on."

Jonah's breath was laborious. "Okay," he managed. "What was the message?"

"He told me to tell you that it wasn't your fault," Katarina told him. "He said that he wasn't angry with you, and is completely at peace. He didn't fault you for trying to save his physical life, but there was nothing that you could do. It was out of your power, and he wanted you to stop blaming yourself. It will probably do your heart a world of good to know that he was even welcomed into the next phase of his life by two of his fellow military veterans. I assisted them all in crossing to the Other Side."

Jonah couldn't speak. He was still deeply saddened, but Mr. Steverson hadn't blamed him. And the spirits of those soldiers had been with him on this Plane for over forty years were now back with him. Brothers in this life, brothers still in the next. "I can't thank you enough, Katarina," he said quietly. "But I got to ask you something. When were you planning to tell me that? You didn't know you'd see me today."

"I would have sought you out," said Katarina with a smile. "I'm not afraid of you anymore, after all."

She looked over at the new Gate Linker, and her smile faded somewhat. Jonah grimaced.

"Katarina, I'm so sorry that the Curaie let you go for helping us," he said.

"Let me go?" Katarina frowned. "They did no such thing. I quit."

"Say what!" exclaimed Jonah.

Katarina smirked. "My time here is done."

"But...why?"

Katarina shrugged. "My eyes have been opened, Jonah. As great as the Curaie have been to me, this job became a comfort zone. Then the comfort faded, and I began to feel like the job was crushing me, especially after I met you guys. I need to do what's best for me, and being in this ethereal lobby day after day, week after week, is no longer going to work."

Jonah looked at her in awe. "Do you want to move to the estate?" he asked. "I know how hard unemployment can be."

Katarina chuckled. "That's not necessary. I will leave the action and wildness to you guys. I'm in a good place, Jonah. I own my house, compliments of the Curaie. Plus, I've saved just about everything I've made, so I'm not broke. I'm just... free."

Jonah was impressed. Katarina didn't have a violent bone in her body, but she was still brave. He initially thought of her as an overly delicate waif of a woman, and while that might have been that much of a stretch, not every brave person in the world was a fighter. He understood that now. "That's really something, Katarina. What're you going to do now?"

"Make more Kirie, keep up my singing, and maybe even sell some of my work," said Katarina. "Also... you know what, never mind. You don't want to hear that."

"Nah, it's cool," said Jonah. "What else?"

"I'm a little... tired of being alone," she admitted. "Maybe—I don't know—maybe I can make a match with someone out there."

Jonah felt his mouth part slightly. Then, he grinned. Katarina frowned at him.

"Why is that funny?"

"It isn't," replied Jonah. "I'm just thinking that I can help you in that department."

"How so?" Katarina raised an eyebrow. "I've forgiven you, Jonah, but I don't think that you're my type."

"Not *me*," said Jonah, with just a little impatience. "I didn't mean me, I—tell you what. Since I'm ethereally grounded, I can't use the

Astralimes. Link up a Gate to the estate, and come with me. We'll talk on the way."

Things settled down well enough in the weeks that followed. All of the estate residents who'd been forced to stay at home all those months were now back. Jonah thought that it was great to see Benjamin, Melvin, Noah, Barry, and everyone else. Of course they were all surprised to learn of everything that had happened as well. The day that Jonah returned from the Median, unscathed, jaws dropped. When it became common knowledge that Jonah stood up to the Curaie and survived to tell the tale, he was looked upon as something of an icon. He tried ardently to explain that raging against the machine hadn't actually been his goal, but it fell on deaf ears. Even when he told them that he hadn't actually gotten away with it, and had been ethereally grounded, his words still had no effect.

People were so relieved to see Jonathan back and safe. Even Daniel, despite his ironclad composure and inscrutable visage. Bast and the heralds were relieved as well, and Bast herself even stopped in front of Jonah long enough to intimate, "*Thank you,*" to him. He still felt like he hadn't done anything noteworthy, but he was thankful that his actions had positive results.

Liz made it clear that heroism had not been her goal, and what she did was what had to be done for Nella. Didn't matter. No one knew that Liz had anything like that in her. Jonah was surprised himself, though he'd never tell Liz to her face. Prior to the events at Blood Oaths, he still viewed her as an innocent girl who needed to be protected; hell, he still remembered the frightened girl who'd fainted in the fire some years back. He even recalled what Rheadne had said in regards to Liz: "*Medics have no place in a fight.*" Well, Liz had acquitted herself quite well. And Bobby, who was wrapped around her little finger already, was even more in awe of her now.

Nella even commented on the matter one day.

"Does this mean that I'm the sweet one now?" she asked with disapproval. "Because I'm not sure that I'm okay with that."

"Just be who you are, Nella," Jonah told her. "In light of recent events, you don't need to be trying to be anything for anyone."

Nella sobered instantly, and let the matter drop.

Suddenly, Spader was no longer the outcast or reject. People were interested in his insights into locks and escape plans, and the way he returned with reinforcements got him much praise. The boy was happy to not be leered at anymore, and very pleased by the fact that Liz now respected him. She didn't even look down on him anymore, and was as civil as could be. He even had the audacity to be smug about it.

"Am I crazy, or is Liz starting to wear down for me?" he asked Jonah and Terrence one day.

"You're crazy." Both Jonah and Terrence said it without hesitation.

But the biggest surprise was Douglas. When it became common knowledge that he'd pulled himself away from the chess board and the golf and did some real fighting, he was tantamount to an overnight celebrity at the estate. Liz had fixed his teeth and nose a day after they returned from the tattoo parlor, but told him that she could do nothing for the residual bruising, and it would heal over time. But Douglas treated it as a badge of honor.

It turned out, though, that beyond the "battle scars," Douglas cared very little about the accolades or praise.

That was because he had been in complete, total bliss ever since Jonah had set him up with Katarina.

Something had changed in Douglas, and though he couldn't see it, everyone else got such a kick out it. They'd already been on four dates, but no one regarded that as an official number, because Douglas spent so much time with her. Reena had even noticed that he had even begun to blow off his grandmother's criticisms.

"Duh," murmured Terrence. "She ain't the only woman in his life anymore. Her opinion is pointless."

They weren't all able to sit as a collective until one evening, when they gathered to watch some news on Balthazar Lockman. Douglas had just had another date with Katarina, and plopped down looking as though he wanted to throw a ticker-tape parade.

"Glad you remembered that you have a life," snickered Jonah.

"Huh?" said Douglas absently.

"Huh?" mimicked Jonah. "You heard what I said. But I'm glad that you guys clicked."

"I am, too," said Douglas.

"You really diggin' this woman, don't you?" asked Terrence.

"Like you wouldn't believe," gushed Douglas. "Man, she's creative…and intelligent…and gorgeous…and perfect. I can't thank you enough for doing what you did, Jonah. But I got to ask you—why did you look out for me?"

Jonah cracked open a soda and placed it on the floor between his feet. "Well, Doug, I knew that you liked her. She was interested in seeing if someone was out there for her, so why not? And, once upon a time, I would have said that you needed an assertive woman, but given your newfound status as a badass, I'd say a dainty, delicate woman like Katarina is just what the doctor ordered."

Douglas smirked, but then started; his phone was vibrating. He looked at it and grinned. "I'll try to keep this short," he promised as he rose from his seat. "I'll be right back."

"Uh-huh," said Terrence. "See ya next year."

When Douglas hurried off, Reena moved forward. "Why did you do that for him, Jonah?" she asked. "I mean, it was cool and considerate of you, but what made you do it?"

Jonah contemplated his soda. "Simply put, I thought they could be great together. Doug was smitten, and Katarina wanted a match. I took a gamble, and sparks flew. I also thought that they just might be made for each other. They needed to get together before life could complicate matters like—" Jonah was going to mention Vera, but there was no point. None of his friends could help him with that. It simply was what it was. "Like Maxine, for instance." He took a different track. "That poor girl still doesn't know where her Christmas present came from."

"Which one?" asked Liz.

"The remastered versions of every *Star Trek*s how there was," answered Jonah. "Even *Andromeda* was there. She has no clue. If she did, she'd be doing the dance of joy. If, of course, she could stop watching them long enough to do so."

"Who *did* give her that present?" asked Spader.

"Felix," said Jonah. "I saw him the night he bought them."

Liz smirked. "If Maxine knew that, she'd pine over him some more."

"Whoa, whoa," said Spader. "Pearson's got a thing for Felix? Get out!" When nobody said anything, he added, "Really?"

"Pleasure to see you," said Reena. "We got here five months ago."

Spader was wide-eyed. "Does he like her back?"

"Hell if I know," said Jonah. "Dude's been alone for so long that the concept of a girlfriend is probably too foreign now."

"Shh!" said Terrence suddenly. "It's on!"

They listened to the news report attentively, which, at least for Jonah, was saying something. Lockman's fall from grace was jarring to people who believed in what he claimed to stand for, and he was in total disgrace. The number of lives he'd ruined by labeling them cultists had come from every direction, forcing the Tenth authorities to put Lockman under twenty-four hour guard.

"That ain't enough," said Terrence matter of factly. "They're gonna have to stick him in a bag and bury him."

The report went on to reveal that although Lockman had sizable assets, they had been frozen. There was a possibility that his funds would go to the people whose lives he'd destroyed, as the lawsuits came from left and right. On top of that, Deputy Feldman up in Dexter City was in hot water as well; an anonymous tip made it common knowledge that he had regularly taken bribes from Lockman dating back almost seven years; allegedly, Lockman had even had a hand in Feldman becoming sheriff. Faulk and the other employees of the Lockman Association maintained their ignorance of Lockman's schemes, and said that they were just as much pawns as the falsely accused. It was going to take some hard work to get them cleared, and they were ordered to surrender their passports just in case they got any bright ideas.

"Kendall told me something this afternoon that I know all of you will love," said Reena when the news report was over. "Reynolda Langford was suspended without pay from the *Ledger* when it became clear that she was in cahoots with Lockman to smear us."

"Suspension without pay?" said Jonah with mock coldness. "It's more than she deserves."

"Don't worry, Jonah," said Liz. "That imbecile woman will never be trusted again. If she ever gets back in their good graces, she'll be lucky to cover a story about the fish factory."

They all laughed over that one, and then spoke amongst themselves about a whole lot of nothing (Douglas never returned). It did Jonah good to do that, because it distracted him from all he had on his plate.

He tried hard to file things away in his mind, but it kept coming back in the strangest ways. Creyton, his gaslighter, or whatever it was, had failed to make him a murderer, so he was now going to bring about an endgame. And Jonah held a place at the forefront. Creyton's side was organized. Jonah's side...well, they had work to do.

It made him wish that he still had Mr. Steverson to talk to. His outsider's perspective was always welcome and helpful.

Jonah walked outside into the yard. The night sky was strewn with stars. The air was fresh, and all was quiet. But Jonah didn't register any of that. Things were heading in a direction that he simply didn't know. Didn't understand.

He hadn't been lying when he told the Curaie that he was scared. He meant what he said about staying on the path, but that fear of the unknown was a powerful thing.

"Jonah?" It was Terrence's voice.

He turned to see both of his brother and sister behind him.

"We had something to ask you, man," said Terrence.

"Alright," shrugged Jonah. "Go for it."

Reena tapped Terrence's shoulder, as though she desired taking over. "Some of us were wondering if...if you needed to clear your head again."

Jonah frowned. "Huh?"

"We figured that—you know—now that Vera was gone, you'd want to head out for a while, too."

Jonah looked around. Several heralds traveled in pairs, doing their patrols. He saw Malcolm heading to the woodshop with a couple of Elevenths he knew were interested in woodwork. With a half-grin, he saw Bobby and Liz, hand in hand, taking one of their strolls across the grounds.

He looked back at his informal siblings and sighed. In all honesty and truthfulness, he had thought of hitting the road again. But it wouldn't achieve anything. Not really. He'd done that already, and trouble found him. Just like Mr. Steverson had told him, sometimes the detour was worse than the path itself.

But Mr. Steverson had also said something else. He'd written it on a piece of paper that would forever be in Jonah's wallet.

You aren't alone. Not now, not ever.

"Nah, I'm fine," he told Terrence and Reena. "If I do manage to get my head on straight, it's going to happen right here. At home."

About the Author

T.H. Morris was born in Colerain, North Carolina in 1984, and has been writing in some way, shape, or form ever since he was able to hold a pen or pencil. He relocated to Greensboro, North Carolina in 2002 for undergraduate education.

He is an avid reader, mainly in the genre of science fiction and fantasy, along with the occasional mystery or thriller. He is also a gamer and loves to exercise, Netflix binge, and meet new people. He began to write *The 11th Percent* series in 2011, and published book 1, *The 11th Percent,* in 2014, and book 2, *Item and Time,* in May of 2015. Book 3, *Lifeblood,* was published next in November of that same year, and book 4, *Inimicus,* followed in August of 2016.

He now resides in Denver, Colorado with his wife, Candace.

Connect Online!

Twitter: @terrick_j
Email: morrisworld18@gmail.com
Website: 11thpercentseries.weebly.com

Made in United States
North Haven, CT
15 August 2023